The Monarch

The Monarch

A Thriller

JACK SOREN

WITNESS
IMPULSE

An Imprint of HarperCollinsPublishers

This is a work of fiction. Names, characters, places, and incidents are products of the author's imagination or are used fictitiously and are not to be construed as real. Any resemblance to actual events, locales, organizations, or persons, living or dead, is entirely coincidental.

Excerpt from *Dead Lights* copyright © 2015 by Martin R. Soderstrom.

EPub Edition DECEMBER 2014 ISBN: 9780062365187
Print Edition ISBN: 9780062365194

10 9 8 7 6 5 4 3 2 1

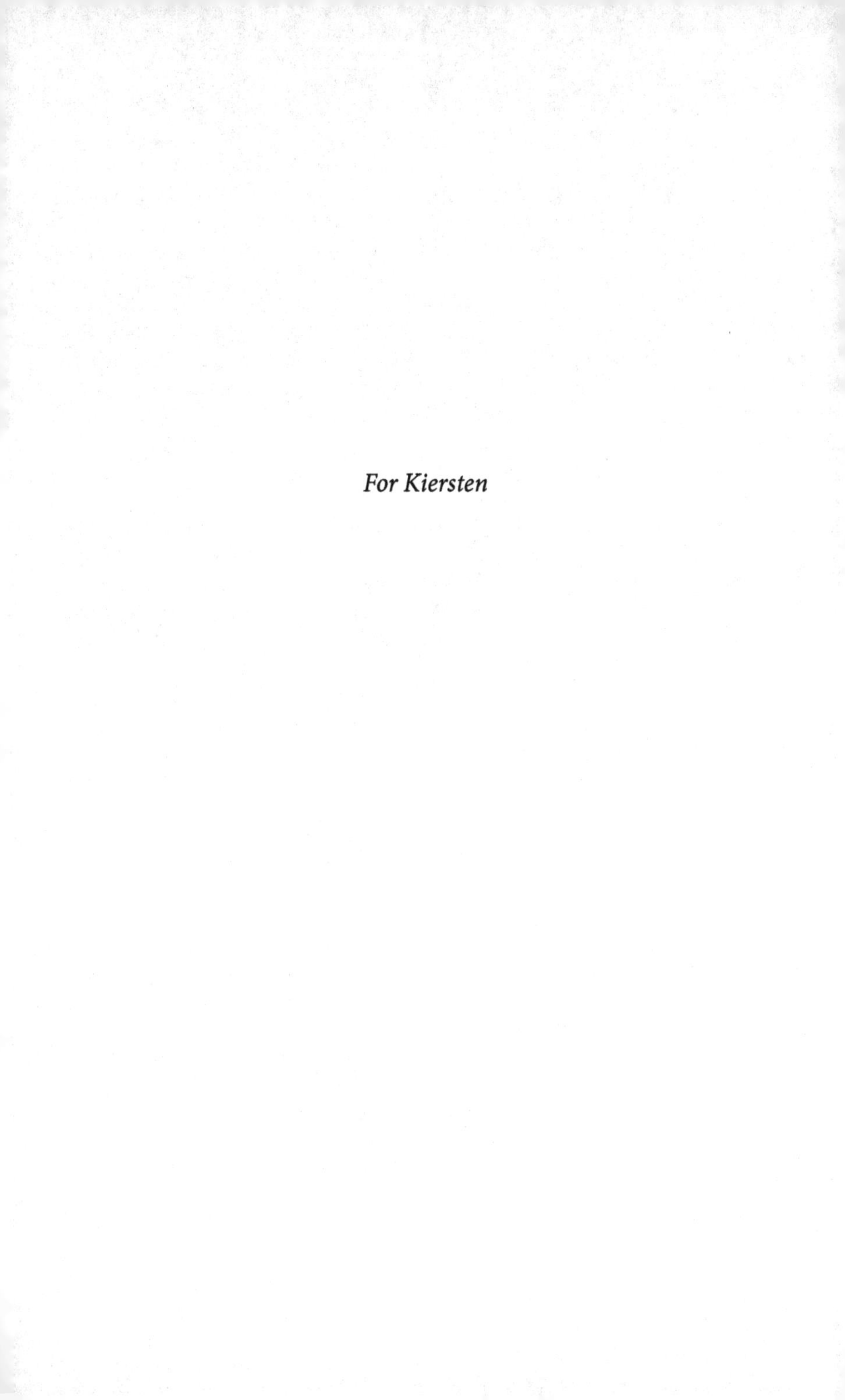

For Kiersten

The difference between stupidity and genius is that
genius has its limits.

Albert Einstein

PART ONE

Friday

1

The Cloisters Museum
New York City
7:30 P.M. Local Time

Joe Wagner noisily flipped through his notebook. He wasn't really looking for anything, he was just trying to distract the museum's curator from constantly looking at the dead guy over his shoulder.

Despite being a New Yorker for his entire life, Wagner hadn't been to The Cloisters Museum in Washington Heights until he was forced to chaperone his son's field trip two years ago. In the end, he quite enjoyed himself, but when he'd first arrived he hadn't even known what a cloister was. He was surprised to find out it was a combination garden and monastery. He found the stonework as intriguing as the fact that the cloisters were brought over, brick by brick, from France before World War I. Even then he thought the place looked more like a transported castle than a museum.

But tonight, he wasn't Joe Wagner, the conscripted parent marching tweens around, he was FBI Special Agent in Charge Joseph Wagner. He was running herd on an entire task force of law enforcement agents, just as he'd been doing for the past six weeks, since the first body had been found. Tonight, blood ran in the egg cup-shaped, cream limestone fountain at the center of one of the outdoor courtyards; a mutilated, half-naked body stretched out across the trickling feature where monks once bent to satisfy their thirsts. Tonight, he was up shit creek and the only paddle in sight was about to come down hard on his career.

"Who found the body?" Wagner asked the museum's curator, Roger Benoit, a small, pale, effeminate man who smelled of baby powder. Wagner's team was asking the other museum staff the exact same question just then, but there was protocol to follow here. If the curator felt disrespected, the complaint would go up the chain fast. That was the last thing he needed.

"Uh, Connie. Connie Baker," Benoit said with a slight European accent. Wagner wasn't sure which country it was from or if it was even real.

"Was she alone?"

"I believe so, yes. She was on her way to the West Terrace and she noticed the fountain sounded muffled. We all heard her scream and came to investigate. The poor woman nearly passed out. Can you blame her?" Benoit kept dabbing at his forehead with a cloth handkerchief, picking up speed when he mentioned Baker. Wagner didn't think it had anything to do with the case but there was something there.

"When was this?" Wagner asked, scribbling in his notebook.

"Oh my, let's see. It must have been about an hour ago. Six-thirty, I guess."

"And why was she going to the West Terrace alone?"

"You don't have to put that in there, do you?"

"We're just trying to clear your people. Make sure no one was involved."

"Involved? Good Lord, of *course* she wasn't involved."

"So why was she alone?"

"She"—Benoit leaned in so he could lower his voice—"she was going out for a cigarette."

"I see."

Wagner asked several more pointless questions and thanked the curator for his time. No one on the staff had anything to do with this, but all the i's had to be dotted very carefully on this one. He made a few more notes and then joined Special Agent Mike Evans by the body.

"Anything?" Wagner asked, putting his notebook away and cinching his coat against the April evening chill.

"Naw," Evans said. He was a little shorter than Wagner, but his crew cut stood straight up, evening their heights. "They're going to need some counseling, but they had nothing to do with it. Half of them are having trouble staying conscious. All they want to do is go home." It was what Wagner had expected to hear.

"Explain to them they'll have to come in and give statements before that can happen. You know the drill," Wagner said, turning to leave.

"Listen, we've got a problem."

"No shit," Wagner said, the aggravation getting the better of him.

"NYPD is screaming bloody murder."

"Have they made the connection to the other killings, yet?"

"That's the other thing. The press were here before we were."

"What?"

"When Duke and I pulled up they were already knee-deep at the gate. We had to chase half of them back off the grounds."

"How—" Evans handed Wagner a fat manila envelope. Wagner pulled the contents out. It was an unmarked file folder and a paperback titled *The Monarch's Reign*. Wagner felt his stomach drop when he saw the cover of the book. The black butterfly symbol on the book's glossy white background exactly matched the bloody butterfly scratched into the victim's chest a few feet away. He flipped through the folder: police reports, FBI documents, and visceral crime scene photos of the first two murders. In a mere six weeks they were already on their third murder, all of them with the same grotesque postmortem mutilation.

"Jesus."

"Yeah. Delivered to just about every media outlet early this morning. We're following up, but so far nothing; no postmarks and no prints."

"When the hell was *this* published?" Wagner asked, flipping through the book's first few pages.

"Couple years ago. Nothing about the murders, obviously. The author, Emily Burrows, lives in Washington Heights. A Brit with a work visa."

"Why didn't we know about this? Scratch that," Wagner said. "NYPD wants something to do? Tell them to get her in here before some reporter gets it in their brain to go find her. If they haven't already."

"Doubt it. Her number's unlisted. We only found her address because of the work visa. It was a lucky hit."

"I'm feeling all kinds of lucky today."

"You haven't heard the bad news yet."

"Of course not."

"The director's on his way down."

Wagner visibly winced.

"Perfect. This aside," he said, waving the envelope, "did you get a look at the corpse's face?"

"No, why?"

"Take a look," Wagner said as they walked over to the corpse where it lay posed over the fountain.

"Son of a bitch. That's Bob Cummings," Evans said, recognizing the newscaster.

"None other. Somebody went to great lengths to make sure we couldn't sit on this one."

"Holy shit, Bob Cummings. NYPD's going to lose their fucking minds when this gets out," Evans said. Aside from being the highest-rated newscaster in New York, Cummings was ex-NYPD, as was Evans.

He leaned forward and looked more closely at the roll of material protruding from the corpse's twisted maw.

"That the cause of death?" Evans asked.

"Probably. ME's on his way. The mutilation is most likely postmortem, like the others," Wagner said, nodding at the crude butterfly symbol scratched into the dead flesh.

"Not exactly like the others, is it," Evans said, pointing to the bruising on Cummings's face. "He beat the shit out of this one."

"Yeah," Wagner said. The other victims had very few marks on them, besides the mutilation. "Not sure what it means, yet."

"Hmm," Evans grunted. He leaned in even closer. "What the fuck *is* that?"

"Damned if I know. Cloth of some kind, looks like. But get a load of this," Wagner said, pointing at a protrusion under the skin of the exposed abdomen.

"No way."

"Whatever it is, it's about three feet long and the only reason we can see any of it is because the killer couldn't push it in any farther."

"SAC Wagner?" a young agent said from the stone stairs that led to the courtyard. Wagner looked up at him. "Director Matthews is here. He's asking for you."

"Sucks to be you," Evans said.

"Not as much as it does to be him," Wagner said, nodding at Cummings's body. But he wasn't entirely sure about that.

"Hey, Pete," Wagner said as he stepped into the museum's foyer, trying to set the tone of the encounter. From the look on Director Matthews's face, it wasn't going to work. Flashing red and blue lights pulsed through the fogged glass blocks around the museum's entrance. The upper drive outside looked like an extension of the Federal Plaza parking garage, there were so many FBI cars strewn about. Beyond the cars, a gaggle of reporters strained at their NYPD leashes.

"Not the way I wanted to start my day, Joseph," Matthews said, staring out at the barricades. The men were the same size and build, but somehow Wagner always felt small around him.

"No, sir," Wagner said.

"You promised me I wouldn't regret the suppression in this case. Do you recall?"

Wagner remembered, all right. Six weeks ago, the first mutilated body had been found by a group of teens on the edge of Central Park; a local artist with no enemies to speak of. Wagner had assumed the killer had chosen the young man at random, the real point being the location in an effort to garner attention. Why the killer wanted attention hadn't really mattered at that point. Wagner had been sure that if they denied the killer his publicity he would make a mistake—a frustrated phone call to the cops or a letter to the media. Something. But as it turned out, the killer was methodical and patient. More patient than Matthews, apparently, Wagner thought. It would have been easy to let the NYPD have the case and be done with it. But Wagner's son had been among the teens who had found the body. It pissed Wagner off, and when he found out the first victim had worked part time for the post office, he used the technicality to take over the case. But worse, he used his old friend to do it.

The second killing had been three weeks ago, an independent art gallery owner again with no discernible enemies. The only connection between the two killings was the art world and the gruesome symbol carved into his flesh. He'd been killed somewhere else and then left strung up in St. Patrick's Cathedral on Madison Avenue, the corpse's arms outstretched like a crucifixion on an invisible cross, the same rudimentary butterfly carved into his bare chest. Still convinced of his tack, Wagner fought to keep that murder out of the press as well, the location making it even harder. Reluctantly, Matthews had finally agreed to go along and even use his influence with the Archdiocese. No small feat.

And now this.

"We're checking the security cameras as well as the traffic cameras in the area, but—"

"But you're not going to find anything. Just like the others," Matthews said.

"No, sir. Probably not. If this is like the others, he has pull like

I've never seen before. The fact that he didn't set off any alarms seems to bear that out."

"You're not helping your case, Joseph," Matthews said. He turned around and faced Wagner. He was at least ten years Wagner's senior and had been a mentor to him when he'd first joined the Bureau, but their rank and methods had driven a wedge between them long before this case came along. "Give me a sitrep and then I have to go meet with the Archdiocese who want to tear a new hole in me for breaking the promises I made to them after the last murder."

Wagner winced as he gave the situation report. He knew Matthews was referring to the work he'd had to do to get the Archdiocese to keep the murder quiet. He'd promised they wouldn't regret the move, just as Wagner had promised Matthews—twice, now.

He told Matthews where the body was, described the scene, and explained who had found it. Matthews didn't nod or even blink through the recitation. Wagner was pretty sure it was taking all Matthews's willpower not to knock him on his ass for putting him in this position. He hoped Matthews wouldn't take any permanent heat for this. The man was made to be the director. If it had been Wagner, he would have taken a swing at hello.

"The vic is Robert Cummings, the local news anchor. He was the cop that beat the corruption charges a few years back."

"Couldn't ask for a higher profile victim," Matthews said.

"No, sir. But that's not all," Wagner said before telling him about the little care package the media had received. Matthews's eye twitched at the news, and Wagner readied himself for that beating.

"Get. That. Woman—"

"She's on her way. I've got the NYPD chauffeuring her here."

"No, not here. Anything we do here is going to be too high pro-file. Clean this up and get the show shut down. I want this museum open by tomorrow morning. The Archdiocese is bad enough without a bunch of rich art patrons whining at me through their pit-bull lawyers. Take her straight to the ME's."

"Yes, sir. Will do. Anything else?"

"I think you've done enough, Joseph," Matthews said before walking out the door, holding a newspaper up to hide his face from the press as he walked to his car.

"Joe!" Wagner turned and saw Evans rushing over to him. He never rushed or called him Joe unless he was excited. And if Evans was excited it was not good news.

"What?"

"I think we got an ID on that murder weapon." "And?"

"You ain't gonna like it."

2

Tallahassee, Florida
9:00 P.M. Local Time

JONATHAN HALL FINGERED the car door's handle again from the passenger seat inside his date's car, fighting the urge to throw it open and run away.

They'd pulled up in front of his modest house over twenty minutes ago, but he was still waiting for a pause in the one-sided conversation, which was foolish. Trudy Malloy hadn't stopped talking since picking him up two hours ago. He had no idea what made him think she was going to run out of gas now.

After the first hour, he'd started playing games in his mind to keep from both going crazy and jabbing a salad fork in his eye to end the night early. It was the first date he'd been on since his wife, Samantha, had passed away almost two years ago, and if this was an example of what Tallahassee's forty-something single women were like, it would be his last.

Left up to him, Jonathan never would have gone on the date. Trudy was a fine-looking woman, there was no doubt about that, but he simply wasn't interested in "finding" someone.

His eleven-year-old daughter, Natalie, had different ideas.

For the past six months, she'd appointed herself Jonathan's personal screening service. There was rarely a day that she didn't come home with a recommendation of a teacher at her school or a friend's divorced mother who would be perfect for him. Trudy fell into both categories. She was the art teacher at Natalie's school and she'd been divorced just last spring.

"And I told Hanna, if you think Paris is the same as New York, you've obviously never been to either place. I mean, seriously. I went to Paris on an art scholarship when I was just seventeen—did I mention that?—and I spent two years in New York studying film, so you just think again before you start throwing around nonsense like that. And do you know what she said? Can you guess?"

Jonathan smiled but made no effort to offer a response. He'd fallen for this rhetorical question trick earlier. He soon realized he was just a bit player in this melodrama. If this were a *Star Trek* episode, he'd be wearing a red shirt. Jonathan looked down and realized he *was* wearing a red shirt. He smiled wider at the irony, which Trudy took to be delight in her tale spinning. *Oh no.*

"—pork meatballs! As if pork meatballs would be on any kind of macrobiotic diet—excuse me—lifestyle plan. I mean—"

Pork meatballs? What the hell was she talking about now? Did she even finish the last story before starting this one? Had he blacked out? Jonathan turned and looked at his house again. It was only thirty feet away, its unkempt front garden and sun-faded siding filling him with hope instead of the usual depressing reminder of his lack of funds. Sanctuary. But more importantly, the person responsible for doing this to him was in there. Natalie would pay for this.

I don't know how it happened, honey. The Guitar Hero controller must have fallen off the shelf all by itself. Hard. Twice. He smiled at the idea, though he knew he would never do such a thing. His daughter's misery wasn't the only reason; those things cost a fortune.

When Trudy started in on her scrapbooking hobby and her latest drama at the art supply store, Jonathan knew he had to end this.

He abruptly leaned over and kissed Trudy, surprising even himself with the ploy. It took her a second to wind down, but eventually there was peace. Ever-loving peace. Suddenly, Jonathan realized this was the first woman he'd kissed since Samantha. Reflexively, he shifted toward her and slipped his hand around her back. Then the past two hours came crashing through his libido and he forced himself to pull away.

He half expected Trudy to pick up her story where she'd left off, but that didn't happen. Her cheeks were flushed and she was panting slightly.

"So, this was fun," Jonathan said, unable to look her in the eye.

"Uh-huh" was all Trudy said. He pulled on the door's handle and made his exit while the getting was good. When he turned to wave to her from his porch, he saw that she was still watching him and making no move to drive away. Maybe Natalie was going to pay for this, but so was he.

He slipped inside and closed the door behind him. After a moment of leaning on the door in relief, he peeked around the curtain in the front window. She was still there and hadn't moved.

"Oh boy."

Jonathan paid the sitter and sent her out the side door. If Trudy was still out there, he didn't want to know about it.

"I knew you'd like her," a voice behind him said.

Jonathan turned to see Natalie on the stairs in her pajamas, a half-melted ice cream bar in her hand. She was at that pivotal age when everything was still simple: Candy was good, school was bad, and boys were yucky.

When her mother had passed away it had been hard on her, but she'd rebounded wonderfully this year. She was pretty much her old self again: funny, mischievous, and bossy. And Jonathan wouldn't have it any other way.

But this recent need to become his personal love doctor concerned him. Something had changed a few months ago to make her suddenly worried about the idea of her dad being alone. He had still been trying to figure out what had changed when a counselor at Natalie's school flagged him down earlier this week.

Natalie had been getting into fights. After bloodying the nose of a boy in her class this week, she'd finally opened up to the counselor. She'd apparently been having bad dreams—dreams about Jonathan dying.

"It's completely normal in kids her age, especially after losing a parent," the counselor had said.

There were two recurring dreams: In the first, she saw Jonathan dying alone; in the second, she saw him with a mysterious woman, safe and alive.

"Natalie sees what happened to her mother as a normal course of events. Her subconscious is extrapolating from that what it feels is an obvious, inevitable progression to your death. That's the first dream. The second is a wish fulfillment. To stop what she perceives as normal, she's injecting another parent into the situation—someone else for death to take instead of you. A decoy, if you will."

The counselor had gone on, but Jonathan had heard enough. It explained the matchmaking. And as far as he was concerned, the only fact that mattered was that he was responsible for this. If he had done a proper job as a father, he would have helped Natalie deal with her mother's death better. He'd obviously dropped the ball. And what was worse, he hadn't even noticed.

He still had no idea how to deal with the problem, so for now he was just trying to be more observant and not to discount any of Natalie's thoughts and feelings. It was the reason he'd agreed to go on the date from hell.

"Talie, I ought to brain you," Jonathan said. "Does she talk that much in school?" He hung his coat up and kissed Natalie on the forehead. She was way too chocolaty to risk a hug.

"Of course she does. She's a teacher!"

"Ha-ha. Very funny, missy," he said, mussing her hair before he walked into the kitchen, Natalie padding after him in her bare feet. He took a brownie out of the fridge and chomped down on the much needed carbs. "Did you finish your homework?" he asked through his own chocolaty mouthful.

"Mostly," Natalie said. She finished her ice cream bar, tossed the stick in the trash, and hopped up on the counter beside the sink.

"Mostly, huh? Mostly as in you thought about doing it, or you just need a little help?"

"So, did you kiss her?" Natalie asked conspiratorially with a big grin.

"Natalie, answer the question."

"The second one. I just need your help with multiplying the stupid fractions."

"Oh, okay," he said. He hated fractions but learned a long time ago that Natalie wasn't the only one going through the sixth grade. He had to relearn whatever she happened to be studying so he could help her do her homework.

"So, did you?" Natalie asked again.

"Did I what?" Jonathan said innocently as he took the milk carton out of the fridge and washed down the brownie.

"Dad! Yuck. Glass."

"Sorry," he said, taking a glass down from the cupboard and pouring the milk into it. He saw that there were bits of brownie floating in it. He made a mental note to pick up milk.

"I don't understand how you guys couldn't get along," Natalie said. "I mean, she's an artist and you're a photographer. That's kind of like an artist, right?"

"Not the way I do it," Jonathan said under his breath. He'd needed a job when he'd left his old life and since he'd typically written "photographer" on the customs forms when he was traveling back then, it seemed as good a choice as any. It didn't take long for him to learn that pretending to be something and actually being it were two very different colored horses. He was awful at it and now they made what money they could from portrait and passport photos.

"What?"

"I said it's time for bed, kiddo." He tickled Natalie all the way upstairs and after making her brush her teeth, kissed her good night and turned off her light.

"Dad?"

"Yes, honey?"

"Don't worry. We'll find you someone."

"Just get to sleep. Let me worry about me. And don't forget we're doing your fractions in the morning."

"Evil!"

Down in the kitchen, Jonathan poured himself a scotch and wandered into the living room to enjoy some solitude. He loved his life with Natalie, but there was something about the night, when it was dark and the house was quiet, knowing Natalie was safe in her bed. After a while he turned on some quiet Etta James and looked at some photos he'd taken of Samantha and Natalie a few months before they'd found out she was sick. Samantha had known all along but had kept it to herself.

Jonathan had first met and fallen for Samantha twelve years ago. He'd tried then to leave his life as the art thief known only as The Monarch, pissing off his partner, Lew. It hadn't worked. They had made too many enemies over the years. One night, while on vacation in Paris with Samantha, his past had come calling. He'd managed to protect her, but his secret was out. He explained everything to Samantha when the ordeal was over. He had to know if she could handle what he was asking her to endure. She said she could, but Jonathan had seen the doubt in her eyes. After one last night together, Jonathan had slipped out of their bed and into the dawn light. He left a note saying how sorry he was and how to contact him if she should ever be in danger—especially if it was because of their time together—but he never saw her again.

That is, until five years ago when she placed the ad on Craigslist that was actually a call for help. He couldn't believe it when he saw that ad.

The same way he couldn't believe that thanks to that last night, he had a six-year-old daughter.

"Hang on. I've got it here somewhere," Jonathan said, digging through his pockets. The lights in the all-night grocery were ridiculously bright and right now each bulb seemed to be focused on him.

He was sure he'd grabbed the five-dollar bill off the table before walking up the street to pick up some milk for Natalie's cereal in the morning, but now all he was finding was pocket lint. He smiled apologetically to the people behind him in line who were feigning either ignorance or patience.

"Here it is!" Jonathan said with a little too much enthusiasm. He knew he shouldn't have gone out after having a scotch on top of the drinks he had at dinner, but they needed the milk. It was why he'd walked, and while he wasn't drunk, he certainly didn't have all his wits about him.

The teenage cashier smiled condescendingly at his triumph as she gave him his change.

"Have a nice day," she said around her bubble gum.

Jonathan grabbed his milk and rushed out of the store, almost knocking over a carpet cleaning display in his rush. Not just from the embarrassment, but because he wanted to get home to Natalie. The house was locked up tight and she was sound asleep in her bed, but he still hated when he had to leave her alone. The reality of being a single dad continually pushed him farther out of his comfort zone than any day had as a thief.

On the walk home he thought about Natalie's dreams again. He was so lost in thought, he didn't notice two men fall into step behind him as he turned the corner off the main drag onto the sparsely illuminated side street that led to his house, still several blocks away. It took his instincts a few minutes to wriggle through the scotch haze in his brain.

Jonathan abruptly stopped and pretended to search for something in his pocket. The men stopped too. He started walking again when his charade was over, and so did his shadows.

Shit.

Most likely he was about to be the subject of a good, old-fashioned mugging. But what were they waiting for?

He looked up the dimly lit street ahead of him and saw the answer to his question. While sparse, the lighting on the side street was sufficient enough to ward off danger. But up ahead two streetlights were burned out. He knew if he waited until they were out of the light, bad things would happen.

He thought about running. He was still in reasonably good shape and it was only a couple of blocks, but nothing said the guys behind him were meth heads. With his luck lately, they'd be part of the Olympic relay team.

There really was only one choice. Confrontation. And pedestrian though it was, his biggest concern was the milk he carried. He didn't have any money to replace it if it ended up on the street in whatever was about to happen. He swayed over to the right of the sidewalk and swung the bag into the top of a hedge. When he was sure the cushy branches had caught and held the bag, he turned and walked back toward his stalkers.

He caught them by such surprise they not only stopped but backed up several steps. One of them was small and overweight and looked like the biggest exercise he got was rolling over to fart at night. He was a pace behind his buddy, and Jonathan guessed their pecking order was evident in that stance. The other one would be a problem. He was huge. Six-four, at least, Jonathan figured, having to look up to meet the guy's gaze from his own height of six-foot-two. He was probably heavier than his buddy, but not in the same way. And he seemed to be pissed. On the plus side, it appeared that if Jonathan knocked him on his ass, his buddy wouldn't be a problem.

Jonathan caught himself. *Maybe we don't start this with assault.* Who knew what they wanted.

"Can I help you boys?" Jonathan asked, his voice neither threatening nor timid. Let them decide how this should go.

The big one seemed to look to his friend for guidance before he answered, and in that moment, Jonathan realized he should have just kept walking. No matter what these guys said or thought when they started after him, they wouldn't have done anything. Whatever happened now was Jonathan's fault, and he knew it.

"Stay away from her, man," the guy said.

"Her? What are you . . . wait. You mean Trudy?" Jonathan was amazed, not at the connection but at the fact that these guys had apparently followed him and Trudy and he hadn't even noticed. *Am I that rusty?*

"Did you fuck her? Fuck her in *my* fucking car, you stupid fuck!" The guy's cool lasted about ten seconds. He was almost crying. This was embarrassing.

"Look . . ." Jonathan mentally scanned through the *reams* of things Trudy had said to him tonight and found her ex-husband's name. "Look, Steve. You've got the wrong idea. Man, have you got the wrong idea."

"Just . . . just leave her alone. Fucker." This guy was a one-note wonder. "She needs to work shit out and she can't do that if you're all smooth and shit in her fucking face."

"Yeah!" the little butterball chimed in.

"I'll try and watch the, uh, smoothness," Jonathan said. He sighed and returned to his milk, figuring turning his back on these guys was about as dangerous as taking a shower without a bathmat.

Then pain suddenly sparked in the side of his head.

"Fucker!" Steve shouted as he and his rotund friend ran off, high-fiving as they did.

Jonathan took his hand away from his head and saw blood on his fingers. He looked down and saw the rock they'd pitched at him.

"What are you? Ten!" Jonathan shouted after them, thinking about going after them for a second, but realizing that leaving Trudy to him was punishment enough.

He grabbed the milk from its hedge resting place and heard a *pop*.

"No, no, no." Lifting the bag up, he saw a thin stream of milk pour out the hole he'd just torn in it. "Damn it!"

Jonathan ran, holding the milk out in front of him like a bomb, all the while milk streamed out of the container and all over him. By the time he made it to his kitchen and grabbed a container, he'd saved about a cup's worth. He carefully put the cup in the fridge and went to get a bandage and some ibuprofen for the pounding lump on the side of his head.

He cleaned up the wound but when he dug under the sink for the bandages all he found was an empty box. Fed up, Jonathan tossed the towel into the sink, stomped into the living room, and opened his laptop. While it booted up, he poured himself another drink to drown out the little voice in his head whining about his promise.

"Come on!" he said a little too loud, wincing both from the headache and the idea he might wake Natalie up. When silence prevailed and the throbbing subsided, he opened a browser window and logged on to a Web site he hadn't been to in years.

The page resolved and asked for his log-in name and password, no logo or text displayed to show the identity of the site. It made sense, since the site didn't know his real identity either.

Jonathan logged in with his numeric username and password, memorized long ago. Another minute of account fetching and the details of his bank account in the Caymans displayed. When the account balance popped onto the screen, it eased his frustration somewhat. Nine-figure numbers tended to do that.

"Enough is enough," he said, keying in a transfer to his local Tallahassee account. He wouldn't take much. No sense in that. A hundred thousand should suffice.

Jonathan licked his lips as he hovered the mouse pointer over the commit button. This would change everything. No more crappy photography. No more insipid clients. No more cutting coupons or counting change. No more stealing gas money from the swear jar.

He looked up at the faces of Samantha and Natalie staring down at him from the mantel, the diffused lamp light making them seem at once disappointed and angry. On her deathbed, Samantha had made Jonathan promise that he would never allow his old life to come anywhere near their daughter. He'd easily agreed, but then she'd added that she also meant his old life's bank account. Jonathan didn't like it, but he understood. She wanted Natalie raised as normal as possible. And while his money wasn't technically stolen, it was the result of less than lawful activities. A mere moment of looking into her eyes made him promise without reservation. But that was then.

After a long, self-deprecating moment, he slammed the lid of the laptop closed, drained the rest of his drink, and fell back on the sofa, a familiar lump where a spring had slipped digging into his back. He shook off the despair and chuckled.

"Look at it this way. It can't possibly get any worse."

3

FCI Yazoo City
Yazoo, Mississippi
9:00 P.M. Local Time

"Have a seat," the warden's secretary said with a smirk. Lewis Katchbrow shuffled over to one of the empty plastic chairs against the wall in his ankle chains and wedged his six-foot, two-hundred-twenty-pound frame into it as best he could. He winced as his hands, handcuffed to the chain around his waist, were squished against the chair's arms. Lew heard the secretary chuckle, but ignored him.

That's how Lew had spent most of his two years in Yazoo, Mississippi's Federal Correctional Institute—below the radar. Minding his own business. Most, until today, that is. He still couldn't believe what had happened in the past few hours.

The cafeteria door had slammed shut, leaving Lew and about twenty inmates hungry, pissed, and milling around in the afternoon rain. A man used to regulations, Lew had planned on just heading back to his cell to wait for dinner, but somebody else's plans got in his way.

Lenny Dyson, an older inmate who used a cane to support a bum leg, stepped out of line and started shouting and swinging his cane around. Lenny normally wasn't violent, which was the reason he could have a cane in the first place, but his shouts grew in intensity until finally he flung himself to the ground and writhed around like he was having a seizure. Everyone, including Rory Dupont, the assistant warden, who was trying to calmly herd the hungry men back to their cells, walked over to see what was happening. Lew stayed put. He'd seen freak-outs before and didn't need to see another one. He cinched his prison-gray shirt collar up against the rain and waited.

Then he saw the real reason Lenny was freaking out. It was an act. He wasn't freaking out.

He was a distraction.

Delroy Thibideau, a lanky black inmate renowned for his temper, marched across the yard with a purpose. At first, Lew thought Delroy was coming for him. He squared off and tried to figure out how he'd pissed this guy off. But Delroy wasn't looking at him, he was looking behind Lew. As Delroy stalked closer, Lew saw him shake something out of his sleeve and into his hand—a shiv. This wasn't a beating. Someone was about to die.

Behind him, Lew saw a little white dude named Mickey King. He hadn't met Mickey either, but knew him through the prison grapevine, a better service than even AT&T offered. Mickey had a big mouth. Probably trying to overcompensate for his size, Lew thought. He also knew Mickey was fond of certain words that no doubt would have made Delroy crazy enough to stick him. In any prison those were unwise nicknames to toss around, but in a fed-eral pen in southern Mississippi, it was masochism.

Lew looked over at Lenny, who was still writhing like a lu-natic. The assistant warden managed to take his cane away, but couldn't calm him down. Lew thought about just calling the AW and ending this, but he knew how long a rat would last. Though just being in a crowd where a prisoner got whacked could make life get more than a little complicated. His parole would be blown, at least. And that just wasn't going to happen.

Delroy eyeballed Lew for a moment, before returning his stare to Mickey, who had no idea what was happening. Lew read the stare as plainly as the evening paper: *Get the fuck outta da way, homey.* Lew feigned a sidestep, giving the impression he was doing just as Delroy wanted. But when they were abreast of each other, and Lew was sure the AW wasn't looking, he struck.

Delroy was already in his backswing, his balance all behind him and to the left. Lew stepped behind him, grabbed the shank with one hand, and pushed on the back of Delroy's opposite shoul-der with the other. Delroy's momentum did the rest. He let go of the shank in an attempt to get his balance and then slammed to the muddy ground. In one smooth move, Lew heaved the shank up onto the roof of the cafeteria building and then turned to walk across the yard toward his cellblock. He heard steps in the mud behind him, knowing there was a pretty slim chance Delroy would let this go. He wasn't out of this yet. He spun around while Delroy was still twenty feet away.

"Heading back, boss!" Lew shouted to the AW. Delroy froze in his tracks, knowing where the AW's attention was now drawn.

"What? Fine, go ahead," the AW said, obviously just wanting the little pimple under his grasp to stop thrashing.

Delroy's stare burned into Lew's face. Lew knew he should have just turned and walked away, but he just couldn't help himself. He smiled and tapped his forehead with two fingers, as if he were tipping an invisible hat. Delroy's eyes widened even more—which was something, considering their already saucer-sized spin—but he remained where he was.

Lew turned and headed back to his cell.

An hour later, as Lew stepped inside the activity room and heard the door slam behind him, he knew it was time to pay for his interference. Then he heard Delroy's signature giggle.

"Ah, crap."

Lew made fists and turned around, readying himself. His fists quickly fell away and he realized he'd walked into something a lot more dangerous than an ambush by some pissed-off cons.

"I think we need to have a chat, *ese*."

Delroy was there, but he wasn't the one talking. He sat on a table by the wall, Lenny beside him, smacking his palm with his cane like a 1920s cop rousting a speakeasy. By the door were two gorillas, bigger than Lew and Delroy put together. All of that was bad. But what was worse—and more confusing—was the leader of the little troop, who stood in front of them facing Lew. Lew looked down into his eyes, which seemed much darker than he remembered.

"Mickey King," Lew said. "Strange way to thank me for saving your life." Lew eased back and sat on the edge of a table. He had no idea what was going on here, but he was pretty sure taking a nonthreatening stance was mandatory to his breathing. The only thing he knew for sure was the murder he'd stopped earlier was no murder at all.

"You just keep runnin' yo' mouth, boy," Delroy said. Mickey

turned and looked at Delroy, who recoiled like he'd just touched a hot stove.

"My associates are a little upset. They were expecting a big payday for our little charade, today. Now they're worried they won't get it. Worried enough to want to take it out of you," Mickey said. Lew watched Mickey pace as he spoke. Not the pace of a worried or anxious man, but the pace of a lecturer, explaining what was what in the world. Lew also noticed that Mickey seemed to have grown a Mexican accent.

Lew had a few comments bubble up into his brain, but he figured if he wanted to stay healthy he'd better keep quiet a while longer. He looked at Delroy until Delroy looked away. That tiny victory aside, Lew thought he was starting to understand what was going on here. And if he was right, things were very bad indeed.

"The only reason you aren't losing blood, *ese*, is because of your intent. You didn't know who I was, or what was really happening, so you took a genuine risk when you stepped in. I'm touched."

"Not like there was any real danger, Mr. Colero," Lew said, taking his shot. If he showed he was smart, he might have a chance. Miguel Colero—known mostly as White Mike, thanks to his complexion and his affinity for coke—had been in charge of a large chunk of the South Florida drug trade until he disappeared last fall. Lew knew this from his penchant of keeping an eye on the law enforcement activity in the Sunshine State—especially Tallahassee. Everyone figured his underlings or his competition had whacked Colero, but with very few photos of him in existence, verification had apparently become impossible.

"And apparently you can also put two and two together. Bravo, *ese*," Mickey said. "But until I'm outside of these walls, I'm still just Mickey King. *Comprende?*"

"*Sí*," Lew said. He was far from out of trouble, but he was still standing and that was something, considering who he was standing in front of.

Lew still had a lot of questions, like how White Mike had ended up in a Mississippi federal pen under an assumed name, or why he was working with nobodies to get himself out, but the only question that mattered was:

"What's the gig?"

"Ah, you see? You see? This is a survivor. A resourceful man adapting to his surroundings. He doesn't whine when he's in a bad situation, he finds the angle," Mickey said, the last of it apparently directed at Delroy.

"Just keepin' it real," Lew said. He sensed there was something spoiled between Mickey and Delroy and he didn't particularly want to watch it go to hell right in front of him.

"The gig is act two. Delroy makes another attempt on Mickey King's life, only this time he succeeds. Your job will be to make sure no more Good Samaritans stick their noses into our production. Simple, yes?"

"As pie," Lew said. "So what happens after? Your coffin rolls on down the road until you pull a jack-in-the-box?" Mickey didn't respond, apparently disturbed that Lew had figured out the plan so easily. Lew made a mental note to dial the smartness down a notch. Being too smart was just as bad as being too dumb with guys like White Mike.

"Time is a factor here, so Mickey King needs to be dead by dinner. A truck rolls out tonight and Mickey's corpse needs to be on it," Mickey said. Talking about himself in the third person was starting to annoy Lew.

"Right," Lew said. "Listen, not to cause trouble or anything. I think it's great that you think I'm such a stand-up guy and all, but you just told me a whole lotta shit that could be dangerous for you. Aren't you banking a lot on your intuition?"

"It's never wrong, *ese*," Mickey said. "But it never hurts to have a safety." Mickey snapped his fingers and Delroy let a plastic baggie unroll in his hand. Hanging down was a shiv in the bag. Lew didn't need to ask where it had come from. Or whose fingerprints were on it.

"How'd you get it off the roof?" Lew asked. But Mickey was done answering questions.

Lew wondered how he could avoid the same fate in store for Delroy and Lenny. He knew they'd be dead before Mickey popped up out of his coffin tonight.

And now the plan included him.

A few hours later, as inmates lined up for dinner, all the players were on their marks—including Lew. He stood in the rain, which had refused to abate, once again.

Delroy was across the yard, looking like a base runner waiting for the third base coach to wave him in. Lenny was there, but he couldn't pull another seizure or this act would never work. Delroy was just going to go for it when he got the signal, right in front of everyone. Lew thought the mob panic that would ensue could only help make the whole thing seem more real. His job was to intercept the assistant warden if he came around.

Mickey, standing in line outside the cafeteria, raised his hands while he was talking. It was Delroy's signal to make his run. Lew looked up and watched Delroy burst out of the blocks. He thought he was going to run full-tilt all the way across the yard, but he seemed to get ahold of himself about halfway and slip into character again.

Lew moved over to the edge of the building and looked around the corner, where the line of hungry men bent. At the end, talking to a couple of inmates, was the assistant warden. The inmates he was talking to had nothing to do with this, so the conversation could break up at any time. And sure enough, Lew saw the AW pat one of the inmates on his shoulder and turn to head toward the main event.

"Damn it," Lew said under his breath as he headed to intercept the AW. He caught him a few feet before the corner, where the AW would have a view of the charade. Lew had no doubt the act would fool the cons, who wouldn't really care if it was real or not, but if the AW witnessed it firsthand, the jig would be up. The doctor was well lubricated with cash, so pronouncing Mickey dead wasn't a problem . . . unless the AW got to the body before the doc did. Lew saw the doc walking toward the cafeteria; his role must've been to just happen to be in the area. He hadn't even seen the doc earlier, but Lew had been concerned about other things.

"Yes, what is it, Lewis?" the assistant warden said.

"I, uh . . . that is, I was wondering," Lew stammered. He knew he should have worked something out before he approached the AW. He could adapt like a banshee with the threat of death over his head, but improv had just never been his thing. He needed the right motivation, and helping someone else escape just wasn't cutting it.

"Take your time, Lewis," the AW said. Lew knew the only reason the AW was being patient was that up until now, Lew had been the invisible man, flying beneath the prison administration's radar. They loved cons who did that. But Lew was about to launch himself smack-dab into their crosshairs.

"I know it's probably against the rules, sir, but I was wondering if I could get a . . ." *A what? A parole? A V8? An amen?* Lew's mind riffled, wondering how long it took to stab someone anyway. Especially when they wanted to be stabbed.

"A what, Lewis?" the AW asked, losing patience. Lew looked past him to the fence in the distance and the line of elms planted beyond it.

"A . . . uh . . . tree. For my cell," Lew said, not even believing it himself. *Really? A fucking tree? Why didn't you just ask for a Jacuzzi and a blowjob!*

"A what?" the AW asked. But the commotion around the corner finally started and Lew didn't have to answer him.

Men were shouting and howling around the corner. It was the prison song of blood, and all the inmates knew the tune. The men in line tried to drift out and around the corner, but the AW knew the song too.

"Back in line! *Now!*" the AW shouted, the nice guy all but gone. Lew just wanted the AW to get around the corner so he could get the hell out of there, partly thinking in the back of his mind that this little show meant he was going to miss another meal. He hadn't thought of that before this.

The AW went around the corner and immediately raised his arm to the tower. Whistles blew and sirens blared. They were going into lockdown. Lew thought better of running out from the crowd on his own with the snipers in the tower alerted. He did what he thought everyone else who wasn't involved would do. He went around the corner to watch a man "die."

Mickey was on the ground, the shiv sticking out of the padding under his shirt, the blood bag he had taped to it turning the mud crimson. The doc was already at his side. He quickly told two trusties to get him to the prison hospital. The doc would pronounce him dead before they locked the last cell.

"You men! Back to your cells!" the AW yelled, obviously worried about how he was going to tell the warden that a guy got stuck on his watch. Guards and trusties seemed to ooze out of the ground to shepherd everyone back to their cells.

"Nice and calm, ladies! Excitement gets you dead," one of the guards shouted to the men, pulling the bolt on his rifle to send his point home. They grumbled and milled around for a bit, but mostly they obeyed, the crowd slowly heading back to their respective cells. Lew joined the crowd, just wanting out of the rain.

"Katchbrow!" someone yelled, and Lew stopped dead in his tracks.

Crap.

Lew turned and saw the AW walking toward him.

"Yes, sir?"

"We've got some talking to do, don't we, Mr. Tree?"

"Hey! Sleepy!" the warden's secretary barked at Lew. Lew opened his eyes and looked at him. "You can go in now."

Lew grinned and nodded before prying his frame out of its plastic chair wrapper. He shuffled over to the door marked "Norman Quinn—Warden" and knocked as best he could. When a voice inside said come in, he opened the door.

"You wanted to see me, Warden?" Lew said.

"Come in, come in," Quinn said without turning away from the flat-screen television he crouched in front of. "Sit down, Lewis."

Lew shuffled over and sat down with a jingle, trying to figure out how everyone seemed to be on a first-name basis with him. He watched the warden fiddle with the television's color settings. It was a nice television. A big fifty-five-inch high-def model. His electronic gadget addiction was no secret, but Lew had had no idea being a warden paid so well.

"Looks like we've got a problem, Lewis," Quinn said. Lew looked out the window behind the warden's desk and saw that he had a perfect view of the cafeteria where their murder-in-one-act had taken place. *I'm screwed.* At the same time, Lew looked at the roof of the cafeteria and saw the shiv he'd thrown up there. *Man, you can't trust anyone.*

"We do?" Lew said, feigning ignorance.

"Ah, that's not right," Quinn said, backing up and sitting in his chair without taking his eyes off the set. "Do their faces look yellow to you?"

"Hard to tell from this angle," Lew said, straining against his bindings. Quinn seemed to notice his cuffs and chains for the first time.

"Gordon!" Quinn called out into the hallway to his secretary. Gordon showed up in his door a moment later. "Gordon, whose idea was this?"

"I don't know, sir. Mr. Dupont, I think," Gordon said.

"No, no, no," Quinn said, shaking his hand in the air. "We don't need these. Get the key."

A few minutes later Lew was unlocked and Gordon was jingling out of the office.

"Close the door behind you, Gordon. And tell Rory I'll want to see him next," Quinn said, coming around and sitting on the edge of the desk holding a remote control that looked as big as a loaf of bread.

"You're not going to hit me with that thing, are you?" Lew said. He was going for lighthearted, but the warden's tight-lipped smile gave him a creepy feeling.

"Not the way you think." He hit a button on the remote and the picture changed from a game show to a grainy black and white image. Lew thought he was watching an old black and white movie until he recognized himself at the top of the screen. He watched himself walk around the corner of the cafeteria and out of frame, where he'd gone a few hours ago to stall the assistant warden.

"This is the good part," Quinn said. "Very realistic."

Lew watched Mickey King's "death" take place in front of his eyes. Almost as soon as Mickey hit the dirt, the prison doctor ran over and waved the assistant warden off, obviously saying King was dead. Even with the circumstances, Lew felt slightly sickened by having to watch it go down.

"But this is by far my favorite scene," Quinn said. He hit some more buttons on his remote and the picture zoomed in on King's dead body. "And now . . ." Lew rolled his eyes.

The supposedly dead King sneezed before going still again.

What the hell's going on here?

At the least, Mickey and Delroy should be in solitary, the doc should be up on charges, and Lew knew he should be back in those chains.

"I have to tell you, Lewis, the worst part of all this—the part that really pisses me off—isn't the deception. The worst part is all of you thinking I'm so gullible that a see-through charade like this would work. Did you really think the morgue wagon would just drive out of here unchecked? Or that one of my charges could be killed right beneath my window and I wouldn't get involved? It's insulting," he said, tossing the brick remote onto his desk, papers and pens shooting off onto the floor on the other side. "Only a moron would be fooled by that!"

"Uh, yeah," Lew said, feeling his face flush. Lew wanted to tell the warden the whole story, but he didn't see the point. It would just sound like prisoner whining. Not to mention make him look like a gullible ass.

Quinn picked up the fallen papers and put them back on his desk. He pulled up his chair and then took a file out of his drawer.

"Lewis Katchbrow," he said flipping through the pages. "What are you doing in here, Lewis?"

"Another three months until today. Now, well, that's kind of up to you."

"You know that's not what I meant. What were you doing pulling an armed robbery in southern Mississippi in the first place? And alone, no less.

"I see how you handle yourself in the yard. Who you talk to and who you avoid. How you spend most of your time being invisible and keeping to yourself. You're adaptable and smart. You just want to do your time and get out of here. Why would you help a bunch of losers and an incognito drug lord with a cockamamie plan like this?"

He caught Lew off guard with that one. Quinn knew who Mickey really was. Lew wondered if this knowledge was the reason Mickey felt he had a time limit on getting out of here.

"Let's just say it wasn't by choice."

"I thought as much," Quinn said, flipping more pages. Then something in the file caught his eye. "Excuse me, *Major* Katchbrow, Army Ranger." Quinn read some more to himself, then read some aloud, as if Lew hadn't heard it before. "Recipient of two Purple Hearts, three Bronze Stars, and a Medal of Valor. Honorably discharged in 1992."

"Look, Warden, what does my service record have to do—"

"You declined your flight home from Kuwait. Just wandered off."

"It says that in my file?" Lew was suddenly curious.

"No, I made some phone calls. And the most interesting thing I heard were reports of you doing some bare-knuckle fighting in Bogotá, Colombia, but then after that . . . poof, nothing. You dropped off the face of the earth until your robbery bust. Where were you for sixteen years?"

"What is this about, Quinn?" Lew said a little harsher. He didn't like someone digging around in his past, especially with what they could find. Quinn looked at him, and then seemed to make some sort of decision, flipping the file closed.

"Simple trade," Quinn said. "You do something for me; I'll do something for you."

"What are you going to do for me?" Lew asked.

"You don't belong here. It's obvious. It's also pretty obvious, today notwithstanding, that for your remaining time you're not going to be any trouble. In fact," Quinn said, leaning forward, "it will probably be difficult to tell you're even *here*."

Lew got the message.

"Are you saying I can walk out the front door? Today?"

"Well, maybe not the front door, but yes, essentially you're correct."

Lew thought about that. He hadn't let himself think about the idea of being free for even a moment in this place. Thinking like that just made you crazy. But he let himself think about it now and really liked the feeling it gave him. He caught himself before the idea got too heady.

"And the price?" he asked, knowing he wasn't going to like it, whatever it was. Quinn leaned back in his chair, put his hands behind his head, and swiveled back and forth.

"Mickey King wants to be dead. Let's give him what he wants."

"You want me to kill one of your prisoners?" Lew said. There was no way he was going to trade a year of boredom for someone's life, no matter how much of a scumbag he was.

"Technically, he's not one of my prisoners. *Mickey King* is my prisoner. But we both know there is no Mickey King. And let's not overlook the fact that technically he's already dead," Quinn said. Lew thought he was rationalizing like hell, but he figured he also now knew where Quinn's shiny new television had come from.

"You don't think I belong here, but you want to make me a murderer. Yeah, that makes sense," Lew said.

"Let's stick to the truth, Lewis. This certainly wouldn't be the first time you've killed someone," Quinn said tapping Lew's file. "But I'll guarantee no one deserves killing more than Miguel Colero. Think of all the damage he's done with his drug trade. The lives he's destroyed. The families he's decimated. You could stop all that."

"Don't try to sell me with the same shinola they used to sell you. Who the hell do you think wants this done? The tooth fairy? Somebody in here recognized him and squealed to some other drug lord. That's who wants King—Colero out of the way. I don't know what you've told yourself, but you're obviously an easy sell. A fucking TV?"

Quinn slammed his hand on his desk and stood up, pointing his finger in Lew's face while his own turned red. "Watch it, Katchbrow! There's a flip side to this coin. I testify that I saw you kill Colero. Maybe I plant some drugs in your cell. I hear they serve great meals on death row. For a while."

"Fuck you. Go ahead, testify. Plant whatever you want. I'd love to have my day in court. Maybe my lawyer goes sniffing around your house or your bank account to see what other new, expensive goodies you've gotten lately. Maybe I talk to a few of Colero's friends and tell them the real story. Hope you didn't get the extended warranty on that piece of shit."

Quinn's face went from red to bleach white. There was an audible click as Quinn's Adam's apple bobbed up and down. He opened his palms and patted the air, apparently trying to calm the room's sudden foul mood. He sat down in his chair and took a deep breath.

"We're getting way off the beam, here. Let's just calm down," Quinn said.

Lew didn't say anything, but he sat back in his chair. Pushing was only going to get him so far.

"Your freedom was on the table originally, and that's what's on the table now. Will you—"

A rapid, frantic knocking on the door cut Quinn off. He scanned the room, looking like a poker player caught with an ace up his sleeve. He grabbed Lew's file and shoved it in a drawer.

"Yes, what is it?" Quinn called out. "Shit!" He grabbed the remote control and flipped off the paused fake murder, the game show returning.

The door popped open and Rory Dupont, the assistant warden, stuck his head in.

"Boss, the inmates have started a fire in Cell Block H. They're threatening to riot over the shanking. We gotta call the state cops. Now!"

Lew looked out the window and saw smoke rising out of one of the far building's windows.

"Damn it!" Quinn headed for the door. "It's our house, we'll handle it."

"What about him?" Rory asked, stopping Quinn and pointing to Lew.

"Leave him here. Give me a set of those cuffs." Quinn handcuffed Lew to the chair that was bolted to the floor. Lew didn't know if it was to keep Lew the prisoner from getting away; or Lew the weapon from being hurt in the blossoming riot. He looked outside again and knew he really didn't care. "Let's go!"

Quinn ushered Rory out of the office and as he was leaving said: "Think about what I said, Lewis. This could be a turning point in your life. Don't blow it over details."

Then he shut the door and Lew listened to the muffled voices beyond the walls fade until he saw the men, armed with tear gas rifles, helmets, and billy clubs, head across the mud toward the smoking barracks, half of them trusties who looked like they wanted to run the other way.

Lew stood up and stretched against the one cuff holding him to the chair until he could see out the window. Men ran every which way. It was pandemonium out there.

That's when he saw it. A reflection in the window. A shape he knew better than his own name. He turned around and saw that it was coming from the television, a news broadcast breaking into regular programming.

A spinning graphic grew larger and larger, until it looked like it wanted to burst out of the screen. Two symmetrical curlicues on either side of a flattened vertical oval, looking for all intents and purposes like an insect.

Like a butterfly.

4

Bogotá
Sixteen years ago

"Baboso!"

Lew heard his nickname and stood up in his dressing room, which functioned during the day as a horse stall. He had no idea what the name meant, but he'd started to like it. And it seemed to give the men no end of glee to say it. Chico, the man assigned to be his manager today, came back and told him to get ready. He'd already had two fights today and wasn't sure he wanted a third, but he'd racked up a higher than usual bar tab over the past few days.

"You fight one more, Baboso. You be rich tonight. Buy us all drinks."

The few men behind Chico laughed a dirty-faced, missing-tooth laugh. Lew wondered if that was his future. So far he'd managed to keep his choppers, but only because he'd made a mouth guard out of old newspapers.

"Whatever, Chico. *Su* asshole, *ma* asshole," Lew said, taking another swig of whiskey. The bottle was almost empty. Lew was glad this was the last fight. He was starting to feel no pain. Bad shit went down when that happened.

The crowd outside rose in volume, followed by both happy and angry shouts. A few minutes later, they dragged a big guy past his stall into the back where a veterinarian would sew him up, if he had enough cash. Lew figured the guy could afford it. He was the winner.

"Let's go!" Chico shouted, clapping his hands.

Lew took one more pull on the bottle and stood up, shrugging out of his full-length, brown leather duster, the only thing he'd bought with his prize money. Everything else he owned he'd come to town with on his back. Underneath he wore khaki army fatigue pants, army boots, and what had been a white tank top undershirt, now stained in sweat, blood, and dirt.

As he worked the kinks out of his powerful shoulders and lightly shadowboxed, the smart-mouthed men scurried out of the way like Lew was fire and they were tinder. Even Chico seemed to lose his management style with Lew towering over him. Lew took the smoking cigarette out of Chico's mouth and put it in his own. After taking a few drags, he dropped it and ground it out on the dirt and straw floor under his heel. Lew smiled and gave Chico a few slaps on the cheek, hard enough to leave a mark.

"Whatever you say. You're the boss, Chico," Lew said. He headed toward the sunlight at the end of the stable, rolling his neck as he trotted in a half jog to wake up his muscles.

He squinted in the afternoon sun glaring down from over the Andes Mountains in the distance. Men waving money and guns parted to form a gauntlet leading into the ring, which was just an open space surrounded by more of the men.

He stepped into the ring and saw his opponent on the far side. He couldn't tell much about him. Someone had tied his hands behind his back and pulled a burlap bag over his head. Every now and then someone would come out of the crowd and spit on him or kick him. The only thing he could tell was the guy was white and dressed all in black, like a failed ninja. He was small too; not short, but not a fighter. He looked more like a swimmer or a gymnast. Lew had seen a lot of things over the past several months, but this was the first time they'd kidnapped someone for him to fight. No, this guy, whoever he was, was in some deep shit. More like he was caught doing something he shouldn't have and now Lew was his punishment. Lew wasn't crazy about that arrangement, but a buck was a buck.

"Is he gonna fight or are you going to hang him from a tree like a piñata? Let's go!" Lew shouted, knowing most of the crowd couldn't understand him. They seemed to get his meaning, though. They untied the stranger's hands and shoved him into the middle of the ring.

He held out his hands, trying to balance himself. It took him a second to realize the only thing holding the bag on his head was gravity. He ripped it off, squinting and moaning from the glare. Apparently he'd been under it for a while. His face was all bloody and his eye looked like it was nesting in a purple goose egg.

Lew dropped his hands and stood up straight. It took the stranger a while to notice the big white guy waiting to beat the shit out of him. Once he did, and saw the crowd, he seemed to figure out what was what pretty fast. He was smart, Lew gave him that.

"What the fuck," Lew said to the crowd, not sure who was in charge, but knowing it wasn't Chico. "The guy looks like someone already beat him. Several times. What's the point of this?"

"The point is you don't get paid unless you fight, Baboso. Now fight!" Chico shouted.

You speak English?" Lew asked.

"Y . . . yeah."

"Then put your fists up," Lew said. "If you don't they'll dislocate your shoulders so you can't put your hands down. I don't know what you did, but I'm going to have to pound on you for it."

"Where am I?" he said, weakly putting up his hands and circling Lew.

"Bogotá. Where did you think you were?" Lew said, throwing a weak punch the guy easily dodged.

"Brazil," he said. "Who are you?"

"I don't think we should be getting too friendly, pal. I feel for you and all, but work's work." Lew threw a harder, more accurate punch, but to his surprise the guy dodged that one just as easily. *Boy's got some skills.*

Lew threw a few more failed punches. The crowd groaned and complained.

"I'm gonna cut you up, Baboso! Fight!" Chico shouted from the side. Lew thought he looked scared, like someone else was warning him. He scanned the crowd of angry, excited faces, but couldn't pick out Mr. Big.

"Looks like afternoon tea is over, champ. I'm going to have to hurt you now," Lew said.

"Man's gotta do what a man's gotta do," he said. "But tell me why short stuff over there keeps calling you a retard."

"What?" Lew said, turning to look at Chico. The stranger punched Lew in the throat and then the temple with his right hand. Before Lew could recover, he swung to the side and followed the initial volley with a left uppercut and a kick to the inside of

Lew's knee with his heel. Lew howled and hit the mud for the first time in his short fighting career. Lew looked up in time to see another kick coming.

He grabbed the foot, lifting and twisting at the same time, his chest muscles straining under the force. His attacker twirled through the air backward. But before Lew could feel too triumphant, the man in black tucked and rolled, using the throw's momentum to help him not only hit the ground softly, but pop back up to his feet in one smooth move.

"Son of a bitch," Lew said. The stranger smiled, but stayed where he was, letting Lew get up. When Lew was on his feet, someone yelled and two items flew through the air from the crowd. The items were identical and flashed reflected sunlight before they fell in the mud, one in front of each of the fighters. Lew bent down and picked up his machete. He swung it back and forth, the air whistling as he cut it.

"What the hell is this?" the man in black asked.

"Best pick it up, friend. They either love you or hate you."

"How's that?" he asked, picking up his machete.

"They must think this is a more evenly matched fight than they expected. So of course they're changing the rules. See all that money changing hands in the crowd?"

"Yeah."

"This is now a fight to the death."

"You mean it wasn't before?"

Man I like this guy. Lew shook the thought away. It wasn't helpful with what he had to do now.

Lew gripped his machete in both hands and cut the air again, trying to intimidate his opponent into making a mistake. It revved the crowd up too. Then the stranger worked his flat sword.

Holding the machete in one hand, he swung it and twirled it like a deadly baton, circling backward and to the side. Lew realized he had some serious training. *Crap.*

"What the hell was that?" Lew asked, circling in the opposite direction so they stayed apart.

"Kenjutsu," he said.

"Gesundheit," Lew said.

"The Art of the Sword."

"Terrific," Lew said. He scanned the edge of the crowd and thought about rushing one of the armed spectators so he could exercise the Art of the Gun, but knew he'd never get a shot off. Suddenly, he was really wishing he had waited until tonight to start drinking.

"We don't have to do this. Let me talk to your boss."

"Sorry, buddy. No take-backs in Bogotá," Lew said. Not that he could have taken him to his boss if he'd wanted.

"Suit yourself."

"Let's do this."

The crowd roared as the men launched at each other, blades glistening in the afternoon sun. The deadly steel clanked and twanged; attack met with block, again and again. Each time, Lew swung with both hands, looking for that one power strike that would end this. His opponent, on the other hand, used only one hand and frequently switched the blade from his left to his right and back again. Lew was pretty sure it was just to get him to make a mistake. And if this went on long enough, he knew it would work.

After a particularly exhausting series of lunges and blocks, the stranger stepped in close; something he hadn't done before. The blades smacked together, only this time he didn't back away. He kept his blade's hilt pressed into Lew's and leaned in.

"How'd you like to get out of here?" he said so only Lew could hear.

"What? Don't talk to me, man. We're supposed to be trying to kill each other," Lew said, though the idea of getting the fuck out of there and being able to let his aching arms drop was more than a little attractive. Right now they felt like lead weights and any moment he thought his shoulders were going to pop out of their sockets.

"We are. We're just taking a little break," the stranger said with a wink. Lew thought it was the most exhausting break he'd ever taken. The altitude wasn't helping. Bogotá was a mile and a half above sea level, and despite how long Lew had been there, he still winded faster than anywhere he'd ever been. Luckily, most of his fights lasted less than a minute. So far this one had been going for almost fifteen. He noticed that aside from the wounds he came in with, his opponent not only wasn't marked from their fight, he wasn't even out of breath.

"What's your plan?" Lew finally said. Something weird was happening. The more they fought, the less he wanted to hurt this guy. *Probably just the booze.*

"Who's in the stable right now?"

"One or two guys hang back, usually. In the back, counting money or fixing wounded fighters."

"Is there a back door?" he asked, swinging the clinched duo around every few seconds. Lew figured he didn't want the crowd to get too restless.

"Yeah, why?" Lew asked, getting tired of just providing information.

"That's our way out," he said, indicating the stable door with his eyes.

"I don't know if you noticed but there's about fifty guys out here who might have something to say about that."

"Leave that to me. Now, I'm going to cut you. Not much, just a nick. You go all roaring bull like you've been doing and come after me, keep swinging your machete, driving me back toward the door. Don't stop for anything, just keep pounding on me. When I give you the signal, run into the stable."

"What's the signal?" Lew asked, actually thinking for a moment this might work.

"I figured I'd yell something like 'Run into the stable.' Not too complicated for you, is it?"

Lew brought a knee up, but the stranger twisted and blocked it.

"Two problems with your little plan. They'll never buy it if I just drop my guard and let you cut me, and if we run into the barn there's going to be a herd of pissed-off, armed gamblers right on our ass. Other than that, the plan's perfect."

"Let me worry about our six, you just run. And I didn't say anything about dropping your guard, I just said I was going to cut you," he said with a grin.

"Tell you what. If you can cut me, we'll try this," Lew said, realizing he didn't have much choice. The crowd was getting pissed with their clinch and starting to throw things.

They pushed apart finally and circled each other again.

Then, moving so fast Lew had a hard time keeping his eye on him, the stranger did a somersault across the mud, coming to a crouch at Lew's side for just a moment before he rolled away, coming back to his feet. It was so fast, Lew almost didn't feel it. He reached down and touched his side, his fingers coming away slick and red.

"Son of a bitch," Lew said, realizing this guy could have carved him up at any time. But there was no more time for wondering. Lew was a man of his word, even if that word was likely to get his head cut off and fed to a pen of pigs.

Lew roared, fire in his eyes, and charged. He brought strike after strike down, the stranger's sword absorbing blow after blow. He drove him back farther and farther down the gauntlet, the crowd roaring with excitement. The closer to the stable they got, the more the crowd liked it.

"Now!" the guy yelled. And there was a moment that could have gone either way. A life-defining moment, for both of them. Lew could keep swinging, pretending to go along and then blindside the guy with his blade. Or he could go along with the plan. A moment later, Lew stopped swinging at him and ran toward the cool dark of the stable.

Out of the corner of his eye, Lew saw him raise his machete. For a moment he had a bad feeling about his decision, but then the guy slammed the blade into a rope running vertically up the huge door frame. Lew hadn't even noticed the rope until now. He kept running, and when he was partway into the stable, the dim went dead black with a crash. He spun around and saw that the stable's door had slammed down, the stranger running toward him. They didn't have much time. The door was massive and would take some teamwork to get it open. With the fervor the crowd had been in, that would take some time to organize. But not much.

The stranger ran past Lew and kept going. Lew spun and ran after him.

"Come on!" he shouted when Lew sidestepped into the stall that had been his dressing room minutes ago. He grabbed his duster and slipped it on before heading back out.

"Seriously?" he said when he saw what Lew had done. "A coat?"

"This is a great fucking coat," Lew said. "A lot of memories are in this coat."

Just then one of Chico's men emerged from a side room. It took him only a second to see what was happening. The stranger, obviously caught off guard, raised his machete, but the man grabbed it with one hand and pulled out a knife with the other. He was thrusting downward when a shot rang out. The bullet caught the man in the shoulder, the blade flying out of his hand. Lew fired again, hitting the wounded man in the forehead. He fell to the ground, dead. The stranger looked up at Lew.

"A lot of memories and one damn fine gun," Lew said with a grin.

"Thanks," he said. "Now, come on."

They ran down the length of the stable and found the back door Lew had mentioned. Never slowing, Lew kicked the door open as they ran. The light wasn't as bright now, the afternoon turning to dusk, but it still took them a second to survey the area.

A dirt road ran past the back of the stable, obviously a service road meant for trucks and horses. To the right the road wound up and then around a bend behind some shacks. To the left it shot straight down a steep incline that seemed to go on forever, but eventually met up with a paved road in the distance that looked like some kind of highway with almost no traffic. Straight across the road was nothing but jungle. This close to dusk, that way was a fool's journey.

"Which way?" Lew asked.

"I have no idea," the stranger said as the first man from the crowd came around the corner, bringing his shotgun to bear on them.

Lew fired twice, wood from the back of the stable exploding over the man's head. The man dropped his shotgun and ran back around the corner. The stranger ran over and picked up the shot-gun, cracking it open to check it—it wasn't loaded. He tossed the useless shotgun to the ground and rejoined Lew.

"What do you mean you have no idea?" Lew shouted, eyeball-ing both him and the corner of the barn. "What happened to your big plan?"

"This was it. Get us away from the crowd and out the back door. End of plan."

"Remind me never to disarm a bomb with you," Lew said, looking at the wall of jungle in front of them.

"Forget it," he said, and motioned down the hill. "We go that way."

"Why?" Lew asked, though he joined him in a light jog as they headed down the road.

"We have no idea what's around the bend back there. Unknown is bad. We like known. So we go this way. Besides, in this altitude, if you have to run, do it downhill."

Lew had things he wanted to ask this guy, but they needed to conserve their energy for the run, so he just listened to the rhythm of their feet smacking the hard-packed earth.

They reached the pavement and stood on the side of the road bent over and panting, Lew more so than his new partner.

They'd almost caught their breath when a truck's lights came over the hill. They flagged him down and the stranger convinced the driver to let them ride in the back of the open-topped cargo truck into downtown Bogotá.

They walked around the back of the truck and the stranger hopped up with Lew's help. He turned around and stuck out his hand to help Lew up. Lew looked at him for a moment but then put up his hands like the offer to help him up was a hold-up.

"Not me, gringo. I'm not done here, yet," Lew said.

"What? What are you going to do, go back to fighting?"

"No, I think you pretty much put an end to my career on this circuit. Hey, don't sweat it. It was time, anyways. You did me a favor. No, I . . . I just haven't found what I'm looking for yet," Lew said, looking off toward the mountains.

"In my experience, if a man gets too comfortable looking for something, he won't recognize it when it finally shows up," he said. Lew looked away but didn't say anything. "Come on, what could it hurt. Let me treat you to a night of the good Bogotá on Uncle Sam's nickel. Then if you still feel the death wish gnawing at you, I'll get you a ride back in the morning."

"Uncle Sam, huh?" Lew said.

"Am I telling you anything you didn't already know?"

"Not really," Lew said. He thought it over for a moment and then reached up and took his hand, but just to shake it.

"Name's Lew," he said.

"Jonathan," the man in black said. Lew made no move to get in the truck.

"Later, Jonny. Don't take any wood—"

A bullet zinged past Lew's head. They looked up the hill and saw a group of about forty men running toward them full-tilt. Another couple of wild shots screamed over their heads.

Lew and Jonathan exchanged the realization, eyes wide. Jonathan pulled and Lew came flying into the back of the already moving truck.

JONATHAN AND LEW leaned back in their chairs on the patio of the Cielo Jardin restaurant in the north end of Bogotá, their stomachs full of red snapper and spicy corn and potato soup. They'd ridden in the truck as far as the farmer would take them, which happened to be far enough away from the angry mob. They walked for a few miles before they came to a phone. Jonathan made a call, spoke a code, and twenty minutes later a car showed up. The window whirred down and an envelope was passed out before the window whirred back up and the car drove off. Inside the envelope was a passport, keys for a safe house, and a credit card paid by the government. Jonathan tried not to enjoy the stunned look on his new companion's face too much. They grabbed a taxi, and fifty thousand pesos later, they were taking a spot on the restaurant's patio.

It was a beautiful night; the sky was clear and the light breeze was kept off them by the long sheets that hung from the top of the patio's pergola, tied off on the railing that ran around the serving area. With each gust the white sheets snapped full and arched, looking more like a ship's sail.

The dinner and the night were on Jonathan. Or, on Jonathan's credit card, which his agency paid. It was the last meal he'd ever have at their expense. He was done with the intrigue.

"So how long were you in?" Jonathan asked before taking another pull on his bottle of Aguila.

"Still shows?" Lew asked, lighting a cigar to go with the whiskey he was drinking. Jonathan had never seen anyone who could hold his liquor like this guy. He was pretty sure Lew was just a lost soul, but it wouldn't be the first time someone was placed in his life to test him.

"Mostly in the way you fight. You don't pick that up on the street," Jonathan said. Lew took a long draw of smoke and blew it up into the air over the table, the wind quickly dissipating the plumes.

"Ten years. Or would have been ten years." Lew didn't expand on that.

"What made you quit?"

"How do you know I quit? Maybe I got drummed out or I'm AWOL. You never can tell," Lew said with a grin and a wink.

"I can. Usually," Jonathan said. He had to admit, Lew was hard to read, but he didn't get the sense he failed at much he set his mind to. "And you didn't answer the question."

"I guess I owe you that much for getting me out of there. Not sure why I didn't leave on my own," Lew said, sounding disappointed in himself. Jonathan knew how that could happen. Sometimes you get into spots that you think you deserve, whether it's true or not.

Once Lew's lips loosened up, they just kept on going. He obviously felt a kinship of some sort with Jonathan, but Jonathan got the sense that Lew had been waiting for a while to tell his story. To anyone.

He'd gone into the military to change the world. To do some good and help people. And he'd spent all ten years doing exactly the opposite. After what he went through in Kuwait, all to preserve the flow of oil to drag racers in the States, Lew had had enough.

"I took a half pension and walked away," Lew said. "Haven't looked back since," he said, raising his glass before downing it. Jonathan knew that wasn't true.

"You know what I think? I think you put so much of yourself into the army that when you left you didn't even know who you were anymore. I mean, you said, 'If I'm not a soldier, who the hell am I?' And you've been wandering around ever since trying to find the answer. Mostly in the bottom of a bottle or at the end of someone's fist," Jonathan said, watching Lew's expression slip from jovial to stoic.

"Getting kinda personal there, Jonny," Lew said. He wasn't

angry, he just seemed unimpressed. "Maybe I should tell you what I think of you."

"Maybe you should," Jonathan said. Sometimes listening to someone talk told you more about him than a profile could.

"All right," Lew said, his grin returning. Jonathan knew his type. If you made it a game, he was up for almost anything. "Let's see. You're obviously a spook. You're not with the major agencies, at least not directly. You're on your own. And you like it that way. But I'm thinking you're about as happy with your career as I was."

"What makes you say that?"

"Those melon heads that grabbed you and brought you to Bogotá. There's a sheen on you that says if you really were on your game, no way they would have gotten you. Or survived to transport you. You let them take you. You wanted to see what adventure they took you on. You were so bored, anything else was better. Especially if there was some risk involved. Which landed you in my little sandbox."

"Interesting theory," Jonathan said, hiding his amazement at Lew's intuitiveness. *This guy is way smarter than he looks.*

The next few hours were filled with more such discussions; some opinion and some confessional. And lots of alcohol. Jonathan told Lew that he did indeed feel the same way. He'd become a spy to fight the supposed evils in the world. But more often than not, he watched the powerful prevail while the weak suffered.

The restaurant owner finally got them to leave so he could close by giving them each a bottle of whiskey to take with them. With no destination and enjoying their newfound friendship too much, they wandered the streets of northern Bogotá, alternately singing and laughing.

Stopping in an alley to relieve themselves, Jonathan fell backward over some garbage cans while trying to do up his fly.

"Jeshus, you okay?" Jonathan said from the ground.

"Yeah, I'm fine. You I'm not so sure about," Lew said, bending over to help him up. Instead, Jonathan ended up pulling Lew onto the ground with him. They laughed and sat up against the alley wall.

They stared at the night for a while. Their wild ride was over and they knew it. Pretty soon they'd fall asleep or pass out, and tomorrow they'd wake up to a world of hurt and unknowns.

"You know my only regret? Well, my recent regret," Jonathan said.

"You weren't man enough to join the army?"

"Ha-ha. No, seriously. When I was in Brazil I was doing a handoff to this fat cat in the government. Guy had a house the size of my old high school. And you could tell by the way he walked around he didn't think anything could hurt him. He was completely untouchable. But that wasn't even enough for him. After the handoff, he had to march me around and show me all his shit. Stuff he'd had stolen for him from all over the world. He was one of these private collectors. Art, antiq . . . antiq . . . old expensive shit, books—you name it.

"He shows me this secret room he's got in the basement where he keeps his best stuff. Stuff that should be in museums. And all I keep thinking is why do you have this stuff if you keep it locked away in a room in your basement? What's the point, you know?"

"Yeah. That's your regret?"

"No, no. In this room, he has this one painting. I kid you not, a fucking van Gogh. He had some guy steal it for him years ago and replace it with a copy he had made. I mean, the museum has been showing this fake to people for years and they don't even know it. All these people who spent their tiny amount of vacation time to go see this work of art, this thing of beauty, and they've been star-ing at a fake. It just made me mad."

"I hear ya," Lew said.

"My regret is that I didn't have the balls to lay him out and take the painting back to the museum where it belongs."

"So why don't we steal it?"

"Yeah, right. We should," Jonathan said, laughing. He looked at Lew's face and saw he wasn't kidding. "Are you serious? We can't do that."

"Why not? Think about it. You're as pissed as I am at how the world works. The rich get richer, the poor get poorer, and it ain't ever changing. And in a few days we're going to go our separate ways and you know as well as I do we're going to either end up dead or doing the same old shit we were doing before. But this could be our chance. Our chance to do *one* thing right. Our chance to feel good about something."

"Yeah, but—"

"You gonna tell me you've never stolen anything as part of an op?"

"No, that's not the point."

"Then what's the point?"

"The point is . . . the point is . . ." Jonathan trailed off and thought about it. Soon he was smiling. "The point is it would feel fucking great."

5

New York City
10:05 P.M. Local Time

WITH A FINAL thump on the thick glass, Emily Burrows fell back into the Town Car's creamy silver leather upholstery, the heel of her hand red and sore from pounding on the glass for over five minutes straight, her throat raw from screaming. The panic rifling through her body aside, she'd never been in such a luxurious car before. At almost six feet tall, her slender frame fit easily into the space, a new experience for someone who spent most of her life banging her head on low ceilings. As her panting eased, she was about to start a renewed assault on her prison when a melodic voice spoke by her ear. She snapped her head around, confirming she was alone in the ample space.

"Over here, Miss Burrows," the voice said.

It was coming from one of the three LCD screens set into the wood grain panel along the front of the compartment, door-to-door smoked glass above it, similar to the glass on the doors and behind her. Unlike most tinted glass, she couldn't see through these at all.

This car was made for kidnapping. The thought renewed her panic and her breathing sped up. She swallowed hard and fought futilely to calm down.

"Please try to relax, Miss Burrows. Have a drink." With that last, a seamless panel opened, revealing a few bottles of water in a refrigerated compartment. Against her better judgment, her dry throat made her grab one of the bottles and gulp down half of it.

Just then, the LCD screen showed the image of a well-appointed study, rows and rows of bookshelves in the background. Sitting at an expensive-looking desk was a man in a black suit, white shirt, and thin black tie. The man wore a mask over his eyes and nose. The kind of mask worn at luxurious masquerade balls: Short, colorful feathers sprouted out the top of the mask, and loops of jewels hung down from the bottom.

On the desk in front of the stranger sat a copy of her book: *The Monarch's Reign.* She could see that more than half of the books behind the stranger in the rows of shelves were also versions of her book. All of the translations and formats were there: hardcover, softcover, book club, Italian, Spanish, French, German, and on and on.

A psychotic fan? Is that what this is all about? If nothing else, she was glad he was just an image on a screen. Actually being in that room would have been too much to take.

"Better?" the man asked, an almost gentle smile below the bizarre mask.

"Better? No, it's not bloody better! You won't get away with this," Emily said, looking at the screen, but slowly reaching into her bag. The water had calmed her somewhat, at least enough to think. She slipped her cell phone out of the bag and attempted to dial without looking at it.

"Please stop wasting time. Your phone won't work in there," the man said, seeming disappointed rather than angry.

Emily stopped moving for a moment when her ploy was spotted. She looked up and saw a tiny camera in the corner of the car's cab. She dialed 911 anyway. After a moment she saw he was right. There were no bars on her phone at all. *Bollocks.*

"Who are you? What do you want? Why am I here?" Emily spouted.

"I just want to talk. I think it will be quite beneficial for both of us," the man said.

"Well . . . you better talk fast. That was a police detective I was with when your thug grabbed me," Emily said accusingly, tossing her phone back in her bag. The detective was taking her down to the chief medical examiner's office on First Avenue to be questioned about the subject of her book when a woman nearby had screamed, distracting him. He'd told her to stay put on the sidewalk while he went to see what was happening, then the thug grabbed her and pushed her into her current prison. The screamer was obviously a ruse.

"Yes, Miss Burrows, I know. Time is shorter than you could possibly imagine. That's what I want to talk to you about. Be reasonable and you'll be back on the sidewalk in just a few minutes. I need your help," the man said.

"My *help*? Are you bloody insane? Why would I—" Emily briefly wondered what would happen to her if she wasn't *reasonable.*

"Or should I call you Miss *Denham*?" the man said softly. Emily's bluster evaporated, her eyes widening and her mouth dropping open at the use of her real name.

Thoughts raced through Emily's mind. *How much does he*

know? Does he just know the name or does he know everything? She knew there was only one way to find out.

"Why . . . why would you call me that? My name is—"

"Emily Katherine Denham," the man said. "Daughter of Sir Richard Denham, curator of the British Museum in London. Thirty-two years old, you studied law and criminology at Oxford University until you were expelled in your third year for . . . poor judgment. Your father used his influence to get you a posting with Interpol as the editor of their Web site, which you did for three years before resigning and dropping out of sight. Shortly before Emily Burrows, ex-Interpol *operative* showed up in New York. You spent the next two years researching and writing *The Monarch's Reign*, which was published two years ago. Did I miss anything?"

Emily drained the rest of her water and then slumped into her seat, deflated.

"You said it would be mutually beneficial. Beneficial how?" she asked.

"Much better," the man said.

A buzzer sounded beyond the obscured glass above the LCD panels. Almost instantly the glass whirred down from the top a few inches. A gloved hand pushed a metal case through the opening.

"Take the case. It's yours," the masked man said. She was tempted to jump up and look at who was in the front seat, or scream, hoping the glass wasn't as thick up there. Not that anyone would notice even if she was right. But with the revelation of her past, especially the mention of her father, she needed to play this out at the moment. He hadn't said as much, but the implication was clear—extortion. Honor was everything to her father and his world. If the truth about her past came out, it would destroy him.

She took the case and put it on her lap. The window whirred back up into place.

"Open it," he said.

She did. And stared speechless at the contents.

"I trust I have your attention," he said.

Emily lifted one of the packets of money out of the case and riffled through the bills to be sure it wasn't a couple of banknotes with newspaper between them. It wasn't.

"What exactly do you want from me?" Emily said, still mesmerized by the cash.

"To give you an opportunity. An opportunity to finish what you started," he said, gesturing with the copy of *The Monarch's Reign*.

The fear and anxiety in her chest now had a new comrade—excitement. *Can it be?*

"I want you to reveal The Monarch's true identity."

The words were so heady and powerful, she thought she might pass out.

"But first, we have some work to do. Or rather, you do."

The other two LCD screens snapped to life, showing several disfigured murder victims. Emily was dizzy with the roller coaster of emotions she felt from the fear of abduction, to the elation of a dream come true, and now to this—revulsion and horror.

"Pay attention, Miss Burrows. You have much to learn."

Eight thousand miles from New York, as Emily was released from her limo prison, Nathan Kring, CEO of Kring Industries, took off his mask. He rose from behind his desk and slowly walked to the floor-to-ceiling smoked windows overlooking his compound's courtyard. He stared at the jungle and then the ocean beyond, the sun just rising in the distance. Paradise.

Any normal man would have been satisfied to forget the world and spend the day on the beach working the burning sand through his toes. He wasn't any normal man. And the disease racing through his dying body would soon overcome the serum pumped into him that allowed him to appear normal. But he wasn't the only one that was dying.

Kring Industries was practically in its death throes, thanks to the past six months. The past six months—and The Monarch. The view outside his pseudo-castle's window and a few small companies scattered around the world were all that were left of the billions in enterprise his father, Bertil Kring, had left him. Nathan could just imagine his father's smug face as he watched his prediction come true. If he were alive, that is. The corner of Nathan's mouth twitched slightly at that last thought. To anyone else it might have just appeared as the first signs that the serum was wearing off. He knew better.

It was a Hail Mary, a final-ditch effort to prove his father wrong, the only thing he really cared about. If not for that, he'd willingly give in to the pain and anguish that was now his daily life and embrace the sweet relief he was staving off. He had to triumph—had to live—to have time to rebuild what he'd pissed away.

But at what cost?

Nathan, whose pride was immeasurable, had not only swallowed it, but had all but bootlicked over the past six months for his one last chance to triumph and fulfill his life's destiny. The only obstacle in his way now was a faceless thief hiding in America.

Nathan shook off the doubts trying to overtake him and redoubled his confidence in his plan. All the pieces were in place and there was no turning back now. Doubts were pointless. He would prevail—prevail and more. And in a matter of days he'd crush the life out of the one thing standing between him and his survival.

The Monarch.

6

NYC Office of the Chief Medical Examiner
10:15 P.M. Local Time

SAC JOSEPH WAGNER pushed through the cold metal doors into the OCME's morgue. Cummings's body lay on a metal table against the far wall. The room was chilled but not terribly uncomfortable. It was actually a little warmer than the frosty April night outside the First Street building. Wagner noticed Dr. Spangler hadn't started the autopsy yet; the familiar Y incision so Cummings's torso could be peeled open like an orange was absent. Several X-rays hung on light boards on the wall above the corpse.

"Cecil! You back there?" Wagner called, easing by the corpse and staring at the X-rays. He couldn't tell a rib from a finger, but the sight of that tube within the corpse's chest cavity was bizarre.

"I'm right here, Joseph. No need to shout," Dr. Spangler said, coming out from his office in the back. He was dressed in a rubberized smock, his hands encased in rubber gloves of the same green latex. A visor was on his balding head, the see-through face plate raised up.

"Sorry," Wagner said, putting away his reflex to shake hands when he saw what Spangler was wearing. "Haven't started yet?"

"I started an hour ago. I just finished moving cadavers around and making apologetic phone calls to the NYPD, CIA, and several insurance companies. Do you have any idea how many cases were in front of this one? I don't like being pressured. You might mention that to Director Matthews the next time you see him."

"I'll be sure to—" Wagner started to say before a voice came from behind him.

"Duly noted, Doctor."

Director Matthews was in the doorway. Among the people behind him was NYPD chief of police Marvin Powers. The only one in the crowd who looked halfway happy was Evans. Wagner knew the more the shit flew the happier Evans got. *He must be delirious with this one.*

The crowd moved into the room, revealing another crowd behind them of lower echelon cops and agents. With the press swarming the lobby, Wagner wondered if they were breaking some New York by-law ordinance.

"Whoa, whoa," Spangler said, holding up his hands to stop the audience trying to form a U around the corpse for a good vantage point of the coming dissection. "About half of you need to leave."

Standing by the corpse, Wagner noticed he wasn't included in the challenge. He thought that made sense, since it was only *his* career riding on this case.

Matthews sent Evans back out, but refused to reduce the numbers any further. Wagner knew Matthews would love to send Chief

Powers out as well, but he'd probably had enough shit storms for one day. Even so, he was pretty sure clear weather was still a long way off.

Matthews and Powers joined Wagner beside the corpse, Powers staring first at the X-rays and then at the tube protruding from the corpse's mouth.

"Anytime you're ready, Doc," Matthews said.

Spangler looked at Wagner and then shrugged. He picked up his pneumatic saw and revved the motor a few times before pulling his visor down over his face.

"You might want to back up a bit, gentlemen," Spangler said. He powered the saw and sliced into Bob Cummings's dead flesh.

Several minutes later, secrets even Cummings himself hadn't known were on display for all to see. Matthews looked bored, but Powers looked like he'd just been on a long sea journey. He was an administrator, not a street cop. Wagner thought he belonged in here about as much as the press.

"To preserve the corpse, I'm not going to fully expose the object," Spangler said, putting down his saw. "We can continue what the killer couldn't finish and just slide it out. Carefully." Spangler slipped his hands under the tube like it was a giant stick of unstable dynamite.

"Very carefully, Doctor," Matthews said, stepping forward. "It must come out intact."

"And so it shall," Spangler said without looking up. Matthews obviously didn't intimidate him at all. Wagner wondered what a world like that was like. "Joseph, could you help me?"

Wagner didn't move. He was fine with watching an autopsy, but he had no desire to touch the bastard.

"Oh come now. A big strong man like you afraid of little old dead body? I find that hard to believe," Spangler teased. Wagner would have let him tease on and not have moved, but then he saw Matthews's stare. Worse, he saw Powers regaining his composure and attempting a grin.

"What do you need me to do?" Wagner asked, stepping forward.

"Pry open his mouth and feed the last bit of the object down his throat. Make sure it doesn't catch on anything."

"Okay."

"As soon as we're done, we're taking it over there, to the basin to rinse off the bodily fluids before they do any more damage."

"Right," Wagner said, reaching for Cummings's jaw with his bare hands.

"Wait!" Spangler shouted. Wagner almost jumped. The only thing that made it worth it was the yip that came from Powers.

"What?"

"Put on the gloves behind you first. In the box."

Wagner did. He found it a lot harder than he thought it would be. When he was finally ready, he gripped the corpse's jaw in his hands, trying to ignore how cold the flesh was even through the gloves.

"And . . . now," Spangler said softly as he pulled the object. Wagner widened the corpse's bite and carefully fed the end down into his ruined throat. It was the strangest last meal he'd ever seen.

With little trouble, the object came free of the corpse. Spangler carried it over to the basin, sprayed it with cool water, and immediately patted it dry with a few soft towels. He leaned in and raised his visor to get a better look at the object.

"My word," Spangler said. The other men came around and stood over the table. "Hold down the edges, Joseph, while I unroll it."

"Gently, right," Wagner said.

"Even more so than before," Spangler answered. Wagner held the edges down and Spangler unrolled the object until it was completely flat. Everyone bobbed their heads back as if they were too close to see it properly.

"Jesus," Wagner said.

"Son of a bitch," Powers said.

"Magnificent," Spangler said.

"What the fuck are we looking at?" Evans, who had snuck back in the room, said from behind them. No one chastised him.

After a moment they all turned slowly in unison and looked at the opened corpse. Then at the same time, they turned and looked back at the object. When their silence stretched on into minutes, Wagner finally shook himself back to reality.

"Get that curator down here, Mike. And I mean now," Wagner said.

"Check," Evans said, heading out and almost running into a guy in T-shirt and jeans, wearing an NYPD gold detective's badge clipped to his belt.

"Sir?" Everyone turned to the door. and Wagner realized the detective was talking to Powers.

"What is it?" Powers asked.

"Uh, there's a problem with *the package*, Chief," the detective said, eyeballing everyone in the room as if he were asking for privacy.

"Out with it. We're all on the same side here," Powers said. Wagner knew of at least two people in the room who wanted to disagree with that.

"Well, Detective Minelli just called. He's had a little problem."

"Damn it, man. What kind of problem?" Powers's anger was palpable and seemed to be pushing the detective farther into the hallway. Wagner knew he just didn't want to look foolish in front of them. He also knew it was too late for that.

"He . . . he lost her, sir."

Powers winced and exhaled. When he opened his eyes, Matthews and Wagner were staring at him.

"Don't worry. I'll take care of this personally," Powers said, heading out of the room.

"See that you do, Chief," Matthews said. And the way he said it kept Powers from replying with anything but a nod.

"Goddamn amateurs," Wagner said.

"We've got a bigger problem than him," Matthews said.

"Such as?"

"The press. If they find Miss Burrows before we do, they'll run with this harder than Obama's birth certificate. We'll never be able to control the release of the story."

Wagner knew of a couple tabloid reporters who were running with the story based on the envelope contents alone already. The only reason it hadn't hit the airwaves in full force yet was that the bigger broadcast news outfits were running the contents of the file folder past their legal departments. But time was running out.

In a matter of hours the killer would have a nickname.

And a following.

DESPITE THE DAMAGE Cummings's bodily fluids had done to the edges of the painting, Wagner found it beautiful and sad at the same time. The group of medieval judges on horseback in the foreground seemed to be milling around in a confined space, waiting for something; the cliff and castles in the background overlooked and judged the judges. But what was most peculiar was the way they all looked off the canvas at something. Wagner wished he knew what they were looking at, but at the same time he was somehow glad he didn't.

After he and Matthews brought the painting down to the Crime Scene Reconstruction Room where it could hang to dry away from prying eyes while they waited for the Cloisters curator, Benoit, to show up, they'd stepped back, sat down, and had been staring at it in reverent silence ever since.

"Joan and I saw this on our trip to Belgium a few years ago," Matthews said. It was weird, because just then Wagner had been thinking about *his* wife, Patti. He couldn't wait to get away from this thing.

"Yeah?" Wagner said. He was a little tired of hearing about their globetrotting. He and Patti went to Florida every few years. They stayed at the same motel and ate at the same restaurants. He liked it that way. And he didn't bore anyone with the details.

"Somehow it seemed . . ." Matthews leaned forward. "Smaller."

"That's spatial reference," a voice behind them said. They turned around and saw Evans with Benoit. The curator wasn't looking at them, but was transfixed by the painting. Even so, he waved his hands and stepped closer to it as he spoke. "You no doubt saw it in its proper context. *The Just Judges* is actually part of a polyptych known as the Ghent Altarpiece. Officially, the title of the piece is *The Adoration of the Mystic Lamb*, in reference to the central painting. It was probably closed when you saw it, Director. In its full glory, when opened, the polyptych consists of twelve separate paintings.

"But this panel is the most infamous. And it would seem its lore is not quite over yet."

"A polyptych?" Wagner said.

"A work made up of several paintings on a set of hinged panels that can open and close," Matthews said.

"Very good, Director," Benoit said. Wagner thought the compliment pissed Matthews off more than it fluffed his ego.

"Okay," Wagner said. "Then how did *part* of a painting from Belgium get inside our friend upstairs?"

"The real *Just Judges* was stolen in 1934," the curator said, moving closer to the painting. "A replica was painted to take its place in the polyptych for display."

"Makes sense. Easier to explain a fake than it is to explain a big friggin' hole," Evans said.

Wagner said, "That still doesn't—"

"The replica is on loan to The Cloisters," Benoit said, finally turning around to face the trio of FBI agents. "I can't tell you what was involved in even getting the replica here. I'm sorry for what happened to Mr. Cummings, of course, but this is a tragedy of grander proportions. I can just imagine what Belgium is going to say when I call them and tell them we didn't even notice it was missing."

"I'm sure Cummings would feel for you. If he could feel," Evans said.

"The killer must have knowledge of the art world, then," Matthews said, "if he grabbed the one painting that was worthless to use as the murder weapon." Wagner knew what Matthews was really saying was that the museum staff was back on the suspect list.

"Oh my, Director, it may be a replica, but it's by no means worthless. It's certainly not worth the millions the original would be if it ever turned up, but private collectors would pay tens of thousands for the replica if it ever went up for auction. Which now, I'm afraid, is a moot consideration," Benoit said.

"*Tens* of thousands?" Evans said.

"Maybe more," Benoit said. He kept looking at them, but Wagner could tell he wanted to turn back to the painting. Wagner exchanged a glance with Matthews and knew they were both thinking the same thing, but it was Evans who voiced it for them.

"Somebody really wanted to make a loud noise we couldn't ignore with this one. A television personality vic and an expensive painting as the murder weapon."

Mozart's Requiem broke the room's mood as it played from Benoit's pocket. The curator took his cell phone out and looked at Matthews. The director nodded and Benoit answered it, turning away from them for privacy.

"Director?" an agent said from the door. Matthews excused himself.

"Any sign of the Burrows woman?" Wagner asked Evans when they were alone.

"Nada. NYPD is setting the town on fire looking for her, though. Have to give them points for that." Wagner expected Evans to try to save face for the cops. "So, you okay on this?" Evans asked, nodding toward Matthews.

"Not even a little," Wagner said. Matthews returned, his face saying good news wasn't on the agenda. "What?"

"MBC-News got the go ahead from their lawyers. FBI counsel got most of the package declined for now, but they're hitting the air in an hour with a piece on the murders. Time's up."

"Fuck," Wagner said.

"Well, check again. That's impossible!" Benoit stomped over to the painting after shouting into his phone. "Connie, I'm standing right . . . *my God.*" Benoit reached a shaking hand out and touched the painting near the bottom before the blood left his face.

"Mr. Benoit?" Wagner said, but the unsteady curator paid no attention to him.

Then Benoit inhaled like a fist had hit his breadbasket. The phone fell from his hand and clattered to the floor as he slumped to his knees in front of the painting, his arm shooting out for purchase. Evans stepped in, catching him. The man looked up, sobbing.

"Take it easy, buddy," Evans said a moment before Benoit grabbed his chest with his other arm. His eyes rolled back in his head and he keeled over, slamming to the floor with an audible crack.

"Jesus! Benoit!" Evans fell to his knees and rolled him over, pressing his fingers to his neck. "Shit, no pulse," Evans said to Wagner.

"Get the doc in here. Quick!" Matthews said to an agent by the door as Evans cleared Benoit's airway and started CPR.

Wagner picked Benoit's phone up off the floor. He could still hear a woman's voice coming from it, calling Benoit's name.

"This is Agent Wagner with the FBI. Who is this?" Wagner demanded. "What did you say to Benoit?"

"It's Connie Baker, Agent Wagner. From the museum. What's happening there?" She sounded genuinely concerned.

"What did you say to Benoit, Ms. Baker?"

"Nothing. I mean, I just told him there was a mistake."

"What kind of mistake?"

"The replica of *The Just Judges* isn't missing, after all."

"You've got the painting there? You're sure?"

"I'm standing right in front of it," Connie said. Wagner looked at the dripping painting and felt his own heart rate skip a beat.

"But if the replica is there, then that makes this—"

"Agent Wagner," Special Agent Duke Roberts, Evans's partner, called from the doorway. "You better come out here. Jesus, what did you do to the museum guy?"

Wagner's head spun. Spangler and Matthews ran in past him and knelt beside Benoit. Spangler took over for Evans, who stood up and moved beside Wagner, catching his breath. Evans leaned in so no one could hear him.

"Fucker's gone," he said.

"Who's gone? What's happening, Agent Wagner?" Connie's voice begged from the phone. Evans grimaced.

"Joe, you really need to come out here," Duke said again.

"What is it, Duke?" Evans asked.

"That woman's out here."

"What woman?" Wagner said.

"Emily Burrows. The one the NYPD lost."

"Told you they'd find her," Evans said with a smile.

"No one found her," Duke said. "She just walked in off the street."

"Agent Wagner!" Connie shouted from the phone. "What is going on?!"

"I wish to hell I knew."

TWENTY MINUTES AFTER Wagner asked Emily Burrows to take a seat in one of the small conference rooms, he returned with vending machine coffee and tea. Getting the beverages only took a minute, but letting her mind work on itself in the solitude was his real goal. That, and an attempt to get background information on her. They had some, but it would be morning before they'd had time to do a full workup. He needed to finish up before the news broadcast ran. It didn't give him much time.

"Tea with milk, right?" Wagner said, placing the tepid paper cup in front of her. He took a seat at the head of the table.

"Ta," she said with a slight smile.

He smiled warmly and sipped his own cooling coffee as he watched her. She was taller than he'd expected. She didn't wear any makeup to speak of, but she had a fresh-faced look; her reddish-brown hair clean and shiny. It bounced slightly when she turned her head too quickly, which she was doing quite a bit. She was nervous and fidgety, but for all he knew that was her normal demeanor. She smelled faintly of powder and lilacs, which unfortunately reminded him of Benoit.

Why isn't she asking why she's here?

"We just need a couple of things for the record before we start, Miss Burrows," Wagner said, opening his notebook. One of the envelopes sent to the media sat on the table. He hadn't decided yet if he'd use it or not.

"Which record is this?"

Wagner ignored her question and continued. "Your full name is Emily Katherine Burrows. You live at 145 Jackson Place, Apartment 3E. In Washington Heights. You've lived there for two and half years. You're a writer and you're here on a work visa from the UK that expires next month. Is that all correct?" Wagner asked.

"Uh, yes," she said.

"Anything else you want to say, anything you think I should know before we begin?"

She shook her head, the curls bouncing.

"What about Detective Minelli? The NYPD officer sent to bring you here. Anything to say about ditching him?"

"Oh, I didn't ditch him. I . . . I'm afraid I just got turned around in the crowds on the street. I tried to find him, but when I couldn't I assumed you'd want me to just come here. As I did," she said, playing with her scarf as she talked.

"Uh-huh," he said. He sat quietly and just looked at her for a minute. He made some notes and then picked up his coffee and leaned back. "Why'd you leave Interpol?"

"To write," Emily said, shrugging. "It seemed like a good idea at the time."

"What kind of writing do you do?"

"True crime books and articles," Emily said.

"Anything I would have heard of?"

"No, I doubt—"

"Does it pay good money?" Wagner noticed her eyes widen slightly.

"It pays fine. Nothing special," she said. She reached for the tea, but took her hand back without picking it up. Wagner made a decision then. He reached into the envelope.

"When did you write . . . this," he said, placing *The Monarch's Reign* on the table between them. She had no reaction to it, which Wagner thought spoke volumes. *She's not asking why she's here because she already knows. But how?*

"About two years ago," she said.

"I see. I've looked at the summary on the back of the book, but I have to be honest, I haven't had time to read much of it, yet," Wagner said, turning the book over to show the blurb he was talking about. "*The greatest thief you've never heard of,*" he said, reading the bold text on the glossy cover. "What exactly does that mean? And what does it have to do with this symbol?"

"I first heard of it during my time at Interpol," she said. "There were rumors—I think you call it chatter here—about a network of black market collectors. They were anonymous, powerful, and dangerous, from all accounts. They didn't care where their items came from, and in fact, would circulate lists of items they wanted."

"To what end?" Wagner asked.

"For all intents and purposes, they were shopping lists. High-caliber thieves would steal the items on the lists, knowing they had a, well, very motivated buyer willing to pay top dollar for items they would usually find impossible to fence. During our investigations, we started to hear about something else. Some*one* else, actually."

"A thief," Wagner said, tapping the blurb.

"Not just *a* thief, *the* thief. The only one with the moxie to steal from the stealers. About sixteen years ago this thief the collectors dubbed The Monarch first appeared. He'd steal items back from these collectors and anonymously return them to their rightful owners."

"Like Robin Hood," Wagner said, his notebook abandoned.

"Not quite. Just like the collectors, The Monarch operated anonymously, but he used surrogates to collect finder's fees from museums and insurance companies. Huge fees."

"How huge?"

"Over the years? Hundreds of millions."

"Of *dollars*?" Wagner said.

"Yes."

"The collectors must have *loved* him," he said.

"Like a plague," she said. "They started offering rewards for The Monarch, some of them higher than the value of the works he'd taken. They were, to put it mildly, enraged. But it didn't work. For sixteen years The Monarch, well, reigned over them. And then about five years ago, poof. He stopped. No one knows why. A few collectors apparently tried to take the credit for stopping him, but their claims never checked out. And to this day, no one knows The Monarch's true identity."

"Amazing," Wagner said, turning the book over in his hands. He realized he wasn't going to get any sleep tonight. "But why did they call him The Monarch?"

"It's in reference to the monarch butterfly."

"Of course," Wagner said, tapping the book's cover art.

"He left it on the walls of the private vaults after each theft. But they got it wrong," she said, catching Wagner off guard. He looked up into Emily's eyes and for the first time he saw a strength in them. She'd been through some sort of ordeal to find out what she was about to tell him.

"How so?" Wagner asked.

"The Monarch's symbol is actually an African symbol."

"African?" Wagner said in surprise. He hadn't seen that coming. "What does it mean?"

"The one who burns you, be not burned."

"What does—"

"It's a symbol of forgiveness."

"Forgiveness?"

"There's no way to know for sure, but I like to think that before The Monarch became The Monarch, he did something he thought was terrible. Being The Monarch was his way of seeking forgiveness. And rather than punishing the collectors and the thieves, he'd forgive them and give them another chance. But it's all in my book."

Wagner shook his head and decided it was his turn to tell her something.

"Miss Burrows, I have something to tell you, which may shock you," Wagner said. He beat the newscast by a few minutes, giving her an overview of what he was already starting to think of as The Monarch case, including the distribution of her book to the media. Through it all she nodded quietly, only seeming taken aback by the distribution of her book, not the murders themselves. But there was nothing conclusive in her behavior. He didn't have a baseline for her so for all he knew she reacted the same way when asked for directions.

He said, "Does it concern you that the subject of your book—the only book on the subject—is a killer?"

"He's not a killer," she said too fast.

"If what you just told me is true, then you don't know that. You don't even know if The Monarch is a he or a she," Wagner said.

"Let's just say it's a hunch. Regardless, I spent two years getting inside The Monarch's head. I may not have discovered his true identity, but that doesn't mean I don't *know* him. Believe me. And I can guarantee you he had nothing to do with these atrocities," she said. Wagner noted the defensive tone in her answer. *She's actually offended.*

After a quick double knock on the conference room's door, Evans stuck his head in.

"It's starting. Just the prelim stuff, but it could be important."

"I'll be right there," Wagner said, closing his notebook and suppressing a sigh. He took one of his business cards out of his pocket and handed it to her. "I'd like you to come downtown tomorrow so we can continue our conversation, if it's not too much trouble. Say ten o'clock?" Wagner said. Of course, it wasn't an option, but he wanted to see what she'd say, given a choice.

"Oh, um, sure. That would be fine," she said, standing up. She wrapped her scarf around her neck and waited for him to dismiss her. *She wants out of here. At least that's normal.* Wagner made a decision then that went against all protocol, but with her reactions throughout their brief interview, he needed to see her reaction to one more thing.

"If you have another minute, I'd like your impressions on something that just turned up. We're not sure what to make of it, but maybe you'll have some ideas," Wagner said.

Emily agreed and he led her down the hall to the Crime Scene Reconstruction Room, nodding to a few people along the way. A couple of NYPD uniforms stood outside the door while they waited for the armored car to transport the painting to FBI Headquarters at 29 Federal Plaza.

"It's not a body, is it?" Emily said with obvious revulsion.

"No, no. Nothing like that," Wagner said.

Wagner yanked the sliding door open and watched Emily's face. For a terrible moment, he thought she was going to pass out. She steadied herself, but her pupil dilations, nostril flares, and the rapid rising of her chest told him all he needed to know.

She turned toward him, eyes moist, and said, "What is it?"

He let her off the hook for the moment and walked her out of the building without making her get closer to the ruined *Just Judges* painting. He was short on time, and he preferred to let what she saw percolate in her mind overnight.

"There you are," Evans said, coming down the stairs to the lobby. "Matthews is looking for you. Did you really show Burrows the painting?"

"Don't worry about it," Wagner said, watching Emily on the sidewalk outside through the lobby's giant windows.

"So what's the verdict?" Evans asked as they headed up the stairs.

"I don't know, yet. She's hiding something. When the newscast is over, send a car over to sit on her apartment. Make sure she can see them."

"You got it," Evans said.

EMILY HALF EXPECTED to see someone following her when she looked back. There were a few people on the sidewalk behind her, but most of them faced the other way. She was being paranoid, but the realization did little to abate the tension she felt.

Thoughts bounced around her head like ricocheting bullets. *It can't be him. It just can't. He wouldn't do that . . . would he? NO! Maybe?* But there was no denying what she'd seen in that room. Wagner had been fishing or she'd still be answering questions. *The Just Judges* painting was indeed associated with The Monarch. It was one of the cases she'd seen cross her desk back at Interpol. But she left it out of her book. It was one of the only times The Monarch was not greeted with open arms by a museum and she thought leaving it out made him look better. She was protecting him, because of how she felt about him—how she felt and the fact that all evidence pointed to The Monarch still having the painting in his possession. Until now.

When Wagner slid that door open, she'd felt like someone had ripped her soul out the bottom of her spine and replaced it with broken glass. At least he hadn't asked her to get any closer. If that had happened, she didn't know what she would have done.

At the corner, she waited with a few other people at the bus stop, trying not to look like a jilted lover. She went over her conversation with Wagner while she waited, trying to remember everything she'd said. But it was all a blur. She couldn't focus on anything except that bloody painting.

The cell phone the man in the limo had given her tweedled in her purse and she almost jumped into the street. Ignoring the odd looks she was getting from the people around her, Emily dug in her bag and took out the phone.

"Miss Burrows." It was the same voice from the LCD screens in the limo, but it sounded different. Tired. *I know how he feels.*

"It didn't work," Emily said, turning away from the other

people at the bus stop. "They treated me like a suspect. I didn't get a chance to suggest anything and I got the distinct impression they wouldn't have listened even if I had. And you didn't say anything about the FBI. We probably shouldn't even be talking on the phone."

"Relax, Miss Burrows. It's an encoded phone, completely untraceable. Even if they somehow managed to pick your signal out of the thousands of signals online right now, they'd only hear gibberish."

Emily tried to relax but it was impossible with everything that was happening. She didn't even have the case she'd been shown in the limo. They promised she'd get it when she got home, since it would have been hard to explain sitting in front of Wagner, but she still thought that was asking for a lot of faith in a man who wouldn't even show his face to her, never mind tell her his name or what his interest in The Monarch truly was. For all she knew, he was the one responsible for the killings, though she wouldn't let herself think about that, yet. She doubted any of this was about the missing chapter from her book. The book had been left open-ended, and would stay that way until the identity of The Monarch was revealed to the world. Something she wasn't sure she would ever let happen.

"But I can't just—"

"We talked about this. It's not going to be easy. You can't just walk in and expect them to listen to you. You need to earn their trust. Just like you earned the trust of the sources for your book. You can do this."

By *this*, he meant inject herself into the investigation even deeper than she already was and report back to him. In return he promised to help her find The Monarch's true identity, finishing the missing chapter and—though still unsaid—protecting her father. But at that particular moment, the only sure thing she had was the phone pressed to her ear.

"I *can't*. How can I possibly convince them—"

"*Miss Burrows!*" The shout was so loud and abrupt she almost dropped the phone. She fought blossoming tears she knew had more to do with what that painting meant than a mystery man's bluster and after a long pause he spoke again, calmer this time. "Remember the endgame. It's what we both want. It's all that matters."

But why does it matter to you?

"I know. You're right," she said, knowing playing along was the only move she had right now.

"Have they shown you anything? Told you anything, yet? About the murders?"

She told him what Wagner had said and what he'd shown her in that terrible white room. It seemed to please him.

"They want to meet with me again tomorrow morning. He seemed a little, well, wobbly."

"Wobbly?"

"Unsettled. Like someone had dropped him into the middle of something he didn't understand. He'd obviously never seen my book before today, but I have no doubt that when we meet tomorrow he'll have read it from cover to cover. He seems very much like a man who doesn't like unknowns." She knew how he felt.

"The fact that Wagner is dealing with you personally is an excellent sign. I'll send you a file on him. Tomorrow, I want you to know him as well as he will know your book."

This man has access to FBI personnel files?

"He's going to know more than my book. My pen name identity has some documentation behind it, but nowhere near enough to fool a government agency. They're going to detain me the second I walk through that door tomorrow morning."

"Let me worry about that," he said. "For now, just go home and get some rest. Read Wagner's file and get some sleep. Tomorrow it's our turn."

He hung up before she could say anything. She put the phone away and turned around to see all the other bus patrons were gone. She'd been so preoccupied with the call she hadn't even heard the bus come and go. She sighed and slumped down on the empty bench to wait for the next bus. As she did, she wondered about the convenience of the murders and the mystery man's requests, but the ramifications were too overwhelming. She pushed the thoughts away as the next bus approached.

"Watch her," Nathan's voice said from the satellite phone held against Thomas Ranger's square head.

Thomas was sitting behind the wheel of the limo. He kept his eyes on Emily Burrows as she waited for a bus.

"Yes, sir," Thomas said.

"She may not be as solid as we'd hoped," Nathan said, sadness tingeing his voice. "We may need to change tactics if she doesn't perform as expected tomorrow."

"That would be unfortunate, sir." Thomas got the message. Nathan rarely explicitly asked him to kill.

"Don't misunderstand, Thomas. We need her alive. But you may need to extract her sooner than planned. Did you get Wagner's file?"

"Yes, sir," Thomas said, glancing at the folder sitting on top of the metal case on the passenger seat. "Our man inside is performing well."

"Good. Deliver the case and file and then put someone on her. You have men on site, yes?"

"Yes, sir, but I can just—"

"I want you back here, Thomas. At least for a little while. You'll be back in New York in time for the event," Nathan said.

"Yes, sir. See you soon," Thomas said signing off. He knew there was no real reason for him to head back to the island. No reason except that Nathan just felt better with his big dog by his side.

He put the satellite phone away and dialed a cell phone. He smiled when he thought about what he could do while back on the island. *Lara.* He wondered what she was doing right then but his fantasy was interrupted by a voice on the phone.

"Go for Bill," the voice on the phone said.

"Change of plans, mate," Thomas said in a less official but still commanding voice. "I'm going to need you to babysit a package for me until I get back into town."

"Roger."

7

Tallahassee, Florida
11:30 P.M. Local Time

THE SANDWICH AND coffee crashed to the ground at Jonathan's feet. The graphic of the butterfly symbol twisted and turned on the television screen until it landed up to the left of the announcer. And there was no mistaking what the symbol really was.

"*Hye wo nyhe*," Jonathan whispered into his empty house. *This is impossible. It's just . . . impossible.*

"According to the FBI, at any given time there are twenty to fifty unidentified active serial killers at large. Eighty-five percent of those are in America. Today, that number, whatever it may be, is plus one.

"Good evening, I'm Robert Kilpatrick with a late night special report.

"A sign of rebirth and renewal, this delicate creature has been chosen as a gruesome calling card by an unidentified killer calling himself The Monarch.

"Our reporter Jan Halton has the story from New York. Jan?"

The image of a well-dressed thirty-something female reporter appeared where the symbol had been. She had one hand to her ear and the other held a microphone. She was standing on what looked like a busy city street, a huge sandstone structure behind her.

"Thank you, Robert. I'm standing just outside Central Park in midtown Manhattan where six weeks ago The Monarch's first alleged victim was found . . ."

Jesus, they've even got the name?

The Monarch. Jonathan hated that name. He thought it made them sound like some kind of jumped-up potentate. But to be honest, he wasn't really thinking about how they were viewed. Right now, as with everything in his life now, he was thinking about Natalie. He needed to insulate her from this. But before he decided to dig in or pull a Casey Jones, he needed to speak to someone.

A very specific someone.

Lew watched the silent images swirl and shift. Scenes snapped from here to there; all of them interspersed with the spinning butterfly symbol as big as his fist on Warden Quinn's giant TV.

As the story progressed, chyron text scrolled across the bottom of the images with the highlights of each segment.

First victim, local artist, found by teens.

Body was posed and mutilated.

Butterfly is the symbol of rebirth and renewal.

The screen switched to a view of a giant, ornate church.

Second victim, gallery owner, crucified.

Church is refusing comment.

Identical mutilation.

A third murder came on the screen. For Lew, that clinched it. The smoke out the window had ebbed, but no one was making their way back, yet. He picked up the desk phone's receiver and heard an abnormal, high-pitched dial tone. He tried pressing 9, and the tone changed to a normal, lower-keyed sound.

Third victim a New York newscaster and ex-NYPD officer.

Museum says nothing stolen.

Lost treasure destroyed.

Lew hesitated before dialing. He knew the number, that wasn't the problem. Dialing this number had consequences. It would send him down a path he'd only minutes ago refused to take. He'd be unleashing something he'd kept bottled up for a very long time. But the real danger was that he might not get the genie back in the bottle ever again. Not alone.

There was a worse possibility, of course. What if what these images were intimating was true? *Not possible. Not him. Not in a million years.*

But he knew if that were indeed true, he wouldn't be hesitating. Or shaking.

11:50 p.m.

JONATHAN WAS JERKED back to reality by his cell phone ringing on the table beside him.

"Hello?" he said, still looking at the television screen.

"You see it?" a voice said. A voice he hadn't heard in almost two years.

"Lew?"

"Did you see it?" Lew asked.

"Oh, I saw it," Jonathan said. He looked at the number displayed on the phone but didn't recognize it. "Where are you?"

"The lap of luxury," Lew said. "Don't worry about it. Listen, do I have to ask?"

"Relax. I'm still in Tallahassee," Jonathan said. He wasn't insulted. Fact was, he'd been thinking the same thing about Lew until he called.

"What the fuck is going on? No way that's a coincidence."

"No shit."

"Listen, I don't have much time. What do we do about this?"

"Do? We don't do anything. We're nowhere near New York. This has nothing to do with us," Jonathan said, not even believing that himself.

"Right, and Oswald was a patsy," Lew said. Despite the situation, Jonathan felt himself smiling. He missed Lew more than he knew.

"Okay, okay. So it has something to do with us. But what? Why now?"

"Hey, you're the thinker. I just break shit, remember?" Lew said. Jonathan knew that wasn't true either.

"I need to think. Figure this out. Get more info. That report was sketchy as hell."

"Said enough for me, thank you very much."

"Why don't you have much time?" Jonathan asked. It was his way of saying he wished Lew was here to talk to in person. Aside from missing his old friend, Lew was the only person on the planet he *could* talk to about this.

"How's Natalie? Did she—"

"Relax, she's asleep," Jonathan said. Despite how Lew had acted when Jonathan told him he was quitting, Lew had always had a soft spot for Natalie. Before he left, she'd even started calling him Uncle Lew.

"I need to wrap this up. Just tell me one thing: Do you need me there?" Lew asked. Jonathan could hear the change in his tone. He knew if he could see him his features would be darker than normal. He wanted to say yes, but from the sounds of it, the price was way too high. Even with what he'd just watched.

"No, I'm good. Like I said, I don't know much of anything right now. Chances are the best move is to just ride it out," Jonathan said, hoping he sounded convincing. There was a long pause on the line.

"Good enough. I'll call again when I can. Give the squirt a hug for me."

"I will, you—" but Lew had hung up.

Jonathan snapped the phone closed and noticed the mess on the carpet for the first time. *Can I really do this alone?*

He looked up at the photographs of Natalie on the mantel and realized there was no digging in and hoping this would pass. He had to make sure none of this—none of his old life—touched her. He'd die before he'd let that happen.

Die or kill.

8

Cuiabâ, Brazil
Sixteen years ago

AN HOUR AFTER making their inebriated decision, Jonathan and Lew climbed aboard a plane and spent almost fourteen hours alternating between making plans and fitful sleep. In the sober light of day, Lew half expected Jonathan to recant and chalk his decision up to drunken courage. Not only hadn't that happened, but Jonathan had taken the lead in their little adventure. That was fine with Lew. He was used to taking orders. Sort of.

"Faster, Spyboy," Lew said from his position at the edge of the villa's balcony. He peeked around the corner at the courtyard below where an evening party was in full swing. From the uniforms and bodyguards sprinkled throughout the crowd, Jonathan hadn't been exaggerating about this guy's connections.

"Don't rush me," Jonathan said as he teased the balcony door's lock with his pick tools. "This is a lot easier when your head doesn't feel like a busted papaya."

"I feel fine," Lew said. He was lying. He actually had to concentrate to keep from falling off the edge of the balcony onto one of the Mercedes parked below.

They'd decided to go in tonight because of the party, their condition aside. At first Jonathan had wanted to wait for a less busy night, but Lew knew if they waited too long they'd lose their nerve. Besides, if everyone was down at the party, they wouldn't be in the house. Or so he hoped. "I guess you just can't hold your—"

Lew stopped talking when he saw he was on the balcony alone, the door open. Lew eased himself back onto the balcony and went inside.

The bedroom—a guest bedroom, Jonathan had said—was immense and looked meant for someone in a royal family. Tapestries and artwork decorated the walls. The floor was a rich caramel gold carpet with an inlaid black and red pattern that looked Mayan. Against one wall was a four-poster bed you'd need a stepladder to get into, the frame and posts a rich red brown oak.

Across the room, Jonathan eased the door to the hallway open and peered out.

"Don't mind if I come in, do you?" Lew said. Jonathan just held his finger to his lips. Lew reached for his gun, but Jonathan shook his head. He waved for Lew to come closer.

Lew stepped lightly to the door and looked where Jonathan was pointing. There was a guard sitting in a chair that looked like a throne at the end of the hall. What Lew noticed most was the machine pistol in his lap. Jonathan eased the door shut.

"The room across the hall is another bedroom. There's a dumbwaiter in it that goes all the way to the wine cellar in the basement.

I don't think it will hold us both, but we can take turns. If we can get over there," Jonathan said in a hushed voice.

"How do you know all this?" Lew asked. "Did he give you a tour or something?"

"Occupational hazard," Jonathan said, smiling. "Even if I'm just doing a handoff, I always gather data on where I'm going—blueprints, staff, security, etcetera."

"What's around the corner from where that guard is sitting?" Lew asked.

"Another long hallway of rooms. Around the next corner is a staircase leading down to the main floor."

"So nobody will notice if he's gone?"

"Unless they come up here."

"That party isn't even half done. No one's coming up here," Lew said. He knew Jonathan understood what he was saying. It was obvious from his face he didn't like the idea. Which made sense. He was a spook. In and out with no traces. Lew was army. Left to him, he'd toss a grenade down the hall and run for the prize when the bits started flying. They needed a middle ground.

"Okay," Jonathan said after he looked around the room for a bit. He obviously saw no alternatives. "What's your plan?"

"Keep it simple. Open the door and yell something in Spanish down the hall. He comes to investigate. We jump him."

"That might work . . . if we were in a country that spoke Spanish."

"Oh. What do they—"

"Portuguese." Lew's Spanish was terrible. He wouldn't know Portuguese if he heard it. "Yes," Jonathan said before Lew could ask him if he spoke Portuguese. "Well, enough to get him to come in here, anyways."

"Works for me," Lew said. He picked a small statue up off a table by the door and held it like a club.

"Don't kill him," Jonathan said before he eased the door open and backed away. Lew put the statue down and nodded that he was ready. "*Ajuda! Alguém me ajude!*" Jonathan called out the door and then backed away himself.

Lew didn't know what he'd yelled, but the next thing he heard were footsteps coming down the hall.

"*Olá? Quem disse isso?*" the guard called as he approached. Jonathan stood with his back to the door, leaning on one of the bedposts, hunched over with his hand to his chest. When the guard entered he raised his gun for a moment, but then lowered it when he saw Jonathan's apparent condition. "*Você precisa de ajuda?*" the guard said. Lew assumed he was asking if Jonathan needed help.

Jonathan turned to reveal his hand wasn't on his chest, but holding an automatic.

"Not as much as you, brother," Jonathan said before Lew grabbed him from behind with a chokehold. A minute later, the guard was out cold.

They tied, gagged, and slid him under the bed.

"Let's go," Jonathan said. They checked the hall and then entered the bedroom across the hall.

It was similar to the one they'd just been in, but light colors and pastels decorated it. In the corner was the dumbwaiter.

"The party looks catered, so they shouldn't need to use this," Jonathan said, climbing in to go down first.

"And if they do?" Lew asked.

"Then you get to kill someone. Probably us," Jonathan said.

"Well, then maybe we should—" Lew again was alone as Jonathan pressed the button for the wine cellar and the door slid shut.

A slight hum rumbled at first, but then it dissipated as the car traveled down.

"That's really getting annoying."

About five minutes later the dumbwaiter started to rumble again and then the door opened. A single bottle of wine sat inside. Lew smiled and took it out, putting the bottle on the floor.

"I'll save you for later," Lew said. He climbed in the dumbwaiter, the wood creaking and moaning. He didn't remember it doing that for Jonathan. "Here we go." He reached around, felt the control buttons, and pressed one. The door slid shut and the rumbling started, much louder from inside the car. It shook and jolted and then started to ease downward.

After what seemed like minutes, the car stopped and the doors slid open. Lew knew instantly he'd pressed the wrong button. In front of him, in a small kitchen, were two people dressed in white chef outfits—mostly. Both their pants were on the floor and one of the kitchen workers was definitely female, Lew reasoned, from the white jacket that was open displaying her mocha breasts. The male kitchen worker had his back to the dumbwaiter and was busy squeezing one of those mounds and making movements with his hips that said he didn't hear his own breathing right now, never mind the dumbwaiter. Lew reached out and made sure he pressed the bottommost button this time. As the door slid shut again, he leaned down to keep his view of the kitchen staff as long as possible.

"Any problems?" Jonathan asked as he helped Lew out of the cramped car.

"Problems? Nope. Easy as . . . pie," Lew said.

They made their way out of the wine cellar and down the stairs to another short hallway, this one with only two doors. Jonathan ignored the doors and walked to the end of the hallway where a basin with flowers sat against the wall.

"What are you doing?" Lew asked.

"Watch."

Jonathan gripped the basin and pulled up. Lew heard a click and the wall popped out slightly. Jonathan slipped his fingers around the edge and opened the wall, which was really a hidden door. He reached in and flipped the switch on the wall. Inside the small room was a vault door with a tumbler and a large wheel handle that looked like the thing you used to steer a ship.

"Did you get the combination when you were here before?" Lew asked.

"Better," Jonathan said. "I saw he was so confident"—Jonathan grabbed the wheel and pulled—"that he never bothers to lock it." The door swung open. As it did, lights inside flickered on. First the ones closest to the vault door, and then farther and farther back in the vault. The click and flicker of the lights echoed in the vastness of the chamber's concrete walls.

"Jesus. We're robbing Batman," Lew said.

Their footsteps echoed as they descended into the vault. It was an awesome sight. Works of art were not only on the walls—each illuminated from above by an individual light—but there were statues and sculptures on pedestals, glass cases filled with jewelry and icons, and bookcases stuffed with the rich, brown leather spines of books, manuscripts, and rolled documents on yellowing parchment. But the centerpiece was at the back of the chamber. Almost glowing under its private illumination, van Gogh's *Sunflowers* hung on the wall. It was one of the most recognizable of van Gogh's paintings and even Lew, who thought dogs playing poker was the height of art appreciation, recognized the painting.

"Unbelievable," Lew said.

"Last year thieves stole twenty van Gogh paintings from the museum. They were supposedly found a few hours later just sitting in the getaway car. The thieves, of course, were nowhere to be found," Jonathan said.

"If they were found, then how is this—"

"It was a scam. The paintings left in the car were forgeries. So good they were works of art in their own right, but forgeries all the same. They had been painted months ahead of time and chemically aged to match their original counterparts. The plan had always been to leave them in the car for the authorities to find. Then the thieves would be free to sell the originals to private collectors like this asshole."

"The best crime is one that no one knows was committed," Lew said.

"Exactly," Jonathan said. He carefully removed the canvas from the frame and rolled it up. He took a plastic tube from his pocket and slipped the painting inside.

"What is something like that worth anyways?" Lew asked. He was starting to wonder if this whole Robin Hood approach was the best idea.

"Ten million dollars," Jonathan said.

"And there were twenty of them!?" Lew was honestly shocked. Then he spotted the jewels in the case by the wall. "Maybe we make this worth our while," he said with a nod of his head.

"You do and you're on your own. That's not why I did this. Speaking of which," Jonathan said, pulling something out of his pocket. Lew saw it was a stick of charcoal. He stepped up to the wall where the painting had been and drew a large flat oval. On either side he drew what looked like mirror images of the number three. When he was done, he stepped back and admired his work.

"I don't get it. What's a butterfly got to do with van Gogh," Lew said, looking at the image.

"It's not a butterfly. Before we crossed paths, I did a few years in Africa, mostly around Kenya and the Gold Coast. There are African symbols everywhere down there, and they're so old no one knows who made them or when they were first used. This is the *hye wo nhye*. It means 'the one who burns you, be not burned.'"

"Sure, whatever you say," Lew said. He didn't get it at all. All he got was that it wasn't okay to steal something you could sell, but it was okay to draw on the walls with a crayon.

"It's a symbol of forgiveness," Jonathan said, as they turned and headed out.

"Forgiveness? You're forgiving this asshole after what you told me about him?" Lew thought he could know this guy for years and would never understand him completely. But he did think it was a pretty cool symbol.

They made their way back out to the balcony without incident, leaving the guard tied up. If they let him go, he'd be shot for sure. Not that he had much chance now. Lew didn't know how Jonathan felt, but he had to admit, taking anything else would have made it a whole different event. He felt like he'd done something good with the skills the army had given him, for the first time in a long time. He'd feel even better once they unloaded the painting and weren't walking around with a ten-million-dollar bull's-eye on their backs.

SEVERAL HOURS LATER, Jonathan hung up a payphone and ran across the street, almost getting clipped by a cab in the morning rush hour. He made it to the table at the outdoor café where Lew was sitting, gnawing down the closest thing to a McMuffin that he could order.

"You look like you just won at the track," Lew said. "Did you set up the exchange with the museum? How'd they take the idea that they've got a fake on the wall?"

"Oh, I set it up all right," Jonathan said, motioning to the waiter for more coffee. Lew thought the last thing this guy needed was caffeine, the way he was bouncing.

"And?"

"They want to do some tests on the one they've got before they buy in, but they're totally on board, trust me. I'm going to call them tonight. We'll probably do the exchange in Amsterdam in a couple of days."

"So what's got you so fired up?" Lew asked.

"Did you know there's a finder's fee for stolen art?" Jonathan asked, holding his cup up for the waiter to fill. Lew had stopped chewing and was eyeing his new friend, trying to see if this was a joke or not.

"What kind of finder's fee?"

Jonathan took his time, taking a sip of his coffee. "Ah, that's good."

"Don't make me hurt you," Lew said. "How much?"

"Since we want to remain anonymous, we had to take a bit of a lower commission, but it's still—"

"How much!?"

Jonathan smiled and leaned forward. "Eighteen percent."

"Of ten million," Lew said when he stopped choking.

"Yes, sir."

"I think I just found my purpose in life," Lew said, holding up his coffee cup.

"You and me both, my friend," Jonathan said, clinking his coffee cup to Lew's like they were drinking champagne, which soon they would be. Lew looked in Jonathan's eyes and knew they weren't talking about the same career. Oh, they'd be doing the same thing, but not for the same reasons.

Not at first, anyway.

PART TWO

Saturday

9

FCI Yazoo City
Yazoo, Mississippi
12:10 A.M. Local Time

LEW MADE SURE the phone was in the exact position it had been before he'd called Jonathan, not that it was likely Quinn would notice if it wasn't. His desk was a mess of papers, receipts, and electronics manuals. Lew pushed the edge of the blotter to the side and smiled when he saw several travel brochures hidden underneath. If nothing else, this wasn't a setup. Of course, that didn't guarantee Quinn would make good on his promise if Lew went through with it. He needed some leverage.

Before he could search the office any further, he saw Quinn making his way across the yard. He only had moments before he'd have to commit one way or the other. After the phone call, he pretty much knew what he was going to do, but if he feigned indecision it might give him a chance to find that leverage he needed.

Lew sat down. He looked away from the television. It was just a rerun of *Match Game*, but the memory of what he'd seen there was still too fresh. He acted bored as he heard Quinn's footsteps approaching.

Quinn, damp and smoky, pattered in and immediately unlocked Lew's cuff. He strained up on his toes and peered out the window like a kid about to steal a cookie. When he was apparently satisfied, he slipped around his desk, fumbled with some keys, and unlocked a drawer.

"Everyone's either locked down or working the fire," Quinn said. "The truck is parked at the loading dock. Get it done and then hide in the back with the body. The doc is busy treating some wounded men. The truck driver is locked down in the waiting room. We couldn't have planned it better."

"What do you mean *we*, paleface. Did I miss the part where I agreed to do this?" Lew said, knowing he could stall for only so long. Quinn was right; if he was on the level, this was the perfect window to get this done.

Quinn took his hand out of the drawer, and Lew looked down the barrel of a snub-nosed revolver. A long moment stretched out before Quinn flipped the gun around and offered the handle to Lew.

"Please," Quinn said. Lew realized Quinn had gotten himself into a pickle and Lew was the guy's only way out. The funny thing was Quinn was *his* way out too. Lew took the gun, careful to remember where he touched it. He'd wipe those spots, and the other fingerprints on the gun would be his insurance.

"Aren't you worried that the autopsy will show a stabbed prisoner is full of lead?" Lew asked.

Quinn's reaction was silent but telling. "Colero's not gonna make it to the coroner, is he?"

"You better hurry" was all Quinn said. Lew stood up, put the gun in his waistband.

"How is Costa Rica this time of year?" Lew asked. The look on Quinn's face was priceless. But the good humor didn't last once Lew thought of what he was about to do.

LEW PEERED INSIDE the door leading to the loading dock. Miguel Colero sat on a beat-up picnic table smoking a cigarette and looking bored. Lew figured he must have greased a few more guards to be here instead of in the morgue. Beyond Colero was the coroner's cube van, the back gate rolled up and waiting to be fed. Inside was a single pine box. Other than that, the van's cargo space was empty, save for a storage locker in each corner for supplies.

He eased through the door and across the concrete floor toward Colero. Lew reached for the gun in his waistband just as his victim turned around.

"What are you doing here, *ese*?" Colero asked.

Lew pulled out the gun and pointed it at him. Colero's demeanor remained unchanged.

"You're probably not going to believe this . . ." Lew said, then, "Holy shit!" Lew looked at the truck with shock plain in his eyes. Colero turned and Lew slammed the butt of the gun into the back of his head.

Colero groaned and fell face first onto the picnic table, like he'd been served up for a feast. Lew ran back and checked the hallway. When he saw it was clear, he put the gun back in his waistband and searched the shelves along one wall. It took him a few minutes, but he finally found some duct tape.

By the time he had Colero trussed up like a shiny gray mummy, the pint-sized drug lord started to come around.

"*Chingada Madre*," he said groggily.

"That's pretty bad language for an accountant, hombre," Lew said. He tore off a foot-long length of tape before he put the roll back on the shelf and checked the door again.

"What the hell are you doing?" Colero said, fighting his bindings.

"I told you, you wouldn't believe me," Lew said.

"Try me, *hijo de puta!*"

"I'm saving your miserable, worthless life," Lew said. He put the length of tape over Colero's mouth and then heaved him up on his shoulder. "But I can see how you'd be confused."

10

Washington Heights
New York City
1:00 A.M. Local Time

"Slow down. You're not making any sense," Emily said.

Dan Cooper, a young man who couldn't have been more than twenty years old, had shown up at her door ten minutes after she'd gotten home.

He was some sort of intern for the *New York Times*. He was short, slight, and had shaved his head and sported a patchy goatee in an apparent attempt to look older. It hadn't worked. He looked like a cancer patient with a dirty face. If he'd paid more than fifty dollars for the suit that hung on him like a sack, it would be a crime. He wore black and white Keds running shoes, one of them with the laces untied. He'd been struggling with a mishmash of folders and rolled-up tubes under his spindly arms when she'd answered the door. But all of that wasn't why she'd let him in, it was what he'd said: "I know who murdered those people."

But he'd been talking nonstop for ten minutes and still wasn't making any sense. Several of his rolled-up tubes were unwound on her kitchen table. They were maps of New York, and Dan had drawn on them with several colored markers.

"I'm sorry. I get excited sometimes. Could I get a glass of water if it's not too much trouble?"

"Help yourself," Emily said. She scanned the maps again while he went to the sink, but her focus waned when she realized Dan was standing beside her oven.

The metal case of cash had been waiting for her on the kitchen table when she got home. Once she got over the idea of someone being inside her apartment while she'd been gone, she looked inside. The cash from the limo was there, along with a folder with a single word on it: "WAGNER." Then the kid's knocking had startled her, and she'd dropped everything on the floor. After quickly scooping the contents back into the case, she'd panicked and jammed the case into her oven before answering her door.

"Um, you still haven't told me how you got past the car out front." Wagner had sent a car to watch her, but the masked man had warned her that might happen. Even so, it had been disturbing to her, so she wondered how this Chihuahua of a person had handled it with such composure.

Dan turned around, holding his glass with a self-assured grin on his face. "I paid a homeless guy twenty bucks to pee on their car," he said with pride before putting the glass of water to his lips. Emily shook her head. Maybe she'd underestimated this guy.

"Brazen," Emily said. "Most seasoned reporters wouldn't have figured out how to get past a couple of FBI agents."

Water shot across the room. Dan almost dropped the glass as he coughed another few ounces out of his lungs. Emily jumped up and went to him, taking the glass from him and patting him on the back.

"F . . . FBI?" Dan managed when he could breathe again.

"Yes. Who did you think they were?"

"Jeez, I just thought it was a couple of reporters. I think I'm going to be sick."

"Not here!" Emily said, grabbing him and pushing him toward the bathroom. They almost made it.

Half an hour later, she'd finished cleaning up the mess. Dan lay on her sofa, his suit jacket hung on the back of a chair, and a cool compress rested on his forehead. She sat beside him and with a motherly touch, checked his temperature by pressing her hand to his cheek.

"Feeling better?"

"How am I going to be a reporter if I go to prison?"

Emily looked at his slight build and thought if he went to prison, a career choice would be the least of his problems. "You're not going to prison," she said, thinking if anyone in that room was headed that way, it was she.

"I am. I know I am. Cripes, they're probably listening to us right now," Dan said. She saw him getting worked up again and tried to think of a way to distract him.

"Tell me about this again," Emily said, walking over to the table. "What do you think you found?"

"It's probably nothing," Dan said, carefully sitting up. But she could tell by his voice he didn't believe that. By his voice and the fact that he was in her apartment. He'd apparently tried to get his coworkers to help him, but they wouldn't listen to him. She was his last-ditch attempt for vindication.

"Humor me," she said. "The dots all along the streets. What are they?"

"Traffic cameras," Dan said, carefully standing and coming over to the table. They sat down. Talking about it seemed to relax him. And the sooner he recovered, the sooner she could get him out of here.

"What about them?" Emily asked, egging him on.

"During each murder, the traffic cameras in the area went dark for a short period of time. Just a few minutes. Just long enough to . . . well . . . do it and get away without being seen."

"Do they know how he did it?" Emily asked, interested in the answer.

"No. Or not that I know of, anyways. But here's the thing, it's a pretty unique trick. So I started thinking, if I was smart enough to know turning off the traffic cameras would let me kill without being seen, what about my getaway?" This was where he'd gotten all excited last time and Emily had lost him. She wasn't sure if she finally got her mind off the money in her oven or something, but this time it was making sense.

"If you can't see him kill, you just look at the cameras outside of the dark zone and you can piece it together."

"Right," Dan said. "My uncle works for the traffic department, so I asked him for a listing of any other dark areas around the same time as the murders."

"Good thinking," Emily said, honestly impressed.

"Thanks. Well, the first two murders were dead ends. No other cameras went dark. I figure he probably got on a bus or went down into the subway or something. But here . . ." Dan flipped through the maps and pulled the one he was looking for on top. Emily could see it was a map of the area of town where the third murder took place.

"You got something?"

"Just after the time the third murder took place, a bunch of other traffic cameras went out in sequence. They started close to The Cloisters museum," Dan said, pointing to the dots he'd marked. Then he drew along the streets with his finger, showing Emily where the line went. "And ended here, near Brooklyn."

"What's the big red X mean?" Emily asked.

"This is where it gets really *Twilight Zone*-y. Just before the last traffic camera came back on, there was a traffic accident right there. A truck hit a car, killing the driver. Then boom, just when the accident is over, the camera comes back on." He stopped talking and smiled, leaving Emily feeling let down.

"It's interesting, but probably just a coincidence. There were likely a lot of accidents during that window."

"That's what I thought at first. Then I saw the police report," Dan said, digging through the papers. She grabbed his hand.

"Just tell me, Mr. Cooper."

"Oh. Uh, okay," he said. "The report said that while they found the remains of the driver of the car, there was no body in the truck. Kind of weird but not unheard of. I mean, maybe the driver fell asleep, woke up after the crash, and took off."

"So?"

"Well, there was this big fire that burned up the truck and car—and the body—so none of it could be identified. But when the camera came back on, they were still burning. I played around with the images in Photoshop and got these," he said, handing her two pictures.

One was of the truck's license plate and the other was a little more blurry but apparently was the car's license plate.

"Okay, the truck I'll give you, but how'd you get the car's license plate? The back end is hidden by the truck and facing the wrong way," Emily said, pointing to the original unretouched photo.

"You can thank the fire for that. Look here," he said, pointing at the window of the coffee shop the truck had smashed the car into. She could just barely see a reflection of the car's license plate, illuminated by the flames on the truck.

"Brilliant," she breathed. She had totally underestimated this kid. She got a sense that it happened to him a lot.

"It was fuzzy and backward, so it just took longer to render. Anyways, I checked them and the truck was stolen the day before."

"What?"

"That's not the best part. The car was licensed to a recent ex-con who was paroled early. I'm still looking into that," Dan said, digging through the papers again. "To this guy." Dan beamed with pride, but Emily didn't recognize the man in the picture.

"Who is he?"

"Are you kidding? It's David Jordan!"

Emily stared at him, her expression unchanged.

"No?"

"Sorry," Emily said, feeling let down again.

"Maybe it happened before you came to New York. The final murder victim, Bob Cummings, you know he was a news anchorman."

"That I know," Emily said.

"Well, Cummings used to be a cop. In fact, there was a huge racketeering case brought against him a few years back. It turned out he was clean, but the assistant DA had gone after him too hard, so he sued. Made a bundle of cash and was exonerated in the public's eye. He became a weird kind of martyr for blind justice. Besides the money, he got famous. Which made it easy for him to get a job in front of the cameras."

"I still don't see—"

"Cummings was exonerated, but his *partner* was guilty. Went to prison for it."

"And just got out," Emily said, feeling a chill.

"Now you're getting it. The guy killed in the car just before the traffic cameras came back on was David Jordan, Bob Cummings's ex-partner."

"Jesus," Emily said tracing her own finger along the map lines backward from the accident to The Cloisters. "Follow the yellow brick road."

"So what do you think?" Dan asked.

He's not the killer, Emily thought. At least, not the one who had killed leaving his symbol in his victim's dead flesh. There was no way to know if he had been driving the truck or not, but Emily's loyal mind reasoned that even if it was him behind the wheel, he hadn't killed but protected—protected his symbol, his reputation, and anyone else from being killed in his name.

"I think you're bloody brilliant!" Emily said, hugging him.

"Don't look at me like that, Church," Emily said when she felt her hulking tomcat's green eyes burning into her. She was standing by the door paging through the pictures she'd taken on her digital camera. Dan had made the mistake of going to the bathroom and leaving his maps and photos lying out on the table. Was that her fault?

Before he'd left he'd told Emily what he wanted from her. A phone call, that was all. A simple phone call to his editors. Somehow he thought her endorsement would make them take him seriously. She knew a call from a struggling true crime author would make no difference whatsoever, but she didn't tell him that. She just wanted to get him out of her apartment. Of course, she had no intention of making the call. Her guilt was easily overridden by her excited conviction that The Monarch was innocent.

Churchill lay on the window ledge staring at her, his tail doing a slow, rhythmic snap every now and then that, to Emily, screamed disappointment.

"I didn't ask him to come here," Emily said, though if he hadn't she wouldn't have had the pressure in her chest relieved.

Despite what she'd told Wagner and her publisher, sometime in her final year at Oxford, during a conversation with her father, Emily had first learned about The Monarch. She'd almost immediately fallen in love with the faceless, debonair outlaw. It hadn't made any sense, but she couldn't help it.

When the masked man had mentioned her "error in judgment," he'd been talking about how she'd taken her school grants and loans and had used them to chase every rumor of The Monarch across Europe instead of finishing her degree. Her goal in life had become to find the object of her affection. Just as, apparently, it had become the masked man's goal. Now that he could use the killings as a way to—

The frightening thoughts from the bus stop rose up in her mind again. What if these killings weren't just a convenient tool the masked man could use? What if he was *responsible* for them? He had power and pull. He also seemed to have a flair for the dramatic. And since almost every murder scene screamed, *Ta-da!*, that didn't bode well for him just being an opportunist.

"There's something bigger going on here than some kid's

dream of being Clark Kent, Church," Emily said, flopping down on her couch.

Churchill rolled off the ledge and thudded to the floor. Emily wondered how he could do that. He just pushed himself into the unknown and somehow always rolled enough to land on his feet. He padded over and hopped up on the sofa, nuzzling his way onto Emily's lap.

"What does this guy want, Church?" Emily asked as she scratched behind his ears. He purred an *I don't know.*

Emily had her suspicions—some of them horrifying—but with thousands of dollars roasting in her oven, it was almost impossible for her to take the righteous stance.

"Maybe he *is* just a fan? Maybe he just wants more of the book?" Emily tried to lie to herself. Churchill twitched like he was trying to shake something off. "Yeah, I'm not even buying that one."

Emily thought for a while longer and finally realized she didn't have enough information—about either the murders or the masked man—to make a decision either way. Her eyes fell on the oven across the room as she thought.

She pushed Churchill aside and took the case out of the oven, placing it on the table. Emily put the file on the table and took the cash out, making a mental note to find a place for it before going to sleep.

If she was lucky, there'd be something here she could trace back to the owner. A serial number, a make and model—something. With the contents out, it just seemed like a run-of-the-mill metal briefcase. The outside was silver aluminum with two latches, each with a keyhole. The inside was lined with black felt and the lid had a couple pockets for files and such. Emily looked in the pockets but couldn't see anything. Just to be sure, she reached in and ran her fingers along the bottoms of the pockets. The first one was nothing but more felt. But in the corner of the second pocket, the one that used the lid as its backing, her finger caught on something.

Emily rooted through a kitchen drawer until she found a flashlight, hoping the batteries weren't dead. The light was dim, but still alive. Before it died, she shone it into the briefcase's pocket. There, in the bottom corner, sticking out through a tiny tear in the felt, was a loop of wire.

Something electronic was hidden in the briefcase.

She dropped the flashlight and backed away.

How could I be so stupid?

This wasn't her first time around the block and it certainly wasn't the first time a source had tried something like this. She tried to run the night through her mind—where they'd been in the room and what they'd said. It had been such an emotional roller coaster that she just couldn't remember it all.

Emily decided against ripping the case apart to get a better look at whatever was secreted inside. The less whoever put it there knew, the better. She was pretty sure she hadn't said anything she didn't want the masked man to know in its vicinity, and it had spent most of the night in the oven. But if the device was sensitive enough, it might have picked up her conversations with Dan at the kitchen table. Assuming it was a listening device and not a bomb. Stranger things had happened; which was why the case went back in the oven.

With paranoia firmly set in, Emily went out into the hall taking only her own cell phone. She made a quick call and returned to her apartment, being careful not to slam the door. If it was a listening device, she didn't want them knowing she'd left. If it was a bomb, loud noises were generally a bad idea, though the more she thought about it, the more she doubted the bomb idea. Still, once her writer brain got rolling it was hard to stop it.

Emily changed her clothes and got into bed with Wagner's file. She propped herself up on some pillows and flipped the file open. For over an hour she read through pages and pages of commendations, reprimands, promotions, and demotions. Wagner's career read like a bouncing ball. Reading between the lines, Emily discerned that he was a man who did what he thought was right, regardless of protocol or the chain of command. Not quite a maverick, but definitely not someone who worried about politics. Normally, he'd be the type of man Emily respected. At the moment—sizing up her opponent—it worried her.

11

FCI Yazoo City
Yazoo, Mississippi
2:00 A.M. Local Time

LEW FELT MORE than heard the driver's door slam. He'd actually fallen asleep after lying in the plain wooden coffin with the taped-up Colero as a pillow. By the time he'd shaken the sleep grog from his brain, he felt the truck pull out and head down the short drive to the prison gate. His training in Iraq, thanks to all the kidnappings of Americans, had included how to determine direction and orientation of a vehicle with a bag on his head. He was pretty sure this wasn't what the instructors had had in mind for his training, but he was grateful for it, nonetheless.

Colero mumbled something under his tape gag.

"Here we go," Lew said quietly, holding the gun at the ready. He'd given up on his fingerprint idea when it just got too hard to hold the darn thing with only two fingers.

Less than a minute later, the van's brakes squeaked to a stop. The door slammed after the driver got out and Lew heard muffled voices for a while. This was the hard part. The waiting. The next sound they heard would either be the driver's door slamming after he got back in, or the dreaded click of the van's back door as a guard opened it to check inside. It could go either way. Lew figured if Quinn was on the level he would have called ahead to the guard. But with the near riot still fresh in the guard's mind, he might decide to check inside the van anyway.

All Lew could hear was the pounding of his own heartbeat in his ears. It reminded him of a time before he'd met Jonathan, before his life had taken a downward spin. His unit was clearing a village in Kuwait when mortar fire hit them. Almost his entire squad was killed except for him and this kid named Olsen, though Olsen had lost most of his left shoulder in the attack. When the shelling stopped, Iraqi troops had come in on foot to check for survivors. Lew pulled Olsen into a ditch and then pulled several dead bodies on top of them. The kid couldn't stop moaning from the pain, so Lew had choked him out to save his life. That's when the boots came out the back door, less than three feet from where they were laying.

Lew had thought he was going to lose his mind from the anxiety. Especially when, to make sure, one of the bastards had strafed the pile of dead bodies with his AK–47. Two of the slugs went straight through Olsen's head, and one of them pierced Lew's leg. Even so, he'd kept perfectly still and quiet. The enemy wandered around the village for two more hours before they left. It was another hour before Lew could get up the courage to climb out of his hole. He put a tourniquet on his leg and walked almost four miles back to base, every one of his buddies' dog tags in his bloody pocket.

And here he was again, hiding with a supposedly dead body in a cheap pine box built for one. After what seemed like an eternity the driver's door opened and closed again. A few jostling minutes later, Lew knew he'd just escaped from prison. But he wasn't free just yet. He surmised that somewhere between here and the coroner, the van would stop. Either because the driver was in on it or because the men who wanted Miguel Colero's dead body had forced him to stop.

Lew couldn't see Colero's face in the dark, but every now and then he heard a muffled grunt and knew the drug lord was trying to talk under his gag. Lew thought about it and realized that if they were ambushed before he could figure out what to do, having Colero free, talking, and on his side might buy him some time, if not save his life. And if Colero went all stir-crazy, Lew'd just rap him in the mouth with the gun and put the tape back on. A win-win scenario, Lew style.

"You got some big *cojones*, I'll give you that, Katchbrow," Colero said when his mouth was untaped. As Lew continued cutting him free, he could tell from the volume Colero was using that he was going to behave. "What's the deal?"

"The warden sold you out," Lew said.

"*Cabron*," Colero hissed.

"Well, there's more," Lew said, trying to keep his bearings by feeling the turns of the van while he talked. So far, they seemed to be on course.

"Like what?"

"Like he hired me to kill you."

"Didn't think someone like you would have a problem with that. Maybe I read you wrong," Colero said.

"You didn't," Lew said, taking neither pride nor guilt in who he was. "But the big issue now is where are we going?"

"*Sí.* Good question."

"Either your enemies are going to meet us and carve you up—and I'm guessing anyone who happens to be with you—or we are headed for the coroner, and when they crack this puppy open we're going to have some fast talking to do."

"You can bet we ain't goin' to the coroner," Colero said. "They must have moved the date up," he said more to himself.

"They?"

"*Sí,* there was a reason I needed to be dead and out today."

"I figured as much," Lew said. Just then he felt a turn and an acceleration that wasn't on his mental schedule.

"What is it?"

"Looks like you're right. We just turned away from downtown. And picked up speed."

For once, Colero was quiet.

THEY HEARD THE driver plead for his life, a gunshot answering him. Then someone pulled open the cube van's roll-up door. Lew tried to peer out through a crack but it was the wrong angle. From the voices he'd heard before they shot the driver, he thought there were three of them. No doubt, one of them was the competition come to claim his crown from Colero. And his pound of flesh.

Somebody shouted in Spanish just before Lew heard a bolt pulled back. The bolt on an automatic weapon.

The repeating of the automatic weapon was deafening in the small space. The smell of gunpowder and ozone made it hard to breathe.

Splinters and smoke filled the air as the shooter yelled like an animal, filling the pine box with holes. When he finally stopped, he kicked the lid off the low-grade coffin. It took some time before the air finally cleared. When it did, Lew imagined the shooter's smile disappeared.

"Impossible!" The shooter sputtered. Lew pictured the three men leaning forward and seeing that the only thing in the pine box was coroner supplies now perforated worse than peg board. Supplies that had been in two storage cupboards at the back of the van's cargo area just two minutes earlier.

Lew and Colero, each in a separate cupboard, kicked the doors open simultaneously. They came thrusting into the cargo area before the assassins knew what was happening. Lew fired his pistol once, hitting the gunman in the middle of his face. His head snapped back and flesh and cartilage exploded up into the air, backlit by the moonlight outside the truck. Lew kept pulling the trigger, but nothing fired. He quickly realized that Quinn had fucked him too.

One of the remaining men turned and ran around the corner. Lew knew that had to be the boss, who apparently wasn't so brave when the chips were falling. The other man reached for the gun hanging in the holster under his arm, but Lew was on him before he could unclip the leather. He hit him at a full run, the two men sailing through the air out the back of the truck and slamming down on the side of the road, Lew using the attacker's midsection as a landing pad for his knees and all two hundred and twenty pounds of his bulk.

Colero, still wearing most of the duct tape Lew had sliced so he could move his arms, jumped out the back screaming and went after the other man, who had run up the side of the truck toward a black Escalade parked across the road. Lew didn't care about him right now. Despite shooting bile and snot into the air on their landing, the man under Lew—who was no jockey himself—was still going for his gun. Lew grabbed the holster and fought with the man. Then he realized he still had the pistol in his other hand.

"Ah, fuck it," Lew said. The gun might have been empty, but it was still a useful weapon. He raised his fist and slammed the barrel down straight into the attacker's eye socket. The one-eyed man screamed and let go of the gun in his holster. "Big mistake."

Lew snatched the gun out of the holster, stood up, and put two shots into the screaming henchman. The screaming stopped.

He turned in time to see Colero coming back around the end of the truck. Behind him, he could see a man lying in the road, lit up by the van's headlights. From the way the body was lying he could tell its back was broken. His head also seemed to be facing the wrong way.

"Guess I wasn't wrong about you after all, *amigo*," Colero said with a smile.

"How the hell did you . . ." Lew looked at the small-statured man and realized there was far more to him than a couple of colorful names. Then he saw that Colero was holding a gun similar to Lew's, each pointed at the other man.

Maybe I didn't think this all the way through.

Time stretched out. Steam rose in the cool night air from their sweaty faces, the corpses littering the street, and the still running engines of the two vehicles. They were on some back road in southern Mississippi. Lew knew if you died there, the only ones that would find you would be the gators and the survivalists.

"What now, *compadre*?" Colero asked, his gun leveled.

"The way I see it there's only one question," Lew said, eyeing

Colero. He figured if the drug king had wanted him dead he would have been in the ditch by now. And it never hurt to have friends in low places.

"And that is?"

Lew dropped his weapon to his side. "I don't suppose you'd let me take the Escalade?"

Colero smiled and dropped his gun as well.

"I like you, Katchbrow. You don't say too much. You can obviously take care of yourself too."

"Seems to me all I've been doing lately is taking care of you," Lew said before he closed the van's back door. He picked up the first man he'd shot under the arms. Colero did the same with the other man. Together they dragged them off the side of the road into the brush.

"That's my point," Colero said. "I could use a man like you."

"Sorry, I like the girls," Lew said.

"I'm serious, *cabron*. Money like you've never seen," Colero said. They headed up to drag the other body off the road.

"I've seen a lot," Lew said. He had the shoulders and Colero had the feet of the strangely folded wannabe drug lord. They swung him several times and then let go, watching him sail into the tall grass. The shape of that man reminded Lew not to push this *little* guy too far.

"I could change your life, Katchbrow. Come with me."

"I can't," Lew said, wiping sweat off his forehead with his shoulder.

"Ah, I know that look. Unfinished business. In that case—" Colero pulled a pen and paper out of his pocket and wrote something down before tearing off a sheet of paper and holding it out to Lew. "Here. For when you're done."

Lew looked at the paper and saw it was a phone number.

"Good luck," Colero said, holding out his hand. Lew shook it. He couldn't think of any situation where he'd need to call a drug dealer, but he stuffed the number in his pocket anyway and drove off into the night.

12

JONATHAN STUMBLED DOWN the stairs, wiping sleep from his eyes as the pounding on his front door continued. It was almost as loud as the pounding in his head. After he'd spent most of the night chasing The Monarch story across the channels, a tiny, paranoid voice in the back of his head now whispered:

Have they come for me?

He shook the nonsense away, fighting it by redoubling his irritation at the intruder. He stomped to the door and yanked it open.

"What is it? Don't you know what time—" The words fell out of Jonathan's brain but missed his mouth. "Seven A.M., but I'm still on Central Time," Lew said.

A smile slowly crept across Jonathan's shocked face before he threw his arms around his old friend.

"Jeez. I know you're single, but you still like girls, right?" Then a quiet came over Lew and he put his arms around Jonathan and squeezed. "I missed you, man."

After a minute, they got hold of themselves and separated, both of them trying to hide their moist eyes and clearing their throats. Jonathan slapped Lew on the shoulder a few times, wearing a grin so big it threatened to be continued on the next face.

"You going to invite me in before the neighborhood watch registers us at Macy's?" If possible, Jonathan smiled bigger. He couldn't believe how much he'd missed that sense of humor. Then he saw Lew's ride sitting in the driveway, full of holes and spewing steam out from under the hood. He read the writing on the side.

"Yazoo City Coroner? Where the hell is Yazoo City? Iraq?"

"It's a long stor—"

"*Uncle Lew!*" They both turned and saw Natalie bounding down the stairs in a flash of brown hair and SpongeBob. She left the ground and landed in Lew's arms.

"Oof!" Lew teetered back until Jonathan grabbed his shoulder and steadied him. "Hey, squirt. What do you weigh now, like eight hundred pounds?"

"Where've you been? Are you staying? Is that your truck? Can I have a ride? How much—"

"Okay, okay, honey. Let Uncle Lew get in the door before you turn on the lights and get out the rubber hose."

"How about I make you Uncle Lew's special cinnamon and chocolate chip waffles?" Lew asked as he walked in carrying Natalie.

Her scream of delight almost shattered the neighbor's windows.

Jonathan, who had been nervous about his pantry stock, was relieved when he had enough ingredients and, more importantly, syrup for the morning feast. They ate and laughed until they could hardly move, most of the conversation and attention on Natalie.

The phone rang and it turned out to be Kayla Swenson, one of Natalie's friends. She and her family were going to Kayla's brother's basketball tournament over in Quincy and she wanted to know if Natalie could go. Kayla's dad was a cop, and the girls had become good friends, so Jonathan said yes. Natalie would only go if Uncle Lew promised to still be there when she got back. He promised and she ran upstairs to get ready.

"Kinda late notice, isn't it?" Lew asked, meaning the invite timing.

"Ha! This is more notice than I usually get. Most of the time they show up in the driveway and Natalie asks in front of them," Jonathan said, still at the sink washing the breakfast dishes.

"Nice. No pressure," Lew said, leaning back in a chair at the breakfast table. He was watching the news on the television perched up on top of the refrigerator.

"I don't mind. The Swensons are a nice, normal family. And it works both ways. Most weekends Kayla either sleeps over here or Talie sleeps over there. Guarantee she'll ask for a sleepover when they get back. You watch."

"I love it," Lew said with a big smile.

"What?"

"You and your domesticity. I didn't think you had it in you, but that's no secret," Lew said. "Especially after Sam died."

"Neither did I," Jonathan said, feeling guilty. He hadn't talked to Natalie about her dreams yet. He wasn't even sure if he ever would, but right now it sat heavy on his shoulders like a yoke laden with buckets of water.

"Tell me something, buddy," Jonathan said, needing to get out of his own head.

"Anything," Lew said, licking syrup off his palm.

"There wouldn't happen to be a prison in Yazoo, would there?"

Lew closed his eyes and exhaled. Apparently he'd wanted to avoid this, or at least avoid it as long as possible. Jonathan knew the feeling.

"How'd you know?" Lew asked.

"All through breakfast you've been protecting your food like someone's going to take it away. I mean, you were never Emily Post, but you broke some sort of land speed record scarfing down those waffles," Jonathan said, trying to lighten the mood.

Lew lifted his coffee mug to his mouth but stopped before putting it to his lips, and set it back down on the table.

"You got anything stronger than coffee?"

It was a little early for Jonathan under normal circumstances, but he thought a little hair of the dog sounded good. They waited until the Swensons had picked Natalie up, even so. The Swensons would have her back by two or three in the afternoon.

With a steaming mug of spiked coffee firmly in hand, Lew told Jonathan everything. If nothing else—and there was a lot else—they were the only people on the planet the other was completely honest with. As they talked, they avoided The Monarch killings completely.

"So I guess we should get that van out of the driveway pretty damn soon," Jonathan said. The only reason Kayla's father hadn't asked about it was because they'd covered it with a tarp. Jonathan could only imagine what a painful explanation that would have been.

"That would be a yes," Lew said.

"Okay, I think I know where to dump it," Jonathan said.

"Then we can talk about going to New York," Lew said.

"Uh, going to New York?" Jonathan said. He hadn't even admitted to himself yet that the idea was swirling around in the back of his head. Mostly because it was simply impossible. And probably not that smart.

"Well, yeah. I know we've been tiptoeing around it like it's a big elephant in the corner, but why do you think I'm here? We have to go stop those murders. Both of us." Lew said it so matter-of-factly that it sounded like he was saying you had to open the door before you walked through it.

"We do."

"Natch."

"But where exactly is Natalie in this grand plan of yours? Waiting in the car? What makes you even think we could find the killer? The FBI and the NYPD seem to be having a few difficulties in that department."

"We're smarter than they are," Lew said with a wink as he downed the rest of his drink.

"Well that's debatable, but I'm thinking having hundreds of agents and millions of dollars in computers and technology might be a bit of an advantage. Come on, Lew. Are you serious? 'Cause if you are, I think you might be using some of your friend's product."

"He's not my friend. I just used him to get out of prison so I could come here. Obviously that was a mistake," Lew said. The monotone voice and the way he kept his teeth clenched while he said it told Jonathan he was pushing too hard. If he wasn't careful Lew would go off to New York on his own. Which was about the only idea worse than them going together.

"Let's just calm down for a second," Jonathan said. "First things first. We'll get rid of that blinking I-just-escaped-from-jail sign you call a van. Okay? We can talk on the way."

"Fine," Lew said, reaching for the scotch to reload his glass. Jonathan snatched it away from him. "Hey!"

"I'm thinking maybe you don't get a DUI on your first day out of prison," Jonathan said.

"Whatever, Mom."

13

New York City
8:30 A.M. Local Time

THE STOREFRONT SIGN said "Pioneer Electronics—Since 1982," but the sign in the window said "Closed." Emily rapped on it lightly with her knuckles anyway. After a moment, a perturbed Asian face appeared in the window. When he saw Emily, he smiled.

"Come in, come in," he said, waving at the air after he opened the door. Emily stepped into the dim computer repair shop and he shut the door behind her. His name, as far as she knew, was Raiden Pioneer, though he'd admitted long ago that he'd taken Pioneer from the sign that was on the shop when he bought it.

"I'm sorry for calling so late last night and for the short notice, Raiden," Emily said, putting her bag on the counter. Bits and pieces of computers lying here or hanging there filled the small shop, but ironically the cash register that sat on the counter was the old nonelectronic type. Emily thought it fit in perfectly with Raiden. What you saw was definitely not what you got.

"Don't be ridiculous," he said, walking behind the counter. "It was a wonderful surprise to get your phone call last night. I've often thought about you over the past two years. You always brought me such challenges, and then poof, you disappeared. I'm happy you are well."

"I'm sorry about that," Emily said. Raiden had been vital to gathering information for *The Monarch's Reign*. She felt guilty about not staying in touch after the book was finished.

"Nonsense," Raiden said. "We are alike, you and I. We have our secrets and we know how to keep them. Now, what can I do for you?"

She pulled out one of the limited edition hardcovers of *The Monarch's Reign*. It had a bookplate signed by her and an expensive leather binding and cover. Very few of them had sold, but they were Emily's favorite of all her book's editions. More importantly, they were also the biggest.

"Ah, how poetic," Raiden said, eyeing the book. "What are we doing? Listening, following or watching?" Raiden asked, rubbing his hands together.

"Following," Emily said. "With a twist. I have no idea where this will be when I need to find it, so if you can do it, I need something that I can follow, even if it's in the next state."

"Hmm. Long distance. Not so easy. Or cheap," Raiden said, examining the book. "You'll have to come back next—" Emily slapped a packet of the bills from the metal case down on the counter.

"I need this in the next hour," Emily said.

"If you have to, you'll be able to follow it to Iceland," Raiden said, running his thumb across the bills.

She sighed and smiled.

"This is for a new book?" Raiden said, sounding excited. "A sequel, maybe?"

"Maybe," Emily said. She just didn't know where she'd be writing it—her apartment or prison.

14

Lost Lake, Florida
9:45 A.M. Local Time

JONATHAN'S CAR BOUNCED along the little-used, unpaved road, overgrown branches from the old cypress trees along the side of the road slapping at the windshield as if trying to stop him. He couldn't blame them. He was about to dump a shot-up van into their midst where it could rot and die.

He checked his rearview mirror and for a minute thought he'd lost Lew and the van, though there really wasn't anywhere to turn off. But if his car was having trouble with the uneven grade, he had no doubt the van was beating the hell out of his old friend. He couldn't help but smile at that idea. Though he knew he'd pay for it once they stopped, which would be in about two minutes if he remembered right.

He hadn't been down this road in over three years. The last

time was with Samantha just before she'd gotten sick. Well, she'd always been sick, but this was just before it had started to show. Being a native of the area, Samantha knew all the nooks and crannies of the landscape, and it seemed that Florida had no shortage of nooks and crannies. Especially in the swamp forest region. It was state land, managed by the Florida Fish and Wildlife Conservation Commission, but was an area so vast that in all the times he and Samantha had come here he'd never seen a ranger. Or another soul, for that matter.

Jonathan noticed that the temperature had dropped several degrees since they'd started down the road, which added to the feeling that they were now in a totally different world. But that feeling was par for the course when he was with Lew.

The guy was stubborn, and once he got something stuck in his head it rarely came out on its own. Jonathan knew the entire ride back, he was going to hear about Lew wanting to go to New York.

He understood why Lew was adamant about it. Lew Katchbrow had had a hard life. Aside from wanting to belong somewhere, Lew had wanted to make a difference in the world. To find a reason for being on this earth. Jonathan understood that all too well. But the fateful night they'd met in Bogotá had changed everything for both of them. What they did together in the following years was special. It had meant something, and he had to admit, if it wasn't for Samantha and Natalie, he'd probably still be doing it. And what this psycho in New York was doing to the symbol they'd chosen—Jonathan, really—was almost physically painful for him, so he could just imagine what Lew was feeling.

But in the end, there was Natalie, and nothing mattered now but her.

Finally, the car broke free of the forest's grasp and was bathed in warm morning sunshine. Jonathan drove a little farther across the sandy rim until he could see their destination below: Lost Lake. He parked and got out of the car, leaning on the side and staring out at the lake while he waited for Lew and the van. It was only a minute or two before Lew came roaring out of the trees. He skidded to a stop and seemed to hunch over the wheel catching his breath. Jonathan suppressed a smile.

"Are you fucking kidding me?" Lew said, getting out of the van and slamming the door. "Are we dumping the van or just beating it into submission?"

Jonathan knew Lew had more to say, but when he got close enough to see the lake behind Jonathan the frustration fell from his face. A look of awe replaced it and he was quiet while he tried to take in the panorama before him.

"Jesus," Lew said quietly, emotion in his voice. This place had that effect on people. Jonathan wondered if maybe that wasn't the real reason he'd brought Lew here. It was one of those places you had to share with someone, but just one person. Jonathan had lost his previous confidant. And now he had another. "Are you sure you want to dump it here?"

"Yeah, I'm sure," Jonathan said, tossing a rock over the edge into the lake. "It's a crater lake. Almost a hundred feet deep."

Lew whistled. "Let's get going, then."

They drove around the rim of the crater, albeit much slower than they had driven through the forest, until they were on a cliff high over the deep end of the lake. Jonathan found a large rock on the edge of the forest and wedged it onto the accelerator while the van was running in neutral. The engine revved like a screaming banshee.

"You want the honors?" Jonathan asked Lew, backing away.

"Why not?" Lew said. He made sure the wheels were straight and then reached in and grabbed the gearshift, leaning his weight out of the van so he wouldn't go with it. "I christen thee the USS *Get Me the Hell Out of Dodge,*" Lew said before he slapped the shifter into drive and jumped out of the way.

The tires spun in the sand for a bit, but then the rubber dug in and the shot-up van took off, its engine sounding happy to be doing what it was supposed to do. It picked up speed and launched itself off the edge, sand smoking off the tires in an arc as it flew to its end with a tremendous splash.

They ran to the edge of the cliff to watch it. The van bobbed up and down as the ripples worked their way out and back from the landing zone. It turned on its side and for a moment they were afraid it wouldn't sink, but then with a *glurg,* the vehicle filled with water and went down nose first.

As it sank out of view, Jonathan realized he hadn't done anything like this since, well, since he'd given it all up for Samantha. He wasn't sorry in the least, but Samantha was gone. Natalie needed him and he needed her, but if he didn't do something with himself—something that made him feel like this—it wouldn't be long before Natalie would want nothing to do with her lifeless father.

"I'll do it," Jonathan said, continuing to stare at the lake.

"Do what?" Lew asked.

"Go to New York."

"Yes!" Lew said, putting his arm around his friend and giving him a half hug as they continued to watch the lake ripple. "I knew you—"

"This can't touch Natalie in the slightest. I mean it," Jonathan said sternly, waggling a finger at Lew.

"Of course. Of course. Come on, this is Uncle Lew you're talking to," Lew said.

Just then something bobbed up from under the surface of the lake. They both leaned in and realized it was the pine coffin from the back of the van. The bullet holes had made it a boat of sorts and it sat pristine on top of the water. Jonathan slowly turned and looked at Lew.

"Let's pretend we didn't see that," Lew said.

"Works for me."

15

Federal Plaza
New York City
10:00 A.M. Local Time

As the elevator rose up 26 Federal Plaza, Emily closed her eyes and took a deep breath. She was thinking about her errand this morning and what she should do next when the buzz of a cell phone emanated from her bag. She dug for her cell phone—now with Raiden's alterations inside—but it wasn't the one buzzing. She flinched when she realized who was calling. She took out the phone the masked man had given her and answered it.

"Do *not* tell Wagner about the traffic cameras," the voice said.

The elevator doors opened. Special Agent Wagner stood in front of her.

"I can't talk right now. I understand. I'll call you soon," Emily said. She hung up and put both phones back in her bag. "Sorry."

"That's all right," Wagner said. "Two cell phones?"

"One's for work and one's personal," she said, impressed by her own quick thinking.

"Right," Wagner said. He had a noncommittal way of saying things, so she wasn't sure if he believed her or not. "This way."

Wagner led Emily to his office. Her thoughts were spinning. Without Dan's traffic camera research she didn't have anything to give Wagner to gain his trust. Not only that, but the voice on the phone confirmed her suspicions about the briefcase sitting in her oven. She tried to take solace in the idea that at least the case wasn't a bomb. Or, at least, not *only* a bomb.

"Thanks for coming in," Wagner said.

"No problem," Emily said noticing her book on his desk.

"I read it last night. Just a wonderful piece of work, there," Wagner said. He wasn't gushing, just stating an opinion. But she could sense there was something unsaid on his mind.

"But . . ." she said.

"You caught me. I really enjoyed it, but it seemed . . . unfinished. I felt like I was left waiting for the other shoe to drop, if you know what I mean." She knew exactly what he meant.

"Thanks. Yes, that seems to be the consensus. Apparently it's what hurt my sales in light of the reviews."

"But I guess this case will be good for business, now that the media is releasing details about your book in the reports on the murders."

"I suppose," Emily said. She wanted to object, but the book signings she had lined up this afternoon agreed with him.

"Don't worry. I'm pretty sure you didn't have anything to do with them," Wagner said to ease her mind. All she heard was *pretty sure.*

"Has he shown up since your book came out? I mean, have any thefts been attributed to him?"

"No," she said.

"Still watching for him, are you?"

"Now and then," she said, trying to act aloof.

"Okay, well in light of what I read—in your book and your Interpol jacket—and our stance on you as not being a possible suspect, I really only have a few questions. It would seem that you're the only world expert on The Monarch. I tried contacting Interpol about him, but they wouldn't even confirm or deny that he exists."

My jacket? The masked man wasn't kidding when he said he'd handle her background. Interpol administrative workers, like Emily, didn't have case files to their credit. Not real ones, anyway.

"As they would," Emily said, nodding. She'd run into the same issues when working on the book. Law enforcement agencies hated the idea of a Robin Hood doing their job for them. And the lack of complaints or theft reports made it difficult for them to even justify getting involved. How do you request budget money when stolen works of art are showing up in museums without explanation? The museums were almost as reticent to talk about it; afraid their Good Samaritan would dry up and blow away. The insurance companies were a different story.

"Well, that being the case, we just need you to advise us on the case. You'd be paid, of course. Not much. It is government work, after all, but I can guarantee an extension of your work visa for the foreseeable future. If that's something you're interested in."

"I think I would enjoy that. Thank you," Emily said, trying her best to act blasé.

"Excellent," Wagner said. "I'll need you to fill out some papers to make it official, but we can do that later. In the meantime, I'd like to get your impressions of what you've seen on the news, so far. Also, any recommendations you have would be welcome."

Is this really happening? She'd thought she was a murder suspect just a few minutes ago, and now here she was ostensibly on the team trying to find the murderer. What a difference a day makes.

"I do have one recommendation off the top," she said.

"Excellent. What is it?"

"Schedule a press conference. The media is running the show right now, no offense. You need to take control back."

"Normally I'd agree with you, but we just don't have anything—"

"Let me talk at the press conference. As you said, I'm the only expert. In a day or two, everyone will know that. Which means if I say something associated with The Monarch, they're going to listen. Or, at least, consider what I have to say."

"Interesting idea. What would you say?"

"The truth."

"Which is?"

"The killer isn't using The Monarch's symbol as a way to get attention. He's not a copycat looking to cash in on an existing fan base."

"He's not?" Wagner said, leaning forward. She had all of his focus now.

"No. The killer *is* The Monarch."

EMILY RETCHED INTO the toilet in the Federal Plaza main floor ladies' room until there was nothing left in her. She took several pulls of toilet paper to wipe her face, and then put down the lid and sat.

What have I done?

But she hadn't done it yet. On Monday at the press conference she was going to do it. She was going to betray the one person in the world that meant the most to her. She knew logically that it made no sense to feel the way she did about someone she not only hadn't met, but had never even seen, but knowing it didn't seem to make a difference.

The masked man had promised that this cooperation would result in her finding out who The Monarch really was. To find him, she had to betray him. Emily pressed the moist tissue to her mouth as more retching threatened to consume her.

When it passed, she bent over and looked under the stall to be sure she was alone. Satisfied, she took out the cell phone and dialed.

"It's done," Emily said.

"Excellent!" The exhaustion was gone from the masked man's voice again. He was exuberant and confident again. "When?"

"Monday at noon. Just like you asked." The contempt was plain in her voice.

"I know how difficult this was for you. But you'll learn there is little that I value higher or reward as significantly as loyalty. And remember the endgame," he said. "Your father would be proud."

"All right, I did something for you, now it's your turn," Emily said, surprised at her moxie. She was surprising herself a lot lately. Something in her had changed—reawakened. She fought to avoid admiring the change, afraid of being even more beholden to this stranger.

"I believe you were paid, Miss Burrows."

"Not payment, exactly. As hard as this is for me, I know the results will far outweigh the sacrifice. And to show my appreciation, I actually have something for you. A gift. But I need two things from you first."

"Two things. Perhaps you should tell me what they are before they double again," he said. She wasn't sure, but she thought he was joking.

"I need a name."

"All in good time. After Monday's press conference, we'll have more than his name."

"Not *his* name. Your name."

Silence drew out on the line. She knew he was evaluating. Reasoning how dangerous she could really be.

"Nathan," he said. That was all. A first name. It was enough. Emily felt good that she'd pulled him out of his comfort zone, made him give up something he didn't want to. But they were only halfway. "And the second thing?"

"I want to meet you. In person. Tonight."

"Impossible," Nathan said with no hesitation. The speed at which he answered told her this was not negotiable. At least, not yet.

"As I said, I have something for you. A gift. But I'll only give it to you in person," she said. She knew she had more pull than the average person after seeing his book collection. But it was no guarantee. If he continued to refuse, there was a line even she couldn't cross, but if the idea of a gift from her intrigued him—

"What kind of gift?"

Emily smiled.

A FEW HOURS later, Wagner and Evans sat across from each other in Wagner's office eating lunch; Evans with a greasy hamburger and fries, Wagner nibbling at a turkey wrap.

"Forgiveness? I don't get it," Evans said around a mouthful of burger after Wagner told him the real meaning of the symbol that looked like a butterfly.

"Burrows thinks it has to do with the whole Robin Hood ethic of The Monarch. You know, he doesn't want to exact revenge, he wants to educate. Show people the error of their ways. Like that," Wagner said.

"Whatever," Evans said, shaking his head as he fired a few more fries into his mouth. "You really going to let her talk at the press conference? Whole thing seems pretty hinky to me."

"I'm still not convinced she's telling us everything, but letting her confirm the killer is The Monarch from the book seems like a win-win for us. We get to take some control away from the media and the killer gets comfortable thinking he's fooled us. Maybe so comfortable he makes a mistake."

"Unless it really is the dude from the book," Evans said. He noisily slurped soda up a yellow striped straw. It wasn't something Wagner hadn't already considered.

"I think that's pretty unlikely. Not impossible, but we're stymied here. I think it's an acceptable risk," Wagner said. The Monarch from the book wanted to teach, not punish. Wagner didn't see any way he would pop up after five years of inactivity in the guise of an executioner. Especially not using the same forgiveness symbol. Not to mention they had no evidence to suggest the first two victims were in need of punishment, in any stretch of the imagination.

"What's Matthews think?" Evans asked.

"I don't know. I haven't talked to him about it, yet."

"Seriously? Ballsy. Dumb, but ballsy," Evans said. Even he knew the heat was on politically over this case, and unsanctioned moves would just give lawyers something to exploit down the road.

"Press conference isn't until Monday," Wagner said in his defense.

"Maybe, but it's already been announced on the news. If he doesn't know already, he's going to pretty damn soon."

"Why don't you let me worry about him," Wagner said, watching Ryan Meed, one of their techs, approach his office. Ryan smiled and stuck his head in.

"Got a second?"

"For what?" Wagner said.

"I've got something you need to see."

Several minutes later and a few floors down, Wagner stood behind Ryan at his workstation, which looked like the cockpit of a space shuttle. Ryan's hands were flying over several keyboards, mice, and control deck knobs. Wagner wouldn't have been able to turn the machines on, never mind use them. But his son, Todd, had highlighted his technical ineptitude years ago.

"We picked up an encrypted cell phone signal in the building a while ago. I didn't think much of it, but then when I did an audit, none of our encrypted phones was in the area at the time," Ryan said, pointing at one of his displays that looked a little bit like the peaks and valleys of a heartbeat on an EEG monitor. Wagner nodded convincingly.

"Right, so what does that have to do with me?"

"We pinpointed the source of the signal as the main floor. Here, watch," Ryan said, playing back recorded security camera video on another monitor. It was black and white, but high quality. It showed a hallway off the main area downstairs. Specifically, the door to the women's public washroom.

Up in the corner of the video a time code spun.

"And . . . now," Ryan said, pointing at the screen. Someone came out the door and then left the hallway, but not before he saw their face clearly.

"Son of a bitch," Wagner said. The face belonged to Emily. "Are you sure it was her on the phone?"

"I ran the recording ahead for fifteen minutes. Nobody else came out. It was definitely her. She signed out a minute later. I checked the log and saw she'd been up here to see you. This something you can use?"

"Oh yeah," Wagner said.

Wagner's cell phone buzzed.

"Yeah?"

"Hey," it was Evans.

"What's up?" Wagner said.

"I just got a call from one of my NYPD contacts."

"What about?"

"Some kid named Dan Cooper took a nosedive off the *New York Times* building this morning. Smashed a taxi flat."

"Jesus. The kid anybody we know? I mean, case wise?"

"Not that I can find, but I think we're going to be involved."

"Why's that?"

"Kid's cell phone survived the fall. Well, his SIM card did, anyway. The last number he called, like a minute before jumping, was to Emily Burrows."

16

Tallahassee, Florida
2:30 P.M. Local Time

THE SWENSONS DROPPED Natalie home just after two. Before they left, Jonathan flagged them down and made his pitch. A sleepover was one thing, but asking a neighbor if your daughter could stay with them for an unknown length of time, that was a whole different ball game.

Jonathan would have loved to take Natalie with them and show her New York, but he had no idea how dangerous things were going to get. Ken Swenson was leery at first, the request seeming to come out of nowhere. Jonathan lied and told him it had to do with finding work before he pulled Natalie out of school. Their financial situation was no secret to the neighborhood. He hit the heart button too, suggesting that after this, Natalie and Kayla might not get to see each other ever again. After that, it was just a matter of time before Mrs. Swenson worked her husband over for Jonathan.

Jonathan knew as difficult as it was selling the Swensons, it was child's play compared to telling Natalie in a way that didn't make her feel abandoned. Even with Samantha's death, if Natalie and Jonathan weren't so close, this would have been a lot easier, but they were more like best friends than father and daughter.

After spending some time with Natalie, Lew headed off to do some shopping. The plan was to catch a flight Sunday morning. The FBI were holding a press conference on Monday and they wanted to be there for that. Use it as a kind of ground zero. Jonathan had less than twenty-four hours left with his daughter, and he hadn't even told her he was leaving yet.

He steadied himself and knocked on Natalie's door. She was inside surrounded by her stuffed animals and drawing. When she looked up he took a mental image of the scene, knowing no matter the outcome of either this conversation or his trip to New York, nothing would ever be *this* again.

Jonathan had never lied to his daughter before, but he just didn't see any way around it. Aside from Lew, the only person who even knew the truth about his past was six feet underground and he and Natalie took flowers to her grave once a month.

"Where are you going?" Natalie asked. She wasn't upset. Not yet, anyway. He led off with the idea of spending a few weeks at Kayla's house, so she was much more receptive to the idea than if he'd just said he was going away. But she was a smart kid, and already she was seeing the nugget at the center of the story. To keep things simple, he stuck to the same lie.

"New York," Jonathan said.

"Why don't you know how long you'll be?" It was a logical

question, and Jonathan could see if he didn't handle the answer just right it could lead to some uncomfortable follow-ups. The main thing he wanted to avoid was giving her any reason to think he wasn't coming back. And with the dreams she'd been having lately, that wasn't going to be easy.

"I could lie and say a few days, babe, but you're a big enough girl to handle the truth. It could take that long just to set up meetings with people. The thing is, it's all up to them. I just have to do it this way. You understand, don't you?" It was basic spy craft. Bury a lie within the truth within a lie. The hard part was keeping it straight and consistent.

"I guess," Natalie said, looking at her stuffed owl and playing with its wings.

"Here," Jonathan said, taking the bag out of his pocket that he'd bought on the way home from dumping the van. He took out a prepaid cell phone made for kids that hung on a lanyard. "You have to promise you'll only use this to call *me*." He slipped it over her head.

"My own phone?" Natalie said, the sparkle returning to her eyes. It was a cheap trick. Jonathan had never liked the bribery tool as a parent, but it seemed he was breaking all the rules today.

"You'll have to make sure you keep it charged. You know, like your iPod. Now promise me you won't use it to call your friends."

"I promise! I promise!" she said, throwing her arms around Jonathan's neck. "I can really call you anytime I want?"

"I'll call you too," Jonathan said, nodding. "If I've got a meeting or something, I might get Uncle Lew to call you."

"Uncle Lew's going too?"

"Sure is. You don't want me to be lonely, do you?" She shook her head no.

"Is Uncle Lew going to live with us in New York?"

"I don't know about that. Maybe at first. He might be lonely all on his own too."

"I don't think Uncle Lew gets lonely too much," Natalie said in that knowledgeable way kids have of talking about unknown things.

"I think you might be right about that," Jonathan said with a smile. "Now let's see if we can pick a good ringtone for you. I'm thinking . . . the theme song from *Sesame Street*."

"Dad, puh-lease!" Jonathan suggested a few more songs that were obviously too young for her. They laughed and roughhoused a bit. Then she put her arms out for a hug. He held her tight. "Thank you for the phone, Dad."

"You're welcome, baby," Jonathan said, hiding the tears slipping from his eyes.

17

Tartaruga Island
12:00 A.M. Local Time

LARA KRING VAULTED out of the elevator and launched herself down the complex's main level corridor, her long Chinese cheongsam dress restricting her movements so she looked more like a ballerina executing a pas de bourrée than an infuriated executive. But she was more than even that. She was Kring Industries' second-in-command, superseded only by Nathan Kring, her father.

Her bone-white hair, stark against the bloodred silk, flowed behind her as if it were spreading her scent of jasmine and coconut rather than trying to keep up with its owner. Her black alligator Manolo Blahnik high-heeled boots—not easy to get on an island somewhere east of Zanzibar—hammered out a typewriter staccato, warning everyone between her and the wide, winding staircase that led to her father's office of the price they'd pay if they tried to intercede. Though at this hour, most staffers were sound asleep.

Her South Asian features were from her late mother, but everything else was from her father. She was his younger female doppelganger in every way, but one: She wasn't dying.

"You're going to *meet* her?" Lara spouted even louder than she'd intended as she burst into Nathan's office, flipping her disheveled hair out of her green eyes.

"Excuse me for a moment, gentlemen," Nathan said, pressing a button on a remote control that muted the voices coming from the displays embedded in the wall opposite his desk. Lara knew the mute also cut off the sound and video going out of the office.

"Is it true?" Lara demanded, holding her clipboard of papers close to her chest, her bluster already threatening to falter in his presence.

"Not that it's any concern of yours, but yes, it's true," Nathan said. He walked around his desk and sat in his leather chair, as if preparing himself to withstand a cross-examination. Lara noticed he'd placed his wheelchair off to the side where it would be out of view of the camera set in the wall above the displays.

"Now? What are you thinking? Shouldn't you be in the data center making preparations?" she said, stalking toward the desk, slamming her clipboard down when she reached it.

"Everything is on schedule. They're not children. I doubt that things will fall apart if I'm gone for a few hours," Nathan said, swiveling back and forth in his chair as he spoke, as if sitting was allowing too much energy to build up in him.

Lara knew she couldn't talk him out of his little field trip any more than she could talk him out of the plan, but he had to know he couldn't circumvent her like this. If the plan failed, she would need to know everything that was happening. Everything. Right down to the last order and penny. But that was defeatist thinking, of course, and he simply wasn't capable of failure; which was one of the faults that had gotten him into this situation in the first place.

Instead of continuing her tirade, she clocked around the desk and put her hand on his forehead. As she expected, he was burning up.

"When was the shot?" she asked.

"Yesterday," he said, pulling his head back from her hand. She knew he was lying.

"Is she monitoring you?" Lara asked.

"Don't concern yourself with Sophia. Your sister knows what she's doing. Look at me," he said, smiling, his eyes ridiculously wide and bright.

Lara cringed inside at the mention of her name. "I wish you would stop calling her that," Lara said. She took her hand away. "You seem fine, but remember the last—"

"I *am* fine," he said, slipping his hand around and squeezing her rear end. "Why don't you let me show you?"

"I'm busy and you're in the middle of a meeting," she said, trying to hide the mix of fear and anger blossoming in her chest.

"It's been so long," he said. She knew the serum was fueling more than his legs.

She picked up her papers and clasped them to her breast, her eyes flicking to the row of faces on the monitors. She knew they couldn't see her, but it was still disconcerting.

"We talked about this. I don't want to talk about it again. Ever," she said, unable to look him in the eye, the memories of all their past encounters assaulting her.

"Fine. Be that way," he said, sitting up straight and smoothing his lapels. "What are you busy with? Anything you need me for?" His tone changed and he was the CEO again.

"No. The consortium is petitioning us again about our reserves. I can handle it, unless you'll change your mind."

"We've been over this. We might be sitting on the only natural gas pocket between here and the mainland, but it's finite. If we manage ourselves, we have maybe fifty years' worth. If we start handing it out, we'll be just like them; reliant on someone else. And you know their proposal is just the start. Next they'll want to use our airstrip or farm the back side of the island. No, I've been clear on this."

"All right, then no, I don't need any help," she said, and began heading out of the room.

"In that case, let me get back to the vultures before they start eating each other," he said. "See if Sophia needs anything. I mean it. She's your sister, whether you like it or not," he said. "And she's crucial to the plan. Without her—"

"All right, fine!" Lara said louder than she meant to, the combined distaste for Sophia and her father wrenching away her self-control.

"And let me know when Thomas gets in," Nathan said, turning back to the screens. She flinched slightly.

"Yes, Father," Lara said. She left his office feeling like the energy had been sucked from her bones. And she realized that of everyone on the island, the one she hated the most was herself.

LARA RAN HER pass card through the card reader, but instead of a green light giving her access to Sophia's lab, it buzzed and blinked red. She tried it again, paying more attention this time, but again it buzzed denial. She examined the card and carefully wiped the strip clean.

"Come on," she said to the device. After five failed attempts the door would lock down for an hour and the guards would come running. She had authority over them, but it would still be embarrassing. "What the hell has she done to this thing?"

She carefully ran the card through a third time. This time, the light turned green and she heard the electronic *buzz-click* of the lock releasing. Perturbed, she pushed through the door and entered her *sister's* world.

The lab gleamed in the dim light coming from a few workstations. In days gone by, the lab had accommodated dozens of scientists and lab techs, but as her father's condition worsened, they'd slowly either been let go or reassigned. Sophia Kring was the only one who inhabited its beakers and test tubes now.

"Is that thing sticking again?" a voice said from deep inside the lab. Lara was almost a foot taller than her sister, but she couldn't see her from the door.

Lara hated the lab. Aside from the knot in her stomach whenever she saw or spoke to Sophia, it smelled terrible. She couldn't even think of what it smelled like. The closest she could guess was rotting garbage.

And all those disgusting animals she has.

She especially hated the little mice, though she'd never show it on her face. Thomas had taught her early in her lessons that rule number one was never let your opponent see your true emotions. *I'm already a black belt in that department.*

Lara took a deep breath and clip-clopped back into the lab. She found Sophia sitting on the floor with a rabbit and two mice in her lap. She wasn't running any experiment, she was just playing with them.

"What's up?" Sophia asked from the floor. She was wearing a

lab coat over her usual sweater and jeans, her glasses pushed up on the crown of her long black hair, which was tied back in a ponytail. Several strands either had never made it into the hair band or had worked their way out through the day.

"He wanted me to check and see if you needed anything," Lara said. She couldn't say Father because that would mean acknowledging that Nathan was Sophia's father too; something she just couldn't do.

"I've done pretty much all the protocols I can for now," Sophia said. "I don't have any more donor material, and since it's the largest constituent in the serum—well, you see my point."

Lara hated the way she talked down to her. Just because Sophia went to university didn't mean she had to rub it in Lara's face every ten minutes.

"Fine. Well, I checked," Lara said, spinning on her heels and heading back the way she came.

"Wait! Hang on a sec," Sophia said, struggling to get up without freeing her creatures. She dropped the mice into a maze, cradled the rabbit like it was a baby, and walked over to Lara.

"What is it?"

"No one's told me what this 'big thing' is, yet. He's taken all my people and just keeps telling me I'll have to work harder. But *you* know, don't you." It wasn't a question.

"You don't need to know."

"Damn it, that's what he keeps saying! Somebody better let me inside the loop or I'm going to . . ." Sophia let her threat trail off. Lara stepped closer to her and stared down into her brown eyes.

"You're going to what?" Lara held her stare until she looked away.

"I don't know. Wait I guess. That's all I ever do," she said, wandering away, patting the rabbit.

"If there's nothing else—"

"Actually, I'm missing a bunch of animal tranquilizers. You don't know anything about that, do you? Or is that need-to-know too?"

Lara turned and headed out of the lab. She got halfway to the door this time.

"He's self-medicating, you know!" Sophia yelled after her.

Lara only hesitated for a moment before using her pass card to open the door. Thankfully it worked on the first swipe from the inside. She'd known about Nathan giving himself shots of the serum for weeks. How the creator and keeper of that serum could only now be noticing was beyond her. As the door shut, Lara heard a muffled "Fuck you too."

That was new, she thought with a smile. She'd been treating Sophia the same way ever since Sophia had returned to the island with her precious master's degrees, but Sophia usually just took it in her own self-deprecating way. Even though it was through a closing door, that was downright aggressive for Sophia.

Before she could think about it anymore, Lara realized what time it was. If she didn't hurry she'd be late for her moonlight swim, one of the few pleasures she had.

Well, that and counting down the hours her father had left.

An hour later, Lara stood naked in the moonlight on her favorite stretch of beach, her bronze skin glistening from her swim. She turned her face to the moist, warm wind, her eyes closed, and listened to the ocean.

"Beautiful," Thomas's Australian voice crooned as he stepped from behind the scant foliage. Lara's breath caught and she felt something run through her body, heating and moistening as it went. She turned around to see that he too was naked, though not as tanned. He was twenty years her senior, but still the most beautiful thing she'd ever seen.

"Baby," she said. She hated that when she spoke to him she always sounded so fragile, nowhere near the alpha creature she was with everyone else. Hated it and loved it. She fought the urge to run to him, feeling her breath deepen and her heart pound.

He was across the sand in the blink of an eye, his mouth hard on hers, his fist firmly gripping the hair on the back of her head. She kissed him back harder, almost hungry. She didn't know who she was when she was with him, but she didn't care. She raised one long leg around his powerful buttocks and then they were lost in each other, slamming to the beach.

When they were both sated and exhausted, he rolled off her onto his back and she quickly took her place at his side, every inch of her pressed into him and her head on his powerful chest as if she were afraid he'd get away. It was always like this right after. It would pass. For now, she enjoyed the moment. No expectations or demands. No father, no disease.

"Why didn't you tell me you were back?" Lara finally managed after several minutes.

"I didn't know I was coming back," Thomas said. She understood. It was typical of her father to give someone a task and then change it at the last moment to keep them off balance. Even so, when it happened now, she was always afraid it had another meaning. She wasn't sure what her father would do if he found out about her and Thomas, but something told her if he did she'd never see Thomas again. And neither would anybody else.

"Wait here," Thomas said abruptly, getting up and trotting over to his pile of clothes. She watched him move in the moonlight and felt herself wanting him all over again. A moment later, he came back with something in his hands, plopping himself back down beside her.

"What is it?"

"I wanted you to have this," he said, holding out a knife in a sheath. He pulled the blade out. It sparkled in the moonlight. He turned it over a few times and then resheathed it and handed it to her. "Just in case."

She understood what he meant. She examined the gift.

"It goes here," he said, taking it back and sliding his hands up her leg. He wrapped the sheath's straps around her thigh and secured them. Caressing the knife, he leaned down and gently kissed her inner thigh before rolling back on his elbows beside her.

"It's perfect," she said, fingering the hilt. Then after some time she said, "When do you—"

"Dawn. He wants my arse back in New York before the press conference," Thomas said. Then he raised his head so he could look her in the eye. "Come with me."

"Thomas—" she said.

"I'm serious," he said, raising up on his forearms. "We'd have at least five or six hours on the flight. We could add supersonic to our mile high club status." He smiled that smile that made Lara feel like she could do anything. Just drop the responsibilities and be—normal. But she knew it was just a fantasy.

"You know I can't," she said, rolling onto her back and resting on her own forearms. She loved him, but with that burning need fed, she could stand to be more than a few inches away from him again. She could tell by the look in his eyes he recognized the shift too.

"Sorry, love. Just got carried away," he said. He was neither angry nor hurt.

The phone in Lara's pack rang. Without a second thought, she sprang to her feet and padded over to it. She took the phone out and returned to the grass beside Thomas, ignoring his resentful stare.

After listening for a moment, she said flatly, "I'll be there," and snapped the phone closed. "He wants me to chopper him to the mainland for this ridiculous meeting."

"You? What about Dieter," he said, referring to Nathan's personal pilot. "Or Sophia? Why is he making you do it?" Thomas asked. Both sisters had been taught how to fly years ago. Lara knew it was so her father would always have someone to do his bidding.

"Because he can," Lara said, lobbing the phone toward her pack.

After a long silence of watching the stars, Thomas said, "He says this plan can cure him. Is that true?" Thomas had known about her father's illness before she had, but it still made her uneasy to talk about it. She kept her knowledge about it to the basics. It was called kuru and it put him in the wheelchair—without Sophia's serum, that is.

Lara could hear the worry in his voice. He would never say it, probably not even to himself, but Thomas was ready for it to be over too.

They interlocked fingers, rested their heads together, and watched as the Earth spun through space in silence. Several minutes later, Lara made up her mind.

"There is something you can do for me."

IT WAS ALMOST 3:00 A.M. by the time Nathan finished with his video conference and left his office. At this hour he could risk wandering the halls of the complex without having to answer any annoying questions. It reminded him of earlier times, when they'd come to the island for vacations. There were no guards back then, or even a staff. It was just him and the girls. And Thomas, of course. He'd had Thomas by his side even before the girls. But times had changed.

The girls had grown into women; Lara deliciously resembling her long-dead mother. Then Nathan's time had run out and the disease he'd known was coursing through his veins reared its ugly head and took hold of him. Though that's what Sophia was for, but she was as moody as she was brilliant. And Lara hadn't helped when she'd found out the truth—or part of it, anyway. Making her second-in-command was the only way to have even a modicum of control over her again. That, and letting her leave his bed for good. It had been a high price, but in the end it would be worth it.

Nathan lighted one of his Cohiba cigars and blew plumes of expensive smoke as he strolled, making the most of his hands while he could use them. This time tomorrow he'd be back in that damn chair. The headaches and a persistent nosebleed told him he'd pushed the medication enough. He had to take it easy or he'd be dead before they reached zero hour. That kind of irony he could do without.

Originally headed to his vault to luxuriate in his few remaining treasures, he somehow found himself crossing the catwalk that joined the complex with the immense hangar behind it that now served as the data center. It was the only room big enough for the expansive server farm. The hangar was the size of a football field. Rows and rows of servers purred as they prepared for their sole purpose in life; some redundant, some masters, and some slaves, just like with any ordered society.

Giant monitors mounted in a semicircle overhead relaying world data in real time cast hypnotic shadows onto the hangar walls. Nests of wires ran up from the server farm and the control center, joining up in the rafters as a kind of web, all blue and gray and black.

He exited the catwalk and surveyed the room. As he'd expected, his head tech Randy Li was the only one at the controls. It disappointed Nathan a little that his staff wasn't there burning the midnight oil, but he supposed everyone couldn't be like him. Even with his illness he had very little use for sleep, sometimes going days with only naps.

"How's our crop doing, Mr. Li?" Nathan bellowed as he descended the stairs leading to the control center.

Randy spun around, obviously not expecting anyone at this hour, especially not his boss. Nathan loved the look on people's faces when they saw him walking around without his wheelchair. Even if they knew he spent time out of it, as Randy did, they still stared as if he were Christ crossing the surface of a sea.

"Good evening, sir," Randy said with his German accent. Nathan had rescued Randy from the Bundeskriminalamt, the German federal police. The BKA had Randy on cyber terrorism charges and were about to lock him away for the rest of his natural life. It was hard to believe that had been almost two years ago. Nathan had always found gratitude a much better motivator than a big stick, though he wasn't averse to either.

"Is everything ready?" Nathan said as he came to rest before the short techno whiz.

"Oh *ja*. All is prepared," Randy said. "But again I must warn you that our time is limited. Once Cyclops detects us and kicks us out, we won't get back in. We need to be precise with our timing."

"Cyclops. How could they give such a sophisticated system such a sophomoric name?" Nathan said. It wasn't the first time he'd mentioned it.

"I like it," Randy said. "I think it truly captures the essence of their system. What would you call a system that merges all of New York's video surveillance systems into a single point?"

"Expedient."

"Yes, well—"

"Until Monday morning," Nathan said, tired of their repeated discussion. "Let me know if there are any problems."

"As I've asked before, if you could let me know the source of the image, we could probably—"

Nathan's stare disintegrated the rest of the words in Randy's mouth. He'd warned Randy about such inquiries. He held his eyes until Randy nervously went back to work.

Nathan looked up at the main display high overhead. A face-shaped image glowered out at the room, like an overlord, as it had for the past few months. But not the same image, exactly. Over time it had been enhanced, spun, inverted, and sharpened. Parts had been softened, brightened and colorized. Other parts had been pixelated and even others interpolated.

Sometimes Nathan wondered if they'd gone too far. If enough of the original remained to be true and useful. After spending hundreds of thousands of dollars in his global search for any information on The Monarch, it had finally paid off. A single image, of a sort, existed. Captured years ago by a security camera in Prague after The Monarch hit another one of Nathan's private collector brethren. But not a direct image, merely a reflection in the glass of a display case. Nathan was confident, with Randy on the case, that it would be enough. It had to be.

Nathan watched as grids appeared and disappeared over the image, sections exploding out, the predictive software looking for any pixel it had missed in the previous thousand passes. They hadn't found anything new in weeks, but Nathan refused to let Randy shut down the process. Randy had explained that the intense mathematics required to process each digital pass over the image occupied a huge portion of the server farm. Data collected over the past six months filled another segment of the farm.

That left just less than half of the data center for the upcoming operation. Their estimates determined it was sufficient. If it wasn't, everyone involved would pay with their lives.

Including Nathan.

18

Unknown

EMILY DREAMED OF paradise. Water as blue as the sky. A white sandy beach. And a warm, tropical wind playing in her hair. It was heaven. And as the fog lifted from her brain, she realized it was also real.

She shook her head and sat up. She was sitting on a beach lounge chair. Twenty feet in front of her the ocean lapped at the white sand in a constant, unstoppable rhythm. The beach ran as far as the eye could see both left and right, and she was the only one on it. Behind her it ran up an incline until it met the ferns, bushes, and palm trees that blocked the view of whatever was beyond.

Emily got up and almost fell back down. She steadied herself, removing her coat and scarf as she sweated in the tropical sun. Her head pounded and there was an odd sensation in her ears. She remembered getting out of the cab for the book signing her agent had set up and the limo pulling up, but then nothing.

No, wait— She remembered pain. Something in her stomach.

She pulled up her blouse and saw two red marks on her skin. That hadn't been a dream. Someone had Tasered her. She looked around and spotted her bag under the lounge chair. She grabbed it and checked the contents. The book was gone. And so was one of her cell phones. The one the masked Nathan had given her. Then out of the corner of her eye, she saw a man approaching. He wore a black suit with a white shirt and a thin black tie—and a mask. Her breath caught.

Nathan.

He strolled toward her, smiling. She saw he was carrying her book and that he wasn't wearing any shoes. Had he been here the whole time? She wasn't sure. It was like he'd materialized out of nowhere. She looked around to see if they were alone and they seemed to be. Feeling defenseless, she hooked her bag over her shoulder and picked up her coat and scarf, holding them over her arm in front of her. She faced him as he approached but stood her ground, unmoving.

As he drew closer, she saw he was tall. At least six-four. His body wasn't muscular but lithe. His step was steady and strong. Confident. He stopped a few feet away and seemed to just watch her. Emily found it unsettling, like he was picking her apart. But more unsettling was the book he carried in one hand.

"Hello," he said. His voice was deep and contained a slight accent that she couldn't quite identify. "I trust this is to your liking," he said, gesturing toward the beach and the ocean.

"I . . . I don't understand. How did I get here? Where are we?" Emily asked, trying futilely to sound indignant.

"Well, now, that would be telling. And we both know how you like a mystery," he said, gesturing with the book. Then she recalled that it had been late afternoon when she'd approached the limo. She looked at her watch. It said it was 10:00 P.M. in New York. But here, the sun was low in the sky. And rising.

"Why am I here?" Emily asked. For some reason, she was calming down. As if she was safe.

"Why, because you asked to be. And thank you very much for the gift. You have no idea how much I appreciate it," he said, once again waving the book. "Of course, I had your little device removed from the spine. I'm a little disappointed. Not that you tried—I expected that—but you used the same shop you did when you were working on your book. Haven't you surmised by now how well I know you?"

He's mad as a hatter. All she wanted to do was go home. It was like her first ride in the limo all over again, but this time he could reach out and touch her if she wasn't careful. But unlike the limo, *she* knew things now.

"My mistake. Old habits and all," she said. She realized why she felt safe now. He needed her. At the very least, for the press conference. She touched her temple as her head throbbed again.

"I am sorry about that," he said. "But I thought drugging you was preferable to having you Tasered over and over again. I think you'll agree."

"Ta," she said, surprised at her cheekiness. "What makes you think I won't scream?" She reached in her bag and took out her remaining cell phone. "Or call someone. The police. Anyone. You could be in serious—"

"Who exactly would you call? The FBI? Your friend Agent Wagner? Go ahead. He has no jurisdiction here, even if you could get a signal. Cell service down here is dicey, at best. A small price to pay, in my view. And as far as screaming, go ahead. Here, let me help you," he said before he bellowed out over the water. "Hmm. I guess the fish police are busy. I do feel foolish, though. When you said a gift I had no idea it would be so special. I feel as if I should give you something in return."

"Take off your mask," she said, tossing her cell phone back in her bag.

"Oh, not yet, I'm afraid. But I will answer three yes or no questions."

"I can ask you anything?"

"Anything," he said, motioning for them to sit down. Emily obliged him and sat. He sat on the lounge chair opposite her.

"Tell me about David Jordan," she said, hoping to surprise him with the name of the man involved in the final New York killing. If she did, he didn't show it.

"That's not a question."

"All right, did David Jordan kill all three of the supposed Monarch victims?" she asked.

"No. Next question." He said it like he was acknowledging that the grass was green. *He's playing with me.* She needed a hard question. Something that could tell her if he was being honest or not. But she had only two chances left.

"Was David Jordan murdered?"

"Yes. I have to say I'm surprised at these questions. You seem obsessed with Mr. Jordan. Be that as it may, one question left."

My God, is he actually telling me the truth? On the off chance he was, she had to make the last question count.

"All right," she said, leaning forward. "If the press conference draws The Monarch out, are you going to kill him?"

"Finally, a good question!"

"So what's the answer?"

"No, I personally have no intention of killing him."

What a strange answer.

"Well, this has been wonderful," Nathan said, slapping his thighs and standing up. She thought he didn't seem as solid-footed on the sand now as he had a minute ago. "But, there is still much to do. You have a long trip and, of course, a speech to write."

Emily stood up. Nathan extended his hand. She thought he wanted to shake hands, so she reciprocated. To her surprise, he took her hand and brought it to his lips, giving a gallant bow as he kissed it.

"I'll treasure this always," he said waving the book as he headed off down the beach the way he'd come. There didn't appear to be anything down there but more beach. She watched him go, realizing she was being left alone on a beach in the middle of who knew where.

She was going to yell after him, but then she saw him stumble. He righted himself, but he had to stop for a minute. He continued his walk slower and more carefully this time, but it wasn't long before he stumbled again, this time falling to his knees. Then he waved at the air.

What Emily saw next was as surreal as waking up on the beach. Men streamed from the bushes, all dressed in black. There had to be twenty of them, several of whom carried unholstered firearms. She realized they'd been watching the whole time. The men ran to Nathan. Then one of them, after Nathan said something to him, waved at the far end of the beach. A helicopter came roaring around the bend, the blades buffeting the air against Emily's chest. The chopper landed on the beach next to the men and they helped Nathan up and into the helicopter. Then, almost as fast as it had approached, the helicopter lifted off and headed out to sea. Emily looked out at the water but could see nothing but liquid blue running to the horizon.

Then she saw the remaining men in black headed toward her. She grabbed her belongings and turned to run, only to see that men had streamed out of the bushes behind her, as well. Before she could say anything, one of them placed a device against her neck that hissed and stung like a bee. She slapped her hand to her neck, but before her fingers reached the wound, the beach swam like it too was water.

She felt herself falling and hands grabbing her, but then she felt nothing more.

PART THREE

Sunday

19

Washington Heights
New York City
6:00 A.M. Local Time

"THIS IS IT," Emily said from the backseat of the cab she'd woken up in. Her head hurt even more. She'd been on two planes in the past fifteen hours. To where and back, she had no idea. When she'd woken up she'd asked the cabbie how she'd gotten there. He'd said two men put her in the cab, gave him two hundred dollars, and said to drive around until she woke up and gave him a destination.

Emily managed her way up the stairs to the front door of her building. As she fished the key out, she saw that the FBI were still watching her apartment.

Once inside, she fed Churchill, who wanted nothing to do with her. He could hold a grudge for days if she accidentally kicked him out of bed while she was sleeping, so who knew how long this would last. Famished herself, she microwaved a couple Jamaican patties and chased them down with some much needed wine.

She took a third cell phone out of her bag and flipped it open. Raiden Pioneer had given it to her. Right after he'd put *two* tracking devices in the book; one a bulky, obvious device in the spine and the other a leading-edge, thin design secreted beneath the book's padded leather cover. It was the same trick she'd used on a source for her book, but she'd decided it was best to keep some things to herself.

The device was a passive cellular piggyback GPS unit. Once an hour it would switch on, ascertain its location, and then use the closest cell phone to send a quick text message to her phone, shutting off right after. It made it almost impossible to detect. But Nathan's comment about hit or miss cell service made her nervous.

She went to the phone's text messages. There were several from when she still had the book, all from a New York City location. And then there were several hours without an expected message. Probably while she was in flight, she reasoned. Then around 10:00 P.M. Eastern Time last night there was another. She felt a chill as she saw where she'd been.

"Bloody *Africa*?" She couldn't believe she'd been halfway around the world and back. Then as she was holding the phone it buzzed the receipt of another message. He was right about hit and miss; she was getting a location message about every five or six hours.

She checked this message and saw that it was from the same vicinity, but several hundred miles to the east. That must have been where the helicopter was going.

Feeling better knowing her long shot was paying off, Nathan apparently none the wiser, she peeled off her clothes and took a shower. She examined the marks on her stomach again as she rinsed the suds off her torso. They didn't look like they'd leave a scar. It made her angry that someone could do that to her with impunity, but she knew that wasn't quite true.

Dried and dressed in a T-shirt and jeans, she checked her answering machine. She had almost twenty messages. The first one was from Dan Cooper.

"Um, hi, uh, Miss Burrows?" Dan's voice said, though it was hard to hear him through the whistling and buffeting of what sounded like a high wind. "It's Dan. Dan Cooper? I'm not sure what . . . that is, I thought you were going to call my editor? About the . . . you know. Anyways, if you could call me I'd sure appreciate it. Or, actually, just call my editor. Please? Okay. Bye."

She deleted it, trying to ignore her guilt over using him, especially since she hadn't been able to use the evidence. The rest of the messages were from her agent. They started off angry but faded into concern. The last message was from Agent Wagner.

"Miss Burrows, call me as soon as you get this. I'd like to speak to you about Dan Cooper's death."

Emily almost burned herself. She'd been in the middle of making a cup of tea when she'd heard the message.

"His what?" Emily said to the empty apartment. She realized that somewhere between the message Dan had left and Wagner's call, something terrible had happened.

Emily jumped on the Internet and after a few searches, found the news story. As she read, her mouth slowly dropped open. By the time she got to the end, she was leaning in so close to the screen the hairs on the tip of her nose stood up from the display's static electricity.

"Bloody hell," she said quietly.

The article described Dan as a loner who didn't fit in. A quiet boy who made his coworkers uneasy. About the time Emily was winging her way to Africa, the naive but enthusiastic boy Emily had met apparently went to the roof of the *New York Times* building and . . . jumped.

She was having a hard time believing it, but then she thought about the whistling wind in the background of Dan's message and realized he'd called her from the *roof* of the building.

"Oh my God."

When the shock eased, she realized why Wagner wanted to speak to her. *They must have a record of the call.*

Suddenly, she was very scared. And she knew what she had to do. It would put her father's reputation at risk, but she just had to hope he could fend for himself. If she allowed herself to think about that too hard—the knighted curator of the British Museum having a fraud and a criminal for a daughter—the guilt would turn her back into a coward. Even the idea of finding The Monarch's true identity became insignificant.

Emily took the case out of the stove; put the money back in it along with her camera with the pictures of Dan's charts. She put on her coat and scarf, poured some extra food in Churchill's bowl, and then headed out to the FBI car watching her apartment.

WAGNER ENTERED INTERVIEW Room F on the twenty-second floor at 26 Federal Plaza, where Evans had put her when the agents he'd put on her apartment brought her in. He looked at Miss Burrows, seated at one of the two chairs positioned at the table. She looked exhausted, her eyes and nose red. Obviously she'd been crying. She sat in the chair facing the mirror, her bag clutched to her chest.

On the table in front of her were several items. He stepped closer and when he saw what they were, he glanced up at the camera as if to say *I hope you're getting this.* On the table was a metal briefcase, a digital camera, a cell phone, and a file folder with several stacks of cash on top of it. Even from a quick glance, Wagner knew it was thousands of dollars. The listening device inside the metal case was inert, disabled by their techs the second she'd held up a note for them that said "Bug in case."

"What's all this about?" Wagner asked.

"Is that camera recording?" she asked. Her tone, though a little shaky, told Wagner she was more mad than sad.

"Yes it is," Wagner said as he sat down across from her. She looked down at the table and took a slow, deep breath like she was bracing herself. He fought the urge to do the same.

"My name is Emily Denham and I've got a story to tell you," she said. For the next forty-five minutes he listened to a fantastic tale.

She told him everything—her first meeting with Nathan in the limo, Dan Cooper's visit, the press conference ulterior motive—everything. She finished off with her abduction to Africa.

When she was done, he didn't respond at all, just got up and left. He joined Evans, who had watched the whole thing through the glass.

"Whaddya think?" Wagner asked. Evans handed him a print-out. Wagner saw that he'd run her supposed real name while they were in there. No priors. Well, that was something.

"If it wasn't for that pile of cash, I'd say she's a writer who got carried away with her own story. She may still be."

"I'd agree with you if it wasn't for that file. That's not a copy or a mockup. That's my original personnel file. Only two ways she could have gotten that," Wagner said, pouring himself a cup of coffee.

"Threats or money."

"Maybe both. Who do you think the rat is?" Wagner asked, knowing someone in the building was in on this. He blew on his coffee and sipped it. It tasted awful and he wished it was cooler so he could toss it back in one gulp.

"Hard to say. My bet would be someone administrative. Outside the action. Easy pickings for someone with enough pull."

"You mean like someone who could arrange to have traffic cameras go dark at the source?"

"Exactly," Evans said.

"What about this Africa trip? Sounds pretty out there."

"Not really. We had a case a few years ago and the guy's alibi was he was in Mexico on vacation with his family so he couldn't possibly be guilty. Turned out his employer owned a supersonic jet. Businesses have been getting into supersonic flight for a few years, now. Fly from New York to Paris in like four hours. That kind of thing."

"No shit," Wagner said. "The more I learn about this Nathan, if he exists, the more I think we should go ahead with the press conference. He wanted it pretty bad to pull something like this. Might be the best way to get anything on him."

"Risky," Evans said. Wagner knew if he thought it was risky it was *really* risky. "Think she'd play along?"

"Yeah, I do," Wagner said, looking at Emily through the glass. "She's pissed. This Monarch, whoever he really is, means something special to her. Look what she risked up until now just to find him. She only balked when she thought Cooper's death was her fault."

"Huh," Evans said with a crooked grin.

"What?"

"Nothing, I think it's the smart play. I just never thought you'd make it."

Wagner responded with a slight raise of his eyebrows and sipped some more of the coffee.

"You want me to contact the authorities in Africa, start getting them involved?" Evans asked.

"Not yet. We don't have much time. Start drawing up a plan for tomorrow. If Nathan tries to make a move, I want him facedown on the sidewalk before he knows what hit him."

"YOU STILL WANT me to do the press conference?" Emily said. She'd half expected them to come in and haul her off to jail. A lot more than half, actually. Technically, she was pretty sure she hadn't done anything illegal yet, even if she had been stupid.

"Just like we'd planned," Wagner said.

"Why would I do that? I told you what these people are capable of, what they've done. You've got the location, why don't you just go and get him?"

"For one, the FBI doesn't have jurisdiction in Africa. For another, what exactly would I arrest him for? All we have is circumstantial evidence and your say-so. And, no offense, but you're not exactly the model of honesty right now. Plus, we have no idea who he really is. Is Nathan his first or his last name? Is it his name at all? We follow that GPS device to your book and we could be arresting some librarian he gave the book to. We've got bupkus. Except—"

"Except for me. You've got me and this press conference that Nathan wants to happen."

"Exactly," Wagner said. "But we've also got something else . . . or we could have something else. With your help."

"The Monarch," Emily said, fear in her belly. *He wants to use me to lure The Monarch, just like Nathan does.*

"This Nathan, or whoever he is, has a hard . . . is motivated to get his hands on this Monarch for some reason. That means if we have The Monarch, we can control the situation. Set up Nathan. Maybe even figure out why he wants him, which could give us evidence and charges against him."

"And what happens to The Monarch?" Emily asked, already knowing the answer. She wanted to see if Wagner would come clean with her. If she could trust anyone in this mess.

Wagner leaned back in his chair and said, "Well, I won't lie to you. If he's cleared of the murders, we'd have to turn him over to Interpol. But from what I read in your book, he'd probably end up skating on that count too. I'm thinking that would be a lot better than whatever Nathan has planned for him."

Emily knew he was right about that. "I'll be honest with you, I'm not crazy about being up on a podium in front of a crowd knowing what I know. I think I'd have a huge target on my back. I'm pretty sure that's why he took his cell phone back. Once the press conference is over I'll be of no use to him anymore and he doesn't want any evidence to connect him to me."

Wagner puffed air through his nose and crossed his arms. He looked at Emily like he was trying to find Waldo.

"What?"

"I'm trying to figure you out. Half the time you talk like a bumbling bookworm, the other half like a cop. Anyway, I already thought of that. We can control the conference—invitation only, controlled area, plants in the crowd. Probably do it downstairs in the lobby. If we need to we can lock it down on a moment's notice. You'd be perfectly safe."

Emily bit her lip and thought about the offer. It was better than anything she had hoped for, but it was less than perfect. Even if everything worked out fine and that Nathan bastard got what was coming to him, getting The Monarch outed and dumped in Interpol's hands wasn't anywhere near the endgame she wanted. Even if he did avoid jail time, he and everyone in his life would have a target on them. She knew there was a laundry list of private collectors willing to pay anything for the chance to get some payback.

But who knew what would happen after Nathan was out of the picture? At the least, she'd finally be able to write the missing chapter for her book. Maybe even the sequel Raiden had mentioned, not that the thought hadn't already occurred to her. She'd take that over the not knowing any day, regardless of the risks.

"I'll do it," Emily said. "On one condition."

"What's that?"

"Keep it open," Emily said. She knew Wagner would know why. The more public the forum, the more chance The Monarch would be in the crowd. Of course, that also meant the more chance Nathan's men would be there too.

"Done."

20

The Cloisters Museum
New York City
4:00 P.M. Local Time

JONATHAN SAT AT the table and endlessly stirred his coffee while he waited for Lew, who was testing the strength of the café's food trays. The museum was closing soon and the Trie Café was almost empty.

"Bad news," Lew said as he arrived at the table. He plunked his tray down. It was loaded with two sandwiches, a coffee, a piece of pie, a piece of cake, and something that looked like rice pudding. Jonathan smiled despite himself.

"They out of whole chickens?"

"Har-dee-har. No, when I was at the cash register, I saw on the news that they've set a location for the press conference tomorrow," Lew said, hitching a thumb toward the television suspended from the ceiling.

"That's bad?" Jonathan asked. He tried to read the television's news scroll, but it was too far away.

"No, the location is the lobby of FBI headquarters."

"Great."

"We'll just have to be careful," Lew said shrugging before he dug into his banquet.

After landing, they'd checked into a midtown hotel and walked to the first murder scene, on the border of Central Park. Jonathan wandered around for almost twenty minutes, finally sitting right where they'd discovered the corpse. There was nothing he could find to show it was anything but a random murder. The view from that location was either of the park or the buildings across the street. Nothing special.

They walked the few blocks to St. Patrick's Cathedral, the site of the second murder. Awed by the beauty and majesty of the cathedral's vaulted ceiling and intricate stained glass windows, they found nothing out of the ordinary. The murder tour was starting to feel like a complete waste of time. Even so, they grabbed a cab and headed for The Cloisters Museum.

They did a bit of the tour, trying to fit in as tourists, but spent most of their time around the fountain where the last body was found. A lot of people were there for the same reason, but when the coast was clear, Jonathan lay back on the fountain in the position they had found Bob Cummings's body. Again, nothing but a wet stain on the back of his shirt. Their investigations were a total bust.

"I don't get it," Jonathan finally said when he tired of stirring his coffee. "I was sure there'd be a theme or a pattern. Something to show what this was all about."

"Well," Lew said around a mouthful of sandwich, "maybe the *who* and the *where* aren't the point. Maybe it's the *how*?"

The song Natalie had picked as Jonathan's ringtone for her started playing out of his pocket. It was her favorite song from the *Guardians of the Galaxy* movie they'd gone to see and was the only song she'd picked that he could stand.

Ooga chaka . . . ooga chaka . . . ooga chaka. . .

Lew looked at him as he took it out of his pocket. "Cute," he said before biting off another hunk of sandwich.

"Shut up." Jonathan chuckled before he answered the phone. "Hi, babe."

Natalie told him about her day. They'd gone go-karting and tonight they were going to a movie. Ken Swenson was sparing no expense in keeping her busy. Jonathan was glad, but at this rate he'd burn through the five hundred dollars Jonathan had given him in a couple of days. They talked and joked for almost twenty minutes, Jonathan reluctant to say good-bye with what he'd possibly be facing tomorrow.

"I have to go, Dad," Natalie said after she mumbled something to someone at the Swensons' house. "We're making popcorn and watching *Frozen*."

"Again? You're going to turn into Elsa if you watch that one more time," Jonathan said, wishing he was there to hear her sing along with the movie.

"I wish! Night, Dad. Good luck. I love you."

"Night, babe. I love you too." Jonathan hung up and stayed lost in thought for another minute before he shook his head and forced himself to focus on the here and now.

"Sorry, what were you saying?" Jonathan asked.

"I said, maybe it's the *how* we should look at. Those news reports didn't have a whole lot of detail. The symbol scraped into the victims' skins was shocking, but hardly life threatening," Lew said, sliding the empty pie plate aside and digging into the cake.

Jonathan just stared at Lew. This was not the same man he'd known a few years ago. In the interim, Lew had become much more reflective.

"Okay, but how do we find out how they were killed before tomorrow?"

"I knew some guys in the NYPD about twenty years ago."

Jonathan was going to say something, but he felt the wind sucked out of him as he looked up from his coffee. He couldn't read the words, but the image on the screen was all too clear and all too familiar.

"Son of a bitch," Jonathan said.

"Wha?" Lew said. He saw where Jonathan was looking and turned around. "Is that—"

Jonathan stood up and grabbed Lew's lapel as he walked past, pulling him to his feet. "Come on."

They walked over to where they could see the screen better.

And there it was, *The Just Judges*—the most stolen painting in the world. And Jonathan and Lew had been the last ones to steal it. Jonathan hadn't seen it in almost eight years. The last time was when he'd pulled it out of his backpack and handed it to the Belgian authorities. They'd thanked Jonathan and Lew and offered to pay them for recovering it, but the authorities had an additional, bizarre request. It was the first time someone asked Jonathan and Lew to *unsteal* something. Well, not really unsteal it, though apparently that would have been all right with the museum as well. They'd just wanted it gone.

Most collectors and experts considered the painting lost or destroyed years ago. It had last been seen in 1935. Apparently there was just too much involved if it suddenly showed up again. Jonathan had refused payment, which had pissed Lew off, and walked away from the job, leaving the painting with the Belgian authorities.

"I told you that painting was bad luck," Lew said, keeping his voice down so the three or four other people who had gathered around them to watch the newscast wouldn't hear. One of the main reasons Lew had balked at not taking the payment was that he'd broken his arm during the theft. It was also the only time either of them had ever been hurt on a job. When they'd walked away, Lew had said it wasn't the last they'd seen of that painting. Jonathan had thought he was just being superstitious. Now he wasn't so sure.

Jonathan was having other thoughts. This painting being used as a murder weapon changed things. This wasn't someone with Miss Burrows's book performing murders they wanted blamed on The Monarch or even someone pretending to be The Monarch. The book didn't even mention the painting. Whoever had done this was sending a very deliberate and very direct message to The Monarch: *I know more about you than anyone in the world and I'm coming for you.*

And it was received loud and clear.

21

Tartaruga Island
3:00 A.M. Local Time

THE HARDEST PART of kuru was the frustration. Before the symptoms arrived in full force, Nathan couldn't appreciate the simple things in life for their complexity—picking up a snifter of brandy or rolling a fine cigar between his thumb and index finger. But what was going on beneath those seemingly simple acts were neurons firing, neuromuscular transmissions rifling down nerve strands to muscles, balance and coordination working in tandem. All of it happening in the blink of an eye. But Nathan sometimes even had a hard time blinking, now.

To be fair, the disease wasn't the only problem. The loss of muscle control and coordination was bad, though not as bad as the involuntary laughing fits. Nathan's ego had suffered the hardest hit of all. At his request, Sophia had come up with a solution for him that had nothing to do with treating his illness.

When he was off the serum, he loaded up with non-depolarizing blocking agents, similar to what anesthesiologists used during surgeries to prevent patients from twitching or moving when scalpels were inside them. The tricky part was keeping Nathan's respiratory system unaffected and allowing him to stay conscious. Eventually, after some seriously close calls, she'd found the right cocktail. His ego could avoid the embarrassment of appearing undignified. But if not for the advanced systems built into his chair, he would've been completely immobile and silent between serum shots.

Now, Nathan worked to rotate his motorized wheelchair so the arm affixed to the side lined up his pass card properly with the access slot keeping the lab door shut. He'd been trying for almost five solid minutes, now. Most doors in the complex automatically detected his approach and opened for him when he was in his chair. Most doors he was apt to use, that is. Not this one. Sophia's lab was her domain.

Finally he oriented the card, gave the subvocal command, and the card slid down through the slot. The door to Sophia's lab clicked open, and he quickly whirred inside. A moment later the door clicked closed behind him.

He rolled down an aisle with science stations on either side, looking like something out of *Frankenstein.* Glass beakers, tubes, and Bunsen burners bubbled and burned away in their stations, oblivious to the stranger among them.

At the end of the aisle he spotted his quarry; a large refrigeration unit. He rolled closer but stopped short when he saw a padlock on it. Even if he'd had the key it wouldn't have helped in his current state. The frustration in him built to a crescendo and he wished he could make a fist just for a moment so he could pound a table with it.

Nathan opened his unwilling, unaligned lips and uttered a moist, drooling howl that might have been cursing in another reality; his chair, confused by the utterance, shimmied back and forth. Just past this tiny loop of metal, inside the refrigerated exterior of the box, sat his prize. The only thing that could make him whole again, if only for a short time.

It might as well have been at the bottom of an active volcano.

"What are you doing?" a sleep-raspy voice behind him said. He turned the wheelchair around and saw Sophia standing there, lines on her face and wrinkles in her lab coat telling him she'd fallen asleep at her desk again. *She may not be my biological daughter, but she sure acts like me.*

"I just want to see it," Nathan's electronic voice said.

"No, you're in no shape to take another dose so soon," she said. "Your body is adapting to the new formula as fast as it did to the others. You'll only quicken the process."

"I feel fine." He was lying. His body screamed in pain. The chair that enabled him to get around and speak was designed for paraplegics but despite his artificial paralysis, he felt everything. "Why is it locked?"

"Because of nights like this," Sophia said.

"I told you, I just want to see it."

"Then why did Lara tell me you wanted a treatment for tonight?" she asked. He knew she was trying to play him. She was the last person Lara would take into confidence.

"Tonight is everything. I have to be at capacity."

"I wouldn't know anything about that, seeing as you haven't told me what the hell you're doing down there. Despite the fact you've turned my lab into a ghost town. Regardless, you're not thinking straight. Maybe . . ."

"Maybe my mind is being affected?" Nathan's electronic voice finished for her. "It's not."

Then something strange happened. Nathan watched Sophia look at him as if she were searching for something or trying to make a decision. Nathan felt like a bug under one of her microscopes. No one had ever made him feel that way before. The moment stretched out and then it was over. She turned away and he was released from her gaze.

"It stays locked. Go to bed, Nathan," Sophia said as she left the lab, presumably to take her own advice, leaving him sitting alone, still shook up from that gaze.

Nathan?

OUT IN THE hallway, Sophia fell back against the corridor wall gasping for breath. She was trying to both stave off tears and calm down. But it wasn't sadness she was feeling. Well, not totally. It was anger.

Earlier that day she had been performing routine tests on a sample of Nathan's blood to try and determine what kind of adjustments she could make to the serum so his body would stop adapting to it so quickly. But she didn't have another blood sample to use as a control, so she used her own. What she'd seen in the comparison had made her feel like she'd been punched in the stomach with an iron fist.

It had nothing to do with the serum. It was the blood samples. Nathan's blood type was O-positive. Sophia's was AB-negative, which she knew was the same as her late mother's. It was a fluke that she even noticed it, but once she did, she checked again and again. There was no mistake.

Nathan could not be her father.

For a brief second in the lab a moment ago, Sophia thought she was going to grab something off a workstation and smash it into his face. Her whole adult life had been devoted to trying to save that bastard's life. Her education, her training and all these years heading up her lab. All of it was for him. For family.

Then the tears won out. She put her hand over her mouth to stifle the sobs and ran toward her room, her lab coat billowing out behind her like a ghost.

22

Hemingway Hotel
New York City
9:00 P.M. Local Time

LEW, A BUCKET of ice under one arm and several cans of soda crooked in the other, bullied his way through the hotel room door. Two of the cans broke free and bounced off the orange and brown carpet. He put the ice and sodas on the credenza by the door with a mumbled curse.

Jonathan sat at the desk against the wall in a bathrobe, his hair damp and mussed, talking on the phone. Lew didn't recognize the language, but could guess that it was Dutch since Jonathan had been trying all night to call the Belgian museum curator they'd left *The Just Judges* with years ago. Lew spun the top off the bottle of Canadian Club he'd bought earlier. He filled a glass halfway and then snapped a Coke open and topped it off. He offered the glass to Jonathan, who waved it away like an annoying gnat. Lew shrugged, took a sip, and then plopped down on a hard orange sofa, putting his feet up on the aluminum coffee table. He eyed the full-length duster coat he'd bought earlier hanging in the closet and raised his glass to it before he swallowed half of his drink.

Jonathan slammed down the phone. "Idiot."

"What's the scoop?" Lew asked.

"The moron sold it to a private collector two days after we left. Two *days*," Jonathan said. "Hey, go easy on that. We've got work tomorrow."

"So I won't drink tomorrow," Lew said. "Did you get a name?"

"Nope. He was too pissed for that. It's three in the morning over there."

"Didn't *he* call *you* back?"

"Yeah, but only because I've been calling the museum, his house, and everyone he's ever known every five minutes all night. I can't wait to see this bill," Jonathan said, crossing to the credenza and getting a glass of Coke with ice. He reached for the CC, but then stopped.

"Go on. Live a little," Lew said, seeing his indecision. Jonathan gave a sly grin, rolled his eyes, and grabbed the bottle. "There ya go."

"Anyways, he wasn't going to give me the guy's name until I threatened to keep the harassment up," Jonathan said, sitting down beside Lew on the sofa. He took a long drink.

"And?"

"Some guy named Canton George," Jonathan said. Lew felt the blood rush out of his limbs. He tried to keep his face from showing what he was feeling.

"Dead end," Lew said after clearing his throat, staring intently into his drink.

"What?"

"What what?" Lew said innocently.

"Lew?" Jonathan said like a father who'd caught his kid with his hand in the cookie jar. Lew tried to keep up the front, but it was short-lasting. Jonathan knew him too well. Besides, Jonathan needed to at least know something about it.

"Fine, yeah I know him. Boy, do I know him."

"Wait a minute," Jonathan said, looking pensive. "George. Son of a bitch!"

And Lew knew the jig was up.

It had been years ago, back when Jonathan had first met Samantha. During that time, Lew pulled one job on his own as The Monarch: the Canton George estate. Things had not gone well. All Lew had told Jonathan was that George was an Australian industrialist and the lead on his collection hadn't panned out.

"What are you holding back, Lew?"

"Nothing," Lew said, not seeing any point in going into the details. Jonathan eyed him while he sipped his drink. Mercifully he eventually broke eye contact, either because Lew had covered his anxiety sufficiently or because he knew pushing now wouldn't be the best tactic.

"That's one hell of a coincidence."

"Yup," Lew said, keeping his eyes down.

"How many is that?" Jonathan asked with a smile, gesturing toward the duster hanging in the closet. "Four?"

"Five," Lew said, thankful the subject was changing. He loved dusters, but they seemed to have a bad habit of attracting knives and bullets.

"I know it's April, but you're going to roast at the press conference tomorrow. Not to mention stand out like a gray pubic hair."

At the mention of the press conference, Lew put his feet down and sat up. "What?"

"I've been thinking about this whole press conference thing," Lew said.

"Yeah? What about it?"

"Look, I know it was my idea to come to New York and all, and I'm glad we're here."

"But . . ."

"But, after seeing *The Just Judges*, are you sure going to this press conference is such a great idea?"

"How do you mean?"

"It's like when Hitler started using the swastika—"

"Excuse me?"

"Let me finish. Before Hitler started using the symbol, it was actually a Hindu symbol of peace. Of course, nobody connects it with anything except the Nazis now. But the difference between what we thought we were getting into before seeing the painting and what we're really getting into is like if Hitler hadn't had a problem with the Jews, but took the symbol anyway and tried to wipe them out just to make the Hindus look bad. You know?"

"Jesus."

"What?"

"I think you just made a good point. Must be the booze."

Lew elbowed him and got up to refill his glass. "I'm serious, Jonny."

"I know you are," Jonathan said, putting his drink down on the table. "But the fact is, seeing that painting and knowing this is targeted—personal—makes me want to stop this guy even more. Can you imagine what would happen if he ever discovered our true identities? Or worse, if Talie found out?"

"What we did was good," Lew said. "We've got nothing to be ashamed about."

"I know, but it won't matter. And even if I could explain it to her, what do you think a judge would say?"

"Yeah, but—"

"I'd never see her again, Lew. I know you care about her, but she's not just in my heart, she *is* my heart. I'd die without her."

Lew knew from the look in Jonathan's eyes that he wasn't exaggerating. He felt something welling up in him that he didn't like, so he tried to change the subject as much as he could.

"Ever read it?" Lew asked, picking up the copy of *The Monarch's Reign* they'd bought on their way back to the hotel. He didn't need to open it. Before being locked up, he'd carried a dog-eared copy with him for over a year. He knew it backward and forward and though he wouldn't admit it, he was more than a little excited at the prospect of meeting the author in all of this.

"Not yet," Jonathan said. "I flipped through it a bit. She never really tries to identify us. Which was kind of weird. You?"

"Come on, be serious," Lew said, tossing the book down with feigned contempt when he found out Jonathan had never read it. "I need more pictures."

"Yeah, right," Jonathan said with a laugh.

"But no kidding, I've still got a bad feeling about going tomorrow."

"I won't lie. There is a risk, but it's also our best shot at finding this guy."

"I don't know about that," Lew said leaning back. "How do you know he'll even be there?"

"Oh, he'll be there," Jonathan said. "Just like arsonists hang around to watch their handiwork burn, he'll be in the crowd, watching what he's done, what he's made happen. Look at the theatrics in his killings. He's all about the accolades."

"Maybe," Lew said.

"Besides, if they knew who we were they would have made a move long before this. And don't forget our secret weapon."

"What's that?"

Jonathan picked his glass back up and before he drank it down he said, "They still think The Monarch is one person."

PART FOUR

Monday

23

Federal Plaza
New York City
11:00 A.M. Local Time

THE FEDERAL PLAZA lobby was already filled with spectators by the time Jonathan and Lew had arrived. Against the far wall a raised stand had been set up, with several chairs and a podium on it. Atop the podium were dozens of microphones, each labeled with a particular news agency's call letters or logos. To accommodate the expected crowd, large flat-screen monitors had been hung from the ceiling at strategic points. Two large monitors had also been hung outside in the plaza so those who didn't care to squeeze through the crowd inside could watch the proceedings. The feed from the cameras was passed directly to the media as well, so they could show the event live without having to jam the space with their cameras. At the moment, all the monitors displayed the FBI logo.

Jonathan couldn't believe the crowd. There had to be two or three hundred people gathered for the press conference.

"Elvis is in the building," Lew said.

"Unbelievable," Jonathan said. They slowly pushed through the crowd. When they were at a point where they could see the outdoor monitors clearly, Lew stopped, but Jonathan kept going. He turned around when he noticed he was alone.

"You're not going in there," Lew said.

Jonathan walked back to Lew so he could talk without being overheard, or at least try to. The din of the crowd was loud and rising in volume.

"If he's here, he'll be in there," Jonathan said.

"Bullshit," Lew said. "You don't know that. You just want to go in there. I think you're getting off on this dog and pony show." Jonathan hated that Lew knew him so well, even after their time apart.

"Don't you?"

"Man, I don't even want to be on this side of town," Lew said.

"Come on. We'll stay by the doors. I just need to see it live, not on these monitors," Jonathan said. He had no intention of staying that far away, but one step at a time. He was going to make up some story about being unable to read people's faces in two dimensions off the screens, but Lew would have seen right through that. Instead, he went for the pity stare. He watched Lew look around the crowd, evaluating their situation. Jonathan knew Lew was running about a hundred different scenarios through his head.

He'd always listened to Lew, who had better survival instincts. Being a spook, even an ex-spook, sometimes made you think you were both invisible and bulletproof. But without an agency, you were alone and vulnerable.

Finally Lew sighed and gave in. "Fine, just remember we're un-armed here." It would have been impossible to bring anything into this crowd. Jonathan knew there would be plainclothes cops or feds passing through the crowds with scanners looking for any-thing dangerous.

Fifteen minutes and many apologies later, they'd made it to the entrance. The revolving doors had been removed to allow free flow of viewers in and out. They passed into the semi-warmth and saw the podium at the far end of the room. Jonathan started toward it and was grabbed by the collar and pulled back. Lew let go and they stood beside the door with their backs to the glass.

"Right here is fine," Lew said. He was being far too serious for Jonathan's liking. Lew wasn't just guessing; he could smell that something wasn't right. That nose of his had kept them alive more than a few times. Jonathan leaned against the glass beside him without argument.

"Yeah, I guess this'll do." *For now.*

A HALF BLOCK east and on the far side of the street, Thomas sat at the wheel of the limo, the engine purring in readiness. He gripped the steering wheel with black-gloved hands, but he was neither nervous nor anxious—not about the mission, at least. Bill Clap-ton, an ex-Navy SEAL Thomas had worked with before, was in the backseat viewing Federal Plaza through binoculars from behind smoked glass.

"Sitrep," Thomas said. They still had a half hour before things got under way, and probably another half hour before the shit hit the fan, but mistakes and anomalies seemed to be following him lately. He wasn't going to be surprised again if he could help it.

"Nothing to report," Bill said. Thomas detected an edge to his voice. He wanted to be inside with his men, but Thomas needed a birddog out here. He couldn't sit at the wheel, ready to go at a moment's notice, *and* use the binoculars. But Thomas knew Bill was too much of a professional to let sulking interfere with the task at hand.

"What is it?"

"Nothing. Well, probably nothing. But those two guys across the street from us are cops or I can't strip an AK–47 blindfolded."

"Where?"

"Eight o'clock," Bill said, indicating the pair across the street and behind them slightly.

"Roger. Keep your eyes on the prize," Thomas said, not wanting them both taking their eyes off of Federal Plaza at the same time. Thomas reached up and pushed the side view mirror's motor control. A muffled whirr sounded as the mirror tilted out so he could see the sidewalk. "Got them."

They were dressed in jeans, hockey jackets, and wool caps. They blended in perfectly with the crowd, appearing to the casual observer like just a couple of guys interested in The Monarch case. But unlike everyone else, they weren't getting any closer to the main event. They were just standing and talking, drinking a couple of steaming coffees out of white and blue paper cups. They also seemed to be looking around quite a bit, instead of looking at each other as they talked.

It was probably nothing, but it was enough to make Thomas look around the area away from Federal Plaza. He spotted three other similar pairs, standing almost equidistant from Federal Plaza as the first pair.

"Shit. We've got a perimeter setup," Thomas said, turning his attention back to the plaza so Bill could confirm his suspicions.

"Got them," Bill said. "Deviate?" Thomas had told Bill and his men that a mission scrub was possible if things weren't going right. He'd lied. This was a one-shot deal. If they failed, they wouldn't have another chance. And neither would Nathan.

"Negative. Keep an eye on them and be ready to use the decoy," Thomas said. He reached across the seat and grasped the handle of the suppressed SIG Sauer automatic lying there as he waited for Bill's response.

"Roger," Bill said. Thomas took his hand off the gun and put it back on the steering wheel. "Decoy looks intact. We're good to go."

Anticipating such a move from the feds, Thomas had put a decoy in place. Posing as window washers, they had carefully pressed a rope of C–4 over the putty holding the main windows of Federal Plaza's concourse in place. The windows were large, and there was enough material in place to blow up a small tank. Unless they brought sniffers out, it would be impossible for anyone to detect. The detonator was the hard part. It had to be passive and close range. If anyone peeled off the sticker in the bottom corner of the glass advertising their fake window washing company, they'd find the inside of the decal lined with wiring and circuitry. But everyone was too worried about a moving threat, which was what Thomas had counted on. They'd never suspect the biggest danger wasn't through the window, but the window itself.

The hard part was going to be timing. The blow rate was going to be unpredictable. Keeping safe anyone identified to him as a retrieval target—The Monarch, Miss Burrows, and anyone else the control center eight thousand miles away ordered him to grab—

was going to be tricky to say the least. And then there was Lara's request. She wanted him to kill Burrows in the confusion that was about to take place. He knew why she wanted him to do it. She wanted to hurt her father. Thomas understood that motivation all too well, but a lifetime of taking orders had him more than a little conflicted about the request.

24

Tartaruga Island
6:30 P.M. Local Time

SOPHIA STEPPED FROM the catwalk into the gallery. Two stories above the data center's floor, she could already see the three giant monitors hung high over one end of the hangar through the gallery's large windows. The central monitor displayed something that looked like a face, colorful overlays dancing across the image; smaller images jumped out of the bigger one for a few moments before they melted back into the whole. The other two monitors flanking the center one, equal in size, each showed a single line of white text on the otherwise black background: "No Feed Detected."

Sophia eased closer to the windows, and the hardware and activity on the floor of the hangar came into view. This was the first time she had come down here since they started the project. Nathan hadn't specifically told her to stay away, but she'd still felt like she was trespassing—seeing something she wasn't meant to see. But tonight she didn't care.

"My God," she breathed as she took in the magnitude of the operation.

A dozen men and women in white lab coats—her reassigned staff—moved through the data center's server farm. Each of them glared at some sort of PDA device as they checked various parts of the computerized labyrinth, no doubt for instructions on what they were doing, since server maintenance and monitoring wasn't their field.

Beneath the monitors, several other lab-coated workers monitored control stations that looked like something from NASA. Hired for their expertise, Sophia only recognized a few of them from brief encounters in the dining hall. At the center of it all were Nathan and Lara, Nathan in his chair, whirring back and forth, and Lara standing tall and erect by his side in one of her trademark dresses, this one sea blue.

Seeing them replaced Sophia's awe with distaste and resolve. Still dressed in her own lab coat, she reached in the pocket and touched the long, sharp object she'd brought.

Sophia buried the fear that someone would spot her and usher her out and descended the long flight of stairs spilling down to the hangar floor. Forcing herself to move at a slow, natural pace, no one seeming to notice an extra lab coat.

She crossed the floor toward her target, nodding to a few other people and ignoring the guards sprinkled around the data center who seemed to be returning the favor. As she got closer, Lara bellowed at the workers.

"Thirty minutes, people!" she said. Sophia could feel the screen overhead glowering down at her like a demented great and powerful Oz. She pulled the object from her pocket as she stepped up behind the arguing pair. *No one even sees me. I'm invisible, just like any other day.*

Lara finally looked behind her just as Sophia swung her arm, but Lara wasn't the target. Sophia slammed the point of the hypodermic needle into Nathan's neck, looked in Lara's eyes to show her the lack of emotion she felt, and then abruptly turned and headed back the way she'd come.

Sophia didn't look back. She'd wanted to kill him, pump his veins full of acid and watch him dissolve in front of her—in front of everyone—but she just couldn't do it. Instead, she'd done the next best thing. She'd diluted the formula. And she'd just made sure he'd embarrassingly go through the change in front of everyone who reported to him. To Nathan, this would be worse than airing dirty laundry for the public to see. This would be airing your dirty laundry and standing naked beside it.

She reached the stairs and headed up at the same slow, steady pace she'd used to descend them, but she knew what was happening behind her: Nathan's brain was exploding with light and heat, his body was shaking uncontrollably, his eyes were rolling up in their sockets, and if he wasn't careful he was biting into his tongue. These were all normal effects of the serum, as it disabled the neuro-blocker that kept his shaking body still before attacking the diseased parts of his brain, temporarily curing him. Very temporarily, Sophia thought as she climbed the stairs. In a fraction of the time the formula usually lasted, he'd start shaking and convulsing, returning to his natural state. And without his wheelchair or the neuro-blocker to keep him still, his greatest fear would come true in front of everyone. Yes, she thought, for him, this would be much worse than death.

Wild chatter moved through the staff like a wave, a few people shouting, and somewhere a woman screamed. Still, Sophia stayed focused on the top of the stairs. She heard running footsteps—first on concrete and then the tinny clang of the metal stairs—as two guards came after her. She remained unhurried. *Do it.*

"Leave her!" Lara shouted. The steps behind her slowed, stopped, and then after a moment started again but headed away from her this time. She knew the only reason Lara had stopped them: Without Sophia, there wouldn't be any more serum.

When she reached the top of the stairs, she glanced back just for a moment and saw Lara staring at her, Nathan sprawled on the ground on all fours fighting the nausea.

Back in the gallery, Sophia tossed the empty hypodermic needle into the trash, a slight blue tinge the only thing revealing the serum inside.

Tears threatened to blur her vision as she crossed the catwalk, but she held them at bay. Not yet. She would let go once she was back in her lab—back home. Which was a sad thought all on its own, making her control even harder to keep.

All she wanted to do now was hold her animals and fall asleep. Ironic, since for the first time in her life, her eyes were open.

25

Federal Plaza
New York City
11:45 A.M. Local Time

EMILY STOOD AT the back of the elevator beside Wagner reading the statement she'd written and trying to ignore the wall of FBI agents around her. Even though she was the one who'd written the statement—and she'd been practicing it over and over—the words were making no sense to her.

"You'll do fine," Wagner said. She knew he meant her nervousness about speaking in front of so many people, rather than her safety. The Kevlar vest they'd convinced her to wear felt like a corset that was making her *more* of a target rather than less.

She smiled at Wagner and continued reading, but her mind just wouldn't focus. It kept drifting off to her real concern. *Is he here?*

Emily had spent years concocting her mental image of The Monarch. His face, his body, his hands. Even his smell. The image would waver now and again, as her imagination refined her desires with her experiences. She knew the reality would never live up to her fantasy, but she couldn't stop herself.

"Here we go," Wagner said as the elevator car slowed and then stopped. The overhead display dinged and a moment later the doors slid open. The noise from the concourse blasted into the car, sounding more like a gaggle of geese than human beings. Emily's breath hitched at the sudden sensory assault. "Stay close."

They left the elevator and moved as a group up the side of the crowd toward the raised platform. Emily looked around at the spectacle. Everywhere people pushed and shoved, standing on tiptoe with their cameras raised high over their heads, flashes blasted over and over at them as the crowd tried to get a peek at this case breaker.

She glanced up at the big screens hung from the ceiling and felt a new fear race through her as she imagined her head filling the displays, every blemish and flaw the size of a turnip. Then she saw that the crowd filling the concourse was just the tip of the iceberg. As they moved and the glare from the windows eased, she saw that the audience filled the plaza outside and beyond. Some stood on the serpentine benches for a better view, pointing and laughing at the spectacle inside. At her.

Am I walking by him right now?

"THAT'S HER," JONATHAN said. Lew followed Jonathan's gaze, which wasn't really necessary with the way everyone was pointing at the woman walking in a sea of blue suits.

"Huh. Not what I expected," Lew said. From the book and

the way she wrote, he'd somehow expected her to look older and tougher. Sort of a thin version of Kathleen Turner, who had gone from beauty queen to scary old broad in a few short years. Burrows was nothing like that. She was tall and pretty in a fresh-faced sort of way. More like Katharine Hepburn in those black and white movies.

Jonathan said, "I'm going to move up closer to the platform. Stay here and watch the crowd." He sidled his way forward before Lew could say anything.

Crap. Lew worked to follow him, his size making his progress a lot slower.

By the time he caught up, they were right behind the press. Any farther and they'd need a press pass. As far as Lew was concerned, this was way too close, their position making an escape almost impossible. Lew tried to identify their best egress, but found himself staring at Emily up on the platform. He didn't even notice when Jonathan drifted to the side of the press corps away from him.

26

Tartaruga Island
6:55 P.M. Local Time

IMAGES FILLED THE two previously dark screens flanking the center one, each individual screen showing dozens of segmented video images coming from cameras a world away—faces, thousands of faces. When a superficial comparison to the face on the center screen matched high enough on their percentage scale, a segment exploded out to fill the center of the screen and a more intense comparison algorithm ran. On completion, a match percentage displayed, indicating the likelihood that they had found someone out in the real world that matched their altered Belgian reflection. From what Nathan could see, they had yet to get above sixty percent.

The pain had passed and he was once again himself. Lara and Randy had done an excellent job of damage control, somehow getting their teams back on task despite the apparent miracle. He'd deal with Sophia later. For now, the screens above him were all that mattered.

"Status, Mr. Li," Nathan said. He could almost feel the data surging back and forth from the server farm behind him to the control center. It was intoxicating.

"They haven't detected us, yet. But our data models showed we'd have a solid ninety minutes before they started to shut us down. We're not even halfway there, yet."

"Good, good," Nathan said, his neck crooked up as he watched the matches fail one after the other. "What about our match confidence?"

"Nothing positive. Highest match so far is sixty-three percent. But there is a problem."

"A problem? What type of problem?"

"There's an incredible amount of data coming across the wires."

"That was expected."

"It's even higher than we expected. The servers can't keep up. As it is," Randy said, waving a hand toward the screens overhead, "we're maxing the buffers out and we're going to have to start dumping data soon."

"English, Mr. Li," Nathan said.

"There are too many faces. The queue is almost full of unchecked captured images. If it keeps up, we're going to start losing images before they've been compared."

"What?" Nathan couldn't believe what he was hearing. They'd been planning this for months and this possibility had never come up. "How?"

"Cyclops must have added new sources—new camera feeds— that we're not aware of."

"There must be something we can do," Lara said, moving beside her father. "What if we reduced the coverage perimeter? We're checking all of New York City right now. Can you limit the source images to a tighter area around the press conference location?"

"Yes," Randy said, his tone indicating he was working out the details. "How tight?"

Nathan looked at the clock and said, "Just the block around Federal Plaza and the building itself. He'll be there by now."

"Give me a minute," Randy said, sitting down at a terminal.

"That's about all you have, Mr. Li," Nathan said, moving behind Randy's chair. After a few minutes of pounding his keyboard, Randy spun his chair around.

"What is it?"

"We can do it. But there are two issues. The first has to do with detection."

"You said we had ninety minutes, minimum. We're not even close to that," Nathan was moving beyond frustration and into anger. He fought to keep control. From past experiences, he knew that too much adrenaline pumping through his system reduced how long the serum lasted. If he wasn't careful, he'd send himself back into the chair before they were done. But the more he thought about it, the more anxious he got.

"We did, when we had a wider footprint. By reducing our presence, if they detect us they'll be able to shut us down faster."

"How fast?" Lara asked.

"We'll essentially be on a single node if we tighten up as you requested," Randy said.

"How *fast*?"

"Seconds. If not faster."

"What's the second issue?" Nathan asked through gritted teeth. It was taking all his willpower not to explode.

"If this is going to work we have to clear out the bulk of the data. We need room for processing, temporary files, indexes—room we don't have right now."

"Meaning?"

Lara answered for Randy. "Meaning we have to start from scratch."

"Essentially, yes. I'm sorry," Randy said looking up at the main display. "But whatever we do, we have to do it now or the choice will be made for us."

Nathan ran his hands through his hair and paced back and forth. One foot in front of the other, twisting and heading in the other direction using back, hip, and thigh muscles. A simple action that, if this failed, he would lose permanently. The cost was too high. He couldn't decide. He stopped pacing and looked up at his daughter. He knew she'd get the message.

Help me.

She chose secret option number three.

"Dump it, Mr. Li. And activate three other nodes—"

"That won't work. I told you—"

"Don't buffer the other nodes. Dump the data as soon as you get it. And if it looks like time is running out, get clumsy with those other nodes. Make them noisy and obvious," Lara said.

"A decoy. That's brilliant!" Randy said. He spun his chair around and went to work.

"We'll find him," Lara said.

They looked up at the main screen, held their breath, and waited.

27

"MY NAME IS Joseph Wagner. I'm the special agent in charge of The Monarch case. Thank you for coming, everyone," Wagner said. The crowd quieted down and all eyes were now on him. He was getting used to the feeling.

"First, I wanted to comment on the package the press received a few days ago. This package, while from all indications contains valid materials, is at this time still from an unknown source. In an attempt to provide the public with as much information as possible, without impeding our investigation, I've instructed the FBI legal department to allow all contents to be published and made accessible by the public. However, this does not indicate FBI endorsement of the contents. In our view, the contents are suspect, at best.

"Second, one of the items included in the previously mentioned package was a book called *The Monarch's Reign*. The author of this work, Miss Emily Burrows, is seated behind me," Wagner said, indicating Miss Burrows for the crowd, though by now it was really a formality. Even so, the sound of camera shutters snapping open and closed rose and then fell. Miss Burrows squinted from the sudden onslaught of flashes.

"I would like to confirm that our investigation has shown that Miss Burrows, aside from being the author of this work, had nothing to do with the package's assembly or distribution. She is as much a victim as anyone in this case.

"That being said, she does have a unique perspective on the individual known as The Monarch. While she has no special access to this case and is not privy to anything the general public isn't aware of, we have brought her on as a consultant. Now, let me be perfectly clear about this," Wagner said, leaning forward. "She is a consultant on The Monarch, not on the murders.

"In a moment, she would like to make a statement and then we'll take some questions. The final point I want to make is that there have been some rumors that a conflict between the FBI and the NYPD has been impeding this case. This couldn't be further from the truth, as represented by the presence of NYPD Chief of Police Marvin Powers," Wagner said, indicating Powers sitting beside Miss Burrows. Powers gave a half smile and a slight nod.

"And now Miss Burrows's statement," Wagner said, stepping away from the microphone and extending a hand toward Miss Burrows. She smiled nervously, stepped to the podium, unfolded a piece of paper, and laid it down, smoothing out the folds with a repeated petting motion. She eyed the crowd.

"Hello," she said, a slight quaver in her voice.

28

Tartaruga Island
7:05 P.M. Local Time

"I THINK WE'VE got something," Randy Li said. It was the third time he'd said the exact same words; each time further processing had dismissed the candidate. They had upped their threshold to almost seventy-two percent, but it wasn't enough.

"The source?" Lara asked.

"Inside the building. Right next to the podium."

"It's not him," Nathan said.

"But Father—"

"He would never be in such a vulnerable position," Nathan barked. He took a second to steady himself. Lara tried to take him by the arm, but he pushed her away.

"Is it wearing off already?" she asked him. It had actually started to wear off a few minutes ago, but he was fighting it. The pain was back and it was getting harder and harder to maintain his balance. *It must be the stress.* The treatment had never worn off so quickly. Then again, he'd never taken so many treatments so close together before.

"I'm . . . I'm fine."

"The hell you are," Lara said. "Sit in the chair." He knew she meant the wheelchair. He'd never get into that thing willingly.

"I said I'm—"

"Detection!" one of the techs called from behind them, an alarm sounding as the warning passed through the system.

"Which node?" Randy asked, jumping out of his chair and trotting over to the technician's console. "It's one of the decoys," he said before the technician could answer him, the result shown plainly on his display. "But if they're on to us, it won't be long, now."

"Sir!" another tech called out. Nathan turned but saw that the tech was talking to Randy.

"*Mein Gott!*"

"What . . . what is it?" Nathan managed, the pain in his head making it hard to talk. This was more than the serum wearing off. He had to repeatedly blink to clear his vision and his left hand was tingling. Something was wrong.

"We've got him!" Randy shouted, pointing to the overhead display. Lara and Nathan looked up. The screen showed the image that Randy had suspected was a good candidate. Beneath the face the comparison confidence display blinked in green: 98%.

"Stage two! Now!" Lara ordered, seeing her father too disoriented to react.

They dropped the connection to the Cyclops nodes, leaving some engineers thousands of miles away frustrated. Randy sent the image on the screen through to zombie processors lying dormant in American databases, planted by Randy. They compared the face to databases of official identification documents—drivers' licenses, passports, criminal records.

"We've got a hit," Randy said after a few minutes. "Wait. This can't be."

"What is it?" Lara asked.

"Shut it down! Shut it all down! Hurry!" Randy attacked his workstation, pounding commands out on his keyboard faster than Lara could read them.

She looked up at the screens flanking the identified face and realized why Randy was so agitated. Their system was warning that an intruder was trying to hack in. Randy managed to shut everything down before the intruder broke through their firewalls.

"What the hell was that?" Lara demanded. Randy collapsed in his chair, panting like he'd run a marathon.

"The face triggered a black response."

"A what?"

"A search and destroy using sophisticated algorithms. Very sophisticated. They were tracing our signal back to its source."

"Why would they do that?" Lara asked. She knew a little about the field after grilling Randy for the past few weeks. Typically system administrators just wanted to keep intruders out or cut them off as fast as possible if they managed to get in. It was only later that other personnel would worry about where the attack had come from.

"The face wasn't found in an American national identity database or in a credit card company's files. It was found in a data center in Langley, Virginia."

"Langley? You mean—"

"That face is a government operative. A spy."

29

Federal Plaza
New York City
12:15 P.M. Local Time

"Target identified," Thomas said from the front seat of the limo. The screen in the limo's dashboard, previously displaying GPS route map information, now displayed a man's photograph, as did the three LCD screens in the back of the limo. The communication from Tartaruga Island to the limo was on a discreet system, protected from the hack happening so far away. "Let me know when you find him."

"Roger," Bill said. Thomas scanned the crowd with his naked eye, but it was impossible to tell anything from this distance. "Got him. Standing to the right of the podium beside a big guy in a duster. Tall and slender. Black windbreaker and jeans."

Thomas looked and saw the man Bill was describing. He was

close to Miss Burrows, but in the wrong position to use the decoy. The exploded glass would fire shards like shrapnel, slicing through everything in its radius. At the moment, that would include the target.

"Tell your men to get on him and be ready to separate him from the crowd. There's some sort of partition to their right."

"Got it. It's a company directory," Bill said.

"Tell your men to be ready to swing the target behind there. It should provide enough cover."

"Roger."

Thomas watched as several men separated from the crowd inside the concourse and made their way across the room.

"They have to get him across the plaza to the curb," Thomas said. Like most official buildings in New York, thick barricade poles protected the entrance, making it impossible to get up close to the building with anything bigger than a dirt bike.

"Them," Bill said.

"What?"

"Get *them* across the plaza. You said *him*," Bill said. "No biggie." But Thomas knew it was a biggie and then some.

Thomas's cell phone rang and he answered it. It was the B team located nearby in the back of an electronics-filled van with a broadcast dish on top.

"We're ready. Image has been superimposed. Just let us know when you want to do the cut-in."

"Stand by," Thomas said, then to Bill he said, "Let me know the second your guys are ready."

"Just one . . . more . . . good to go," Bill said. Thomas put the cell phone back to his ear.

"Play it."

12:20 p.m.

Jonathan watched Emily Burrows clumsily answer questions from the reporters about The Monarch—a situation he found more than a little surreal—when he heard his name. He saw Lew ignoring Miss Burrows and looking up at one of the huge displays overhead. When Jonathan saw what Lew was looking at the hairs on the back of his neck prickled.

" . . . *a photographer from Tallahassee, Florida. It's not yet known what motivated this mild-mannered family man to take up a ritualistic killing spree. Again, for those just tuning in, the killer known as The Monarch has been identified by the FBI as Jonathan Hall . . .*"

A fist slammed into Jonathan's face just below his right eye. The world swam, and Jonathan was only peripherally aware that someone grabbed him and dragged him away. Even in his delirious state all he could think about was Natalie. If that broadcast wasn't nationwide now, it would be in minutes. Soon, everyone in Tallahassee would see it. He'd lose her for sure.

As more and more of his senses returned, Jonathan knew he had only one chance. Get to Natalie as soon as he could. If he could just explain things, maybe she'd understand. Either way, they could run. Whether that was any kind of life for an eleven-year-old would be something he'd anguish over later. Right now he needed to stay out of a prison cell.

"Get your shit together, Jonny," Lew said. "We've got to get you out of here."

Jonathan's vision returned as Lew led him toward the door. He looked down at Lew's hands gripping his arm and noticed they were bloody and bruised. He looked back and saw two men with earpieces lying on the ground, bloody and broken. Past them, he saw that four armed men had jumped out of the crowd and up onto the raised platform by the podium. The FBI agent called Wagner and the NYPD chief of police were on the ground, not moving. Two of the men had their guns pointed over the crowd, and were intermittently shouting and firing into the air.

Two other men had Emily Burrows and were dragging her out like they'd tried to drag him. If not for Natalie, he might try to help her, then a thought occurred to him. He got his feet under him, shook off the remaining bells in his ears, and pushed Lew off him. A few more bullets thunked into the ceiling and pieces of cement crashed around them. They raised their arms over their heads to deflect the debris, the crowd screaming and running every which way. Jonathan's was the only face up on that screen right now. They—thugs and cops alike—would only be after him right now. He had to keep it that way.

"What the hell are you doing?" Lew asked.

"Get Burrows. She's in danger."

"Who the fuck isn't? Come on," Lew said, trying to grab Jonathan's arm. Jonathan's wits and reflexes were back and he slipped out of the grab easily.

"I'm serious, Lew. Go help her. Something's fucked up here and I'll be damned if I'll let one more person get hurt in our name," he lied.

Lew hesitated for a second, then said, "Aw, fuck!" and ran over to help Emily.

Jonathan turned and pushed his way through the crowd out of the building and into the concourse. He had to get out of there and as far away from Lew as he could.

He dodged through the people in the plaza, fighting off the odd person who made the connection between the images on the big screens mounted overhead and this lunatic running by. It wasn't hard, but if the crowd got too thick he wouldn't have room to maneuver. It would be pile-on-the-serial-killer, and he knew there wouldn't be enough left of him to pour into a jar for a court date. But even if he got through them and to the street, he'd still be up shit's creek.

I need a diversion.

Just then the front windows of the federal building exploded in a mass of noise, smoke, and glass, the blast wave hitting Jonathan in the back and knocking him to the ground. His senses dulled by the concussion, he distantly heard screams of pain and panic, bodies both slamming and flopping to the ground around him like someone had opened a window high overhead and alternately pushed and thrown them out.

By the time he raised his face off the pavement again, his ears were ringing just slightly louder than the sound of all the car alarms around him going off.

He got up, shaking the dust and glass off himself. He had been far enough away from the blast seat that the crowd had blocked the worst of the projectiles from him. Then he saw the carnage. It was horrific. Half the people who had been standing in the plaza—the people he'd just run through—were all on the ground, either deathly still or writhing in moist pain. Blood was everywhere. The glass had cut them to shreds. He knew the people inside the concourse were probably worse off, but smoke still filled the enclosed area and he couldn't see anything.

"Lew!" Jonathan called, jumping up on one of the serpentine benches, trying to see inside. "Lew!" He waited, fearing the worst. After what seemed like forever, a dusty and bloody figure stumbled out over the bodies wearing a duster. *Thank God.*

"There he is!" Two men over to the side started toward Jonathan. Their appearance and unwounded state said they hadn't been here for the explosion. It still wasn't safe to be around him. Knowing Lew was alive, Jonathan turned and ran.

When he got to the street, a limo came screeching to a halt in front of him. The back door flew open and a man with a gun inside said, "Get in or you're dead."

Jonathan kicked the door closed, turned, and ran up the sidewalk.

LEW TRIED TO run but he was still too fuzzy and just ended up falling onto someone on the ground. He pushed himself up and looked into a woman's panicked eyes. Glass from the explosion had sliced into her face and neck. Blood gurgled out of her wounds as she fought for breath.

"Help . . . hel . . ." And then she was gone. The dead and dying littered the plaza. He shook his head and got back up to his feet.

When the windows exploded he'd been standing behind the company directory. The initial fireball had eaten all the oxygen in the area and sucked in more hungrily, slamming him headfirst into the structure. He reached up and touched the pain in his head and his fingers came away warm and wet. It wasn't the first time he'd cracked his skull, but it always hurt like a mother.

Through the smoke he saw Jonathan kick a car door closed and take off up the sidewalk. Then the car peeled out, jumped the curb, and drove after him. Lew was running before he realized it, cutting across the plaza, stepping around the human obstacles scattered before him. He had no idea where the Burrows woman had been during the explosion, but he didn't care anymore. Whoever had done this was after the closest thing to a brother he had.

But he only had one emotion right now, and it was pure rage.

He didn't know who all was involved in this despicable event, but he knew some of them were in that car.

He left the plaza and sprinted across the road, his lungs screaming. He hadn't run full-out in a long time. He'd let the only thing he'd ever really been able to count on atrophy over the past few years, but he still had the skills to put the pain into a corner of his mind and lock it away. His heart would have to explode before he'd stop running.

He rounded the corner and saw Jonathan turn around just as the car caught up to him. He thought it was going to run him down, but at the last moment it swerved and a door on the car opened, slamming Jonathan to the pavement like a ragdoll. Lew kept running.

Someone got out and scooped Jonathan up, carried him over to the car, and tossed him in. The man looked up and saw Lew coming like a locomotive. He pulled a gun and fired a few wild shots as he backed into the car after Jonathan. And still, Lew kept running.

The door closed and the car pulled off of the sidewalk, but had to stop as traffic cut it off. Horns blared and people shouted. The limo slammed into the car blocking its exit, then backed up so it could take off using the space it had created. Lew reached the car just as it was backing up and before it could take off, he leaped onto the roof.

The car sped away through the gap it had created with Lew on top. He gripped the sides and hung on, wishing he had any weapon besides his hard head. He'd be shaken off if the car ever got out of the lunch hour traffic, so he balled up his fist, wound up, and slammed it into the driver's door window. The window exploded into the car and Lew felt the bones in two fingers break. He put that pain away too.

Someone shouted and then two bullets fired up through the roof from inside the limo. They missed him and went through his duster. He rolled to the side as two more shots blasted through the roof where he had just been a moment ago. Then he heard a shot inside the car and the shooting stopped. Lew was even more frantic, but his busted hand was making it hard to hang on. As if they'd heard his thoughts, the limo start careening from one side of the street to the other, bouncing off the parked cars as it went.

On the third bounce, Lew lost his grip and found himself airborne. He slammed into the side of a parked truck and felt consciousness slip from him before he landed on the pavement.

JONATHAN, WEDGED DOWN on the floor of the backseat of the limo, plastic ties around his ankles and wrists, watched Lew fly off the roof of the car. Beside Jonathan lay the man who had grabbed him and tied him up—dead with a bullet through his forehead.

While he'd been shooting at Lew on the roof, Jonathan pulled his knees tight to his chest and kicked out. The shooter turned, rage in his eyes, and pointed his gun at Jonathan. A second later, without even turning his head, the driver had swung a gun around and killed his accomplice.

"That's a hell of a guard dog you've got there, mate," the driver said now. He had an Australian accent, but not a thick one, like he'd been away from home for a long time.

"You have no idea," Jonathan said.

"Just sit back, be quiet, and we'll have no problems," the driver said.

"No *more* problems, you mean," Jonathan said. The driver didn't physically react, but his silence told Jonathan he was right. This little operation might have netted him, but it hadn't played out as planned. "Relax, I know how missions can go sometimes. You can't foresee everything. I'm sure your boss will understand."

"I'm not going to tell you again, mate. Shut it." Jonathan was getting to him. He was taking a bigger risk than he normally would, but after seeing the driver kill his partner for threatening him, he'd lay odds he was wanted alive and well. Then he remembered, just before all hell had broken loose, a couple of thugs going after Emily Burrows.

"No problem," Jonathan said, and then after a beat, "Miss Burrows probably wasn't that important to him, anyways."

"You were warned," the driver said, swinging his arm back with the gun gripped in his fist.

"Wait—" Jonathan had forgotten alive and well didn't necessarily mean conscious. The gun slammed into the side of his head and a bright explosion in his mind radiated out until his brain overloaded and everything went dark.

30

New York Downtown Hospital
New York City
9:00 P.M. Local Time

ALMOST NINE HOURS after the massacre, Emily waited until Wagner's family left, crying and supporting each other as they shuffled down the hospital corridor, before she tentatively made her way into his room. The scratches on her face beneath the few small bandages still stung, but they weren't the reason tears filled her eyes. She blamed herself. For all of it.

The banks of machinery beside the bed were dark and silent, making her breathing sound even louder. She walked around the far side of the bed so she could watch the door, paranoia still strong in her after today. Part of his hand was visible outside the sheet. She delicately uncovered it and took it in both of her shaking hands. He was still warm. The touch, the human contact, was the final brick. Her sobs took her, tears rolling down her face as she silently fought for breath.

"I-I-I . . ." She tried to say she was sorry, but speech failed her. She crumpled to her knees in slow motion and pressed her forehead to his hand. She had known very few good men in her life. Truly goodhearted souls interested only in right and wrong, not how the decisions would paint them. She knew in her heart that Wagner was one of those. His entire team had seemed like protectors rather than law enforcers. And now they were gone.

As the sobs eased she sniffled and took a tissue from the bedside table and wiped her face. She got up and pulled a chair over, sitting beside him. She didn't know why she was here or what she hoped to accomplish with her vigil. She knew his family could come back, which would make for some very awkward explanations. She also knew that someone would soon come to move him down to the hospital's morgue, though it was no doubt filled to capacity today, and they might just leave him where he was.

There were no final tallies yet, but the last news report she saw put the dead at forty-nine, with dozens injured, their fates unknown. Strangely, there had been no further mention of The Monarch's true identity.

The blast had not only blown out the windows, but destroyed much of the concrete around the windows, causing part of the building front to collapse. An on-site FEMA engineer had assured the public the damage was superficial and the building wasn't in any danger of falling. Even so, they had evacuated the area. Since she'd been knocked unconscious almost instantly by the blast, all of this was secondhand knowledge for Emily. The last thing she remembered was pulling away from the man who had attacked Wagner. She'd spun and ran right into Wagner's arms as he got up. Then there had been a loud *whump* before Wagner pushed her down and threw himself on top of her. The next thing she knew, she'd woken up in the ER, surrounded by chaos and screaming.

"I just want you to know, I'm going to do what I can to make this right," Emily said to Wagner's body. "I don't know if it will do any good, but I'm going to tell the story—the real story—to anyone who will listen. And if it's the last thing I do, I'm going to find Nathan. Find him and make him pay."

"Do you mean that?" a voice said from the door. Emily sat up with a start, and looked at the stranger. He was big, dressed in some kind of long canvas coat that made him look like a cowboy. His left hand had two finger splints on it under white hospital tape, and bandages were wound around his head. She assumed he'd been hurt in the blast.

"I . . . I'm sorry. Did you know Agent Wagner?" Emily said, standing up and working her way toward the door with the intent of leaving.

"Only from the newscasts," the man said. Emily nodded, then shook her head.

"Then why—"

"I'm here to see you, Miss Burrows."

"See me? Why?" Her paranoia ramped up.

"My name's Lew. Lew Katchbrow," he said, holding out his hand. By reflex, Emily shook it. It was strong, but gentle. "The Monarch sent me."

She felt her knees buckle slightly, but Lew's damaged hand slipped around her back and held her up.

"He sent you? For me?" This had to be a mistake. Or a trick.

"We have a lot to talk about, but I don't think this is the best place. Have you eaten?" She literally couldn't remember the last time she'd eaten.

"How do I know—"

Lew cut her off, apparently anticipating her question. "He said to tell you that leaving *The Just Judges* out of your book was a good idea. Especially since the Belgians sold it to someone two days after he gave it back to them."

"My God," she said, taking a quick breath. "You *do* know The Monarch."

"You have no idea, lady. But we really need to go," Lew said.

She let herself be led away from Wagner's room by Lew, but hesitated in the hallway. She looked back at the nurses' station at the end of the hall, and her common sense said to run toward it.

"You can trust me," Lew said, apparently sensing her worry. "Any public place you want to go is fine. Lots of people and no tricks. Promise."

After a long moment she said, "Lead the way." She stayed five steps behind him all the way so she could make a run for it if he tried anything, but something about his eyes and the way he talked about The Monarch made her want to trust him. Still, her common sense hadn't exactly been brilliant lately.

31

Tartaruga Island
4:15 A.M. Local Time

"Welcome back," Lara said when Nathan opened his eyes. He looked around and saw he was in his bedroom. The last thing he remembered was trying to get out of the hangar before anyone saw him collapse.

"What—how long?" he rasped, surprised for a moment that he could talk at all without the healing power of the serum running through his veins. But of course he wasn't just missing the serum, but the neuro-blocker as well.

"About nine hours. You collapsed in the hall. Randy and I found you and brought you here," Lara said, pouring him some water from the carafe by his bed. "I described your condition to Sophia. With a little convincing she said it sounded like you might have had a transient ischemic attack—a mini-stroke." Lara held the glass to his lips. Nathan drank hungrily despite the heavy feeling that something was caught in his throat. He'd grown used to that symptom years ago.

"She also admitted giving you a half-strength serum dose. Not only didn't it last long, it didn't fully deactivate the neuro-blocker in your system. She said it was like running a car with your foot on the floor and the emergency brake still set. If it matters, she seemed upset at the result of her subterfuge."

"*Described* my condition? She didn't examine me?" was all Nathan said.

"I've had her restricted to her lab. I didn't know what you wanted to do but assumed you didn't want her sneaking off to the chopper while you were . . . recovering."

Nathan didn't like the idea of Sophia being a prisoner and he didn't want to know how Lara had *convinced* her. Of the two of his girls, he'd always thought Lara was the one most like him, but now he was thinking Sophia was showing hidden promise. For now he let it go.

"Give me an update. What did I miss?" Nathan said, awkwardly pushing himself up in the bed. He was having trouble holding still. Lara filled him in on Jonathan Hall's past profession and the attempted cyber attack they had thwarted.

"We've located current information on his residence and occupation from the DMV. We'll be in position within the hour."

"I got him?" Nathan asked, both excited and a little melancholy the chase was over.

"You got him. A ninety-eight percent match. Definitely The Monarch," Lara said. Nathan took a cleansing, relieving breath. His calm lasted about two seconds before he noticed the look in Lara's eyes.

"Hall and Burrows en route, yes?" Nathan said. His suspicions were confirmed when instead of answering, Lara got him some more water. He clumsily turned his head away from the glass. "What's wrong?"

Lara explained about the explosive miscalculation and losing their own men.

"The news reports have the dead set at forty-nine," Lara said. "I'm afraid Miss Burrows was—" A tweedle from her cell phone stopped Lara in mid-sentence while she read a text message. For a moment, he thought she was going to pitch the device across the room.

"What is it?"

"Uh, nothing," she said, putting the phone away. "As I was saying, Miss Burrows wasn't acquired. She got away."

Nathan's chest heaved. At first he thought he was having a coughing fit, but then he realized he was laughing. Hard. A side effect of the disease. If he didn't get a neuro-blocker shot, he'd be laughing inappropriately all the time, now. Tears ran down his face. Lara knew about the condition, but even so she looked uncomfortable in the face of it. When he found it hard to breathe, the laughter finally subsided.

"Where's Thomas?" Nathan said between pants.

"He's still in New York awaiting further instructions."

"Tell him to get Burrows back here ASAP. At all costs. Do you understand? She's integral to this. Without her—"

"I understand, Father. Consider it done." He could tell by the look on her face that she didn't understand at all. She didn't need to.

He sent Lara away to *convince* Sophia to give him the neuro-blocker. A little later, while trying to get himself some water,

Nathan caught his reflection in the cabinet of rare books against one wall. He watched himself shake and twitch.

If this didn't work, he'd take a final dose of the serum, light a final cigar, and hobble into the natural gas holding tanks beneath the complex. One throw of a switch and it would all be over.

Mercifully over.

32

New York City
9:30 P.M. Local Time

LEW DIDN'T KNOW if Emily could help him find Jonathan or not, but right now she was the only lead he had. At least she'd stopped looking like a scared rabbit that was going to bolt at the tiniest noise.

"You've hardly touched your food," Lew said, seeing her plate when he finally eased back from the pile of dirty dishes on his side of the table.

"I just don't have much appetite after today," Emily said, picking at her spaghetti.

"You need to eat," Lew said. "Especially after today. Nothing drains a body more than shock." He watched her poke at her food some more, but the fork never made it up to her mouth.

"You still haven't told me why we needed to get out of the hospital," Emily said. Lew had shined her on about the question earlier, more intent on getting food into his grumbling belly.

"Let's just say that whoever took Jonny might be interested in me."

"You were with him, then. How well do you know him? Why was he here in New York? And how does he know me?" Emily said in rapid-fire succession.

"Easy, Geraldo. I'm going to be honest with you. I'm still not sure I can trust you."

"Trust *me*?"

"Jonny said to protect you when he saw the shit going down. I don't know why, but he usually has pretty good reasons for doing the things he does. So I figure maybe we can help each other."

"Oh," she said sounding disappointed.

"Who's Nathan?" Lew asked abruptly, hoping to catch her off guard.

"How do you know that name?"

"Back in the hospital room you said if it was the last thing you did you'd find Nathan. And make him pay. Pay for what?"

Emily sighed, drained her wineglass, and then told Lew everything about Nathan's bribe, his request, and even the abduction and her meeting on the beach. Lew listened quietly, letting her finish, each stage of the story fascinating him more than the last. When she was done, he refilled both their wineglasses.

"You think it was Nathan that grabbed Jonny?" Lew asked.

"It would seem likely. More than likely, actually. But you have to believe me that I had no idea what his endgame was."

"From what you've told me, I don't think we've even glimpsed his endgame yet. Can you contact him? Do you know where he is?"

"No. . . . wait. Yes, I do know where he is," Emily said. She explained about the book and the cell phone she'd given to the FBI.

"They still have the phone, but if we could get it, we could locate Nathan. I'm sure of it."

"They have it? The FBI? In the building that was just blown apart? Yeah, we're not getting in there anytime soon."

"We may not have to," Emily said, a faraway look in her eye.

RAIDEN PIONEER PEEKED through the glass a few minutes after Emily knocked. She was relieved he was there so late. At first he smiled, before he noticed the big man standing behind her. Emily nodded. Raiden eyed Lew again, but unlocked the door.

Emily sat with Raiden at the counter by the old-fashioned cash register while Lew wandered around the small shop, poking at the computer guts hanging everywhere. As Emily spoke to him, Raiden never took his eyes off Lew.

"A new phone's not going to help you," Raiden said.

"It can't pick up the signal?" Emily asked.

"It'll pick it up, but what you want is the log of the previously texted locations. That's on that particular phone's SIM card. A new phone won't have that."

"Bollocks, you're right," Emily said. "Wait, what about Bluetooth?"

"Hmm, yes. That might work. You'd have to get within about twenty feet of the original phone, but if you could get a connection, it would only take a few seconds to grab the data."

Emily wasn't sure how she could get that close to the original phone, but at least it was possible. When Raiden told them the price, Emily looked at Lew, who was trying to push some wires back into an old motherboard he'd apparently unplugged.

"What? It was like this," Lew said.

"No, money. The FBI took all the cash Nathan gave me. Can you pay Raiden?"

"Oh. Yeah, sure."

"So that's all you need?" Raiden asked.

"Guns," Lew said, approaching the counter.

"Excuse me?" Raiden said.

"He just does electronics, Lew," Emily said.

"Look, this is a nice shop and all, but this computer crap is all show. It's staged. Most of it has a couple months' worth of dust on it. Meaning it's garbage. Your pal here is a businessman. And I'm willing to pay a fair price. But without an automatic and a box of shells, no deal. Bank's closed."

"Lew, please," Emily said emphatically, embarrassed by her new partner's behavior. "Raiden is a friend, and he's willing to help us. But—"

"Glock okay?" Raiden said to Lew.

"I guess," Lew said, not seeming surprised that he'd been right. "I'd prefer a SIG P226 with a .357 clip, if you've got one.

"Nice weapon, but lower capacity than the 9mm," Raiden said. Emily felt as if she weren't even in the room anymore.

"You give me .357 slugs and I won't need as many shots," Lew said.

"True. Let me see what I've got," Raiden said, going into the back of the store.

"You'll catch flies," Lew said as he pulled a wad of cash out of one of his coat's pockets.

Emily realized her mouth was hanging open and closed it. It had never occurred to her that Raiden did more than electronics. But the really shocking thing was after only a few minutes of wandering around the shop, Lew had known more about Raiden than she did.

"What exactly did you do for Jonathan?" Emily asked. She was starting to get used to the idea that The Monarch had a name, but she just couldn't bring herself to call him Jonny. In fact, she wished Lew wouldn't either.

"*For* him? Well, if you listen to him, most days I just messed with his blood pressure," Lew said with a smile and a wink. Emily didn't know how he could be so . . . so amiable after what had happened this morning. She was having trouble not hyperventilating whenever she thought about it.

Raiden brought out a selection of guns, and Lew examined each, selecting two of them. He also purchased a couple of boxes of ammunition, extra clips, and a couple of underarm holsters. He offered to buy Emily a gun, but just the idea of having a weapon made her light-headed. After the arms deal, they waited another half hour for Raiden to prepare their Bluetooth-hacked phone.

They left Raiden's shop and Lew tried to flag down a cab. Under his coat, she couldn't even see the new weapons. It made her wonder how many unseen things she passed every day without realizing it.

"Where are we going, now?" Emily asked as a cab slowed and pulled to the curb. Lew opened the door and stepped back.

"You're going home. I'm going to try and get close to that phone of yours," Lew said.

"What? But I thought we were—"

"A team? Sister, let's just say I don't play well with others. You've done enough. No offense, but aside from that phone of yours, you'll just get in the way. And I think it's pretty obvious things are far from safe. Just go home. Work on a new book or something. Have a nice life," Lew said. He turned around, his coat flapping dramatically in the morning breeze, and headed up the street.

Emily was furious. She felt like a tag-along little sister being sent home. But worse, whatever fate had befallen Jonathan was her fault. There was no way she could just go home and let that lie. Not after the promise she'd made to Wagner. And she knew there was only one thing Lew would understand. She marched after him, spun him around, and slapped his face even harder than she'd meant to, the frustration of the past few days all summing up in her swing. She saw red images of her fingers appear on Lew's cheek.

"Jesus, lady! I knew you were trouble," Lew said rubbing his cheek.

"Look! You wouldn't have an inkling of where to go if it wasn't for me. I'm as deep in this as anyone, if not deeper, so don't you dare try to dismiss me. What if by some bloody miracle you do get the location? Do you have any idea what Nathan looks like? You stick your head up down there asking stupid questions, and if you're right about them wanting you as much as Jonathan, you'll get it shot off. Nathan will talk to me. Hell, he's practically in love with me! So you just get your arse in that cab and stop this cowboy bollocks!" She yelled so loud and with such vitriol she almost lost her balance. Lew reached out and caught her by the arms.

"Okay, okay. Relax," Lew said. He walked back to the cab with a slight hunch to his shoulders, like a scolded schoolboy. They got in and Emily slammed the door behind her before she crossed her arms, still fuming.

"Where to?" The driver asked. Silence drew out in the cab. Emily realized she had no idea what they were supposed to do next.

"If I give him directions are you going to hit me again?" Lew asked. *Why is he so damn likable?* Emily did her best to stifle a smile. Apparently Lew took that as a no. "Hemingway Hotel."

"Why there?" Emily asked as the cab pulled away from the curb.

"Clean up," Lew said, rubbing his cheek.

PART FIVE

Tuesday

33

Unknown

JONATHAN SNAPPED HIS head up and fought the inky tendrils trying to drag him back down into the darkness. His cheek ached where the Australian had pistol-whipped him. He tried to reach up to feel his wound but handcuffs running through the metal arms of his chair prevented him from moving his hands more than a few inches. He gripped the arms and pulled as hard as he could, but they wouldn't budge. The chair didn't rock either, apparently bolted to the concrete floor under his feet.

He bent his head down so he could touch his wound. It had crusted over and was already healing. He'd been out for at least a day, something that no pistol-whipping could accomplish. He'd been drugged.

The fuzz rapidly lifting from his senses, he looked around the dimly lighted cavern he was in. It was huge, empty and lit only by emergency lighting. The air was hot and smelled moist and salty.

Streamers of wiring hung from the ceiling, both power lines and blue CAT-5 computer network cabling. Whatever had been here had sucked a lot of power and had been computerized.

"Good afternoon, Mr. Hall," a man's voice boomed out above him from speakers. He involuntarily looked up, but the ceiling was so high and it was so dim he couldn't see anything. "May I call you Jonathan?"

"No, you may not," Jonathan said. He winced as the act of speaking made his head pound even more. "What you may do is get me out of this fucking chair."

"John, John the leprechaun. One shoe off and one shoe on," the voice said. Jonathan frowned at the nonsense.

"Was that supposed to be a joke?"

Muffled voices argued over the loudspeaker. A man and a woman. A disconcerting giggle. More muffled voices, then the female voice said: "Just give him the shot!"

After that, minutes passed with no sound at all except Jonathan's own heartbeat, which felt like it was in his eye sockets.

"Apologies, Mr. Hall," the male voice said a few minutes later. "I'm sure you have a lot of questions."

Jonathan remained silent and still. He'd tried bending this way and that, leveraging here and pulling there, but he was too well secured. Physically, he was at their mercy. Mentally, he might have the edge.

"First, allow me to introduce myself," the voice said. A light snapped on in a large window high overhead. The light streamed down, spotlighting Jonathan. He squinted and turned his head away slightly. "My name is Nathan Kring, this is my island, and I'm the one responsible for finding you—for finding The Monarch."

As Jonathan's eyes adjusted to the brightness, figures took

shape in the window. A seated man dressed in black looked down at him. Behind the seated man was a tall, slender woman with striking bone-white hair.

Island. That explained the sea air, but it still didn't tell him where he was or why he was here. Jonathan remained silent, getting the definite sense that Nathan was waiting for a reaction. After a minute or two of waiting, Nathan continued.

"Yes, well, I would have preferred this meeting to be more cordial, but your hidden identity made that impossible. Nevertheless, on to business. I have a job for you, Mr. Hall. A job you are uniquely experienced to perform. I want you to steal something for me from the Canton George estate. An easy task since The Monarch already robbed Mr. George. Once you've done that, you'll be free to go and handsomely rewarded, of course."

Canton George? Jonathan suddenly wished he'd pushed Lew harder back in the hotel room, not that it would have helped. Lew was a bulldog in a lot of ways, but if Jonathan was here because of that failed job, he had even more problems than he'd thought he had a moment ago.

"You really need to say something. Acting like a petulant child is not the response I expected from The Monarch." Jonathan could hear the disappointment in Nathan's voice.

Did he really think I'd congratulate him for finding me?

"That's probably because I'm not The Monarch. I have no idea who you're talking about or why you think—"

"Please. You were taken from the press conference about The Monarch. And let's just say I've gone to great expense to verify you are, indeed, who I think you are. Great expense. And I've done things no one else had the . . . wherewithal to do. I know you're The Monarch, just as I know you'll help me."

Cocky bastard.

"Hey, I just saw a crowd and wandered in to see what was going on."

"Fine," the voice said, obviously perturbed. "You leave me no choice."

Jonathan didn't care what he did, there was nothing that would make him—

Ooga chaka . . . ooga chaka . . . ooga chaka. . .

Jonathan felt a chill race down his arms and legs as his breathing deepened.

No, it can't be.

"You should really answer that. It might be important," Nathan said, derision dripping from his voice.

Jonathan leaned down so his handcuffed hand could reach his pocket. The name on the call display sent a chill through him. He pressed send.

"Is there anything a father wouldn't do to protect his child?"

It was a woman's voice. Jonathan looked up and saw the woman behind Nathan holding a phone to her ear. Then a light in another window snapped on. Natalie stood there alone; a blindfold covered her eyes and headphones were over her ears.

Jonathan lost it. No training in the world could have prepared him to handle the shock his system took seeing his little girl blindfolded in this place. He pulled at the handcuffs, slammed his back against the chair, and flailed his legs out like an animal caught in a trap.

"You son of a bitch! I'll kill you. I'll kill every motherfucking one of you!" Jonathan continued to struggle for a few minutes before his adrenaline eased, allowing him to stop thrashing. With exhaustion came defeat. The rage left him, replaced by the rawest, purest angst he'd ever felt in his life.

"Please settle down, Mr. Hall. You're going to hurt yourself if you keep this up. And then I'll have no reason at all to keep young Natalie alive."

Despair overtook his angst, tears blurring his vision.

"She . . . she's just a kid. Leave her alone. She's got nothing to do with this."

"Oh, but she's got everything to do with this. She is going to be my honored guest while you complete your task. She's my little insurance policy to make sure you don't run off to some corner of the world and disappear. Now, do we have a deal? Will you take the job?"

All Jonathan could think about was what Natalie must be going through. There was little else he could say.

"What do you want me to do?"

34

Hemingway Hotel
New York City
12:45 A.M. Local Time

"CHECK UNDER THE beds," Lew said. He'd gone through the bedroom already, but hotel rooms had a habit of eating socks and paperback novels. He didn't want any evidence remaining that they'd ever been there.

He'd packed both his and Jonathan's belongings; his in a khaki duffel bag; Jonathan's in a large messenger-style, black leather shoulder bag. A shopping bag full of their disposable items—bottles, cups, wrappers, and newspapers—sat by the door. He'd dump it on their way out.

Lew cinched his duffel bag closed by the room's sofa, noticing a strange hesitation in Emily's movements. She was an odd woman; filled with potential and the instincts of a private detective—

which was obvious from the details she'd dug up for her book—but something had happened, either to her or in her. Everything she did was tentative and unsure. Lew found it an attractive thing to watch, but he imagined it must have been hell to live that way.

As he watched her, he realized that without meaning to, his eyes were wandering up and down her body. He caught himself and shook his head to clear his thoughts. There was no time for that.

Besides, she's smart. She'd never go for someone like—

Lew stopped his wondering when he saw her do something strange. She picked up one of the pillows and pressed it to her face, like she was smelling it. Lew turned away before she caught him looking, but he couldn't help wondering whose scent she was trying to capture.

"Everything okay in there?" Lew said, keeping his gaze away from the room, busying himself with tidying things by the front door. He picked up the last bottle of Canadian Club and saw it still had a finger's worth of amber fluid in its base. He spun the cap off and slugged it back, the burn as it rode down making him feel better. Without Jonny around, he thought way too much.

"Is that wise?" Emily said, coming back into the room. She had a T-shirt in her hands. "Found this under one of the pillows."

"Too late to matter," Lew said, holding up the empty bottle before he dropped it in the bag with the others. He took Jonathan's shirt and tossed it in his bag. "I think we're good to go."

They grabbed everything and left the room. Lew dumped their garbage and noticed a newspaper in the receptacle. He took it out and flipped through it.

"Weird," Lew said.

"What is?" Emily asked as they waited for the elevator.

"There's nothing in here about Jonny."

"Maybe it's old."

"Nope, it's got a bunch of stuff about the explosion and The Monarch, but no mention of Jonny being identified as him."

"What's it mean?" Emily asked.

"I'm not sure. But if I went to all that trouble to identify someone so I could kidnap them, it would sure help if no one else was suddenly looking for him."

Emily looked at him in that weird way again, like when someone spent hours looking at one of those magic posters and finally saw the sailboat raise itself up off the page. He didn't like it. It made his throat dry.

The elevator bell rang and the door opened. They entered the car and both reached for the ground button at the same time. A half turn each and their faces were only a few inches apart. He could smell her scent; not perfume or cologne, but just a coppery, unique smell that was all hers. She held his gaze a few moments too long, her lips parting just slightly.

"Sorry," he finally said, clearing his throat and stepping back to give her room to press the button. She pressed it and the door slid shut. They rode down in silence, each staring at the floor, the air in the car seeming thicker than it had on the way up.

They were headed back to the scene of the crime—Federal Plaza.

While Lew had policed the hotel room, Emily had called Donald Hinton, a junior FBI agent she'd met while preparing for the press conference and one of the few agency people she knew was still alive. She found out he was going to be bringing evidence on the case from Federal Plaza to the temporary FBI HQ in Lower Manhattan. Including the tracking phone. As much as Lew hated the idea of going back there, if they could get close enough with their Bluetooth hack device, Hinton wouldn't even know what had happened.

It was a long shot, but it was all they had. If it didn't work, Lew knew he'd never see Jonathan again.

35

Tartaruga Island
8:00 A.M. Local Time

"I WANT TO see my daughter," Jonathan said, holding fast. The guards walking behind him stopped and raised their weapons. Nathan swung his wheelchair around. Jonathan made a conscious effort to not appear threatening—he just wasn't moving until he talked to Natalie. Maybe that wasn't even she. She'd been so far away and blindfolded, it could have been any little girl. Yet his rationalizations didn't hold much water when he considered the phone call.

"In due time. Please, let's continue. It's so infrequent lately that I have guests I can show around," Nathan said. Jonathan evaluated his "host." It was disconcerting to talk to someone when his lips didn't move. And with the way his head lolled to the side, it wasn't even possible to look him in the eye most of the time.

"Move," Lara said.

"Did you kill the Swensons?" Jonathan asked.

"Who?" Nathan said.

"The family that was looking after his daughter," Lara said.

"Ah," Nathan said. "I'm afraid you'll have to ask Lara that."

Jonathan looked at Lara, who was apparently the old man's daughter, and waited.

The smart play would be to shut up and keep walking. He was being given an opportunity to reconnoiter the enemy's lair, by the enemy himself, no less. But when it came to Natalie, he was rarely logical. Like the outburst when they'd shown her to him, it was raw emotion; no filter and no thought. If he'd been unbound and close enough, he actually would have killed them. With his bare hands, if necessary. Death was no stranger to him, but Jonathan had never killed or harmed anyone in anger in his life. But right now if he knew where Natalie was he'd dump this old, used-up pile of flesh onto the floor and beat him to a pulp with his own wheelchair.

"Lara?" Nathan prompted. She continued her staring contest with Jonathan for a while longer.

"They're fine," she said. "A little . . . bruised, but fine." She grinned beneath her hooded gaze.

Well, that's something, Jonathan thought. He was carrying enough guilt right now. Assuming she was telling the truth.

"Now for the last time, *move*," Lara said, squaring off.

When Jonathan didn't comply, Lara nodded her head. One of the guards snapped out a telescoping club and swung it into the backs of his legs. Jonathan kept the scream in, but his muscles betrayed him and he fell to his knees.

"Lara!" the old man said in what passed for a shout from the electronic voice mounted to his wheelchair. He swung around to face the guards. "Leave us."

At first they didn't move. Jonathan looked up and though the old man missed it, the guards only obeyed the command when Lara nodded again.

"My apologies. My daughter can be . . . impulsive. Lara, help the poor man up," Nathan said. Lara grudgingly took Jonathan by the arm and helped him stand. Jonathan took note of her stance as she did. She appeared to be helping him, but she positioned herself so she could knock him back down with a single blow.

"Thanks," Jonathan said, looking into her green eyes. He made sure nothing that was going on inside his head was evident on his face. She sneered anyway, releasing him and returning to her father's side.

"I promise you, your daughter is safe and close by. You'll see her shortly. And later, I have something very special to show you. Something you will uniquely appreciate," Nathan said.

They continued the tour, Jonathan limping slightly from the welt he could feel rising on the back of his leg. Lara positioned herself so she was always within striking distance of Jonathan.

"As I was saying," Nathan said. "My father bought the island from the Australian military after the war. The base was used for intelligence gathering by Z Force, a joint—"

"—Australian, British, and New Zealand commando unit," Jonathan said.

"Yes, I see you know your military history. In any case, once Z Force moved out, there was little left besides this complex, a few remote stations around the island stripped of equipment, and one of the few island runways in the region capable of supporting jet traffic. That and about a million turtles. I wasn't sure why he bought it, but I know he thrust himself immediately into controversy by stripping the island of the turtles. The act was being brought to the world's attention and things looked bad until the U.S. military did the same on Diego Garcia off the coast of India. But in U.S. fashion, they upped the ante and instead of depopulating turtles, they stripped the island of all indigenous humans."

"How fortunate for your father," Jonathan said.

"He was lucky like that. In life and in business. They say he had the Midas touch, turning any enterprise he attempted into a gold-producing venture against all odds. Over and over again. After he died, I used the island mostly as a sanctuary. Somewhere to come and recharge when corporate life got to be a little too much."

They rounded a bend in the wide corridor and came upon an elevator. Inside, Jonathan saw the complex had four floors in all, but the numbers on the control panel were inverted, with 1 at the top. Right now, they were on the second floor.

We're underground.

· Once they were all inside, the button for the fourth floor lit up all on its own. The doors shut and they descended. When the doors opened, Jonathan saw that most floors, at least the ones he had seen, had an almost identical layout. Simple, utilitarian efficiency common in the military. But the floors were huge, with crisscrossing corridors. If he could get free, finding Natalie would be no small feat—never mind getting out of there once he did.

"We're not going to the third floor?" Jonathan asked. The omission of the area made him curious. Lara gave a side glance to her father but remained silent.

"It's just the living areas. Nothing of much interest," Nathan said. They moved around the corner and headed down the now familiar long corridor at a slow pace. "When I became ill, I moved my corporate headquarters here. It was supposed to be temporary, but once I'm well I think I may keep it here."

"Once you're well?" Jonathan said. He couldn't believe that someone who looked like Nathan did would ever be well again. He looked like he needed to be in hospice so he could prepare to die. "If you don't mind my asking, what exactly do you—"

"Ah, we're here," Nathan said as they turned the far corner in the corridor. They had arrived at a door with an access panel. Unlike the other hallways and rooms, this door didn't open automatically as they approached. A guard stood vigil outside the door, straightening up when he saw them approaching.

"Lara, if you'd be so kind," Nathan said. Lara took out a pass card and after two tries, unlocked the door. They went in and Jonathan saw it was a laboratory of some kind. The layout and equipment didn't interest Jonathan as much as the stunning woman in the lab coat with the black ponytail, at the far end of the lab.

Nathan brought his wheelchair to a stop and said, "Mr. Hall, I'd like you to meet my other daughter, Sophia. She's the scholar of the family." Jonathan noticed that Lara sneered as much at her sister as she did at him.

Sophia came over. She had the saddest brown eyes he'd ever seen. But not just sad, they seemed almost—broken. *Maybe that explains the guard outside the door.* She gave Jonathan a half smile.

"No problems with the neuro-blocker?" Sophia asked, not really seeming to care one way or the other.

"It's working fine, as usual. I was hoping you could keep Mr. Hall company for a little while. I need to speak to Lara on another matter," Nathan said. Jonathan noticed Lara's eyes widen slightly. Sophia reached up and pushed an escaping strand of hair behind her ear. It immediately fell down again. He didn't know about Nathan's plans to use him to rob Canton George, but right now he was pretty sure Nathan was using him as a lever between the two sisters.

"Father, do you think that's wise?" Lara said.

Sophia said, "I don't know. I'm busy with some animal trials and—"

"Nonsense. It will only be for a few minutes. Think of it as a break," Nathan said, turning around and wheeling his way back to the door. "Lara?"

Lara's face went from a sneer to a pucker as she exchanged glances first with Sophia and then with Jonathan. He didn't know what Sophia's said, but he understood the look she gave him perfectly. Lara puffed air from her nostrils and reluctantly joined her father, opening the door and following him as he whirred away. As the door closed, Jonathan saw there were now two guards standing fast outside the lab.

He wasn't going anywhere.

9:00 A.M.

WHAT ARE YOU doing?

Sophia brushed through her hair and pulled it back into a strand-free ponytail, snapping the hair band tight to keep it that way. Her freshly rinsed face now had a light powder coating it hadn't had when she'd first come in. She'd rolled fresh deodorant under her arms, but refrained from squirting the little perfume she had left on her neck. She put her lab coat back on, smoothing out any wrinkles with her hands and plucking off the odd animal hair she'd missed with the lint roller. She looked at herself in the mirror of her lab's bathroom and then made a face at the perturbed reflection.

She'd left him out in the lab, saying she'd be back in a minute. Her father—she desperately wanted to think of him as only Nathan, but after all these years it was hard—probably would be upset that she'd left him alone.

But why did he leave him here with me in the first place? Especially after last night.

Sophia opened the door but stopped short when she saw Jonathan standing in her office by her desk. She eyed her unmade cot against the wall and her pile of clothes on the floor. He turned and smiled disarmingly when she entered.

"Sorry. Didn't mean to startle you. Would it be all right if I . . ." He motioned toward the bathroom.

"Of course. Go ahead," Sophia said. The second he closed the door, she scooped up her laundry and tossed it under the cot. She pulled the blanket up and saw there was a salsa stain on it from the burrito she'd had last night. She put her pillow on top of the stain and shook her head. Of all nights to be a slob.

The door opened and she stood up so fast her glasses fell off. She bent to get them, but Jonathan beat her to them. He smiled and handed them to her.

"Should we go back out?" Jonathan asked.

"Yes. Sure," Sophia said. Jonathan motioned for her to go first. She thanked him and left her office with Jonathan close behind.

"How do you know my father, Mr. Hall?" Sophia asked when they were back in the lab. He seemed more interested in her animal cages than in her. He answered without turning around.

"I don't. And call me Jonathan."

"You—"

"So what is all this about?" Jonathan asked, waving at the cages and the maze table.

"It's for my research."

"This whole lab is just for you?"

"I used to have a staff. In fact, most of the initial work was done at Kring Laboratories, a research facility in Nigeria, but things . . . changed."

"I'm assuming the change has something to do with the guard outside your door. He's not keeping people out, is he." It wasn't a question.

Who is this guy?

"If you don't know my father, then how—"

"You show me yours and I'll show you mine."

"Excuse me?" Sophia said, feeling her face redden.

"Give me the Cliff Notes version of your research and I'll tell you anything you want to know. Deal?" he asked, putting out his hand.

Sophia shook it and agreed, noticing how soft his hand was. She doubted revealing the research to a stranger was what her father had in mind when he asked her to stay with Jonathan. Which was exactly why she agreed so quickly.

"Do you know what a prion is?" she asked, wiping off a white-board and grabbing a marker.

"Something to do with the brain, isn't it?"

"Yes, that's right. Basically," she said, drawing something that resembled a string on the board, "there are harmless proteins in all of us—you, me, animals, plants—everything. For these pro-teins to assume a functional shape—be able to do anything—they have to fold, sort of like this."

Sophia drew a kind of coiled ribbon beside the string, trying her best to simplify the process for Jonathan. He nodded, so she assumed she was doing all right.

"For some reason—nobody really knows why—sometimes one of these benign proteins will fold abnormally," she said, continuing to draw. "But the really interesting part—and the real danger—is not that a protein can fold, but what an abnormally folded protein does after it folds. They're capable of coopting any other proteins they come in contact with, making it a copy of itself."

"Like a zombie," Jonathan said as Sophia finished drawing something that looked like an untied shoelace.

"Exactly, but a microscopic zombie that will never get a movie deal. It travels through the body, changing perfectly healthy proteins into copies of itself. When these misfolded prions get into the nervous system and the brain, you get prion diseases like Creutzfeldt-Jakob disease, fatal insomnia, and even some types of Alzheimer's."

"You can die from insomnia?"

"Um, yes, but it's not the kind of insomnia you're probably thinking of. Only twenty-eight families in the world have been identified with the gene responsible for—but I'm getting off topic," she said, batting the air like she was erasing what she just said.

"Sorry. Prions. You were saying," Jonathan said.

"Yes, someone with a prion disease experiences impaired brain function causing memory changes, personality changes, dementia, and problems with movement. All of these get worse over time," she said, putting down the marker and walking over to where the cages lined the wall.

"Is that what your father has?" Jonathan asked.

"Yes, he has kuru, a type of prion disease that used to be quite prevalent in New Guinea back in the 1970s."

"The seventies? How long has he known he had it?" Jonathan asked.

"He was diagnosed shortly after returning from New Guinea around 1973. Even though they could detect it in his blood, kuru has a long incubation period before symptoms start to show up. Decades," she said. She left out the part about that being the same year she was born—partly because with her recent revelations, she wasn't all that sure about the veracity of what she'd always assumed were facts about her early childhood. And partly because she wasn't that crazy about admitting to Jonathan that she was over forty.

"Wait a minute. Kuru. Kuru. Why do I know that name?" Jonathan asked, but he didn't appear to be asking her. Then it seemed to come to him. "Kuru. I think I played a video game that had kuru in the backstory a year or two ago. In fact, I think it was set near Papua New Guinea. But they must have embellished. It was a zombie game. The characters only turned when they—"

Jonathan stopped mid-sentence. Sophia was pretty sure it was because of the look on her face. Even with her connection to Nathan being fictional, she was mortified at the idea of the truth coming out. But she knew the best thing she could do was face it head-on.

"Kuru was at epidemic levels in the 1970s because of the indigenous tribes' practice of ritualistic cannibalism. I'm not familiar with the video game, and I'm sure they did hyperbolize for effect, but it was based on fact. Kuru is very real. And so is the fact that to contract it, Nathan had to have consumed human tissue, including brain."

Jonathan was apparently trying to control his reaction, but when his eyes slightly widened she knew she had to keep going or the emotional turmoil of the last few days would push her over the edge.

"Once symptoms start to show, they typically increase with intensity over several months until they finally result in death. When his symptoms first showed he was told he had six to eighteen months to live," Sophia said. She turned away from Jonathan, took a moment to steady herself, and then opened one of the cages.

"When was that?" Jonathan asked with an even tone. Sophia couldn't be sure, of course, but she liked the idea that he was ignoring the elephant in the room for her sake.

She turned around holding out two tiny white mice, their pink noses furiously sniffing the air. "Five years ago."

"Five *years*?"

Sophia put the mice down on a table rimmed with six-inch Plexiglas. Jonathan came over beside her and they looked down at her creatures. One was inquisitive and almost hyperactive, zipping here and there in the enclosure. The other lay on its side, pawing at the air and rolling its head back in semicircles, its mouth opening and closing.

"My father had an advantage over others afflicted with a prion disease. He knew it was coming long before the symptoms showed up. It gave him time to prepare."

"Prepare?"

"Yes. His subvocally controlled chair, for instance. He had it developed especially for him."

"Vocal? I can't even see his lips move," Jonathan said.

"Not vocal, *subvocal*. Like when you read to yourself. The brain still sends electrical impulses to the vocal cords even if you don't speak out loud. The neckband picks those up and translates them into commands—speech, movement—like that."

"Amazing."

"And his voice synthesizer. Most people have to make do with a canned, tinny electronic voice. Even with advancements in the field, the vocal generator always sounds artificial."

"You mean like Stephen Hawking," Jonathan said.

"Sort of. They've actually offered Mr. Hawking much more advanced and natural-sounding voice synthesizers, but he keeps his antiquated one since so many people identify its tone and sound with him. But my father was never one for nostalgia. He spent almost two years recording his own voice so that if and when it happened, his artificial voice would sound like his own. But he also had other advantages."

"You mean money."

"Yes. He had resources others didn't. For the most part, there's next to no research into prion diseases," Sophia said, picking up the hyperactive mouse as it scaled one of the Plexiglas walls in an attempt to escape. She gently put it back down next to its immobile brother.

"Why not?"

"Economics. The law of averages, really. Prion diseases are very rare. Only about three hundred cases are diagnosed in the United States every year. With so many other diseases affecting so many more people in the world, it's hard to justify funding for research."

"Unless you're a gazillionaire who has it," Jonathan said.

She chuckled and agreed.

"So why are we looking at mice?" he asked. Sophia thought he seemed more agitated than before, like he was in a hurry.

God, I'm boring him.

"This is Charlie and Lucy," Sophia said, pointing out that Lucy was the hyperactive mouse. "Can you tell me which one has the prion disease?"

"Charlie looks like he does, but I'm guessing it's a trick question. I'll say Lucy."

"Both answers are wrong."

"Huh?"

"They both have a form of kuru. They've had it exactly the same amount of time and at the same density."

"You cured Lucy?"

"Not yet," she said, walking over to a refrigerator. She took out a bottle filled with blue liquid and returned.

"She looks pretty cured to me," Jonathan said.

"Watch." She filled a hypodermic needle with some of the blue fluid and then injected Charlie with it. For a moment, nothing happened. Then Charlie's convulsions became much more violent. He looked like he was going to tear himself apart.

"Hey," Jonathan said.

"Wait for it," she said.

Then, as abruptly as they'd started, the convulsions stopped. But more than that, Charlie seemed to be under control now. He got up off his side and scampered over to sniff what Lucy was doing. They were identical now, in every way. It was impossible to tell them apart.

"That's not a cure?" Jonathan asked.

"Not yet. The serum, in its simplest form, is healthy proteins from Fred's brain."

"Fred?"

"One of their companions I euthanized earlier. Unfortunately, it's impossible to harvest the proteins needed from a live donor. They're not cured, but they have lived longer than any of the other subjects with the disease."

"And any brain has the proteins they need?"

"No, unfortunately. At first, our tests were all over the map. Sometimes it worked and sometimes it didn't. It was frustrating. Then I found the commonality in the successful cases: I had trained all the positive result donors how to run the maze. The ineffective ones had no training at all. Learning or intelligence has an effect on the brain's proteins. But the donors who did the best on the maze—the *smartest* donors—produced the best results."

"This formula of yours, that's how your father has survived so long?" Jonathan said.

"Yes," Sophia said. "But I just tweaked it for his specific needs. The original serum, including years of trials, was done in Nigeria."

"I think there's something wrong with your formula," Jonathan said. Sophia looked at the mice and saw one of them convulse and fall over onto its side. "Charlie's down again."

"That's not Charlie, it's Lucy," Sophia said. "Though in a few hours, the same thing will happen to Charlie. It's one of the problems I haven't worked out yet. The final problem, really. The effect is fleeting."

"Still, if you can transfer this to humans it would be worth millions. Billions. Incapacitated patients given their faculties again, even for a few hours, is groundbreaking. Have you published your findings anywhere?"

Sophia felt the familiar pang in her stomach when she thought about the groundbreaking research trapped, like her, on the island. She picked up the mice and returned them to their cages.

"You haven't gone public with this, have you? Any of it," Jonathan said. "He's got you doing all of this just for him."

Sophia just looked at him and didn't say anything. Even without speech, Jonathan seemed to get the message.

"Wait a minute. Christ, he can get out of that chair and walk around? Even for a little while?"

After looking at Jonathan for a few more silent moments, Sophia finally said: "Yes."

"But if the same donor restriction applies to humans . . ." Jonathan trailed off. She figured he either reasoned it out for himself or didn't want to know the answer. She wished she didn't.

For years, pristine donor samples had arrived in a prepared state, neatly packaged and labeled "Kring Laboratories: Human Samples." But a few months ago, like so much of Kring Industries, the research facility was sold off. When the inventory of samples was exhausted, new samples started to come in. Sloppily prepared and sometimes damaged samples. No packaging. No labeling. For fear of hearing what she thought she would, Sophia had kept her questions to herself and buried herself in her work. Something that now tore at her soul.

Unable to keep facing him, Sophia turned away from Jonathan and closed the animal cages. She looked at the creatures behind the bars through blurring vision, realizing for the first time how similar to her they really were. But before her melancholy could reach a crescendo, she felt Jonathan's arms slip around her from behind. Her breath caught and she reflexively leaned back into him, feeling his warm body against her back.

Then she felt the cold steel against her throat.

"What—"

"I'm sorry, but I don't have any choice," he said. "You seem like a good kid and it's pretty obvious you're not aligned with your psychotic father, but he is your father. I'm betting if he sees a knife to your throat he'll let me and my daughter out of here, no matter what he had planned for me."

"I . . . I don't understand," Sophia said. "Your daughter? Who's your daughter?" She resisted the urge to fight, not wanting the blade to dig into her neck.

"You really don't know, do you?"

"Know what?"

"Your father wants me to steal something for him. He's holding my daughter somewhere in this complex as leverage."

"What? That's . . . that's impossible," Sophia said with little conviction. Kidnapping? Was he really that far gone?

"I don't want to hurt you, but if I can't speak to her, make sure she's okay . . ."

Jonathan turned Sophia, keeping the steel pressed to her throat, and slowly walked her toward the front of the lab. No doubt to make an impression on Nathan and Lara the second they walked back through the door.

"You don't know where she is?" Sophia asked.

"No, but I'd bet she's on the third level. It's the only one your father didn't show me in his grand tour."

Then Sophia had an idea. An idea that might get the knife off her throat and let her take a swipe at Nathan.

"I'll take you to her. Let me help you," Sophia said. She felt the metal against her throat ease up.

"You'd do that? Go against your father?"

"Yes."

Moments stretched out while he considered the offer. It was an odd situation. Even with the steel against her skin, she felt sorry for him. She knew firsthand what her father could do to people. He pushed them to their breaking point and beyond, then sat back and observed their reaction like she watched her animals react to experiments.

"How do I know I can trust you?" Jonathan said, the edge eased from his voice.

"You don't," Sophia said, knowing there was nothing she could say to guarantee her veracity. If she lied to manipulate him, even in this situation, she'd be no better than her father.

Then she felt the cold steel lift from her skin as he took his arm away. He gently pushed her away from him. The backs of her thighs, her buttocks, and her back seemed to burn in the cool air from their loss of contact. She turned around and saw that the knife at her throat had actually been a metal ruler he'd taken from her desk when she was in the bathroom.

He tossed the ruler on a workstation, seeming almost out of breath from the episode. No, not the episode. Worry for his daughter. He looked like he was feeling physical pain over her plight. Sophia fantasized about what it would be like to have a father like that.

"So how do we get past the guards?" Jonathan asked.

"Follow me."

9:20 A.M.

"YOU'RE NOT THINKING straight," Lara said as she followed her father into his office.

"Sit down," Nathan said. Lara ignored him, which he had tolerated in the past, but it had been happening more and more.

"Who knows what Hall's doing down there right now. And Sophia, don't get me started about her. He's probably filling her head full of—"

Nathan rammed his desk with his wheelchair. Mementos and stacks of paper slid off and crashed to the floor, along with most of the copies of *The Monarch's Reign*, which fell from the shelves and revealed his real library of books behind them.

"I said sit down."

After a moment, Lara slumped into one of the chairs in front of his desk. Nathan's gaze never left her as he did his best to convey his anger in his current state.

"Well? What is it?" Lara asked when the silence drew out.

"I called Canton last night to give him an update and to know when to expect his guests," Nathan said.

"You . . . you should've let me take care of—"

"Lara," Nathan said. Lara looked like she'd been caught not only in the cookie jar, but burning down the cookie factory.

"What did he want?" Lara said, eyes wide.

She's good.

"It was a very interesting conversation. Very enlightening. It seems Canton wants to amend our deal. Now he wants three million dollars in cash added to the original agreement. Why do you think he would do that?"

"I don't, um, I don't know," Lara said, adjusting her position in the chair.

"See, I know Canton, and the fact that he's a greedy bastard is no surprise. But three million dollars? That's a fairly odd amount to add to a deal between a couple of billionaires, don't you think?" He tried not to think about the fact that he wasn't technically a billionaire anymore.

"I suppose he . . . maybe he just wanted to make a point?"

"Oh, he made a point, all right. In fact, he made such a point, I decided I had better find the answer to these questions before the deal took place. And you'll never guess what I found. It seems that someone from Tartaruga has been calling Australia. Fairly regularly. And not just Australia, but Canton's private line," Nathan said. His chair turned and whirred around his desk so he was right beside Lara's chair. "Who do you suppose could have made those calls?"

"Thomas is from Australia. Maybe—"

"Honestly, Lara. You expect me to believe after all these years, Thomas would sell me out for a paltry three million? No, this was someone else. And I'm willing to bet the three million is just a gratuity on the real arrangement. What did he offer you?" Nathan said, tired of playing. He turned and rolled back behind his desk.

"Me? Seriously, Father. You don't really believe I would ever do something like this, do you? It sounds more like something Sophia would do."

"First Thomas and now Sophia. You're running out of scapegoats, Lara. Sophia doesn't have a traitorous bone in her body. You, on the other hand, could teach a master's class on the subject. And don't insult me by denying it. I already checked with Ruby and she's confirmed it was you calling Canton."

"Ruby? Who's Ruby?"

"Canton's personal assistant. She's been on my payroll for years. She doesn't know why you were calling or what you two talked about, but she knew enough. So again, what did he offer you? Or more importantly, what did you offer him?"

Lara sat in silence, her cheeks flushed and her eyes moist. Nathan waited in silence as well. He had more experience than she and could wait her out. He was pretty sure what the offer was, but if she wasn't forthcoming, he had an ace or two up his sleeve.

"The three million dollars was . . ." Lara said it, but trailed off so quietly he couldn't make out her words.

"Speak up, girl."

"The three million dollars was for me!" she almost shouted.

"Why?"

"Because you're taking too long," Lara said.

"Taking too long to what? Recover?"

"No."

"To find The Monarch?"

"No," she said, stronger.

"Then what am I taking too long—"

"To die! All right? You're taking too long to die!"

Nathan fluttered his eyelids like he'd been slapped in the face. He hadn't expected that. Not from her. But now that he heard it, he was sure he knew what the deal was. He fought for control, glad that he wasn't jacked-up on Sophia's serum. If he had been, Lara would surely be dead right now. She *was* dead to him now, but she was still useful. Even more so now, actually. He wouldn't have to hold back. He could swing her at his enemies full force, and if she shattered . . . there were always more weapons.

"Let's see if I understand your little conspiracy," Nathan said. "You convinced Canton to renege on our deal. Not a hard endeavor. Then you told him if he cut you in, you'd give him your shares of Kring Industries. With the inheritance you envision from my death—an inevitability without this deal—you'd sell him controlling interest. For what? Power? Money?"

"He said he'd keep the company as a separate entity and let me head it. The three million was a sort of signing bonus."

"And all you needed for your dreams to come true is for me to die," Nathan said.

"Can you blame me? You treat that little gutless bitch down there better than you treat me! And you sure as hell didn't drag her into your bed. Why would I care what happens to you?"

God, she had it backward. He did all those things because he loved her, not because he didn't.

"You're a fool," Nathan said.

"Excuse me?"

"Let me tell you how your deal would have really gone down if I hadn't found out about it. Canton would have given you everything you asked for."

"I know," she said.

"What you don't know, or aren't considering, is what happens *after* the deal. He'll drain Kring Industries of everything worth having, and then he'll short the stock. The company will dissolve with the guts ripped out of it, and when the stock is decimated he'll make more money than if it had been successful. And you, my dear, will have long spent your three million dollars. You'll have nothing left but your tight dresses and an attitude."

"That's not true."

"Have you even considered the thousands of employees and families that work for us? Or the thousands of peripheral industries we support? What happens to them because of your arrogance and shortsightedness? Do you really think the only reason I'm doing all this is to keep breathing?"

"It's not?" she said, challenging his convictions. He ignored it.

"It doesn't matter."

"Why not?"

"Because you would never have the shares to give him in the first place."

"What?"

Nathan pushed every fiber of his body to the breaking point and fought the neuro-blocker as much as he could, doing his best impression of leaning forward.

"You don't own any stock. And you never would have. Do you really think I'd leave my company to someone who didn't have my blood running through their veins?" It was a lie. Nathan had fully intended on leaving everything to Lara, with a healthy portion left to her sister, of course. But everything was unraveling: going behind his back to Canton, Sophia discovering he wasn't their biological father and attacking him. Ironically The Monarch—the thing he'd been trying to destroy and blaming for his financial downfall due to the expense of the search—was looking like the only thing that could save him.

"*What?*" Lara hissed more than said, her breath coming in gasps.

It was time to get in front of this thing.

"Sophia, who you seem to think is oblivious to everything and naive, has figured something out you haven't—I'm not your biological father. In fact, legally, I'm nothing to either one of you, since I never adopted you either."

Nathan, to send his point home, took his eyes off of her and rolled over to the window, looking out on his jungle. A few guards were moving about, their loyalty bought and paid for. Lara sat slack-jawed, staring at the floor.

"Almost forty years ago, when the doctors first detected kuru in my blood, I bought Kring Laboratories and set them to work. Never being one for half measures, I wanted someone in-house with my best interests at heart. Someone who would fight for me, regardless of a paycheck. I had no idea how long I had before the symptoms would start showing up. So I assembled a team of scientists and sent them to scour these islands looking for just the right person.

"Someone young and malleable, someone with off-the-chart intelligence but controllable—someone without a father."

"Sophia," Lara said softly. Nathan wheeled around to face her.

"Sophia."

"But Mother said—"

"Pearl was an exceptional woman. She knew a once-in-a-lifetime opportunity when she saw it. Your life on the Maldives was less than luxurious, and the future that lay before you and your sister was anything but bright. Your mother and I made a deal, a business transaction. Beneficial to everyone."

"You . . . you *bought* us."

"Not *us*. Sophia. Originally I was just going to take her, but your mother was savvy and if I didn't take both of you there was no deal. She impressed me and I agreed, bringing her along in the bargain. And don't be mistaken, I came to love your mother, dearly. As she came to love me. It was a tragic irony when a disease she was carrying took her from us," Nathan said, feeling melancholy at the remembrance of holding Pearl's hand at her bedside while cancer destroyed her.

"Then I was—"

"Baggage," Nathan said, being deliberately cruel. She had to be punished.

Lara visibly recoiled in her chair. She looked around the room as if waiting for someone to let her in on the joke, her mouth opening and closing as she gulped air.

"How did you think I would react?" Nathan asked. His biggest problem right now was not Canton George. He was sure he could handle that old snake even in his present condition. The real problem was that he still needed Lara. It would soon be time to clean up the loose ends, and he couldn't do it alone. Sophia, though brilliant, was no killer. Neither was Lara at the moment, but if he spun this situation right, that would change.

"In any case, I'm willing to forget this momentary . . . lapse in judgment. You may not be my blood, but you're still mine."

Lara winced and closed her eyes. "As long as you do as I say and keep me alive, you'll continue to have the money and power of the Kring family at your disposal."

Nathan drove forward until he was right beside her again. She turned and looked at him. Nathan assayed her eyes for a moment. The fire was gone. She would do as he said from now on. He realized once all this was over it would be child's play to get her back into his bed.

"You'll have a job for life," Nathan said. "My life."

9:45 A.M.

"WHAT'S DOWN THERE?" Jonathan asked as he and Sophia passed a ladder that led below. They were in the bowels of the complex, a core area that ran the full height of the installation, where the life-blood of the complex coursed in and out. Bands of pipes hugged walls and ceilings, running up, down, back and forth. From what Jonathan could tell, they carried water, sewage, steam, hydro cables, and natural gas. The smell was terrible, but not nearly as bad as the noise.

"That's where the generators are and the holding tanks for the natural gas," Sophia shouted, though he barely heard her. "Come on."

Sophia waved for him to follow. They turned one of the corners in the poured concrete tunnel—which seemed to be made of nothing but corners—and she led him to a ladder. Jonathan had lost track of their way a long time ago. He didn't even want to think about being in here without Sophia.

She pumped her thumb up. Jonathan was glad he got the message, because he couldn't hear a thing.

He climbed up the ladder, with Sophia close behind him, until he reached a closed hatch. He reached up and turned the circular handle a few times and then pushed up. When the hatch was all the way open, he climbed up out. Sophia followed, shutting the hatch behind her, muffling the majority of the noise.

"Thank you," Jonathan said, wiggling a finger in his ear.

"It's been almost twenty minutes," Sophia said. "Let's go. If they come back while we're in here noise is going to be the least of our problems."

Back in her lab, she'd led Jonathan to a vent that had looked welded shut, but had opened easily. Sophia said she and Lara used to play in the tunnels when they would visit the island as kids. But then her father had discovered the natural gas pocket under the island and dug out a newer, deeper level to manage the gas and house several giant generators. After that, her father had welded most of the vents shut except for a few larger access panels in the corridors. Sophia didn't explain why, but a few years ago she'd used some of her chemicals to break the weld around the vent in her lab. If they found Natalie he wasn't going to be able to hold her, but he could see her and talk to her. That would be enough until he could figure a way out of this mess.

He really wished Lew was here.

"This corridor runs along the guest rooms. If she's here she'll be in one of these," Sophia said.

Jonathan crouched and trotted over to the first one, but saw no one inside. The next three were the same. Then, in the second to last room, he found her, his breath catching in his throat when he saw her.

The room was bright, fake sunshine coming from phony windows on one wall, an impossibility this far underground. The color scheme was bright as well. All golds and yellows. It resembled a hotel room, with a dresser and writing table against the wall. In the middle of the room was a large bed and on it sat Natalie. She was busy drawing.

He opened his mouth to call to her, but stopped himself at the last second.

"What is it?" Sophia asked. Jonathan gently led her away from the vent so they could talk without Natalie hearing them.

"I can't say anything to her," Jonathan said, standing close to Sophia so he could keep his voice down. She smelled of chemicals and animals. He thought it odd that it was about the best thing he'd ever smelled.

"Why not?"

"What would I say? 'Daddy's been kidnapped and has to go be a thief. Remember to brush your teeth.' It's ridiculous," Jonathan said. He'd explained about The Monarch when they first entered the tunnels. His honesty was Sophia's price for helping him, though he felt she would have helped him regardless.

"She'll understand," Sophia said.

"No. She won't. Besides, even if she did, as hard as it is for her right now, how much harder would it be knowing I was out here somewhere? How could I explain why she has to stay there? No, it has to be this way."

Sophia looked at him, her head slightly tilted. She looked almost . . . awed.

"All right. If you say so. Whatever we're going to do, we have to do it now."

"Just let me look at her again," Jonathan said, turning and easing back to the vent.

Jonathan smiled as he watched her. Then, out of nowhere, Natalie started singing. Just a silly, repetitive children's song, but it was more than Jonathan could take. He backed away from the vent, blinking tears from his eyes.

"Okay. Let's go—" Sophia put her arms around him and hugged him. Part of him wanted to let go and sob, another part of him wanted to do something very different. He took the middle ground and just accepted the human contact. When she let him go, he saw she was crying and knew it wasn't just for him.

"Come on," she said.

11:00 A.M.

SOPHIA AND JONATHAN got back to the lab ten minutes before Nathan and Lara returned. An hour later, Nathan dismissed the guards. Alone, he took Jonathan on what he thought would be another tour. Jonathan expected Lara to complain again, but she remained silent. Even her stance was different on her return than before they'd left the lab.

Level five, accessible by a separate, private elevator at the far end of level four, held something Jonathan had never expected to see in such a place. But he was starting to realize that this island and Nathan's life were filled with the unexpected.

"My father started this collection before I was born," Nathan said as he rolled over to where Jonathan stood. "He never divulged its existence to anyone, including me. I stumbled upon it years ago when I was expanding the complex. On the first day of excavation, we found this chamber. It was a very special day."

Jonathan had no doubt. And if he knew this man at all, he also had no doubt that the workers who had been present that day no longer drew breath.

The room was a treasure vault.

"I don't suppose it ever occurred to you to return these items to their rightful owners," Jonathan said.

"And who would that be? The country that pillaged their neighbor hundreds of years ago? The men these articles were taken from before they wound up here? In the case of the religious icons, the Catholic Church? We all know what pillars of honor they've been through the centuries."

"Those are weak justifications, and you know it. These treasures don't belong to you, no matter how much you paid for them. Even if you didn't pull the job yourself, you're a thief. And so's your father."

"And you're a Supreme Court justice? Please, you've made your living and your fame as a thief."

"That's different. I've never kept any of it. It's all where it rightfully should be," Jonathan said, examining a van Gogh he'd never even heard of.

"And you've never taken a finder's fee?"

Jonathan didn't say anything.

"My point exactly," Nathan said. "I'm sorry you can't appreciate this for what it is. I think it was a mistake showing it to you. Let's go. Dinner will be ready shortly. And you have a job to do." It was hard to tell through the electronic device he used to communicate, but he thought Nathan was insulted.

"Hang on," Jonathan said, coming around a large display case of royal jewels. He was only halfway into the room, but the treasure seemed to stop there. The display cases and pedestals continued on to the far wall in the distance, but they stood empty. "Where's the rest of it?"

"What do you mean? That's all of it. Isn't it enough? You seem to think there shouldn't be anything here and yet you're complaining about the depth of my collection?"

Jonathan walked up to an empty display case and saw a plaque describing what wasn't there and a clean area within the dust on the pedestal.

"The items have been taken out. Wait. You've been *selling* them," Jonathan said, realizing what was happening. Nathan's endeavor to find him had been so costly he'd had to start selling his prized collection, piece by piece.

"That's enough of your impudence, Mr. Hall. Leave. Now. Or I won't be responsible for what happens to *your* treasure."

Jonathan felt the blood boil up into his face. He fought the urge to strike out and forced himself to walk silently to the door. He'd found Nathan's Achilles' heel and he'd foolishly poked at it.

As they headed to the private elevator, Jonathan couldn't help but wonder how whatever Nathan wanted him to steal could possibly be worth half a roomful of treasure. Canton George had something Nathan was willing to financially ruin himself to get. Anytime someone wanted something that bad it made him dangerous and unpredictable.

But nowhere near as dangerous as the man who already had it.

36

"Is that him?" Lew asked from behind the wheel of the liberated car. Emily had been less than thrilled with the idea of stealing a car. Probably about as thrilled as Jonathan would have been to find out that the woman he'd asked Lew to protect—the final thing he'd ever said to Lew—was sitting in that stolen car staking out a police cordoned-off federal building waiting to follow an FBI agent.

Lew knew what he should have done was dump Emily off with the cops where she'd be safe, but when he thought about it, she hadn't done so well under their care the last time. They had managed to get a few hours' sleep in the car—Emily more than Lew— but as it got close to the time when the junior agent was supposed to show up, Lew would wake Emily up and ask if anything that moved was the guy they were waiting for.

"For the fifth time, no," Emily said. Lew was not a watcher. He was a doer. This recon stuff was Jonathan's thing.

"Hey, I'm just asking," Lew said.

"That's not even a man," Emily said, sounding like her frustration level was reaching its breaking point.

"It is so." Lew leaned forward and looked closer. "Son of a bitch. I guess if you can make it here you can make it anywhere." She'd stopped laughing at his bad jokes about an hour ago.

Lew was actually glad their frustration levels were so high. The first few hours of sitting in the car had been uncomfortable in a different way. The space in the front seat seemed interminably cramped and when their hands accidentally brushed each other it was as if a spark lit up the car's interior. Ever since that moment in the elevator, all he could think about was what it would be like to hold Emily. Lew was sure his time in Yazoo was to blame, but that fact didn't help. At least now, as he deliberately annoyed her and made her snap at him, he was starting to lean back toward wanting to push her out the door and go on alone. At least, a little.

"There he is!" Emily said, grabbing Lew's arm in her excitement. Her hands felt hot all the way through his duster's sleeve.

"Okay, okay," Lew said after swallowing. "He still has to go up and get the stuff. Let's hope he's not being paid by the hour."

They watched Hinton flash his ID to the cops at the blockade before they moved the yellow sawhorse out of the way. He pulled his green Ford up in front and got out, slipping on a construction hardhat before entering the building.

"Make sure that thing is ready," Lew said.

Twenty minutes later he came out of the building carrying two office file boxes. He put them in the back of the Ford, got in, and headed back for the barricade.

"Here we go," Lew said as he pulled out and drove in the opposite direction.

"What are you doing?! He's back there," Emily said.

"Relax. I've done this before," Lew said. As he drove he kept an eye on his rearview mirror and slowed down gradually. Pretty soon the green Ford was right behind them. If he'd pulled out after the agent had left, the cops would have noticed him. This way he was just part of New York's morning traffic.

"Use the mirrors. Don't look back," Lew said. "Do we have a signal yet?" If the phone was off or out of battery power, this was all for naught.

"I don't see . . . wait! Yes, I've got a signal," Emily said. "Signals."

"Signals?" Then Lew realized they were in New York and there had to be hundreds of Bluetooth devices around them—phones, headsets, Walkmans, you name it. "Can you identify the phone?"

"No," Emily said. "I have no idea . . . wait, something's happening." Lew tried to look at the device but he had his hands full with the traffic and keeping an eye on the green Ford, making sure he didn't get more than twenty or so feet away from it.

"Yes! I love you!"

"Uh, what?" Lew suddenly felt his cheeks flush.

"Oh, not you. Raiden. He coded the device to the phone. It's eliminating erroneous signals. And . . . there. Got it. It's locking on now and . . . no! The signal's gone."

"Gone? But he's—" Lew looked up and saw that the green Ford was gone. He'd taken his eye off it for just a second. Lew slowed and spun his head around. "There he is. Four cars back. On your side."

Emily looked in the mirror and nodded that she saw him. Lew

slowed to the point where the cars behind him started honking, but he didn't care. They were getting closer. Then the green Ford pulled out and started to pass on the outside. Lew would actually prefer if he got ahead of them. At least then he could . . . oh shit.

"Get down!" Lew shouted.

"What?" Emily said without taking her eyes off Raiden's device.

"He's passing us. If he sees you he'll recognize you for sure."

"I've got the signal back," Emily said, seeming to ignore him. She was too focused. As the front bumper of the green Ford started to pass them, Lew reached out and grabbed Emily, pulling her down so she was out of sight, more than a little aware that her head was now in his lap. Once the agent had passed them, he pulled in behind the Ford and let her up.

"Sorry," Lew said with a grin.

"I . . . That was . . . um . . ." Emily looked back at the device. "Signal lock!"

"Do we have the data yet? This traffic is getting hairy." Lew pulled up tight to the green Ford's bumper to keep another car from cutting in between them. He ignored the flurry of honks and birds flipped at him. Then the pair of cars came up on a traffic light that had turned yellow. "Finally," Lew said. He pressed the brake but saw the green Ford accelerate.

"He's running it!" Emily said.

"Hang on," Lew said, punching the accelerator. He stayed within thirty feet of their target, but there was enough space that the light had turned red and cross traffic had already entered the intersection. Horns blared as he spun the wheel, fishtailing out of the way of an approaching taxi. Then he spun the wheel back the other way and nudged an SUV with his side of the car, but he kept going. Incredibly they made it through the intersection.

"Man, that was—"

"Stop!" Emily yelled over him.

Lew didn't realize she wasn't shouting at him until the truck hit them broadside. His head smacked against the window and he felt the side of the car buckling in around him. Then everything went white.

Lew opened his eyes what he thought was a few seconds later, a high-pitched whine in his ears.

"Emily," he managed, shaking the fuzz out of his brain. But when he looked beside him he saw he was alone in the car. Emily and the tracking device were gone, the passenger door still open. The view of approaching pedestrians was hard to see through, but he could tell the green Ford was long gone too.

His door wouldn't be opening without the Jaws of Life. He tried to climb out the other way, but his leg was wedged against the steering column. He could taste blood in his mouth. He'd bit the inside of his cheek in the crash. As his head cleared, he realized the wailing wasn't in his head at all, but was the sound of the approaching ambulance. Exhausted, Lew just wanted to sleep. Maybe a ride in an ambulance wasn't such a bad idea?

"Lew! Help!"

The sound of Emily's voice snapped him out of his funk. He squinted through the windshield and saw someone dragging her toward a pickup truck parked across the street. A pickup truck with a bashed-in bumper.

Adrenaline shot through Lew's nerves. He pulled harder but his leg was stuck fast. He grunted and smashed the steering wheel. It moved but just a bit. Realizing he couldn't pull his leg out, he instead pushed sideways on the steering column, pulling it aside at the same time. When it started to move he got his other foot up against the wrecked door for leverage and shoved. He'd free himself or break his leg. Either way, he wasn't going to just sit here and watch that bastard take Emily.

After what seemed like forever, something snapped. It was the steering column. Lew pulled and wrenched himself free, scrambling out of the open passenger door. He fell on the pavement, but got back up, and ran with only a slight limp toward the pickup truck, pushing onlookers' hands off him. He'd almost made it when the pickup truck's brake lights flickered. Wheels spun as it fishtailed away, knocking several pedestrians down as it went.

And then she was gone. He'd failed her. And he'd failed Jonathan.

Lew ran, knowing the only thing he could save now was his freedom.

37

Tartaruga Island
3:00 P.M. Local Time

EVERY INSTINCT HE had told him not to eat or drink. The plateware or silverware could be compromised. Jonathan didn't listen to any of it, or rather, Jonathan's stomach didn't. He couldn't remember the last time he'd eaten and if he was about to pull a job—alone, at that—he was going to need all the sustenance he could get his hands on. And what sustenance.

Green asparagus and purple artichokes surrounded presentations of roasted blue lobster, chicken fricassee, and sea spider crab. Several bottles of Penfolds Grange, 1951, dotted the table.

The dining room was just as impressive. A vaulted ceiling surrounded an ornately complex crystal chandelier hanging over the dark wood of the dining table. Matching teak sideboards lined both sides of the room, each covered with silver platters, those in turn covered with detailed engraved silver lids. Paintings from the Baroque period hung on the walls, and light chamber music emanated from recessed speakers in the ceiling. There were ten chairs placed around the table, but only three place settings. One of them was vacant.

The dining room was nestled on the third level of the complex. Hunger aside, it was difficult for Jonathan to concentrate knowing Natalie was just a few rooms away, but he wasn't supposed to know that. Lara, at the opposite end of the table, hadn't said more than a few words to him beyond that something was delaying Nathan and he would join them when he could. Jonathan wanted to ask where Sophia was and if Natalie was being fed as luxuriously, but doubted he would get a useful answer.

If he could get some more time with Sophia, he was pretty sure he could turn the tables on this whole situation.

Jonathan cleaned off his second plateful, drank a third glass of wine, and then leaned back with a satisfied sigh. What he saw next almost sent him toppling back in his chair onto the ornate carpeting on the floor.

"Good evening, Mr. Hall. I hope my absence . . . ah, I see you went ahead without me. Good. You're going to need your strength," Nathan said. And not out of an electronic box. In fact, his wheelchair was nowhere to be seen. He stood in the doorway in a tuxedo, the jacket unbuttoned and open. He had one hand in his pocket, while he held a cigar in the other. "I trust the smoke won't bother you. I ate earlier and I just couldn't resist my Cubans. Old habits and all."

Jonathan realized his mouth was open. He closed it as his host, obviously jacked up on Sophia's serum, entered and sat next to him.

"Uh, yes. I mean, it was very good. Top notch," Jonathan said, unable to take his eyes off Nathan. It was like he was meeting him for the first time. "But I was wondering where—"

"Sophia and your daughter are having an equally satisfying supper. Trust me. I just thought it might be better if we discussed business without having to make a lot of explanations. I believe your daughter is unaware of your . . . past. Is this not so?"

Jonathan nodded, wondering how he'd come by that little tidbit of information.

"Yet something else we have in common," Nathan said as Lara dropped her silverware on her mostly empty plate and got up from the table.

"If you'll excuse me," Lara said, practically gritting her teeth.

"I was hoping you'd stay for the briefing, Lara. You could help—"

"I have things to attend to, Father," Lara said. She tossed her napkin down and marched out of the dining room. Jonathan wondered if that woman was ever happy, though he had to admit he was glad she was gone.

"Children," Nathan said, though Jonathan could see by Nathan's face—now that it was animated and not lolling to the side—that he was not pleased with his daughter's behavior. "Enjoy young Miss Hall's preteen years while you can. They go so quickly. But on to business."

Nathan got up and poured himself a snifter of brandy from a collection of bottles on one of the sideboards. He held the bottle up, offering Jonathan a drink. Jonathan shook his head and declined.

"Probably best," Nathan said. He took a long sniff of the liquid, swirling it in the glass as he held it in his palm. "As you know, Canton George is a collector."

Jonathan nodded, nervous. *How much information does he have?*

"What you probably don't know is that Canton and I used to be business partners. In fact, there was a time when we were the best of friends. I won't bore you with the drama, but that time has passed. We've spent the last twenty years trying to put each other out of business. And I'm not too humble to tell you that I was achieving that goal before my condition flared up." He tilted the snifter back and sipped his drink. Afterward he closed his eyes and almost groaned in ecstasy. This was a man who enjoyed all the experiences life had to offer. Jonathan thought the wheelchair was probably an experience he could have done without.

"What's the target?" Jonathan asked. He was worried, but not just about Natalie's safety. If Nathan came after The Monarch because of his history with Canton George, Nathan was going to expect him to know things that he didn't. Lew hadn't shared much of anything about the job, except that it had not gone well. Jonathan had always assumed that meant nothing had been stolen.

"Part of his collection. I'm afraid I can't tell you what it is, yet, for reasons that will become obvious in time, but rest assured Canton has something that belongs to me. And I want it back." That didn't make sense to Jonathan. If Nathan and George were rivals—enemies, even—how did Nathan even know about a theft George would have certainly wanted to keep quiet? With so many unanswered questions, Jonathan was starting to blame himself for not probing Lew harder about the botched job.

"How am I supposed to steal something when I don't know what it is?"

"His items are catalogued and labeled. Have you forgotten? Item CS–231 is what you'll be stealing."

Damn it! Have to be more careful.

"How big is it?" Jonathan asked.

"About the size of a hatbox. Like so," Nathan said, showing Jonathan the general dimensions with his hands.

"Okay, what's his security like?" Jonathan caught his mistake a second too late. "It's been a while and people tend to beef up security after a robbery," he said, trying to cover his slipup. It seemed to work.

"Minimal, same as before. Living in the middle of nowhere like he does, he doesn't think he needs much in the way of security. Maybe four or five guards on the grounds and a mediocre security system."

"When do we go?" Jonathan asked wanting to end this little exchange before he made a mistake he couldn't cover.

"Tonight. I know that doesn't give you much time to prepare, but the timing is unavoidable and I'm hoping your previous venture there will make up for it."

"I'm going to need some equipment."

"I'll have Lara get you whatever you need. We anticipated your requests and should have everything on hand," Nathan said.

"What about transportation? Not just to Australia, but in and out of the area?" Jonathan asked. It was his first blatant attempt to find out where exactly he was. Or, at least, to find out where he wasn't.

"We've got that covered, as well. And let me save you some time, we're in the Indian Ocean, a few hundred kilometers east of Africa," Nathan said, apparently seeing right through Jonathan's ruse. Jonathan nodded.

Why's he being so forthcoming? Jonathan wasn't sure he wanted the answer to that question, but he figured he'd better strike again while the gate was open.

"All right," Jonathan said, rising and pouring himself a coffee from the sideboard behind him. "Cards on the table. What's with all the fake cordiality?" He sipped the coffee. It was about the best cup of coffee to ever touch his lips—dark, rich, and not too bitter.

"I'm sorry? What makes you think—"

"Let's not fuck around, Kring. You killed people in New York to find me. A *lot* of people. Near as I can figure, it cost you millions. You kidnapped my daughter to force me to help you. And to top it all off, you decide to give me a tour and have dinner with me? What the fuck are we waiting for?" Jonathan was trying to shock Nathan into dropping his facade, but he was also letting out some of his pent-up anxiety.

Nathan pursed his lips and stared. Jonathan felt like a bug under a microscope, Nathan's cold stare pulling him apart, layer by layer. He stood his ground and stared back, fighting the chill that wanted to race up his spine.

"Fine," Nathan finally said. "Let's clear the air. First off, I had no intention of killing anyone with that explosion. It was supposed to be a simple diversion. People I trusted let me down."

"What about the others? The ones that put The Monarch into the spotlight to draw me out? Those were no accidents."

"No, they weren't. Sacrifices had to be made. For the greater good."

"The greater good being your revenge on Canton George," Jonathan said.

"No. The item you're stealing is not just part of Canton's collection. It's the only thing that can save my life."

"That's the greater good? You justify killing those people to save yourself? Because you're worth more than them?"

Nathan's solemn facade slipped away and he was suddenly laughing a deep, hearty laugh. But it was a laugh relegated to just his mouth and chest. His eyes didn't crinkle up with joy. Instead, they looked panicked and helpless.

"Again, my apologies," Nathan said when his laughter subsided. "My disease has a disconcerting symptom of inappropriate laughter. It would appear my mobile and lucid state is about to leave me." Nathan made his way to the far end of the room, seeming to have trouble making his legs obey him, and pressed a call button on the wall.

"How can item CS–231 save your life? What is it?" Jonathan asked quickly since Nathan looked like he was going to collapse.

"My plans need to change," Nathan said, slumping into a chair. "You'll be leaving shortly. Good luck to you, Mr. Hall. Remember what's at stake. Both for me and for you."

The door to the dining room opened and Lara and several security guards flowed in, two of them grabbing Jonathan by the arms and holding him while the others ran to Nathan's side.

"Now just wait a—" Jonathan didn't get to finish. Lara stormed in and roughly pulled a black cloth bag over his head.

Then she put her lips to his ear.

"Fail him and I'll personally cut her heart out."

38

Pioneer Electronics
New York City
9:00 A.M. Local Time

LEW DIDN'T HAVE many options. In fact, near as he could figure, all he had was *option*. And even that was a long shot. Jonathan was gone. Lew's only link to him was Emily. Emily was gone. Both of them had been taken right from under his nose. But if Emily could track someone with her phone, then maybe—just maybe— she could be tracked too.

Everything had been going well. Raiden Pioneer's shop was open and no one else was around. Lew thought he was finally catching a break, as he explained the situation to Raiden in his shop bathed in the early morning sun streaming through the dirty windows. But when Raiden came out from behind the cash register he didn't have a phone in his hand. He had a gun.

And it was pointed at Lew's heart.

"Put the gun away," Lew said, raising his hands. Raiden Pioneer's glare and unshaking gun hand told Lew this wasn't the first time the unassuming man had held a weapon. He was also pretty sure Raiden wouldn't have a problem pulling the trigger if Lew cornered him.

"In the back," Raiden said, wiggling the gun toward the curtain that separated the front of the store from his workshop. Raiden circled around behind him, staying at least six feet away, and locked the store's front door and turning over the "Open" sign.

This guy's no amateur. Generally people who were new to holding guns on other people used their television-acquired training and always stood close enough to press the weapon into their target's back. That invariably made it easy to overpower them, especially if you had close combat skills.

"Look, Hopalong, all I want to do is help Emily. She's in trouble and I need your help to—"

A colon-twisting *snick* echoed in the little store as Raiden cocked the gun's hammer.

"I don't know what you've done with Emily or why you're here, but I'm turning you in," Raiden said.

"Turning me in? For what?"

"For mass murder." Lew's eyes narrowed.

"What are you talking about?" Lew asked, afraid of the answer.

"It's been on the news for the past hour. A tourist came forward and turned a video of the Federal Plaza disaster in to the police when he couldn't sell it to the news stations. He didn't film the explosion, but he got a great shot of someone jumping onto a limousine and smashing the window as he ran from the scene. Someone wearing a duster. It wasn't hard for me to guess who it was after meeting you earlier. Your description is on every channel now. And I'll bet there's a nice reward involved."

My duster? They didn't have my face or name. That's something.

Lew was doubly glad he hadn't waited around at the accident for the cops to show up. But time was ticking and Emily's kidnapper could be anywhere by now, never mind where the hell Jonathan was. This suspicious little opportunist was his only hope. Though he wasn't going to get anywhere as long as Raiden had that gun.

"Things aren't always how they look," Lew said, taking a tentative step forward.

"That's far enough," Raiden said, seeing his idea plainly. "In the back!" Raiden waved his gun toward the curtain that led to the back of his shop.

Lew hesitated, but knew he had little choice. He turned around and stepped toward the curtain, his hands in the air.

"You're making a mistake," Lew said.

"Let me worry about—"

As Lew parted the curtain with one of his raised hands, he abruptly dove through the material out of Raiden's sight. The workshop was small and cluttered, a workbench against the wall beside the curtain, a few tables covered with electronic guts along the other walls and a door opposite the curtain. Lew saw through the door's window that a dark alley lay beyond. An easy escape that his flight muscle was begging him to take. But getting away was the last thing on Lew's mind.

Still, he opened the door, then doubled back and hopped up on the bench. Raiden had taken too long following him. Lew figured he was either just calling the cops from the store or he wasn't as steady with that gun as he'd appeared. Lew remained where he was, silent, hoping whatever was going to happen would hurry up because his accident-bashed knee was killing him from crouching on the bench.

After what seemed like minutes, the tip of the gun finally appeared through the curtain. Lew forced himself to keep waiting. When the entire gun hand was through the curtain, Lew slammed his good hand down on the gun so the webbing between his thumb and index finger jammed between the hammer and the gun. Raiden reflexively pulled the trigger. The hammer slammed down and tore into Lew's flesh. He howled in pain and wrenched the gun away from Raiden, rolling off the workbench onto the floor.

"Son of a bitch! Fuck! Shit!" Lew, who had been shot more than once, had never felt pain so excruciating. He cocked the trigger and released his hand.

Raiden had backed against the wall, fear and the gun in Lew's hand keeping him from making a run for it. Lew continued to rage, the pain pushing buttons in him he tried to keep buried. He kicked a stool across the room and cleared everything off the workbench and the tables. Raiden remained where he was, his eyes growing wider and wider as he watched. Suddenly, Lew vaulted across the room and press the gun's barrel into Raiden's forehead, panting hot, rapid breaths through clenched teeth.

This was as close as he'd been in years. Close to losing himself. The aggression and mindless, numbing violence had been a necessity on the battlefield, but it had followed him out of the army too.

All he wanted to do was pull the trigger. Over and over. Just keep shooting until his frustration—and Raiden's head—were history. But then he'd be a self-fulfilling prophecy, condemning Emily and Jonathan to their fates because of his ineptitude. *No! I'm not that man anymore.*

"All I want. Is to find. Emily," Lew managed with stilting, deep breaths. He forced himself to stop clenching his teeth, his head pounding from the effort. He stumbled back a few steps and then did what Jonathan would do. He took a risk and trusted someone else. He flipped the gun around so he was holding the barrel and held the butt out to Raiden. "Can you help me or not?"

A LITTLE WHILE later, Lew sucked wind through his teeth, clenched for a different reason now. Raiden had sewn up his hand and was taping the final bandage into place. It still hurt like hell, but now it was more of a throb than a stabbing that made his toes curl. Raiden had offered Lew whiskey to drink during the procedure, but he'd refused, which had made his thirsty liver kick him a few times. He had to stay clear. When this was over, no matter what the outcome, he was going to go on the mother of all binges, but for now, he took the pain.

"Where'd you learn to do that?" Lew asked, examining Raiden's handiwork while the electronics expert put his portable ER away.

"North Korea," Raiden said, the tone of his voice saying he didn't want to share the details. Lew understood and let it go.

Lew got up and put his duster back on, easing his broken and damaged hands through his sleeves. Raiden handed him the tracking device he'd whipped together in less than five minutes. Watching him work had been awe-inspiring. His hands had flown from tool to part to tool as if he wasn't even looking. The closest approximation Lew had ever seen was when he'd been in his prime, stripping and reassembling an M–16 in record time, over and over.

"This will find her?" Lew asked.

"Its range and signal attenuation is limited. If she's been taken out of the tri-state area, I'm afraid she's gone." Lew flipped it on, a blip showing up three-quarters of the way down the screen. Raiden looked on and said, "She's headed for New Jersey."

"Do you know what's in that area?"

"Uh, let's see. Industrial mostly. And a private airport."

Crap.

Airport meant ID check. If Warden Quinn wasn't dead by now, Lew's deal with him certainly was.

"We may have a problem," Lew said. He explained he couldn't travel under his own ID without going into details as to why. He knew Raiden didn't need to hear them and would understand.

"Do you know anyone who can do papers in—"

"Stand against the wall," Raiden said. Lew backed up and watched Raiden take out a Polaroid camera, *Is there anything this guy doesn't do?*

A few minutes later, Lew had a driver's license and a passport in the name of Sven Longren. He turned the documents over and whistled, impressed by their quality.

"Sven?" Lew said.

"You're big and blond . . . Hopalong," Raiden said with a smile.

"Gotcha," Lew said, smiling back.

"Do you have a car?" Lew asked. He needed new transportation, especially if he was going out of state.

"No, but I've got a motorcycle. The helmet would probably help you get out of the city without being spotted."

"Perfect. I don't know how to thank you," Lew said. But Raiden knew. Lew coughed up most of his cash and gave him a promissory note for twice as much once he was back. Lew didn't have a problem with signing; in all likelihood, he'd be dead before this was over.

Lew put on the black helmet, straddled the bike, and started the motor. He twisted the accelerator a few times, liking what he heard. He'd be there in half the time now, which still might not be soon enough. The blip on the tracking device wasn't moving anymore. Raiden and a few seconds on Google confirmed it was the airport.

"Thanks again," Lew said over the engine's roar in the alley.

"Just take care of Emily. She has a good heart but your helmet has more street smarts," Raiden said. Lew knew exactly what he meant.

"Count on it," Lew said. He flipped the smoked visor down and kicked the bike into gear, the engine howling as he flew down the alley, his duster flapping behind him like a superhero's cape.

39

Drummond Field Airport
New Jersey
10:00 A.M. Local Time

LEW SHOT THROUGH the afternoon, the drone and whine of the machine between his legs thankfully washing out any self-deprecating thoughts from his brain. Traffic had been heavy, but Lew had weaved in and out without much trouble. Once out of the city and across the state line, he rocketed to the airport in record time.

Drummond Field, a small airport dedicated mostly to cargo flights, rose up on his left as he came out of a short tunnel cut through the bedrock. A high chain-link fence ran around the airfield, the entrance a few hundred yards up ahead. Lew gunned the throttle and saw that the tarmac was a busy place. Planes taxied this way and that, figures in bright orange vests wearing big yellow ear protection waved batons with both arms, directing their charges. Most of the planes were mid-sized cargo jets, some plain and some marked with familiar shipping company logos. A smattering of private and corporate jets rounded out the complement.

As Lew passed through the entrance and turned toward the buildings at the base of the control tower, he saw what he was after. The plane stood out like a sore thumb—even the other pilots and crews stood around on the field to observe the sleek, red-striped supersonic jet. Lew could care less about the plane's cosmetic beauty. As he pulled into a parking spot, the plane taxied out onto the runway. He put the helmet on the bike's handlebars and ran inside to the airport's information counter.

It was early and with the airport mostly serving private jets there was next to no walk-in traffic. Which explained the minimum-wage, long-haired attendant who was more interested in his phone than what was happening out on the tarmac.

"Dude, I can't stop it. It's already been cleared for takeoff by the tower," the young man behind the counter said in response to Lew's demand.

"Look, it's an emergency. I have to get on—"

"Dude," the man said, pointing outside. Lew turned and saw the red-striped plane arc up into the sky, the roar of its engines practically shaking the building. "Jesus, that's sweet."

Lew slammed his fist down so hard on the counter, several pens down the other end hopped up in the air.

"Uh, are we cool? I don't have to call anybody or anything, do I?" The man had backed away from the counter a few steps and was reaching for the phone.

Calm down, Lew. You can't help anyone if your ass is in jail.

"Sorry, man. I'm cool. It's just—" Lew leaned in and motioned the man to come closer to share his secret. "I'm going to lose my job if my boss finds out I forgot to secure the sample," Lew said, almost in a whisper.

"Sample?"

"It's not contagious or anything. Yet. But I really need this job. It's been a rough year, you know? Lost my last job last month. Those deaths were not my fault. CDC even said so. Think that saved my ass? Not even a little." The young man's eyes were getting wider with every tidbit of story Lew laid on him.

"So what's this sample?" the young man asked, whispering himself.

"I've already said too much. I don't want to put you in danger. Maybe if . . . nah," Lew said turning to leave.

"Wait! Maybe if what? Come on, dude. I can help."

"Well, if I knew where that plane was going, maybe I could meet up with it. Secure the sample there, you know?"

"No worries. I've got it right here," the young man said with a smile. He punched the keys on his computer for a second. "Stop over in Pensacola, Florida, then on to Zanzibar, Africa. Oh. You're pooched."

"Why's that?" Lew said, having the information he needed.

"It's supersonic, dude. They're already halfway there. No way you'll catch it."

"Do you have any flights going out to Pensacola I can hitch a ride on? Cargo or something?"

"Well, yeah, we've got several today, but like I said, you'll never—"

"You get me in a jump seat and let me worry about that," Lew said, holding out his bandaged hand. The man shook it. "You just saved my job. Maybe even some lives. You're like a hero, man."

"Nah," the man said, practically digging his toe into the sand. "Just helping out."

"That flight?" Lew said, nodding toward the computer.

"Oh, right," the young man said before he went to work.

It took what cash Lew had left, but he got the seat. He had forty-five minutes to wait for his flight out, but if he didn't get that plane held up in Pensacola, he was done. A supersonic jet would be in Zanzibar in a couple of hours, though he doubted that was its actual destination. More than likely, it was nearby.

"It's Lew Katchbrow. Let me talk to him," Lew said into a pay phone a few minutes later. Then a voice Lew thought he'd never hear again came on the line. "Save the pleasantries. I need a favor. And I mean now."

LEW EXAMINED HIS duster as the cargo plane bounced in for a landing in Pensacola three hours after it took off. His collision with the truck back in New York had all but torn out the lining on the left side. On the right side, down near the hem, there were two bullet holes. Lew groaned. It had only been a couple days and it was already practically ruined. And he knew he wasn't done yet.

A few minutes later, the plane came to a stop. He undid his seat belt and waded through the tied-down boxes and crates in the plane's hold, toward the back cargo door. A loud clunk echoed through the plane's cavity and the aircraft shook and rumbled as the entire back end of the plane slowly levered down to the tarmac. Warm air blew in ruffling Lew's short hair. He closed his eyes and enjoyed the moment. Spring in the Northeast sucked. He'd been cold the entire time. This was a climate he could tolerate. There was even something about the aroma of jet fuel and burning rubber that soothed him. Jonathan called it his army brain. Lew stopped his mind from wandering. He didn't like how he felt when he thought about Jonathan just now. He had to focus on Emily. Which was no problem at all.

The slowly descending tailgate finally gave Lew a view of the airport. Sitting on the tarmac behind the plane was the man he'd called. He was dressed in a white linen suit, had his arms crossed, and was leaning back against a shiny black Hummer, a huge smile on his face. Lew walked down the ramp, his damaged duster flapping behind him in the Everglade breeze. He smiled despite himself. They'd accomplished something together, which always bonded people, regardless of their characters.

"*Ese*," Miguel Colero drawled out as Lew approached. "You look like a freakin' cowboy." His Latino accent was still hard for Lew to take, and part of him would always think of the man as Mickey King.

"Subtle," Lew said, glancing up at the huge vehicle behind Colero. They shook hands, both men squeezing harder than they had to. "Couldn't you find anything bigger?"

"I'm back and people need to know. Trust me, *ese*, in this thing, they know."

"I'll bet. I wasn't sure when I called if you'd even be alive. Your competition has been dealt with, I take it."

"Yes, and there are some very fat and happy alligators to prove it." Lew didn't need to know more. And with the small talk over, he got down to business.

"You held the plane?" Lew asked.

"*Sí*. But this was not easy, especially with your no-kill request. Whoever you're fucking with has some serious juice."

"But the plane is here."

"*Sí*, on the other side of that building. But we have to go now."

They drove around the back of the building and as they came around the far corner, the supersonic jet came into view. They were in a remote area hidden from the rest of the airfield. Colero pulled the Hummer to a stop on the edge of the tarmac.

"Where's the crew?"

"Inside, but they are seriously pissed. Especially the Australian. He only calmed down when we let him make a phone call."

"Who'd he call?"

"No idea."

"You didn't find a woman on board?"

"No, just two men, including the pilot. But we just pretended to search it when they were off."

Lew stared at the plane for a few moments, trying to hide his concern. She had to be on board, still. Unless . . . no, if they popped the door on a supersonic jet in flight, it would be ripped apart. She was definitely still on board. Whether she was alive or not was a different story.

"Did you bring my toys?" Lew asked, deciding to continue with his original plan.

"Right here, *ese*," Colero said, opening the console between their seats. He pulled out two pistols and some spare clips and gave them to Lew. Lew pocketed the clips and put the weapons into his empty holsters. He'd pressed his luck pretty good back in Jersey, but there was no way he could've ridden in a jump seat if he was packing.

"Okay, ten minutes after I'm on board, let them go," Lew said. He held out his hand and Colero shook it. "We're even, brother." Colero squeezed hard and didn't let go, Lew's stitches aching.

"We passed *even* when you had me get the DEA to hold the plane, never mind the guns, *ese*."

"The DEA? They're not your guys?"

"My guys can't hold a plane. Ever heard of the TSA?"

"So they're actual DEA agents. That work for you."

Colero just looked at Lew and neither confirmed or denied anything.. In a flash Colero's eyes had gone from friendly to feral.

"What do you want?" Lew asked.

"When you've done whatever good deed you're doing, I want just one thing."

"What's that?"

If he says my soul I'm going to shoot him in the face.

"The ride," Colero said nodding toward the supersonic jet. Lew didn't hesitate at all.

"Deal."

Colero smiled and let go, his eyes instantly softening. "*Buena suerte*," he said, wishing Lew good luck.

Lew got out of the Hummer and, after checking the area, made his way to the plane. He thought about what he'd just promised. If he came through he'd be creating the first supersonic drug dealer in the world. But in reality, he knew he'd be lucky to get out of this thing with his skin, never mind the plane.

Lew slipped on board and after a quick check saw that the plane was indeed empty. Of course, he knew from the years he and Jonathan had slipped artifacts around the globe that just because something looked empty, didn't mean it was. It took him only a couple of minutes to find the false floor. He raised the panel—aware he only had about five minutes—and felt something tighten in his chest. There she was. Emily was tied up, wearing a gag and a blindfold.

He wanted to lift her up and run out of there, but if he did Jonathan would be lost. There was still a chance they weren't going to where Jonathan was, but it was all he had.

He thought the blindfold made her even prettier, if that was possible. *She's probably scared out of her mind,* Lew thought. He had only a moment but he wanted to put her at ease, let her know that he was there and nothing was going to happen to her. He leaned down next to her ear.

"It's okay—AH!" The second she'd heard a voice next to her ear, Emily had slammed her head forward and head-butted Lew above the eye. "Jesus, it's me, Emily. Lew."

Rubbing the welt forming over his eye, Lew got her to calm down, explaining she had to sit tight for just a while longer. She struggled at first, but eventually calmed down when he held her hands.

"I promise I'll keep you safe, but right now you have to be quiet or this whole thing is going to be blown."

Lew put the panel back in place, looked out the window, and saw the men leaving the building. Time was up.

Knowing true smugglers always have more than one hiding place, Lew moved to the back of the plane and looked for an empty place to hide. With moments to go, his fingers slipped under the edge of a wall panel. He pulled and the panel came away. It would be a tight squeeze, but he'd fit.

Lew wedged himself in and pulled the panel shut behind him, the clips that held it in place clicking just as he heard voices on the other side. He leaned back, got as comfortable as he could, and then pulled one of the weapons. He checked that it was loaded and then slid the clip back into the handle. He pointed the weapon at the panel and waited.

40

Tartaruga Island
9:30 P.M. Local Time

SOPHIA SAT ON the floor in the back corner of her lab, gently stroking Lucy's twitching head. She knew in Lucy's current unmedicated state she probably wasn't even aware of the caressing, but the strokes weren't really for Lucy.

The door to the lab buzzed, telling Sophia someone had used their pass card to unlock it. She quickly got up and put Lucy back in her cage, then busied herself at one of the stations. A few moments later, Nathan and Lara came in. Nathan had a metal box in his lap.

"Sophia?" Nathan's electronic voice called. "There you are," he said when she walked out from behind the station.

"Hard to be anywhere else with your Gestapo outside the door," Sophia said. Lara rolled her eyes, but that was all. No snide comment or derisive banter. And she kept flicking her gaze to Nathan. Sophia thought she seemed antsy. Almost nervous. A state Sophia had rarely seen her in.

"I want you to do a DNA profile on the eyes in this case," Nathan said. Lara took the box from his lap and put it on the counter. "I'll have another sample for you soon. You'll need to profile that one as well and cross-match the two—make sure they're from the same donor. If all goes well, you'll need to prepare one more serum. The *final* serum."

"Final serum?" Sophia repeated, knowing what that meant. "How can you be sure that—"

"I'm sure. That's all you need to know."

"Who's the donor? Where are the eyes from and why don't you have the other sample yet?" Sophia asked.

"Don't worry about the details. You just take care of the science," he said.

"Wait a minute," Sophia said as Nathan wheeled away with Lara behind him. He stopped and turned back. "I want to know what's going on." She would have preferred to do this one-on-one with him. She could feel Lara's eyes burning into her.

"Sophia, you're told what you need to know, just like always. You know I'm a busy man and I don't have time to explain everything. Now get to work. You don't have much time."

"That's not good enough," Sophia said, stepping forward, her recent revelations fueling her uncharacteristic backbone. It was such an unusual stance for her, both Nathan and Lara jerked back a little. "You have time to explain things to Lara. I'm . . . just as much your daughter as she is." Her voice cracked a little, but she cleared her throat to cover it.

"Oh please, Sophia. Play your games on your own time. We've got work to do," Lara said.

"And what I'm doing isn't work? But that's beside the point. Where's Jonathan? And for God's sake, why is his daughter here? And why wasn't I invited to dinner? What did you talk about that I couldn't know?" The questions riffled out of her like vomit. Once she started she couldn't stop and they just came faster and faster. "And the guards. Since when is there a guard posted outside my lab? I gave you the neuro-blocker. Is he protecting me or keeping me in? I don't see why—"

Lara stepped forward and slapped Sophia across the face. Hard.

"Get a hold of yourself. You're acting like a fool. Do as you're told," Lara scolded.

That was the last straw for Sophia. Her anxiety, fear, and anger came rocketing up out of her chest in the form of a closed fist punch into Lara's face. Lara's head rocked back and she stumbled for a moment before righting herself.

"You little bitch!" Lara lunged at her, but Sophia was ready.

"Stop it. Stop this," Nathan said, rolling to the left out of the way of the fighting women. He seemed to be more interested in protecting the sample than in stopping them from hurting each other.

Arms locked on each other's shoulders, the girls spun around, a blur of black and white. Lara had the training and height, but Sophia had fear and anger, a powerful combination. They danced around the lab, slamming into workstations and sending glass flying where it smashed on the floor. Then the other would get the upper hand and they'd dance the other way, sending more glass smashing to the ground. They were destroying the lab, which was almost as satisfying to Sophia as the idea of strangling Lara.

"Stop this. Stop acting like children. Lara. Sophia. Stop it," Nathan said again, spinning his chair this way and that to avoid the whirling dervish crashing through the lab.

"I hate you! You're a weak, pathetic fool!" Lara shouted as she fought.

"At least I'm not sleeping with Thomas so I can hear Father's secrets!" Sophia shouted back,. It was a guess—Thomas had come into her lab more than a few times reeking of Lara's perfume—but she could tell by Lara's reaction she'd hit pay dirt.

Lara howled at the revelation in front of Nathan, who went silent when he heard this. She said, "I'll kill you, you ungrateful bitch!" Lara lunged, her eyes wild with rage. Sophia dodged the attack at the last second. But Lara had put so much into her lunge that she couldn't stop. She slammed facefirst into the workstation counter, blood shooting into the air, and fell to the ground dazed.

Sophia took the opportunity and jumped on her back, hooking one arm around Lara's throat, both women being cut by the broken glass scattered all over the floor.

"Who am I supposed to be grateful to? You?" Sophia demanded, holding her sister in place.

"I'm not the one who was sent to university. I'm the one that had to stay here. I'm the one that had to—" Lara let that last go unfinished as she pulled on Sophia's arm, trying to free herself.

Sophia reached down and picked up a long, pointed hunk of broken glass and pressed it to Lara's throat.

Everyone got very quiet.

"Do it," Lara hissed. "Destroy me, then maybe you'll see who Father really is."

But she already knew. Didn't she? Regardless, Sophia couldn't do it. She realized as she held the shard to Lara's throat, slicing her own palm until blood ran down her arm, that it wasn't Lara she hated after all.

The hesitation was all Lara needed.

Suddenly she grabbed the shard and bucked backward, throwing Sophia off—right into Nathan's wheelchair, knocking it over and sending him sprawling onto the ground.

The sight of the helpless Nathan squirming on the ground took the fight out of both of them. Sophia called the guard in and they got Nathan back into his wheelchair.

"Get yourself cleaned up," Nathan said to Lara. "We don't have much time."

"But Father—"

"Now."

Reluctantly, Lara turned to leave, but before she did, she leaned in to Sophia and said, "I wouldn't have hesitated." Then she flipped her bone-white hair back and marched out of the lab, still gripping the bloody shard that had almost ended her life.

"Get your hand cleaned up and then get the eyes profiled. We need to be ready." Before Sophia could say anything more, Nathan spun around and left with the guard at his side.

Sophia rinsed her sliced palm in one of the lab's sinks and wound gauze around it to stem the bleeding. Then she swept up as much glass as she could, getting the lab if not clean at least tidy enough so she could work. Before she could start the DNA profile, the anxiety rose in her again, but instead of anger, this time all she felt was despair and loneliness. She crumpled to the floor against the counter, crying. She didn't cry just because she was trapped, she cried for the loss of a father she'd never really had in the first place; she cried for her sister, not Lara but the girl she used to be who had been dead and gone for so long; and she cried for a little girl she hadn't even met, but only viewed from a distance through the eyes of a distraught father. She cried for them all, but mostly she just cried because it felt good and it was hers. Hers alone.

They were insane. She didn't know what their little project was, or who would pay the price, but she knew what the endgame was—Nathan's life. And she knew they'd do anything to achieve it. Even if that meant endangering an innocent little girl.

The final serum.

If that were somehow possible, Sophia wondered what would become of her if Nathan didn't need a cure anymore. She was pretty sure the reason he'd kept Kring Laboratories and, more recently, her additional research quiet was to make money off it once the work was complete. But while he needed the research, what about her? Would she serve any purpose once the work was completed? If she wasn't working to save him, she wasn't even sure who she would be. Part of her thought she might just cease to exist.

Cried out, a calm came over her, but her mind kept reeling. She needed to work, needed to be busy. She got up, washed her face, and then took the eyes Nathan had brought her to the DNA profiling workstation. She had been using the DNA-testing-on-a-chip method and apparatus developed by FBI scientists for months now, and knew the DNA test would take only a few hours, but Nathan didn't need to know that. She could use the extra time. She had plans.

Sophia injected the fluid sample from one of the eyes mixed with a chemical onto the chip that was the size of a large postage stamp. Then she put the chip into the testing system, a peripheral computing device that looked more or less like a small inkjet printer. Connected to her laptop by a USB cable, she ran the testing software and sat back to wait for the results. It took her only a few minutes to make her decision.

When her work was complete, she would leave the island with the research—not just what she'd done, but *all* of it. She was finished with this insanity. It was time to help others. And she would start by helping a scared little girl a few floors above her.

"Is it true?"

Lara had been so lost in her fury after leaving Sophia's lab, she hadn't heard Nathan wheel into her room. She turned around to face him.

"Yes," she said. She'd thought about denying Sophia's accusation, but one of the benefits of what he'd told her in his office was that now, aside from keeping him alive, all bets were off.

"How long?"

"Almost a year," she said. Nathan was quiet and seemed to be struggling to look at her.

"Do you love him?"

"Would it matter? I know what has to be done," Lara said. Even before the illness, her father had been one of the proudest and most vain men she'd ever known. It made sense that he wouldn't want anyone around who had witnessed him at his weakest, but it had been a long illness and the list of witnesses was just as long, but she knew her little revelation had just thrust Thomas's name to the top.

"There will be others," Nathan said. "Men of better standing. Men worthy of a Kring woman." She knew he was talking about himself.

"I know," Lara said.

"When he returns from Australia, we'll know if it's time. Best get some rest," he said.

Lara forced a smile, stepped forward, and kissed him on the cheek.

"I'll be ready."

41

Somewhere east of Zanzibar, Africa
1:30 A.M. Local Time

THREE MINUTES AFTER the voices faded away, Lew kicked the panel off and rolled out onto the plane's floor. He hadn't spent this long in the fetal position since he was in diapers, and now he was just as cranky. He groaned as he stretched his legs and back out straight again, hollow cracks emanating from his joints and old wounds. He rolled his neck and looked around the plane's interior.

It was empty and moonlight shone in through the tiny windows and the open door. The air smelled salty and humid, perspiration breaking out on his upper lip. He wiped it off with the back of his hand and stood up.

Through the windows on one side of the plane, Lew could see the tarmac and a jungle beyond lighted by the runway lights. On the other side he saw a small outbuilding and a paved road that led away and down over a crest in the landscape. No one was visible outside the plane anywhere. Worrying that he was too late, he hurried to the false floor and lifted the cover. He exhaled when he saw Emily still bound and alive.

Click.

The door to the cockpit opened without warning. Lew froze. The pilot was still on the plane.

Looking at something on the instrument panel as he pulled the door open, he hadn't seen Lew yet. Lew eased the false floor cover down and duckwalked two yards back into the plane, quietly rolling behind two of the big leather seats. He couldn't be sure that he hadn't been seen or that the pilot wouldn't come back there, so he pulled one of his guns and eased the hammer back, pointing the weapon where he thought the pilot would appear at any moment.

Lew steadied and slowed his breaths until the only sound he made was the blood pounding in his ears. He listened for the pilot's approach. He heard the sound of the cockpit door closing. Then the squish of loafers treading on the plane's lush carpeting— coming toward him. The pilot reached his hiding spot and stepped into full view.

The pilot was facing away from Lew, looking out the windows on the other side of the plane. Lew applied more pressure to the gun's trigger, then he heard a car's engine approaching. If he had to shoot, it would bring everyone running. He thought about trying to jump the pilot, but from the size of his arms and the prison tattoos, he knew it wouldn't be a quick or quiet fight. All he could do was wait.

The squeak of brakes.

The slam of a car door.

The rattle of a tailgate dropping open.

Every sound brought Lew's finger ever closer to pulling the trigger. All through it, the pilot continued to look out the window.

"Dieter! Get your arse out here and help me!" a voice called.

"Bugger me," the pilot said. He spun on his heel and marched back up to the front of the plane.

Lew eased off the trigger and rested the cold barrel against his forehead as he breathed again.

He got into a crouch and looked out the window, staying out of sight. The pilot was just reaching the man who had called him, a tall, blond-haired military type with a beat-up pickup truck behind them. Two uniformed guards stood beside it, a tall, thin form between them with a black hood over its head. Lew knew immediately it was Jonathan from his clothes and stature.

"Yes!" Lew said louder than he meant to. He couldn't help it, the relief pumping through him like a shot of morphine easing his pain. Memories of the first time they'd met threatened to take his attention, but he worked to stay focused, knowing they weren't out of the woods yet. Not by a long shot.

Lew watched them argue for a minute before the pilot reached in the back of the pickup and took out a large metal case. It was heavy from the look of it. The blond-haired man took Jonathan from the guards and they headed back toward the plane.

"Ah, crap," Lew said, holstering his gun. His plane ride apparently wasn't quite over yet. He turned and headed back to his hiding place, seeing the panel lying on the floor and realizing it was a miracle the pilot hadn't noticed. Or had he? "Shit!"

If the pilot had noticed and just figured the panel came off in flight, putting it back in place now would only attract more attention. If he hadn't noticed and he left it where it was, that could cause them to search the plane.

In a flash, Lew decided he couldn't risk touching the panel again. He left it on the floor and looked for another place to hide. In desperation, he opened the lavatory door. Hiding in there had obvious pitfalls, but as it turned out he didn't have to worry about it. There was another door on the other side of the lavatory. He closed the first door behind him and opened the other one into the baggage area in the tail of the plane. *Jackpot!*

Lew stepped in and quietly closed the door behind him. The compartment was completely empty, save for an uninflated raft held to the wall with Velcro straps. On the other wall, secured while it wasn't in use, was some cargo netting. There was nowhere to hide if anyone came through the door.

A few minutes later, he felt the plane's engines rev to life. After warming up, the plane began to move, turning around in preparations for takeoff. It was just about then that Lew realized there was something else missing from the cargo hold—seat belts. The engines revved higher and higher, the uninsulated cargo hold echoing the sound until Lew thought his fillings were going to shake loose. He finally felt the plane roll forward, slow at first but then faster and faster. Lew stood with his feet apart in an effort to maintain his balance.

This isn't so—

The pilot slammed the supersonic engines into full throttle and the plane shot forward like a bullet. Unfortunate Newtonian physics kept Lew in one place, and though he thought he slammed into the back of the cargo hold, it was actually the other way around.

Just as the sonic boom echoed from outside as they broke the sound barrier, Lew's intestinal fortitude ran dry and he passed out.

PART SIX

Wednesday

42

Canton George Reserve
Thirty miles north of Sydney, Australia
12:30 A.M. Local Time

DISORIENTED DIDN'T EVEN begin to describe what Jonathan was feeling. With a booming in his head louder than a steel drum, he'd pulled the bag off his head and opened his eyes to a wild and wondrous moonlit world. He was deep in some kind of jungle, but it was like no jungle he'd ever seen. And for Jonathan, that was saying something.

Greens so deep and rich they were almost black painted the alien foliage around him. Strange-shaped trees stretched up toward the sky, ankle-deep in what looked like giant ferns. A creek babbled in a meandering line through the small clearing, making the scene almost idyllic.

Jonathan touched the back of his head and felt lump number

two left by his Australian friend. After being led into what Jonathan guessed was a plane, the Australian had leaned in close and said through the black bag "One more time, asshole," and then Jonathan had momentarily felt pain explode at the base of his skull before losing consciousness. He put his anger and pain away for now.

On the edge of the clearing, standing out like a rock in a carton of eggs, was a large metal suitcase. It stood on its end, and on top of it was a clamshell DVD player. A little yellow Post-it note was stuck to the screen with two words printed on it: "Play Me."

But the most bizarre sight in this tropical oasis was what lay at his feet. Emily Burrows struggled against her bindings, periodically moaning softly.

How the hell is she still alive?

"Miss Burrows, I need you to get up on your feet. Can you do that?" Jonathan said after untying her and removing her gag and blindfold. He didn't wait for her to agree. He put her arm around his shoulders and gently worked her up. She must have been trussed up longer than he because she was having trouble keeping her legs under her.

Jonathan walked her back and forth along the creek bank, which at first was more of a drag, but eventually she started to work her legs. A few minutes later, she pushed off Jonathan to stand on her own.

"What's going on? Where are we?" Emily asked groggily. Jonathan tested the creek water—a complicated process of him tasting it. It seemed okay, sweet and cool. He scooped some up and splashed it on her face, then scooped some more and let her drink it. When the water hit her system, she suddenly stared in shock at Jonathan. "Oh my God!" she said, backing up, her eyes widening.

"Take it easy," Jonathan said.

"But you're . . . you're *him*. You're The Monarch."

"Please calm down, Emily. We're in a situation here. A bad one. But there's a little girl out there who's in a worse spot. Her life depends on what we do next. And for the record, I'm not The Monarch." She seemed to work that over in her mind for a bit, seeing how it tasted.

"Then who are you?" Emily asked.

"My name's Jonathan Hall. I was at that press conference with you in New York, there was an explosion and then I woke up here. That's all I know," Jonathan said. He was trying to align himself with her. Make her believe he was in the same situation as she, hoping that would break down any defensive walls and get her to trust him quicker. "That and I think we should obey the sign," he said, pointing at the DVD player she had yet to notice. He didn't know what they'd see, and he was pretty sure whatever it was would almost instantly deconstruct his little psychodrama, but it might have the answers they needed.

Emily agreed, though Jonathan noticed she was still casting the odd sidelong glance at him. She was more savvy than she appeared. They took the Post-it note off the DVD player and pressed play.

The screen came to life, showing Nathan Kring sitting behind his desk, bookcases behind him displaying a wide variety of tomes. He'd obviously taken a dose of the serum before turning on the camera, as the wheelchair was nowhere in sight. Nathan seemed to contemplate the camera for a moment before speaking.

"Hello, Mr. Hall. Miss Denham," he finally said, leaning forward and tenting his fingers.

Denham?

"One of two things is about to happen. Either you're going to not only save yourselves, but myself and young Miss Hall in the process; or you're going to be delivered into the clutches of someone vastly worse than how you must currently view me. Which path you take is completely up to you."

Jonathan meticulously analyzed everything in the image, from the background to the facial cues Nathan displayed as he spoke. He couldn't afford to miss a thing. Emily's breathing had quickened and she was leaning heavily on him for support.

"First off, allow me to apologize for my ruse, Miss Denham. As you can see," he said, motioning behind him, "my admiration for your work was disingenuous, though I did come to like you in our short exchanges. You have a keen mind, and in a different world . . . well, there's no point in reverie now. Canton George, the man you are about to meet, is indeed a fan, but not in the way you would hope, I'm afraid. Ever since The Monarch came into his life, it's been his singular goal to erase him from existence. Unfortunately, when your book came out lauding The Monarch for his endeavors, the crosshairs fell on you, as well."

Typical of his ilk, Jonathan thought. He was trying to focus but he couldn't help but wonder what the hell Lew had done to enrage George so.

Jonathan put his arm around Emily reflexively. Despite her shock, he thought she was holding up remarkably well. Meaning she hadn't passed out or thrown up.

"Mr. Hall, it was a pleasure hosting you for the little time you were here. But on to the matter at hand. The assignment I laid out for you wasn't a complete deception. Should you choose the right path, there will indeed be a job for you. Dare I say, the most important job of your life. Now for the choice.

"Option number one—the path I hope you choose—is for you

to indeed break into Canton's estate and steal the item we discussed. Of course, this will be no mean feat, since he knows you're coming. But I'm sure you're up to the task. Bring it to me intact and I promise to release all of you, including your daughter. I'm afraid this is the only option that ensures her safety. Miss Denham doesn't really have a role in this option, but of course you can use her as you see fit."

"Use me?" Emily said, but Jonathan shushed her.

"I'll have my man wait with the plane until sunup. You'll find a map in your pocket with the location indicated. Show him the item and he'll fly you all back here. Show up empty-handed and he'll kill you all," Kring said without emotion. Jonathan checked his pockets and found the folded map he hadn't even known was there.

"Option number two is more straightforward, but less . . . fruitful. In the suitcase you have with you is three million dollars. Head up to Canton's estate and deliver the money, Miss Denham, and yourself to him. Please don't attempt to run off. I'm pretty sure that's what he wants. You see, this is a hunting reserve. Canton has always seen himself, despite being black as night, as the great white hunter. He's placed men throughout his reserve to hunt you down, though he'll no doubt want to execute the kill shot himself. He has promised that if you take the payment directly to the house he'll make . . . it . . . quick and painless. I highly doubt this will be the case. He's also promised to deliver the item to me if you do this, but I hesitate to believe him. Oh, and be aware that if you choose this option I will do my best to care for young Miss Hall. She'll want for nothing as long as I draw breath, which unfortunately won't be long without the item. Which would mean—well, you've met Lara."

Emily had her hand to her mouth and was having trouble breathing. Jonathan's concern for her lessened when Natalie was mentioned. He was fighting a powerful combination of fear and anger, digging his nails into his palm to keep it in check. He figured it was a pretty good bet that regardless of the option they chose, Natalie wasn't going to get much older.

"Choose wisely, Mr. Hall. I hope to see you again. For everyone's sake. Good-bye and good luck." The screen went dark.

Jonathan laid the suitcase down and opened it. It was overflowing with euros. He closed it and picked it up.

"Come on. We better get going," Jonathan said, holding his hand out for Emily. He had no idea how to get out of this, but he knew the first smart move was to not have seasoned hunters chasing you for kicks. Then of course there was the issue of not having any idea how to get to the estate, since he'd never been there before, but a path leading out of the clearing seemed to be the best place to start.

"Are you insane? I'm not walking to my own bloody funeral!" Emily spouted. "Who's Natalie? And how do you know where to go?"

Jonathan could tell by the way she crossed her arms and planted her feet, they weren't going anywhere until he answered at least a few of her questions. He put the case down and took a deep, cleansing breath. With Natalie in the balance he just wanted to run—run and kill. He knew that wasn't the way to anything good, but the urge was overwhelming. Emily needed answers and he needed to calm down. He knelt down at the creek and splashed cool water on his face. It helped a little.

"Natalie is my daughter," Jonathan said, trying to bottle up the emotions hooked to her name. "Kring is holding her hostage on his island. If he doesn't get what he wants . . ." Jonathan trailed off, unable to voice the obvious.

"Your daughter?" Emily said, her tone changing.

"But Kring's wrong on one count, at least. I've never been here before."

"Then why does he think you have?"

"It's . . . complicated. What did Kring mean by his short exchanges with you? What's your involvement with him?" Jonathan asked.

Emily told Jonathan about her encounters with Nathan over the past few days. Everything from the limo enlistment to the bug she planted on him. Through the explanation, Jonathan just listened and nodded, taking it all in. He was fitting it into his current knowledge and trying to figure out if there was a way to use the information. He had no doubt that the limo in her story was the same one that had abducted him.

"And why was he calling you Denham? I thought your name was Burrows?" Jonathan asked, aware of the time passing.

Emily explained her background, leaving out the part about hunting for The Monarch and throwing her degree away.

Jonathan reciprocated with his story of what he had seen in Nathan's complex. He told her about Lara and Sophia and the mice in Sophia's lab. He even told her about the serum that, for a short time, cured Nathan's symptoms.

"He's in a wheelchair?" Emily said. Jonathan could tell she was picturing the man as she'd met him on the beach. She told him about Nathan's stumble near the end of their encounter.

Jonathan had more questions but before he could ask them, they heard the sounds of someone crashing around in the brush just beyond the edge of the clearing. The hunters were starting already. Emily backed up and then stepped behind Jonathan.

Jonathan picked up the DVD player. He hefted it a few times. It might make a satisfactory weapon if he hit the mark. It might at least slow them down enough so Emily could get away.

"Get behind the tree," Jonathan said. When she just stared at him, not understanding, he pointed to the tree then swung the DVD player like a club. She nodded and scampered behind the tree. He moved over by another tree closer to the noise. "When I tell you, start making a racket back there."

"What kind of racket?"

"A loud one. Recite the Lord's Prayer, scream like a chicken, I don't care. Just get their attention."

"Oh, right," she said.

Jonathan ducked behind his tree and listened. When the thrashing was about to break into the clearing, he gave the signal. Emily started making a racket like none he'd ever heard. She seemed to be imitating a whooping crane. Badly.

Jonathan raised the DVD player over his head and was about to step out and hurl it when he heard the sweetest sound in the world.

"What the fuck is that?"

Can it be?

Jonathan's eyes widened and his mouth dropped open when he heard Lew's voice. He stepped out from his hiding place and couldn't believe his eyes. There he was with that same wise-ass grin he'd always had. It was obvious he'd been through the ringer to get there; both hands were bandaged, his duster looked like it had gotten caught in some machinery, and he had a welt over one eye. Jonathan's first impulse was to run over and hug the big lug, but he stuffed that down, cleared his throat, and did his best to act unimpressed.

"About time you showed up," Jonathan said. He smiled despite himself and shook hands with Lew. "I was starting to think they'd popped you when you were on the roof of the limo."

"Yeah, I love you too," Lew said, pulling twigs and vines off his duster.

"It's all right, Emily! You can come out," Jonathan said, letting himself chuckle at her diversion now. Emily stepped out from behind her tree. "This is—"

"Lew!" Emily shouted, rushing by Jonathan and throwing her arms around Lew.

"Easy," Lew said, though he hugged her back. "I'm still recovering from that rocket we rode over here."

"I take it you two have met," Jonathan said.

"Yeah, when we were looking for you, back in New York," Lew said, still having the stuffing squeezed out of him.

"How hard did you look?" Jonathan asked, eyeing the embrace. They finally let go and both of them seemed extremely uncomfortable all of a sudden.

"What do we got?" Lew finally asked.

Jonathan and Emily brought him up to speed on Kring and the deal he'd made with Canton George. They told him about the DVD recording, the suitcase full of cash, and the options they were presented.

"Nice guy," Lew said.

"It gets worse," Jonathan said.

"Doesn't it always?" Lew's grin faded as he looked at Jonathan's face. "Jesus, what—"

"They've got Natalie," Jonathan said, his voice quavering.

"Fuck," Lew said, horror and anger apparent in his tone. He put a hand on Jonathan's shoulder. "No forgiveness this time."

"Not even a little," Jonathan said, trying to stay focused. If they let emotions rule their actions they'd never get out of this.

Before they could continue, Emily interrupted.

"Hang on a second. This isn't making any sense," she said, shaking her head.

Jonathan prepared himself. He'd known this was coming. Emily pointed at him.

"You said you weren't The Monarch."

"That's right, but—"

She continued before he could explain. This time she pointed at Lew. "You said you work with The Monarch and you know Jonathan. In fact, you *called* The Monarch Jonny back in New York!"

"Yeah, that's because—" Lew tried to say, but failed.

Jonathan, despite the stakes around them, found himself smiling at the silliness of the situation. It was like watching a Three Stooges episode and it was just what he needed right now. He also took note that though both he and Lew were offering to explain, she wanted to work it out on her own. He admired that.

"Wait a minute," Emily said, like a puzzle piece that wouldn't fit had finally been turned the right way and *snicked* into place. "You mean you're *both* The Monarch?"

"Yes," Jonathan said with a smile. She turned and looked at Lew.

"Bingo," Lew said with a wink.

"Of course! Oh my God, why didn't I see this. The conflicting descriptions from witnesses, the complexity of the thefts. I thought it was just the unreliability of eyewitnesses or the victims trying to muddle the investigations to protect themselves. It all makes sense now! It would *need* to be two people to work at all."

"You got that right," Lew said.

"What exactly happened here, Lew? No bullshit," Jonathan said, referring to his one-man Monarch job.

"There was . . . an accident," Lew said.

"What kind of accident? Did you kill someone? George's kid or something?"

"No, jeez, no, man," Lew drawled out. "I didn't kill anyone. I don't think."

"Jesus, Lew, would you just say it!"

"I sort of, um, burned down his mansion."

"Sort of?"

"Well, completely, actually. I was bypassing the alarm and I guess I got the wires crossed or something. I'm pretty sure everyone got out."

"And his collection?"

"No, no way. I was the last one in there before the roof came down. That's gone."

"Jesus!" Jonathan kicked the suitcase, leaving a dent in the side. "No wonder he wants us."

"Look, let's get going while I still remember the way out of here," Lew said, changing the subject.

"Going? The only place I'm going is up to Canton George's estate," Jonathan said. "Take Miss . . ." Jonathan looked to Emily to see which name he should call her, but her wide eyes and slight head shake told him she didn't want that information disclosed to Lew just yet. "Take *Emily* out of here, while you can. But watch yourselves. If there was any truth to what Kring said, they'll be looking for us soon."

"I can take care of a couple of well-heeled hunters," Lew said. "But why the hell would you go there?"

"I'm staying," Emily said, both men snapping their heads around when she did. "The deal was for both of us. If he sees just you coming, you won't have a chance, whatever you're planning." She was right about that.

"The only chance for Natalie is up there," Jonathan said to Lew.

Lew took a gun out and tossed it to Jonathan. Then he took out another one and pulled the automatic's slide back, loading a bullet into the chamber.

"Mind some company?"

Jonathan smiled, though he'd known all along his friend wouldn't let him down. He slapped Lew on the shoulder and then looked at Emily.

"Okay, here's the plan . . ."

1:45 A.M.

"HOLY CRAP," LEW said from his position on the hill looking down over the estate. The jungle ended in a cliff, spilling down onto several acres of flatland. George had rebuilt what Lew had destroyed, but *rebuilt* wasn't the right word. *Manifested* better described what had taken the place of the large ranch-style home that had been there before. Now it looked like an English castle, complete with observatory dome on top. Huge floodlights illuminated the mansion and the grounds.

In the distance behind the mansion, Lew could see a tennis court and an in-ground pool complex, the outbuilding looking more like a health club or a temple than somewhere to stow wet bathing suits. To the left of the sports complex was a large grove of mature trees, somehow green on the flat, brown grass that surrounded them. The front of the property was alternating huge patches of grass and concrete, and while there were trees and retaining walls, the trees were decorative, shaped and sparse. With all the windows in the four-story face of the mansion, a surreptitious approach from the front would be almost impossible. The trees in the back were definitely the way to go.

Lew worked his way along the top of the cliff, looking for guards as he went. He hadn't seen any, yet, but he couldn't believe he was that lucky. Unless the message on the DVD meant all the guards were out in the jungle on the off chance Emily and Jonathan had decided to make a run for it. That would be bad. There'd be no telling how many there were, how they were armed, or when they would decide to come sauntering back to the house.

The plan was for Lew to take out any guards and then work his way into the house to get the drop on George and anyone inside. Jonathan and Emily, as requested, had walked up the road with Kring's payment. But with a place this big, even once he got inside, it could take Lew an hour to find them. He was liking this plan less and less.

Twenty minutes later, Lew had worked his way around back and down into the grove of trees. When he reached the last tree, he was still fifty feet from the house, and as it turned out the back of the place had even more windows than the front. He'd have to take a chance.

Lew crouched and darted out of his cover, heading for the large granite staircase that sloped away from the house into the yard. It was the closest point, and it would get him onto the terrace that ran along the back of the house halfway up. Once inside, moving from the top down was preferred to trying to work his way up.

Lew made it to the stairs and crouched on the first few steps, his back to the solid granite railing, concealing him from anyone unless they happened to come down the stairs just then. He caught his breath, his nose tickling from the heavy scent of chlorine in the air, and then ascended the stairs in a crouch, his gun drawn.

Flattened against the back of the house, Lew peered around the edge of one of the huge, decorative windows. The inside of the house was just as still as the outside. He moved along to the closest of several doors. In the years since the incident at the previous house on this very site, Lew had made it his business to learn how to bypass alarms. At first, he'd tried it the way Jonathan would approach it. He'd studied alarm manuals and schematics until his head hurt—about a minute and a half—and realized if he was ever going to be successful at this, he'd have to do it *his* way. And so with that approach, he'd practiced and studied until he'd become a craftsman at his way. And that's what he used here.

Lew raised his boot and stomped down on the bottom hinge of the door. Two stomps later the doorjamb cracked, releasing the hinge. He then pressed just above the height of the busted hinge on the center of the door with one hand, and slipped the fingers of his other hand under the bottom of the door and pulled—pulled *hard*. His damaged hands ached and throbbed but some grunting made that go away for the moment. The door was metal but hollow, thankfully, and a minute later the entire bottom third of the door was bent out high enough for him to crawl under.

Once inside—with no alarm sirens sounding—Lew brushed himself off and looked around. He was going to have to hurry now, before anyone noticed the L-shaped door sticking out onto the terrace.

He was in the kitchen, or at least *a* kitchen. It seemed too small for a house this large. He figured this must be a guest kitchen. Doorless entryways led off in several directions, but through them was more dark and quiet. Lew was more nervous than when he'd left Yazoo Penitentiary. Something was definitely off. To the left was a small spiral staircase leading upward. He continued his trek to the high ground and quietly ascended the wrought-iron Slinky.

Lew eased the door at the top of the stairs open and found himself in an empty ballroom larger than a high school gymnasium, the hardwood floor shining in the twilight beaming through several large bay windows. Three chandeliers hung from the ceiling and several glass doors displayed the house's top level as empty and dark. He made his way to the far side and was about to open the door when he saw an alarm control panel on the wall. A green LED glowed on the panel. The alarm was off. Lew rolled his eyes.

When he opened the door, he heard muffled voices coming from below. *Finally.* He had started to feel like he was in a horror movie. The circular hallway wrapped around an empty, railing-lined space that looked down over the main floor. He looked over the edge, feeling a bit of vertigo from the eighty-foot drop, and listened. The voices seemed to be coming from a doorway one floor down. Slowing his pace, he eased his way down the stairs and peeked around the edge of the open doorway.

It was another two-story-high space, a wooden landing running all the way around three sides of the large, square space. Everything in here was shiny, caramel wood—the walls, the doors, the floor—everything. A single chandelier hung down in the center. Below was an equally wooded great room, a fireplace set into one wall and a large patterned carpet on the hardwood floor, various sofas, tables, and chairs scattered around it. On the far side of the room, the only way down was another spiral staircase, this one wooden like everything else. This was as close as Lew would get and stay out of sight.

He eased through the door in a crouch and peered down at the odd scene below. Jonathan and Emily were on their knees by the fireplace, their fingers laced behind their heads. The suitcase was on a coffee table, open and displaying the cash. Lew recognized Canton George, the short and thin black man in a khaki safari outfit standing beside the case. The first odd thing was that George too had his fingers laced behind his head. The second odd thing was the three bodies, dressed similarly to George, lying to the side. Lew could see a few smears of blood on the floor, and from their lack of movement, he assumed they were dead. The only other man in the room, also dressed in khaki, was holding a gun on George.

"Claude's taking care of them, don't you worry," the armed man said. The news didn't seem to console George much. It didn't take a genius to see that one of George's men—or maybe more, depending on who Claude was—were cashing in a little early retirement bond. Lew understood. Despite working in such a luxurious environment, furnishings were hard to pawn, especially when you had to haul them hundreds of miles to the pawnshop. A big case full of cash was another matter and obviously too tempting for them to turn down.

Lew knew the smart move would be to stand up and pop the lone thief now before Claude or anybody else showed up. But seeing Emily kneeling down there stopped him. He didn't want her to see that side of him if he could avoid it. It was stupid and adolescent, but something inside wouldn't let him shake the feeling. He'd have to find another way. Lew thought about going back into the ballroom and crossing the wires in the alarm panel, hoping he could set it off as a distraction, but the last time he did that here . . . no, that wouldn't work.

"How can you do this, Dennis? I treated you like a brother!" George said.

"Shut up!" Dennis said, smacking George in the mouth with his pistol. George fell to his knees and held his bloodied mouth. Just then, another man dressed in khakis came in from outside, a rifle slung over his shoulder. "Did you get them all?"

"Aye, mate. They'll be ripped apart by morning," the rifleman, obviously Claude, said. Lew figured he'd killed whoever else had been waiting in the jungle in case Emily and Jonathan had run, leaving the disposal of their bodies to the wilderness.

Now there were two targets. Things were getting complicated, and his reasons concerning Emily aside, jumping up and shooting was now out of the question.

"What about them?" Claude asked, nodding toward Jonathan and Emily. Lew knew that if they hadn't been searched, Jonathan would still have access to a gun. Lew had put it in Emily's pocket, hoping George would see her as less of a threat. But pulling it now would be a death sentence. Dennis turned his gun toward the kneeling pair, and Lew knew the time for sensibilities and contemplation was over. Out of ideas, he acted on instinct.

Lew crawled up the landing to a set of double doors that led to a sitting room. He opened them both carefully and went in. There was nothing he could use as a weapon, but that wasn't why he'd gone in. He walked as far back as he could, tucked his gun into his waistband so it was snug, and then turned around and faced the open doors.

"Kill them," he heard Dennis say from down below. Lew summoned his courage and with an emboldening shout, he took off. He ran as fast as he could, his thundering footsteps no doubt garnering the attention of everyone in the great room. When he was almost to the railing, he stomped both feet and dove over the railing into mid-air, howling like a maniac, his duster flapping in the air behind him.

"What the fuck!" Lew heard someone yell, but he was too busy to figure out who it was. Arcing down, he snagged the chandelier, ignoring the pain in his damaged hands, and swung toward the wall with his momentum, bullets zipping past him as he reached the swing's apex. One of them cut through his collar and creased his shoulder. He kicked off the far wall, spinning around. The gunman's eyes widened as he saw what was coming, but realized it too late. Lew kicked hard with his boot and caught Dennis under the chin, lifting him off the ground. He slammed to the floor, either out cold or dead, but now Lew was swinging the other way with his back to the room. He braced himself for the gunshot from Claude.

At least Jonny will be able to save Natalie.

The gunshot came and went, but Lew didn't feel anything. As he swung back, he let go at the bottom of the arc and hit the ground in a crouch. He pulled his gun from his waistband and spun around to see if anything was coming at him, but all he saw was Claude lying on the floor, a hole in his forehead. Lew turned to thank Jonathan, but saw Emily holding the smoking gun, the reality of what she'd just done sinking in. Jonathan took the gun from her. Lew was surprised that, despite looking like her knees might buckle at any moment, she was holding her own. But they were so focused on Emily that they forgot about George.

Lew heard the gun's slide pull back behind him. He turned in time to see that George had grabbed one of the dropped guns. He wasn't coming at them, though. He turned toward the man he'd just called a brother, the man who had just hit him in the mouth, and returned the favor. Only George did it with three bullets into Dennis's face. He probably would have fired more, but Jonathan came up from behind him and stripped the gun away.

George turned toward them, panting with what appeared to Lew to be anger. He wiped a trickle of blood from the corner of his mouth with the back of one hand, his eyes flicking back and forth among the intruders in his home. His glare finally came to rest on Lew.

"Who are you? How'd you get in my home?" George demanded.

"Yeah, you're welcome," Lew said. "Maybe you'd like Dennis and his buddy Claude, there, back. Have yourselves a little pistol-whipping party."

"No, of course not," George said, but Lew got the feeling his demeanor change was a show in reaction to his situation, not something he really felt. "My apologies. I think you can understand I'm not myself right now. Perhaps a reward, yes?"

These assholes, Lew thought. Always with the money.

"Sure," Lew said. "How about three million euros?"

"Wait, how do you kno—"

"What about Kring?" Lew said. The phony smile fell from George's face.

"Kring? How do you . . . wait, you're with *them*?" Jonathan pressed the still hot barrel of the gun against George's neck. "Ah!"

"The item you promised Kring. Or my friend here gets careless with the wiring again and burns this place to the ground," Jonathan said.

"Your friend? But I thought you—"

"We're just full of surprises," Lew said, walking over beside Jonathan, though he wasn't sure he liked the idea of this guy knowing it was just he who had taken out his last collection. Then he remembered the image of Emily kneeling with a gun to her head. Nope, he liked this just fine.

"Nice, by the way," Jonathan said, motioning at the still swinging chandelier.

"Thanks. I think I may need to change my pants."

2:50 A.M.

JONATHAN PACED BEFORE a massive oak desk, the automatic held slack at his side. George sat behind the desk, his hands flat on top as Jonathan had ordered after telling him to sit down. There was something odd about George's left hand. It looked natural, but its sheen and lack of movement betrayed the disguise. Jonathan could see by the myriad of photographs hung around the room showing George on various hunting parties that the prosthesis was a fairly recent occurrence.

Following the decor of the great room upstairs, the office was also a cocoon of oak and teak. The air smelled of polish and wood. High up on all four walls were mounted heads of George's kills. His hunting prizes, but Jonathan knew that, like other men he'd met over the years, George's real treasures were not on display.

"How is she doing?" Jonathan asked Lew. He was seated on the love seat beside Emily, who hadn't said much since the shooting. At least she didn't look nauseous anymore. Lew held one of her hands between both of his, which seemed to be helping.

"*She* is still trying to keep her bloody lunch down," Emily responded.

"Sorry," Jonathan said.

"Hell, she's doing better than me," Lew said, stretching his neck. He reached under his collar, winced, and pulled slightly bloody fingers away. "Ain't serious but hurts like a . . ." Lew stopped himself with a side glance to Emily. "Just hurts. We'll both be better off once we get out of this freak show."

Jonathan nodded. He'd never seen Lew affected by a woman like this. Lew had certainly had his share of dalliances, but his behavior and manner never faltered. In fact, it was usually magnified. Emily was special to him. And it seemed to be mutual.

"I hear that," Jonathan said, offering Emily a slight smile. He turned back to the desk, rapping on it with the barrel of the gun. "Let's go. The item. Now."

"This desk was a gift from a British earl. It's over three hundred years old," George said to Jonathan, though he kept looking at Lew. Jonathan easily distinguished George's South African accent, a smattering of lightly rolled r's and hard consonants.

"Is that so?" Jonathan said. He raised the gun and fired a bullet into the wood, garnering George's full attention. The South African shielded his eyes from the explosion of splinters. "The item!"

"*Kak!* You're insane. How do I know you won't kill me the second I give it to you?" George said, looking at the ruined corner of the desk. A darkness slid across his eyes and Jonathan knew if given the chance, George would kill them all without batting an eye, which of course had been the plan all along. This was not a man used to being told what to do.

"You don't."

"Give us the item or we'll call the authorities and you can explain how you helped kidnap a little girl and launch a terrorist attack on New York," Jonathan said, playing the only hand he had.

If George played hardball, they'd have to find the vault themselves and break into it. That would take time. Lots of it. Time they didn't have—time Natalie didn't have.

"I had nothing to do with that. That was all Kring. All I did was tell him what I wanted. His methods were all his own. The man is diseased and unstable."

"And you took advantage of it," Jonathan said. "But he's not just crazy, he's motivated-crazy. You had something he wanted. Something he thinks can save his life. He created a phony serial killer to find The Monarch. Killed dozens of people in the process. All so he could hand The Monarch over to you. But no matter what Kring paid or gave you, I'm guessing you wouldn't have given him what he wanted."

George's stoic mouth formed what might be a smile. Jonathan hated men like this. Men who thought their power and money made them invincible and godlike. No matter what they did, their hands would always stay clean. They were just the orchestrators, the manipulators. Men like this were why he and Lew had created The Monarch in the first place.

"You're a monster," Emily said. "You and Kring, both."

"I say we kill him and get out of here," Lew said, after whispering something to Emily.

"I've got a better idea," Emily said. "Why don't we call Kring and see what he'd be willing to offer for his friend, here. I'm guessing he'd pay even more than he has already. And I'll bet there's a pretty good chance he knows where you keep the item."

Jonathan nodded, understanding their ruse. He picked the phone up off the desk and pretended to dial Kring.

"Wait," George said. Jonathan kept dialing. "Ag, wait, goddamn it!" George slammed his hand down on the receiver.

"Change of heart?"

"If I show you my vault, I need assurances you'll just take Kring's item. Nothing more."

Jonathan looked at Lew and Emily. Lew nodded and shrugged.

"Deal," Jonathan said.

3:20 A.M.

Canton George led Lew, Jonathan, and Emily down a staircase hidden behind a gun display. The passageway was tight and smelled moist.

"How do you know Kring?" Jonathan asked as they walked down. After Kring's psychodrama of sending him in here, Jonathan had no idea if all, part, or none of what Kring had told him was true. Not that he thought he could trust George any better.

"We were business partners—friends, actually. It was many years ago and we were both very different men back then," George said. Jonathan detected something else in George's voice—regret?

"You boys have a lovers' quarrel?" Lew goaded.

The billionaire gave that little almost-smile again, showing he despised the fact someone would talk to him like this. Especially Lew. He stopped, turned, and looked Lew dead in the eye over Jonathan's shoulder.

"Actually, I left him for dead in the Papua New Guinea jungle. But the man just doesn't know when to die," George said. Jonathan recalled his discussion with Sophia and knew what George meant.

"Move," Jonathan said, shoving George ahead.

"Why the hell would you . . . Holy crap," Lew said as they

rounded the corner at the bottom of the stairs. At the end of a short hallway was the door to the vault. But this was unlike any private vault door Jonathan had ever seen. The door was round, six feet in diameter, and made of some kind of blue-green metal, trimmed with copper. The metal shone even in the dim lighting. There were two combination tumblers set into the door, and a standard vault wheel. It looked more like the door to a bank vault. George's smile grew slightly, obviously proud of the impact his baby had on his unwanted guests.

"I hope you understand if I ask you to wait here while I open it," George said. Jonathan didn't see the harm and stood with Lew a few feet back while George approached the behemoth. From the looks of it, the door weighed in at over a ton, so there was little chance George could pull the door open faster than they—or their bullets—could traverse the space between them.

Jonathan looked at Lew and nodded toward George. He wanted Lew to continue their conversation about Kring, prying out every morsel of information that he could. Lew got the message.

"So you were saying, you left your best friend to die in the jungle. Why?" Lew said.

"It wasn't quite that simple," George said as he spun the first combination lock. "We were best friends back then and we'd made the same mistakes. We'd both played the part of billionaire playboy, ignoring the companies our fathers left to us. It was almost a competition to see who could destroy their family heritage first. As it turned out, we tied.

"Nathan heard about a cache of gold lost in the Papua New Guinea jungle during the war. If true, it was a treasure that could have saved both of us. Seeing our way of life coming very quickly to an end, we teamed up and went after it, spending every dime of what we had left. It was a foolish endeavor and I don't think we really expected to find anything. It was more a final adventure before reality came crashing down," George said, moving to the second combination lock.

"Let me guess, you found the gold and left your friend to rot so you could keep it all," Lew said.

"You're partly right," George said, turning to face Lew. "We found the gold, all right. But what I didn't know was that Nathan had made an arrangement with our guides. Halfway down the mountain, tribesman surged out of the jungle. They spirited Nathan away and then proceeded to kill everything that moved. I lost most of my party, but our firepower managed to turn the tide. When it was over, I assumed Nathan was either dead or doomed—the Papua New Guinea tribes back then still heavily practiced cannibalism—and I wasn't about to wait around for the tribe to regroup so they could attack again. We left with the gold.

"Two years later, Nathan surfaced. He wanted his share. By then I'd learned what he'd tried to do, so I told him to go to hell. The only thing he had left was that island of his. I figured he'd retreat to it and die like he should have done years ago."

"But he didn't," Emily said.

"He found his father's collection," Jonathan said.

"Yes," George said, his face showing he was as surprised as Lew and Emily that Jonathan knew that part of the story. "The collection was more valuable than all the gold we'd found."

George finished opening the second lock and then spun the vault's pegged wheel, clanks and scrapes echoing in the small space.

"You can imagine my surprise and delight when Nathan came to me six months ago. Apparently I had something he needed. He offered me millions, but I turned him down. Then I realized a man like Nathan, his network, and how he did business, was the answer I was looking for."

"What was the question?" Lew asked.

"How to get revenge on The Monarch," Emily said.

"Exactly," George said, pulling on the massive vault door. Perfectly balanced, it didn't seem to take much effort at all to open it. As it swung open, lights inside the vault flickered to life. "But if I can't have that, I'll take solace in helping you destroy Nathan."

"The enemy of my enemy," Jonathan said, not really buying it. You didn't spend the time and money George had, just to suddenly abandon your goal for something else entirely.

"Maybe not friends," George said, stepping into the vault. Just inside the door, he turned around and spread his arms. "But I'll settle for cohorts."

They stepped inside, making sure to keep themselves between George and the door. Getting caught in here would be a final mistake.

The inside of the vault reflected the door's opulence and shine. Blue-green metal edged with copper lined the walls and ceiling. Halogen bulbs ran in semicircles around the ceiling. The floor was bright alabaster marble. Even the few chairs and stools scattered here and there continued the color scheme. There were a few tables around the grocery store-sized confines of the vault, presumably for viewing items. Controlled and cooled air flowed inside, a slight breeze wafting out of a few vents around the room.

But this was like no collection Jonathan had ever seen before. There were no paintings or sculptures, no gold or jewels. Not even any antique documents. The entire collection consisted of about a dozen pedestals, displaying their treasure beneath glass cases. The treasures themselves were not immediately identifiable.

"What the hell is this?" Lew said, as he and Emily leaned in close to the first case by the door. Inside it was a blackened, misshapen item, held in place by copper prongs, the entire contents of the case immersed in some sort of clear fluid.

"My collection has changed somewhat since your . . . cleansing. I have you to thank, really," George said, his hands behind his back as he rocked on his feet, like someone waiting for a recipient to guess what present they'd just been given. The smile was back too.

"Thank? Thank me for what?" Lew said.

"For the clarity you gave me. My previous collection consisted of works produced by others. By-products. Waste of the true treasures."

"True treasures," Lew repeated. Jonathan could tell by the look on his face he had no idea what George was talking about. Jonathan wished he didn't. "This . . . briquette is a treasure?" Lew said, hitching his thumb at the item.

"Most assuredly. It's the first and, for obvious reasons, the closest to my heart. Though nowhere near the most valuable in dollars."

"But what—"

"Oh my God," Emily said, stepping back from the case.

"It's his hand," Jonathan said.

"His . . ." Lew trailed off as George raised his artificial hand so Lew could get a good look at it. "You mean?" Lew looked closer at the item again and recognition fell across his face as he apparently discerned the fingers and thumb at the top of the burnt appendage. "Jesus Christ!" Lew jumped back from the display.

Instead of being offended, George was titillated, laughing as he walked deeper into the vault.

"And all of these?" Lew asked, pointing at the rest of the displays in the collection.

"Human body parts," Jonathan said.

"Oh, but they're much more than that," George said. "These are pieces of genius. Think about it, what would have more value—van Gogh's paintings, or the ear he cut off? A scroll from the 1200s, or the actual heart of a Templar? The cup that caught Christ's blood at the crucifixion, or the actual blood the cup held?"

"This is sick," Lew said.

"Actually . . ." Emily began.

"Don't tell me you agree with this lunatic?" Lew said.

"It's not something new. The sale of famous, historical body parts has been around for hundreds of years. Probably longer," she said.

Emotionally, the idea turned Jonathan's stomach as much as it did Lew's, but logically, he could understand the concept.

"People actually pay money for this?" Lew asked.

"A great deal of money, trust me," George said. "But commerce aside, almost every Catholic Church has relics, usually embedded into their altars."

"Relics?" Lew asked.

"Pieces of saints' bodies. The Vatican distributes them as a kind of reminder that miracles, at least at one time, actually happened," Emily said.

"And let's not forget the mummies. Egyptian body parts are on display in every museum around the world," George said.

"Whatever," Lew said shaking his head.

"What did you promise Kring?" Jonathan asked George, all too aware of the time slipping away from them. "Where's item CS–231?"

George remained silent, obviously having second thoughts.

Jonathan nodded to Lew.

Lew walked up to a display case with what looked like a lump of clay in it, and tapped the barrel of his gun against the glass.

"How much did this one cost you?" Lew asked.

"You wouldn't! You promised—"

"So did you. Play hardball and you'll have a steel box full of garbage. The choice is yours," Jonathan said.

Canton George's face turned lobster red, his hand clenching and unclenching. He paced back and forth, panting like a caged animal. He was powerless and he knew it, but he was so used to being in control it must have been like a foreign flavor on his silver tongue.

Without pretense, Lew smashed the display. Glass shattered and fluid rushed out onto the floor, the item flopping to the ground like a dropped oyster.

"No!" George screamed, moving toward Lew. Jonathan raised his gun and stopped him.

"Uh, uh, uh. The item."

When George remained stubborn, Jonathan nodded to Lew and he stepped over the mess to the next display case, a larger one with bits of bone in it. Lew tapped the glass. Emily turned away, apparently preparing for another crash and splash.

"Going once, going twice—"

"Stop! Fine, I'll give it to you. Just take this maniac out of my house."

George went to the back of the vault and unlocked a cabinet. He took out a contraption and brought it over to one of the tables.

"What is it?" Emily asked.

"It's a transport case for Kring's item, nitrogen cooled," George said. He punched a code into it and the contraption hissed open, oozing cold vapor. Then he reached around behind a nearby display and pressed something. The glass around the item also hissed open, more cool fog blossoming as the interior mixed with the vault's room temperature. Using a pair of copper tongs, he took a small lump out and put it into the cryocase, sealing it inside. "There. Now go."

"What is it?" Jonathan asked as Lew picked it up.

"The anterior prefrontal cortex from the greatest mind in human history," George said, his mood seeming to lighten at the prospect of telling someone about one of his treasures, even if he was about to lose it.

"Whose mind?" Emily asked, moving closer to the item.

"Albert Einstein's," George said, his chest practically swelling with pride.

Jonathan's, Lew's, and Emily's mouths dropped open simultaneously. Lew took the case out from under his arm and held it out in front of him with both hands, like it might explode if he wasn't careful. A long time seemed to pass before anyone spoke.

Incredulously, Emily said, "*The* Albert Einstein."

"Is that even possible?" Lew asked, shifting only his eyes to Jonathan.

"Back in the fifties," George said as he paced, the gun pointed at him unable to deter his lecture, "when he died, Einstein left instructions that stated he was not to be autopsied. He wanted to be cremated and his ashes secretly dispersed. He was not fond of the rock star attention he'd garnered by that point and was afraid that he'd become an even bigger postmortem celebrity."

"So how—"

George cut Lew off. "He left instructions, but it's very difficult to make sure the world follows your wishes when you're dead. The pathologist on duty that night in the Princeton Hospital lied. He said he had permission to perform an autopsy. No one is sure why.

In any case, during the autopsy the doctor removed Einstein's brain and eyes."

"His eyes?" Jonathan said.

"Yes, apparently they're still in a safety deposit box somewhere in America, but no one knows for sure. It's all just rumors. But the really interesting thing is that the pathologist didn't even have the skill or training to remove and preserve a brain, much less a brain revered by the world as the epitome of genius.

"Einstein's son did end up giving his permission after the fact. Again, something that didn't fit what everyone at the time expected to happen. Isn't that delicious?" George asked, grinning widely now.

"As a phlegm sandwich," Lew said.

"Yes, well, in any case, the legal issues were handled. The extracted brain was sectioned and kept in a basement for years before anyone agreed to do any kind of study of it. When it was finally examined, the results showed that Einstein's brain was just an average brain. In fact, a little less than average in size, weight, and density."

"Huh? But how could someone that supersmart be—"

"Aha, because it *wasn't* his brain," George said, appearing incredibly pleased with himself. "The sectioned brain wasn't Einstein's. The theory is, there was a switch, and Einstein's brain—the real one—was extracted and preserved by a true expert who later sold it at auction. The supposed pathologist of record was just a paid-off stooge. Sometime after that, someone cut the real brain into pieces so they could sell it several times and make more money. Over the years, the pieces have vanished."

"Jesus," Jonathan said.

"This is the last known piece in existence," George said, waving his hands and practically saying, *Ta-da*.

"How do we know you didn't just give us a lump of cheese?" Lew asked.

"There's a letter of authenticity in the base of the cryocase. Beyond that, I'm afraid you'll just have to trust me," George said.

Jonathan worked to process everything they had just been told. That story plus the cryocase, which meant the item was still viable, explained why Kring wanted it. If what Sophia had told him was true, it was the extra step Kring needed for a cure. A *permanent* cure. It was the last thing Jonathan wanted to give the bastard, but the only thing on the planet that could save Natalie's life.

If they weren't already too late.

43

Tartaruga Island
9:30 P.M. Local Time

Sophia stood just outside Nathan's office, summing her courage to confront him about Jonathan's daughter. She knew he'd be mad that she'd slipped past her guard, but she didn't want to risk asking to leave, only to be denied. She also knew she was in the right, but even with her recent revelations, facing off with the man who had been posing as her father all these years practically terrified her. She'd almost calmed herself enough to enter when she heard something that terrified her even more. It froze her to the spot where she stood.

"Call Thomas. Tell him Mr. Hall and Miss Denham are coming and they've got the item. He's to meet them on the tarmac," Nathan said.

"You're not really going through with this, are you?" Lara asked.

"And tell Sophia to be ready with the DNA profile from the eyes Thomas brought back from Pensacola. I have no doubt George's item is authentic, but we have to be sure," Nathan said.

"But—"

"Enough! The future—our future—hinges on what we do in the next few hours. I need you to listen and obey. To the letter. Do you understand?" Sophia had a feeling "our future" didn't mean her future.

"Yes. I understand," she said.

"Good. The exchange will occur in the courtyard. I want you to position our two best sharpshooters on the roof around the courtyard. When I give the signal, they are to open fire." Sophia put her hand to her mouth to stifle a gasp.

"Their targets?" Lara asked.

"Everyone but you and me. No one gets out of that courtyard alive."

"Even the girl? Natalie?" Lara asked, sounding more surprised than shocked.

"Especially the girl. Give orders to shoot her first. I want to see it in Hall's eyes. I want to see him realize who the best man is. Just before The Monarch dies."

Sophia pressed back into the shadows as Lara left her father's office, a determined resolve in her stride. When Lara reached the elevator and the door had closed, Sophia ran the other way. If Lara was going straight to the lab, she had only a few minutes.

I have to get Natalie out!

At the end of the hall, Sophia gripped the grating covering the access way to the bowels of the complex and pulled it open. She hurried inside and pulled the grating closed behind her.

Hunched over, Sophia ran along the cramped tunnel to one of

the ladders that connected the levels. She climbed down as fast as she could, but knew she'd gone no faster than the elevator. At the bottom, she jumped off the ladder and ran, the pounding of the generators beneath her feet tickling her ears. She reached the access panel to the lab, kicked it open, and crawled out.

She ran to the door, pulling out her access card as she went. She could hear footsteps on the other side, but it was impossible to tell how close they were. Sophia collided with the door and ran her card upside-down through the slot twice in rapid succession. The light above the reader blinked red. She continued running the wrong side of her card through the slot reader. After the fifth pass, the panel emitted a long beep and the light turned solid red. She'd forced the electronics to lock down the mechanism. It would be an hour before the reader would accept a valid card again, though she doubted Lara would wait that long. Sophia looked at her watch as she ran to her computer. She figured she had about ten minutes before Lara had the guards break the door down.

She dug through a drawer filled with miscellaneous junk, finally finding the little USB hard drive. She plugged it into her computer and started to copy the data. She had to save Natalie, but there was no way she was leaving without the research.

As she watched the progress bar on the computer screen slowly crawl toward one hundred percent, she heard someone trying to use a security card on the lab door. After several tries, someone banged on the door and cursed. When the door went quiet, Sophia checked her watch again.

While the data transferred to her drive, Sophia ran to the refrigerator and took all the remaining serum and baselines over to the sink. It was probably futile, but if she failed to save Natalie, she thought it would at least be harder for an unmedicated Nathan to execute his plan. She put one vial of the serum into a bag she grabbed from her office and dumped the rest into the sink. When it began taking too long, she just smashed the glass and ran the water, flushing her work down the drain.

The data transfer was barely at fifty percent.

She stood running her hands through her hair. What was she forgetting? Nothing could be left behind for them to reconstitute her serum. She saw her shelf of logbooks. There was no time to shred them all and she couldn't carry them.

She pulled a large garbage receptacle over by the exhaust fan and then ran to the shelf, pulling down all her notes. She dumped them all in and poured in a bottle of sulphuric acid. The books smoked for a minute before bursting into flames. Most of the toxic smoke went out the vent, but some of it leaked into the lab. Sophia coughed and covered her mouth and nose with her sleeve.

The computer beeped that the data transfer was complete. Sophia grabbed the USB drive and put it in her jeans pocket. Then she initiated the wipe command—a security protocol that would wipe the hard drives of their data and prevent their recovery by all but the most dedicated computer forensic team.

Suddenly a bell sounded and the sprinklers in the ceiling burst to life, showering everything in the lab with a combination of water and fire retardant foam. Sophia grabbed her bag and slipped the eyes Thomas had brought for her to test into it, along with a few personal items. This wasn't how she'd wanted to leave her life in the lab, but there was no time for melancholy. She wiped water and foam from her face. Darting to the back of the lab, slipping and almost falling, she unlocked all her animals' cages. Everyone went free today.

Stepping carefully over the fleeing animals, she hurried back across the lab and into the access panel. It wouldn't shut properly, so she just pulled it closed as best she could. She'd kicked it open a million times as a child, but her mature leg muscles had damaged it in her rush.

Out of the foamy rain, Sophia took off her lab coat and used it as a towel, wiping the water and foam off her face and body. Then she headed back down the tunnels to the ladder and headed up to level three.

The alarm was still sounding when she crawled over to the welded vent that led to Natalie's cushy prison cell. She peered in and saw that though Natalie could hear the alarm, it just seemed to be an annoyance to her rather than a danger.

Tough kid.

Sophia took the small vial of sulphuric acid out of her bag and carefully poured it along the vent's welded seam. As the acid drew the moisture out of the metal, slight toxic smoke rose into the air. She stepped back so she wouldn't inhale the poison. When she gave the vent a kick, the remaining seam cracked and the cover sprang free. She slipped inside, the screeching alarm hiding her entrance from both the guard outside the door and Natalie.

Sophia eased up behind her and put her hand over Natalie's mouth so she wouldn't scream. The girl looked up with wide, confused eyes.

"Relax, honey. I'm a friend of your dad's," Sophia said. "I'm going to take my hand away. Okay?"

Natalie nodded, her wide eyes narrowed as she evaluated this stranger's story.

"How do you know my dad?" Natalie asked.

"He helped me with a recent . . . problem. So I'm returning the favor. How'd you like to get out of here?" Sophia said, unsure of what exactly she would do if Natalie said no. It didn't matter. Natalie smiled and nodded.

They gathered up Natalie's drawings, put them in her knapsack, and then slipped through the vent into the noisy tunnel. Sophia closed the vent cover, which unlike the one in the lab, married up well with the severed seam. She turned around and took Natalie's hand, leading her deep into the complex's innards, to a place Sophia had never shared with anyone.

44

Australia
4:45 A.M. *Local Time*

"THERE IT IS," Lew said from the backseat of the Land Rover they had liberated from the Canton George Estate. After calling Kring and telling him they were coming, they'd locked George in his own vault. Jonathan glanced back and saw Lew's new toy in his lap: a sniper rifle from George's gun cabinet.

Jonathan, driving with Emily in the passenger seat, didn't see the car Lew said he'd stolen to get out to the reserve, but he drove up a rock outcropping on the side of the road Lew pointed at anyway. The three of them got out of the Land Rover, Lew taking the rifle, and walked through the long grass lining the dirt road. It was cool in the early morning dim, and Jonathan wished he had his own duster about then. In the distance, Jonathan could hear traffic on the main road, though it was still out of sight. Behind the rock outcropping, Jonathan saw Lew's stolen car covered in branches. Jonathan helped him clean it off.

"You walked from here?" Emily asked as she watched them work, awe in her voice.

"Jogged, actually. If they hadn't been hauling you two over their shoulders, I never would have caught up to them. Well, in time. They left a trail through the jungle like a herd of elephants running from a mouse." Lew tossed the rifle in the back of the car. Jonathan held out his hand, but when Lew shook it he didn't let go.

"What?" Lew asked.

"Nobody dies," Jonathan said. He wasn't just talking about them or expressing a consideration for human life. They needed the pilot and they had no idea if Kring's man had made arrangements to contact Kring en route or not.

"No worries," Lew said with a smile. Jonathan would have felt better if Lew didn't seem like he was enjoying all of this.

Abruptly, before Lew could get in the car, Emily kissed him on the cheek. Jonathan thought Lew looked like someone had sent a jolt of electricity through him.

"For luck," Emily said, her eyes darting to Jonathan before her cheeks flushed red and she headed back to the Land Rover.

Lew cleared his throat and seemed to avoid Jonathan's glare as he got in the car. He started the engine and rolled down the window.

"Remember, give me ten minutes," Lew said, his arm crooked out the window. Lew was going to position himself at the airport so he could cover Jonathan and Emily when they arrived at the plane.

"What do you want, a kiss? Get the fuck out of here," Jonathan said with a wink, slapping the roof of the car before backing away.

"Asshole," Lew said before gunning the engine, shooting dirt up into the air and heading on down the road. He gave the horn a toot and waved his arm as he went.

Jonathan joined Emily at the Land Rover as they watched Lew's car disappear around a bend.

And then the longest ten minutes of Jonathan's life began.

"You had to do it," Jonathan said when he thought he saw Emily retreating into herself. She looked at him and smiled sadly.

"I know," Emily said. "I was just thinking about how I'm going to tell him that my bio and name are phony."

"Right," Jonathan said. It was then he realized Lew and Emily might be feeling more than the bond of two people in the same kind of trouble.

"I finally—" Emily started to say before she sighed and opened the passenger door. "Never mind." She got in and closed the door, slumping in the seat with her arms crossed.

While she sat alone in the Land Rover, Jonathan stood beside it, leaning against the hood and staring at the beauty around him as the sun started to come up. He thought about Natalie's dream about him being with a mysterious woman who saved him from dying. Just a child's wish in disguise. Or was it? Strangely enough he found himself thinking about Sophia Kring. What side would she be on when they got to the island? He thought he knew, but you could never tell. He felt a strange flutter in his chest as he thought about her, but turned his mind to other things. Checking his watch, Jonathan took one last look at the landscape and got into the Land Rover beside Emily, and started the engine.

"Here we—"

The explosion rocked the Land Rover like it was doing the watusi. Jonathan thought they'd been double-crossed, but aside from the rocking and an echo across the Australian morning sky that sounded like a rocket full of thunder, the event seemed to stop. He looked over at Emily, but she was looking out the window behind them.

"Oh my God," she said. "Isn't that about where we just were?"

Jonathan spun around in his seat and then got out when he saw the cauliflower-shaped cloud rising up into the sky. Emily was right. It was the George estate. Or what had *been* the George estate, judging from the size of the cloud.

"What could have happened?" Emily asked when Jonathan got back in the Land Rover.

Jonathan pulled off the shoulder and accelerated down the road. Every now and then his eyes would flick to the rearview mirror to look at the smoke. He had an idea of what had happened but it didn't matter. Nothing mattered except getting to that plane.

45

Canton George's Estate
5:15 A.M. Local Time

CANTON GEORGE WOKE up covered in glass and human flesh. The vault had saved his life, but he'd still felt the blast. He couldn't tell from where he was, but he was pretty sure he could guess what had happened.

"*Kring, jou bliksem!*" he said, calling Kring a bastard. They'd left the metal case of euros up in his office. If they had just been thieves and not after the brain, they would have taken that damn thing with them. As it was, he had no doubt there wasn't much of his house left up there.

It was all gone. Every last human treasure lay scattered on the vault floor, exposed to the air, with glass and debris slicing into everything. At the time of the explosion, George had been partially inside one of the vents, attempting to crawl through. He'd been slapped around inside the vent before falling back into the vault, his torso and face laced with broken glass and stinging from the preservation chemicals.

He couldn't really feel the pain. Not with so much rage boiling up inside him. Rage for both Kring and that oafish half of The Monarch who had destroyed his collection so long ago. What had they called him?

"Lew," George said like he'd tasted something bad. Suddenly, he knew what he was going to do. It would be expensive, in both dollars and favors, but he was so angry he couldn't focus.

George pulled himself up and limped to a panel in the middle of the vault that thankfully had been mostly spared from the blast. After the loss of his last collection—and his hand—he'd taken precautions. Like having the vault supplied with an air circulation system, and an emergency communication line that ran underground all the way to the forest in the back compound where an antenna was secreted atop one of the trees. Those close to him had thought he was being paranoid. If nothing else, this would shut them up.

But he wasn't calling for help. Not yet, anyway.

"A Reaper? Have you lost your mind, George?" the voice on the phone said. His name was Colonel Rudyard Maitland—pedophile, murderer, and base commander of Diego Garcia, the U.S. Navy's base a thousand miles south of India. "I can't launch a military drone on a civilian target, for Christ's sake!"

"You can if you want your secrets kept, Maitland," George said. Even as he uttered the threat, he continued to scan his mind for other ways to entice him and any other impediments. Money wasn't the problem. A fully loaded MQ-9 Reaper drone—or UAV, as the military called them—cost the military about twenty-nine million dollars, though Maitland undoubtedly knew George would pay considerably more.

"I . . . I can't. There's no way to protect myself. My career would be over, at the least!"

"Your career *is* over as of today no matter what you do, Maitland. But it's up to you whether you'll have enough money for retirement in paradise under a new name, or if you'll spend the rest of your life in a cell."

"Oh Jesus," Maitland muttered.

I'm losing him.

And then thinking back to his childhood in the Capetown slums, he realized he could offer something else. Something uniquely tailored for a man such as this.

"How about some playthings too, Maitland. All yours, to do with as you please. No questions asked."

The silence on the line was deafening. If he didn't go for it, George knew he'd—

"How many," Maitland said, breathing as if he'd just run a marathon.

Canton George smiled.

46

Tartaruga Island
10:30 P.M. Local Time

THE CHAIR'S WHEELS crunched and popped as they rolled over the broken glass on the lab floor. The mélange of chemicals mixed with fire retardant foam and stuck to the wheels' rubber, riding up the arc, and making them look like whitewalls. The alarm and the sprinklers had shut off before the door had finally released its lock, not that it made any difference. The damage was done. Nothing of any use remained.

Movement caught Nathan's eye, a twitching mouse sitting on a lab bench across the room. A healthier mouse ran around and around, pausing now and then to stop and sniff the invalid before returning to the important work of showing off. Fury blurred Nathan's vision and he looked away, blinking his eyes clear.

Normally resilient to a fault, Nathan in better days would have already been planning his recovery from such a tragedy. It was how he'd lived his entire life. There was always an alternative, a route back to the top. Always, except now. The absent serums and the blinking computer screens shouting "ERROR ERROR ERROR" all around the lab told him Sophia had taken the research too. Even if they found her, someone who would do this to her own lab would never cooperate again. Without that, he'd have to start all over. But Nathan knew he didn't have time. Even if he could find the money to hire a new staff and restock a new lab, he wouldn't live long enough to see the first trials happen. Without the serum, he'd be dead in a few months, *if* he lasted that long. She'd killed him as surely as if she'd plunged a knife into his heart.

"My God," Lara said from behind him, seeing the destruction for the first time.

"What is it?" Nathan said. He just wanted to be alone, bathe in his despair and depression. Decide on the best way to kill himself.

"She took the girl too," Lara said. "We'll find her."

"Don't bother," he said. Sophia wasn't the one responsible for this. It was Hall. Nathan's plan had backfired; Hall had planted something in Sophia's brain during those few minutes they'd spent together. Lara walked up behind him and put her hands on his shoulders. It was the first time she'd touched him in over a year.

"We need the girl," Lara said. "If you want to lure him in, you need her as bait."

Lure him in. Yes, lure Hall in and use him and his daughter as leverage to force Sophia to cooperate. He'd kill Hall in front of her, just like he'd killed that Bobby at her university. Then he'd hold a gun to the girl's head and Sophia would do whatever he asked. And once she'd done it, then he'd kill the girl. And he'd kill Sophia too. Slowly.

Nathan felt the despair fade and mutate, become something white-hot burning the depression away. The girl was the key.

"Find her," Nathan said. Lara took her hands off his shoulders and headed out, stopping by the wall.

"I think I know where to look," she said. Nathan spun his chair around and saw Lara standing by the bent maintenance tunnel access panel.

"Nothing fancy," Nathan said, rolling out of the room. "They'll be here in a few hours. And Lara . . ."

"Yes, Father?"

"I want them both alive," Nathan said.

"Yes, Father," Lara said, her voice strained.

47

Australia

5:30 A.M. Local Time

"ON YOUR KNEES!" the large Australian shouted.

Jonathan and Emily knelt beside each other with their hands behind their heads for the second time in the past few hours.

"Just take it easy," Jonathan said.

"Shut up," the man said. Jonathan could see into the plane from his position. It looked like there was only one other person in there, a man sitting in the pilot seat busy at the console in front of him. "Where is it?"

Jonathan turned to Emily and whispered, "Stay where you are. Don't give him any reason to do anything."

Jonathan rose to his feet.

"What are you doing? Get down—" Jonathan waved his hand and two chunks of asphalt exploded in front of the Australian's feet.

"The next shot goes through your heart," Jonathan said. "Put your gun on the ground and kick it over here. And tell your pilot to get out here."

This was always a tense moment for Jonathan. The subject would either comply or open fire. But the fact was the pilot was the only one they needed. If push came to shove, this guy was expendable—but that didn't mean he couldn't get a few shots off before Lew took him down from his sniper position.

"Drop it!" Jonathan shouted. He felt ridiculous ordering an armed man to drop his gun when the only thing he was holding was air.

The man scoured the hills around the airstrip, clearly trying to find the source of the shots. Jonathan hoped he could do the math. The hills were several hundred yards away and he was holding an automatic handgun. Even if he spotted a muzzle flash, his situation was untenable.

Elongated seconds stretched out; the man massaged his weapon as he tried to decide what to do. Finally, he gave up on the hills and stared at Jonathan and Emily.

"Dieter! Get out here!" The man put his gun down on the tarmac with a flourish so whoever had him in their sights could tell what he was doing, then kicked the gun over to Jonathan. He picked it up and held it on the Australian and the pilot, who had joined his comrade, as they waited for Lew.

He came out of the forest on the hills, his rifle slung over his shoulder. When he arrived, they tied and gagged the pair and put them in the cargo hold. The pilot went willingly, but the big Australian was obstinate to the end, dragging his feet and continually hooking his legs around the plane's seats as Lew walked him toward the back of the plane. When he'd apparently had enough, Lew grabbed him and slammed him hard against the bulkhead.

"Look, dickwad, don't give me a fucking reason," Lew snapped into the man's ear. "We need your buddy, but you're just dead weight." The man grudgingly nodded and allowed himself to be put in the hold beside the pilot.

"Sorry about that," Lew said to Emily.

Their captives secured, everyone sat around a table to make their plans. Jonathan could feel the time slipping away, tick by tick.

"Okay," Jonathan said, drawing on a piece of paper to help him think. "I never saw the outside of the place, but I got a good tour of the inside."

"Tour?" Lew said.

"Don't ask," Jonathan said. "Kring said there's a runway on the north side of the island. We land there and head down a road to the main compound. There's a courtyard outside the main building. Place looks like an old control tower. That's where the exchange will take place."

"You can't give it to him!" Emily said. "It's practically a national treasure."

"Pretty gross treasure," Lew said.

"I don't care what it is," Jonathan said. "If it gets Natalie back, he can have it. And I'm not going to risk trying to con him. This is a guy who has figured out all the angles. If either one of you have a problem with that, you better speak up now."

No one said anything.

"All right, then."

"Shouldn't we contact the authorities? There are only three of us," Emily said.

"Which authorities?" Lew said. "We don't have any idea who has jurisdiction over Kring's island. Hell, it might be a damn nation on paper."

"Lew's right," Jonathan said. "Besides, there isn't time. Kring knows we're coming and how long it takes to get there. I'm not giving him any reason to pull a fast one."

A banging noise reverberated from the cargo hold, along with muffled shouting.

"Shut up back there!" Lew said. The banging stopped.

"We need to hurry," Jonathan said.

"Okay, so where am I in all this?" Lew asked.

"I figure no matter how aboveboard we play it, he's going to try and get the upper hand. I don't know how many guards he's got working for him, but I saw at least three different ones. You got to figure there are shifts and some I didn't see. We're probably looking at ten."

"At least," Lew said.

"Why don't we ask *them*?" Emily said, looking at the door to the cargo hold.

"That would be nice, but anything they say would be suspect. Bad intel is worse than no intel," Jonathan said.

"If that's the case, how can we be sure they'll even take us to the island at all?" she countered. Jonathan liked the way her mind worked.

"I'll ride up in the cockpit and watch the compass. It's the best we can do. Besides, Nathan wants our care package pretty bad," he said, and then looked at Lew. "As for you, I figure we play it the same way we did here. Give you a head start so you can get into position. Hopefully we'll get a look at the place on a flyover before we land."

"Works for me," Lew said.

They talked about a few more details and worked out the kinks in the plan. Jonathan offered Emily a gun, but she declined.

"Okay, let's get this show on the road," Jonathan said. "I'll see if there's any grub in the galley. I don't know about you but I'm starving."

Lew headed back to get the pilot. The plan was to just leave the big guy back there where he couldn't do any harm.

Jonathan found some sandwiches and bottled water and was loading up a tray when he heard Emily scream. He came running, gun out.

Emily was sitting in the cabin, looking whiter than she had when she'd shot that guy back at the estate. Jonathan made a motion with his hands, asking what was wrong, then followed her eyes. She was looking through the restroom door out into the cargo hold.

"You better get in here, Jonny," Lew called. Jonathan entered the cargo hold and saw what had made Emily scream.

His hands still tied, the Australian had worked his gag off. Blood covered his face. And it wasn't his blood. The pilot's corpse lay bleeding out on the floor.

"Jesus."

"Do you need me now, mate?" the Australian said, spitting out blood. He'd leaned over and bitten through the pilot's neck. Jonathan realized that's what the banging had been.

"You piece of shit," Lew said. "I ought to—"

"Easy, mate. Touch me and you're not going anywhere."

"We'll just get another pilot. The delay will be worth it if it means I get to kill you," Lew said, grabbing him by the lapel and cocking his fist back.

"Go ahead. But good luck finding a pilot. There are maybe fifty pilots in the world that can fly this baby. Well, forty-nine," he said with a smile, his teeth still covered in blood.

"And you're one of them?" Jonathan asked.

"That I am."

"I still say we—"

"Lew!" Jonathan commanded more than shouted. Lew looked at him and hesitated, but eventually let go. He vented his frustration by pounding the bulkhead a few times.

"Fine. But if you so much as turn on a fucking light without checking with us first . . ." Lew said, pressing his gun to the Australian's forehead.

"I get it," he said.

"So you'll fly us to Kring's island?" Jonathan said.

"On one condition."

"Condition? Are you fucking—"

"Lew, go see if Emily's all right," Jonathan said.

"This is a mistake," Lew said to Jonathan before he left, casting a final glare at the Australian.

"Boy's got a temper," the Australian said.

"He's cheerful compared to what I'll be if you fuck this up for me," Jonathan said. "What's the condition?"

"I want the girl. Lara, Kring's daughter. I don't know what you lot are planning once we get there, but I'm thinking there aren't going to be any survivors."

"That's it?" Jonathan asked, finding it hard to believe anyone would want that sneering Hitler in a dress. Sophia, he could understand, but Lara?

"And a ride out of there."

"Done," Jonathan said, and knelt down to untie his hands.

"But take my advice, mate. Whatever you plan, make sure killing Kring is part of it. If he's even got one breath left in him, you, your family, and everyone you've ever known are dead."

"Right," Jonathan said sarcastically.

"Don't dismiss me. You see that explosion after you left Canton George's place?"

Jonathan nodded, getting a bad feeling.

"George wasn't useful to Kring anymore. That metal case of money was lined with C–4. There's nothing left back there but a deep hole. And the same thing will happen to you once you're no longer useful to him."

Jonathan wanted to ignore it as an empty threat, something just to throw him off, but he couldn't. The Australian's voice was edged with pure fear as he talked about Kring. He wasn't scared for Jonathan.

He was scared for himself.

48

Tartaruga Island
6:30 A.M. Local Time

SOPHIA'S EYELIDS SLIPPED down again, her pupils rolling up as exhaustion and the oppressive heat of the tunnels tried once more to put her to sleep. Her head rocked forward and then snapped back up when she caught herself at the last possible moment. She opened her eyes wide and shook her head, taking a deep breath. If she gave in and went to sleep, she and Natalie might never wake up.

Deep in the bowels of the complex, they were in what Sophia used to call her happy place. It was a nook no bigger than a prison cell. At just four feet high, it was only accessible by squeezing through a tight stand of pipes. Though she had played with Lara in the tunnels as a child, even then Sophia had needed a safe place for when Lara went into one of her rages. She'd stumbled onto this nook one day, and had originally intended on telling Lara about it until she'd found her cutting the heads off of Sophia's dolls again, so she'd kept the find to herself.

Whenever things got to be too much, this is where she'd come. Wriggling back into the nook—no small feat for her mature hips now—was like traveling back in time. A young hand's crayon and marker drawings covered the walls. A pictograph representation of her early years. The pictures not all that dissimilar to the ones Natalie now drew, she noticed.

Natalie lay asleep on an old blanket while Sophia sat with her back to the wall. The air was wet and hot, but the concrete was cool on her back. This far from the generators, their throb was reduced to a soothing massage.

Sophia watched Natalie sleep, her back rising and falling. Gently, she brushed a few strands of hair out of her face. Sophia envied this little girl, even in the predicament they were in; both for her blissful childhood naïveté and for her loving father. For a moment, Sophia wondered what Nathan would have done if she'd been kidnapped as a child. She shook the idea away, depression serving no purpose in their current situation.

When Nathan and Lara were meeting with Jonathan in the courtyard, she'd take Natalie out through the data center. The exit let out behind the complex. There was a path that led through the jungle there, which ended several miles away at a helipad. They used the helicopter for hops to the mainland and while she'd hated taking the lessons at the time, she was grateful today.

Natalie coughed and opened her eyes, looking around in that way kids do when they first wake up, as if rebooting their memory takes a moment. She looked at Natalie and smiled.

"Is my dad here yet?"

"Not yet, sweetie," Sophia said, rubbing Natalie's back gently. "Go back to sleep."

"M'kay," Natalie said, her eyes closed before her head was back down on the blanket.

Sophia wondered what had happened in Natalie's life to make her able to handle what she'd been through in the past few days with such aplomb. Kids by nature were resilient, but Sophia thought it was more than that. She wondered if Natalie knew her mother better than Sophia had known hers. Sophia couldn't even picture her mother's face anymore, it had been so long. She relied on a picture in her wallet, which was apparently the only picture of her mother in existence. Nathan had tried to take it from her, saying it wasn't healthy to live in the past, but Sophia had stolen it out of the trash and kept it secretly all these years. She used to feel affection about that for Nathan, thinking he was trying to protect her, but now she wondered what she'd been told about her past, if anything, was true. How had she and Lara really ended up a "Kring"? Was her mother even really dead? Did Lara know any more about this than she did? These and a million other questions zipped through her mind, but before she could spiral further, sounds snapped her back to the here and now.

Voices echoed in the tunnel beyond the pipes again, the guards sweeping past, looking for them. She knew they were safe where they were, but her heart still pounded in her chest as they drew near.

"I tell ya, I did three tours in Iraq but this bitch scares the shit out of me," one of the guards said.

"If we were smart we'd kill her and the old man and then get the fuck off this rock while we can."

"Yeah, and have Thomas hunt us down? No thanks." Sophia heard the squawk of a radio.

"*Delta team, report.*"

"Delta team. All clear. Heading back topside."

"*Roger. Relieve Alpha team at the helipad.*"

"Roger. Out," the guard said. "Let's go. At least we'll get some fresh air. Smells like ass down here."

The guards moved away, and Sophia slumped against the wall. They were guarding the chopper. Plan A just went out the window, no doubt Lara's doing. The problem was, there was no Plan B.

Sophia reached in her pocket and took out the USB hard drive with all the kuru research on it. Could she buy their freedom with this? Her life's work for a little girl she barely knew. Sophia dropped the drive into her bag and rubbed her eyes hard. She was so tired it was difficult to think.

Maybe if she shut . . . her eyes . . . just . . . for . . . a . . .

49

Somewhere over the Indian Ocean

"How much farther?" Jonathan asked from the copilot's seat. Lew and Emily were back in the cabin trying to get some sleep. Jonathan was tired, but he'd had enough pistol-whipped sleep in the past week to last him the rest of his life.

"About ninety minutes, give or take," Thomas said. Jonathan's gun, along with the one he took from Thomas, were in his jacket pockets. He still didn't trust Thomas, but it would take the killer longer to unfasten his seat belt and get out of his chair than it would for Jonathan to draw down on him.

Before takeoff, Thomas had helped them draw a rudimentary map of the complex. Once Lew knew how to get in and where they were holding Natalie on the third level, that was all he'd needed. Jonathan, on the other hand, wanted more. He wanted to know what kind of man could do the things Kring had done, simply for a chance to survive. Not only to him and Natalie, but to his own children. In the coming hours, he was pretty sure information was going to be just as powerful as, if not more so than, bullets.

"How long have you known Kring?" Jonathan asked.

"I've known *Mr.* Kring for almost twenty-five years," Thomas said. It was obvious he didn't like the disrespect Jonathan felt toward his boss.

"Long time," Jonathan said. "Then you knew him before he was sick. Physically, I mean."

"Yeah, well, not really. He'd already contracted kuru when I joined up with him. He just hadn't started to show any symptoms until a few years ago. That's when everything changed."

"You must really love her. To turn on Kring like this, that is. Without our little gift package, he'll probably die. I suppose, in a strange way, you'll be killing him."

"No, no, it's not like that," Thomas said.

"Don't get me wrong. I'm all for it. It's probably the only chance my daughter has, I just don't know if I'd be able to do it if I were you. All those years and the things you've done for him. That's loyalty. Except for now, of course," Jonathan said. He couldn't push any harder if he wanted to land safely. He sat quietly and let the silence between them work on Thomas; the drone of the engines and the hiss of the conditioned air pumping into the plane were the only sounds.

"There was a time when I'd gladly point this plane at the sea and throttle up for him. I could tell you stories all the way to Tartaruga and you still wouldn't be able to understand the kind of man he was. How he singularly and completely defined the word *power.* That man could kill your daughter in front of your eyes and have you thank him for the act," Thomas said, his eyes far away and glistening with emotion.

"*That* man?" Jonathan said.

"That man is dead. He died just about the time his Frankenstein daughter started experimenting on him. I'm betraying no one by helping you. In fact, I'm rectifying something close to betrayal that's been going on for years. I'm not helping you at all," Thomas said, turning slowly until he looked Jonathan dead in the eyes. "You're helping me."

The phone Jonathan had taken from Thomas rang.

"Easy," Jonathan said, picking up the phone and seeing Thomas twitch like he wanted to grab it. He read the display. "Who's Blane?" Thomas seemed to pale.

"You better let me answer that, mate," Thomas said.

He explained that Blane was his man in the U.S. military, stationed at the naval base on the Diego Garcia archipelago. He used him mostly for personnel intel, but every now and then Blane would call him. And whenever that happened, some serious shit was about to go down, and Blane wanted a big payment to cough up the details. Considering the current situation, Jonathan let him answer it, but on speakerphone.

LEW WAS ASLEEP for a solid two hours before he woke up in the luxurious recliner in the plane's cabin. Emily was still asleep next to him, her head resting on his shoulder. He looked down at her face, inches from his own. After a moment, her eyes flitted open and looked up into his.

She smiled at first, but then apparently realized what was about to happen and her smile was replaced with an earnestness. "Are we . . ."

Lew leaned forward, still too close to dreamland for his defenses and self-deprecation to stop him. Emily's lips parted and her eyes moistened. Then she abruptly pulled away.

"I'm sorry," Lew said. "I'm a jerk."

"No," Emily said softly, touching his face with her open palm. "It's not that. I just . . ."

Lew raised his eyebrows and shook his head slightly as if to say, *What is it?*

"If we're going to . . . that is, before we . . ."

"You're kind of freaking me out, Emily. What is it?"

"You need to know the truth. My name isn't Emily Burrows. It's Denham," she said almost despondently.

"Your name is Denham Burrows? Kind of masculine, isn't it?" Lew said. He was being deliberately obtuse, trying to put her at ease. He really didn't care what her name was. Lord knew he'd gone by more than a few names over the years. She chuckled, the attempt seeming to work.

"No, silly. It's Emily Denham."

Then, speaking barely above a whisper while holding his hands, she told him the whole story. Through the whole thing all Lew could think about was how soft and warm her hands felt. And how warm it was getting in the plane's cabin.

"That's it?" Lew said when she was done. "Baby, I don't care about any of that." Though it did make Lew think about everything he'd eventually have to tell her about himself. Now *that* bothered him.

"Really?"

"What do you think?" Lew said, pulling her to him. Again their mouths parted as they came closer and closer.

"Lew!" Jonathan's shout broke the moment and they both jerked apart.

"Uh, yeah!" Lew called, sitting up.

"Get up here. Quick!"

Lew made a face and smiled, Emily pretty much doing the same. He stood up, rolled his neck, and took a cleansing breath.

"To be continued," he said before turning and heading up to the cockpit. As he walked he heard a voice behind him.

"You better believe it."

As Lew entered the cockpit, he saw Thomas holding a cell phone. Jonathan looked very intense. Lew wasn't sure he wanted to know what was going on.

"What's all the—" Both Thomas and Jonathan simultaneously shushed him.

"Are you still there, Blane?" Thomas said.

"I'm here, but you're cutting in and out, man. Are you . . . pay or not?" a man's voice squawked stiltedly out of the device's speakerphone.

"You're breaking up too. Tell me what I'm paying for again," Thomas said at Jonathan's silent urging.

"U.S. Navy is . . . an attack on Tartaruga. You want details, then you pay," the voice said.

"An attack?" Lew said. Their looks shushed him again. He shrugged at Jonathan, who just waved a hand, motioning him to be patient.

"How much?" Thomas asked.

"Fifty. Same account . . . last time," Blane said. Lew could guess they weren't talking about fifty dollars. Thomas was greasing someone in the forces.

"Deal," Thomas said. After a long silence, he said it again. "Did you hear me, Blane? What's the info? I'll pay. You'll have the money in the morning."

"That ain't good enough," Blane said.

"It'll have to do," Thomas said. Jonathan pointed at Thomas

in a scolding way. Thomas waved him off this time. After another silence, Blane finally responded.

"All right. In the morning. We launched a . . . per an hour ago. Should be . . . ere seven-thirty, your time," Blane said.

"Say again. Launched a what?" Thomas said, then, "Shit! We lost the connection."

"Get him back!" Jonathan said.

"I'm trying," Thomas said.

"What the fuck is a *per*?" Lew said.

"Could be anything," Thomas said as he repeatedly dialed. "A Clipper, a chopper—anything. Point is, we're going to have about an hour to get the hell out of there after we land. Ah, it's no use," he said, tossing the phone onto the console.

"What do you mean it's no use?" Jonathan said, picking up the phone. Lew looked at the display and saw there weren't any bars registering on the signal strength meter.

"Look, I'm amazed we got any signal at all up here."

"What about Tartaruga? We'll just call from there," Lew said.

"Blane's not exactly the reliable type. We'll be lucky if he answers."

"Great," Lew said. Jonathan looked up at Lew, his eyes showing the fear there. In all the years he'd known him, Lew had never seen Jonathan afraid of anything. But he knew the fear wasn't for himself, which just made it all the worse. Lew put his hand on Jonathan's shoulder. "Why don't you get some rest? I'll stay up here."

"I'm fine," Jonathan said. Lew looked at Jonathan's hands and saw they were shaking.

The weird thing was, so were his.

PART SEVEN

Thursday

50

"THERE IT IS," Thomas said. "Off to the left."

Jonathan leaned forward and looked down at the seemingly endless sea. At first he couldn't see it, then he spotted the foam outline around Tartaruga as the ocean lapped at the green and brown growth on its surface. It was hard for Jonathan to believe he'd spent hours down there, never mind that his daughter was even now below him.

"Circle around and make a low pass," Jonathan said. "I want to see what we're dealing with."

"Okay. Just let me swing away to reduce our airspeed," Thomas said. After heading away from the island for a bit, Thomas began to bank the plane and head back. They were moving slower now and were much lower. Jonathan could see the white caps on the waves below.

"Lew! We're doing a flyover. Have a look," he called back into the cabin.

"Roger," Lew said. He had his duster off and was sitting on one of the small tables while Emily dabbed at the wound on the back of his neck with some cotton. The first aid kit was open on the table beside him. They both turned and looked out the window. Jonathan could tell there was something real happening between them. He was glad for Lew, he just hoped it wouldn't get in the way.

As the plane turned, they got a slow, full view of the island. It looked like a turtle, which was probably where it got its name. Near the tail, a bald swath cut across the green canvas covering the island like someone had taken an electric razor and made one pass from beach to beach. It was the paved landing strip. A few small mountains rose up where the apex of the turtle's shell would be, though Jonathan could see nothing there besides jungle coverage. At the head was what looked like a dock, vacant of boats.

They swung around the back of the island and Jonathan saw the complex and the courtyard where the exchange would take place. He couldn't see any people, but he could make out the buildings. There were two smaller outbuildings and one larger, flat edifice with a hangar attached to the back corner. The hangar was almost three times the height of the complex, but Jonathan knew the most impressive part was underground. He figured the hangar was where they'd first taken him.

"It's huge," Lew called from the cabin. "You say it goes four levels down?"

"Five," Jonathan corrected, counting Nathan's vault and the generators.

"It's a good thing you know where Natalie's being held. If we had to search that place we'd be toast. No way could we do it in just an hour," Lew said.

"Okay, take us in," Jonathan said to Thomas. He walked back into the cabin. "You guys ready?"

"Just about," Lew said, shrugging and wincing back into his duster.

"You're sure you don't want a gun?" Jonathan asked Emily, though he pretty much knew what the answer would be.

"I'm sure," she said.

"Okay. Are we all clear on what we're supposed to do? If you have any questions or doubts, now's the time—"

"Jonny," Lew said, putting his hand on his arm. "It's going to be fine. In and out like grease through a goose. We'll be long gone before the attack gets here. Just please tell me we're not really saving this psycho's girlfriend." Jonathan looked over his shoulder to be sure Thomas wasn't listening. He was busy bringing the plane in for a landing. Jonathan turned back and shook his head no.

"Atta boy."

"We better get our seats for the landing," Jonathan said. "Everyone but you, of course." Lew smiled. The stakes were high—higher than they'd ever been before—and victory, despite what Lew said, was not even close to a foregone conclusion, but Lew looked like he was having the time of his life. Jonathan recalled that he'd always looked like this on jobs when things were at their worst. He gave Lew Thomas's cell phone number so they could stay in touch when the shit hit the fan, if need be.

"See you soon," Lew said, shaking Jonathan's hand. Jonathan headed back up to the cockpit. By the time he strapped himself in and looked back to the cabin, he could see Lew bent over out of sight by the chair where Emily was sitting. Lew stood up and saw Jonathan watching him. Lew winked and headed out to the cargo hold, closing the door to the bathroom behind him.

The wheels touched down with a slight thud and squeal, the nose gear bouncing down a moment later. Now they were racing down the short runway at incredible speed, trees on both sides of the plane smearing past. Jonathan felt himself thrust forward as the brakes caught. When they were almost halfway out of runway, Thomas flipped a switch sending a chime through the plane. It was Lew's signal. A few seconds later they felt the plane rock slightly as Lew threw open the door in the cargo hold. The plane had slowed considerably, but it was still moving at a good clip. They couldn't see the rear of the plane, so they had to have faith that Lew had made it.

If they had waited any longer, the security cameras at the east end of the airstrip would have picked up Lew rolling out of the plane and scurrying into the jungle.

The plane came to a full stop and Thomas powered down the engines. Through the window, Jonathan could see a single small building at the edge of the jungle near a dirt road that led over the rise and disappeared into the trees. Parked by the building was a beat-up, military-issue Humvee.

"Now we just—wait!" Thomas said, but Jonathan was already swinging the pistol at him. He hit him in the jaw and knocked him cold.

"Now we're even," Jonathan said. He tied Thomas up and then he and Emily made their way to the Humvee with their prize.

There was a note pinned under one of the wiper blades. Emily took it and read it aloud.

"Follow the road to the clearing and wait. Do not enter the

complex or your daughter dies," she said. Emily looked like she wanted to say something, but she didn't. They got into the Humvee and looked down the runway to where Lew had jumped out. There was no movement down there. Jonathan took solace in the fact that there wasn't a body lying on the tarmac.

"He's fine," Jonathan said as he started the engine.

"I know," Emily said with false bravado, hugging the cryocase in her lap.

Jonathan put the vehicle in gear and they bounced along the rough road, disappearing into the jungle.

6:45 A.M.

LARA SEETHED AS she stood near the ladder to level four, rage flowing hot through her veins like the steam racing through the pipes surrounding her. Sweat covered her body and the humidity had turned her hair into a white mass of tangles and kinks. She'd passed thirsty about an hour ago and was having trouble coming up with enough saliva to moisten her cracked lips. She checked her watch and realized there was no more time left for the hunt.

Nathan's order to take Sophia and the little girl alive had been frustrating. She'd hoped Sophia would stick her head out and an exhausted guard would ignore his orders and shoot her. Several times, preferably. It would have tied everything up neat and tidy and Lara would've gotten what she wanted without having to dis-obey her orders.

The only reason Nathan wanted Sophia alive was so he could get the research she'd no doubt taken with her, but a bullet or two to the head wouldn't harm whatever she was carrying. Lara imagined Nathan's beaming face—metaphorically speaking, since his facial muscles didn't move noticeably anymore—when she handed him the research, along with the news that Sophia had been tragically killed.

But no, Sophia couldn't cooperate. She had to stay hidden with the little brat. And any second now, her father would call Lara on the radio and the game would be over.

Lara kicked a stand of pipes in frustration. There was no point searching anymore. They'd been through the tunnels repeatedly and found nothing. Somehow she'd gotten past them. She was probably in the jungle by now. Lara was just about to double the guards at the helipad when her radio squawked with her father's simulated voice.

"Go ahead," she said into the radio.

"They're here. Are the men in position?"

They weren't. She'd pulled the shooters off the roof to help with the search.

"On their way," Lara said.

"Did you find them?" Nathan asked. It was a rhetorical question, but he wouldn't let up until she said it out loud.

"No. I'll keep some men searching, but—"

"Never mind. Just get up here. If you can find your way," Nathan said. Lara squeezed her eyes shut.

"Yes, Father," she said.

"SON OF A bitch," Lew said to the corpses.

The smell had assaulted him as soon as he'd entered the hangar. The stench wasn't new to him, not after Iraq. It was a long time ago, but a million years wouldn't be enough time to cleanse his palate of that smell.

Inside a storage room off to the side of the hangar's massive, wire-strewn interior, he'd found them. Over a dozen dead, all in lab coats.

Lew ran across the expanse to the long metal staircase leading up to a series of windows. He ran up the stairs and then along the balcony to an opening between the windows. Once inside, he headed straight for stairs that led to the roof.

It was vacant. He crouched by the door and checked his watch. Just over half an hour before the attack, whatever form it was going to take. The sound of a vehicle echoed from the jungle. Lew saw the open-top Humvee come bouncing out with Emily and Jonathan inside. After they entered the courtyard they drove out of sight. He'd have to get closer to the ledge to see any more.

A noise on the other side of the door stopped him and he pressed back flat against the wall. A few seconds later, the door opened, and two armed guards, each with a rifle over his shoulder, came out. They crouched low and duckwalked toward the edge of the roof.

Shooting wasn't an option, so Lew put his gun away and just walked up behind them.

"Lose something?"

The guards looked at each other and then spun around, trying to pull their rifles off their shoulders.

Lew focused on the bigger of the two, punching him in the throat and the eye. He went down hard and wouldn't be getting up for a while. In the meantime, the other guard got his rifle free from his shoulder and swung the butt toward Lew's head. He caught it with one hand and kicked the guard's feet out from under him. The guard went down hard on his back, knocking the wind out of him. As he gasped for breath, Lew pulled the rifle free and slammed the butt into the side of his head. The guard grunted and then stopped gasping.

They had handcuffs on their belts, which Lew used to hook them to some pipes by the door. Then he took the firing pins out of the rifles and tossed the useless weapons on the ground After scoping out the area, Lew headed back in.

On the third level, Lew found the room where they'd been keeping Natalie. It was empty. He looked under the bed in case she was hiding and found one of her drawings.

"Son of a—"

Voices sounded in the hallway.

Lew eased up to the doorway and peered out into the hall. A grate lay open and Lew watched two men and a woman with wild white hair climb out. *What the hell?*

"Head downstairs and work your way up again. Find Sophia and the girl," the woman said.

"Alive?" one of guards asked.

"We need the child alive for the exchange. Nobody says she has to be unharmed," the woman said.

Natalie's alive!

"And Sophia?" the guard asked.

"I need what she has on her. If an accident happens, so be it. Understand?"

"Yes, ma'am!" The guards practically saluted before heading off down the hall. Lew eased back into the shadows as the woman passed by. He wanted to reach out and wring her neck, but there'd be time for that later. When he was sure she was gone, he called Jonathan.

"You survived, did you?" Jonathan said when he answered.

"Barely," Lew said. "From now on I only jump out of airplanes that are ten thousand feet off the ground."

Lew told Jonathan about the bodies he'd found, Natalie not being in the room, and then about the conversation between the woman and the guards.

"Yeah, that's Lara, all right," Jonathan said after Lew described her. "Piece of work, huh?"

"We're doing the Aussie a favor by leaving her here," Lew said. "What should I do, now? Look for Natalie?"

"No, you'll run into guards for sure. Get back up here and cover us for the exchange."

"Okay," Lew said. He always said that when Jonathan gave him instructions he didn't like. Apologizing later was quicker than arguing.

"Lew," Jonathan said. "I mean it. Get back up here. We don't have time to be looking for you and Natalie when we're done here."

"Of course. Be right up," Lew said, hanging up the phone. He looked down the hall at the grate Lara and her guards had emerged from. Why were they in there? He checked his watch and then hurried over to it, slipping inside the complex's tunnel system.

7:00 A.M.

"DAMN IT," JONATHAN said under his breath.

If only there was a way to reach Sophia and—

He looked at the phone. At *Thomas's* phone.

Jonathan quickly scrolled through Thomas's contact list, and sure enough, he found her number. He selected "Sophia" and pressed send. The phone rang with a soft *brrr* in his ear. Then again. And again. Then he realized if she had Natalie, Thomas was probably the last person she wanted to speak to. He quickly switched from the phone app to messaging and sent a text:

Sophia, it's Jonathan calling. Pick up!

Then he called her again. This time it rang only once.

"Jonathan?" Sophia's voice said on the line. She sounded exhausted.

"Sophia, thank God. Is Natalie—"

"She's with me. We're just waiting for a chance to get past the guards."

"No, there's no time. I can't explain. You have to get her out. *Now.* I'm in the courtyard and—" Jonathan abruptly hung up and stepped out from behind Emily, putting the phone away and taking out his guns.

Movement in the complex's doorway had caught his eye. Nathan rolled out, flanked by two guards. Jonathan heard Emily's breath catch when she saw him.

"You okay?" he whispered.

"I'm fine. I know you told me about the wheelchair, but seeing it . . . I just wasn't ready, I guess," Emily said. Jonathan had felt the same way when he'd seen Nathan stroll in for their dinner, so he understood. He scanned the area behind the trio but couldn't see anyone back there.

"Hello again, Mr. Hall," Nathan said. "Please put the guns on the ground at your feet."

"Where's my daughter?" Jonathan said.

"Guns first, then we talk," Nathan said. Jonathan thought he was being awfully calm for a man facing two automatic weapons. Then again, Nathan thought he had sharpshooters protecting him. Jonathan knew he could easily pop the two guards before they knew what was happening, but there was no need for that. Yet. He put the guns at his feet.

"That's better. Much more civilized," Nathan said.

"Where is she?" Jonathan said, playing along with Nathan's charade, now that he knew Natalie was indeed with Sophia.

"Close by. Don't you worry," Nathan said before he ordered one of his guards to take the cryocase from Emily. One approached while the other kept a gun pointed at them.

"Hang on," Jonathan said, stepping in front of Emily. "Show me my daughter and then you can have the case." If he didn't react properly, Nathan would smell a rat. Sophia and Natalie would lose vital minutes they needed to get to safety.

"The case first," Nathan said. "I have to verify what you have. I'm not about to turn over all my cards when you could be bluffing."

The guard stood almost nose to nose with Jonathan.

"Please," Nathan said. When Jonathan didn't move, he said, "Shoot the woman." The other guard swung his gun toward Emily.

"Wait!" Jonathan said as Emily let out a gasp. He eyed Nathan with all the contempt he could muster, fighting his instinct to grab the guard to use as a shield. Jonathan stepped out of the way and let the guard take the case from her.

The guard returned to Nathan's side.

"Very good, Mr. Hall. You're a smart man."

"You've got your prize, now where's my daughter?"

"She's just inside. Go on in and get her," Nathan said.

Jonathan and Emily took a step together but Nathan stopped them.

"Just you. Miss Denham will wait here with us."

"Forget it," Jonathan said.

"It's okay," Emily said, stepping backward. "Go get your daughter, Jonathan. I'll wait here."

Jonathan looked at her, shaking his head slightly. He had no time to explain that Nathan had no idea where his daughter was, and even if he did he wouldn't just hand her over like this. Heading across the courtyard would be a death march, but if he hesitated, they'd be dead anyway. With the rooftop guards incapacitated, maybe he could get into the complex before anyone else shot him and maybe these guards would leave Emily alone and chase him. A lot of maybes. But it was the only play.

Jonathan walked toward Nathan. He stepped past him and the guards, waiting for the crack of a rifle to tell him he was about to die. He was halfway to the door when he heard Nathan order the rooftop guards to shoot him. When nothing happened, he gave the order a second time.

"Shoot him. Now," Nathan said, and Jonathan knew he wasn't talking to the rooftop guards anymore. He turned around and saw both guards on the ground bringing their guns to bear on him. They were too far away to rush and the complex was still too far behind him to make a run for it.

He'd failed. He was about to die, but that wasn't the worst of it. Emily would surely follow, and then they'd scour the complex and find Natalie. Jonathan wouldn't be surprised if Nathan had his own daughter shot in the process.

"I'm sorry," Jonathan said, closing his eyes.

Two shots rang out. Jonathan braced for the impact but it never came. He opened his eyes and saw both guards lying dead beside Nathan. On the other side of the courtyard Thomas cocked a rifle, the spent shell shooting up over his shoulder to land with the first one on the jungle floor, ropes still hanging from his wrists.

"Get the girls," Thomas said, pointing the rifle at Nathan. Jonathan held out his hand and Emily ran across the courtyard to him. "Hurry, mate. There's not much time left."

He didn't need to tell Jonathan twice. They ran inside the complex, leaving Thomas holding a gun on his former employer.

Thomas watched Jonathan and Emily disappear inside the complex. If they came out without Lara, he'd put a bullet in each of their brains without a second thought. He might even do the same if Lara was with them. And he was sure Lara would help him do it.

When they were gone, he kept the gun trained on Nathan, but he couldn't bring himself to make eye contact with him. He knew this was not the man he'd met so many years ago, the man he'd served faithfully every moment since then, but it was still the same shell. And he still had the same manipulative skills. If Thomas wasn't careful he'd end up shooting himself before they came out.

"What are you doing, Thomas?" Nathan finally said.

"Shut up," Thomas said, shifting his view from one side of the courtyard to the other, taking a few steps away from the man in the wheelchair.

"Do you really think she'll go with you? Do you think she'll come out and see you holding a rifle on her father and thank you for the act?"

"I'll make her understand," Thomas said, cursing himself for responding.

"You're a bigger fool than I thought if you think a tryst can surpass a familial bond," Nathan said, rolling sideways slightly in his wheelchair.

"Stay where you are!" Thomas said. He'd meant to just say it, but somehow it came out as a shout.

"Are you afraid of me? Afraid I'll magically launch out of this chair and overpower you?" Nathan said. And then a beat later, "Look at me."

"What about Sophia's familial bond? Or have you killed her already?" Thomas said, ignoring the taunts.

"Look at me," Nathan said again. Thomas gritted his teeth, knowing he was a fool to try and exchange barbs with him. Then despite every mental scream not to, he looked Nathan in the eye.

He wanted to pull the trigger. Pull it over and over again. He wanted to destroy this thing that had taken the place of the greatest man he'd ever known. Maybe the greatest man ever. But it would have been easier to shoot Lara. When you've been in a cage for so many years, you don't need bars to keep you incarcerated. The memories are enough.

"If you get in our way, we're all going to die. Even you," Thomas said.

"We're all . . . what are you talking about?" Nathan asked.

As if on cue, a faint buzz drifted down from above. At first it seemed almost imaginary, like a mosquito that kept flying in and out of earshot. Then it gradually grew louder, until it sounded like a small plane. Thomas wanted to think it was just some tourist flight taking in the sights, but he knew better. He looked up at the brilliant, cloudless blue morning sky and edged sideways, trying to see the source of the sound. It took him a minute or two, Nathan forgotten, but finally he spotted it. High up in the heavens, flying a large circular pattern, it looped around and headed back. Just a shiny spot against the indigo of the sky until it finally turned out of profile and Thomas saw it in full frontal view.

"Fuck me," Thomas said, a chill dancing across his skin. He took out the cell phone he'd taken from a guard to call Jonathan, but before he could dial his own cell phone's number, both the phone and the rifle fell from his hands, a searing pain in his back sucking the wind from his lungs and the strength from his muscles.

Thomas coughed blood, rivulets dripping down his chin. He looked down at Nathan, who was smiling. He spun around and came face-to-face with his attacker. It was Lara, but no Lara he'd ever seen before. She was dirty, slick, and her hair looked like a madwoman's. She looked up at him from beneath hooded, dark eyes smeared with ruined mascara. Her face completely blank of expression. No joy. No sorrow. Just slack.

"Per . . . Reaper," Thomas said, each breath a gurgle of pain. Then he fell over facedown on the pavement, the knife he'd given Lara sticking out of his back.

7:15 A.M.

SOPHIA CLIMBED OUT of the access panel, a little confused by the phone call from Jonathan. It had lasted for only a minute, and for all she knew he'd had a gun to his head and it was a trick to get her to come out of hiding. But there was something in his voice.

"Where are we going? Where's my dad?" Natalie asked as they carefully made their way down the hall. Sophia ignored her questions. With her lab and personal living quarters no doubt guarded, they were heading to Lara's room for some supplies. It was a little risky, but she doubted Lara would be spending any time in her room right now. She used what little sulphuric acid she had left, burned through the lock, and took Natalie inside.

"Sit here. I just need to grab some things," Sophia said, indicating Lara's bed.

"But my dad—"

"He's close, honey. You'll see him soon." Sophia grabbed a large backpack out of Lara's closet and filled it with a few articles of clothing and some supplies.

With the chopper out of the question, she'd come up with Plan B. When they were kids, Nathan would sometimes take Sophia and Lara camping on the island up in the mountains. She still loved camping, though now she rarely had time and usually went alone. Lara never went anymore, but as she'd hoped, her camping supplies were still in her closet. If it turned out Jonathan's call was a hoax, a few days in the jungle should be enough time for things to calm down. They could live for a few days off the fruit in the jungle and there was a freshwater stream. Then she could grab the chopper or use a radio to call for help. It was risky, but it was all she had.

"Who's this?" Natalie asked. Sophia looked up from her packing and saw Natalie holding a picture from Lara's nightstand. She stopped and sat on the bed next to Natalie.

"That's me and Lara when we were about your age," Sophia said, her eyes far away. "I didn't think she still had this."

"You both look happy. I didn't think she was ever happy," Natalie said. Sophia knew she had spent only a few minutes with Lara when she was first brought to the island and put in her locked room, but somehow in that short time, Natalie had discerned Lara's everyday temperament. Sophia took the picture and held it, remembering when it was taken. It had been just before her mother had died.

"Lara used to be the funniest girl I knew. She'd play practical jokes on the guards that would drive Na— my father crazy. She was my best friend in the whole world," Sophia said, the last barely above a whisper.

"What happened?"

"Not long after this picture was taken our mother died. Lara never got over it. She stopped laughing and joking and pretty soon she hardly talked anymore." Sophia again wondered if her mother was truly dead, but she was starting to think that was just wishful thinking.

Then after a long, quiet pause Natalie said, "My mother died too."

"I didn't know," Sophia said. "I'm sorry, honey."

"S'okay. Everything dies. I didn't smile for a long time either."

Sophia looked away. Then instead of putting the picture back on the nightstand, she packed it with her other things. When the pack was full, she changed into a khaki blouse and hiking shorts. She tied a bandana around her forehead, laced up a pair of hiking boots, and tied a camping knife in its sheath around her thigh. Lastly she transferred the kuru serum research into the new knapsack.

Now they just had to get away from the complex.

They could go through the hangar, but then they'd have to take the elevator up to the second level. Still, she didn't want to risk going back into the tunnels. There could still be a few guards in there looking for them.

"When we get out of the elevator, I need you to be very quiet, okay?" Sophia said, pressing the button to summon the elevator. Natalie nodded. Somehow she knew what they were doing wasn't a game. Sophia reached out and gave her a one-armed hug. "Good girl."

The elevator door opened and when Sophia looked up, she was staring down the barrels of two guns.

7:20 A.M.

LEW CHECKED HIS watch as he ran down the tunnel, anxiety rising in his chest to match the pounding of machinery around him. He turned the corner, hoping to see the ladder leading up out of the maze he'd trapped himself in, but all he saw was more tunnel running parallel to several huge, thumping generators. He'd lost track of which level he was on but didn't really care. He just wanted out.

"Damn it!"

He took out his cell phone and tried again, but he still couldn't get any signal in the cinder-block and pipe-lined tomb, not that anyone could have heard him with all the noise, anyway. With little choice, he continued on, sweat pouring down his back from the sweltering heat.

"What the hell have you done to yourself now, Lew," he said, rapidly losing hope of escaping the maze before the attack came. It didn't take a genius to know that whatever form the attack took, being down here when it happened was a bad idea.

Two more corner turns—sure he must have traveled in a complete circle by now—and he saw what he thought looked like the vent he'd used to enter this hell.

The vent was welded shut. He kicked at it a few times, but did little more than dent it. Spotting a fire extinguisher on the far wall, he grabbed it and then used it as a battering ram against the perforated metal. On about the twentieth bash, the seal finally let go on one edge. A few minutes later he'd managed to bend the edges back far enough to allow him to squeeze through.

He heard a tearing sound as he pulled his legs out and realized he'd ripped his duster. Again. Or so he presumed, since he couldn't see anything. The room he'd entered was darker than the tunnels, but thankfully it was cool and relatively quiet. His teeth still buzzed from the pound of the generators.

He flipped open his cell phone and used the glowing display as a dim flashlight. He made his way around the edge of the room, seeing what looked like empty display cases every few feet. Following a bend in the wall, his extended hand slipped across something cool and metallic. He felt around and realized they were elevator doors. But better than that, he found light switches on the other side of the elevator. He flipped them on and squinted against the glare until his eyes adjusted to the brightness. When they did, he couldn't believe it. He was in Kring's private vault. Of all the places to end up! The irony annoyed him.

Lew looked for the button to summon the elevator, but couldn't find it. The only thing near the door besides the light switch was a numeric keypad.

"Seriously?" Lew said, looking back up at the door. He wasn't going anywhere.

"DAD!" NATALIE RUSHED into the elevator under the guns Jonathan was holding and hugged him. He put the guns away, dropped to one knee, and squeezed her. Then he pushed her back so he could look at her, while Emily held the elevator door open.

"Did they hurt you? Are you all right?" Jonathan asked, checking her for wounds.

"I'm fine. Sophia saved me!" Jonathan stood up and looked at Sophia, who appeared to be heading out for a camping trip.

"Is that true?" When the elevator door had opened, all Jonathan had seen was someone standing there, so he'd instinctively stepped in front of Emily and pointed his guns. Sophia, seeing the guns, didn't cower or run. Instead, she'd shielded Natalie from the sudden threat with her body.

"I didn't do anything," Sophia said, looking at Emily.

"Oh, Emily, this is Sophia. Sophia, Emily," Jonathan said introducing them. "And I somehow doubt that."

"We need to get out of here," Emily said, looking at her watch. They had minutes, at best. And no idea where Lew was.

"What about Lew?" Emily said, as if reading his mind. Jonathan looked at the two women and his daughter and was suddenly very aware he was the only one with a weapon. Then he made a hard choice.

"Emily, we have to go. Our time is up," Jonathan said. Emily looked at him and then down at Natalie. She finally let go of the door and they stepped into the elevator, heading up to the surface.

"Thomas flew you here?" Sophia said when Jonathan explained how they'd gotten there. She was standing with her back to the elevator door as the car slowly crawled up. "And he's going to fly you out of here?"

"That's the plan," Jonathan said. The elevator dinged that they'd reached the main floor.

"Where's your sister?" Emily asked Sophia.

"I have no—"

"*Down!*" Jonathan shouted as the elevator doors opened. Lara stood twenty feet away, a gun leveled at them. He wanted to pull his weapons and shoot, but his first reflex was to protect Natalie. He grabbed both Natalie and Emily and pushed them against the side wall, gunshots already echoing. Jonathan looked up and realized Sophia was still standing there with her back to the door, looking at them without understanding what was happening.

The first three shots slammed into the back of the elevator, chips of Formica and aluminum ricocheting around the elevator car. The last three hit their mark, the slugs thunking into Sophia's backpack. She grunted as she was smacked against the back of the elevator before she collapsed to the floor. Natalie screamed.

Jonathan went to pull his guns, but he realized one was missing. Emily had already grabbed one and was firing wildly out of the elevator. He grabbed his remaining weapon and came around the edge of the elevator door firing. The sound in the confined space was excruciatingly loud, but their shots were in vain. Lara had already run out the complex's front door into the courtyard. After exchanging an incredulous glance with Emily, Jonathan checked on Sophia, while Emily kept her weapon pointed out the elevator door. Blood on the back of the elevator wall told him at least one of the bullets had found its mark.

He unhooked her backpack and tossed it away so Sophia could lie flat. The pack's interior had captured two of the slugs, but one had passed through into Sophia's shoulder. The shot looked through-and-through, but she was bleeding a lot. Jonathan wanted to help her but precious seconds were ticking away.

"Put pressure on her wounds. I'll be right back," Jonathan said, running to the courtyard door and pressing himself against the wall. Something bumped him and he realized Emily had come with him and was pressed against the wall beside him. *Lew, I hope you're okay because this is a match made in heaven.*

"Wait here," Jonathan said before he jumped out, ready to fire. But there was no danger in the courtyard. No Lara. No Nathan. But it wasn't completely empty; Thomas lay on the ground at the far edge, a knife sticking out of his back. Jonathan looked around to be sure he wasn't walking into a trap, and then made his way around the perimeter of the courtyard. His cell phone rang when he was halfway. He answered it as he continued to walk, scanning the area for attackers.

"Where the hell are you? We've got trouble up here. I need your help," Jonathan said, a strange buzzing coming from the phone.

"Yeah, that's going to be a problem," Lew said.

Jonathan reached Thomas's body and knelt beside him. He put two fingers on his neck.

"Looks like there's no rush," Jonathan said, standing up. "We just lost our ticket out of here. Thomas is dead."

"What? Who killed him?"

"I didn't see it, but my money's on his psycho girlfriend," Jonathan said, realizing the buzzing wasn't coming from the phone. It was above him. He eased back toward the complex, scanning the skies, until he found the source of the sound banking toward them from the east. It looked like a small airplane but before he could identify it, the craft seemed to buck up in the sky as something fell away from it.

"What the hell?" Jonathan said.

Then the missile's engine ignited. It screamed across the sky, leaving a vapor trail behind it. And it was headed right for them.

"Jesus!"

Jonathan jumped up and ran straight inside the complex, not caring if someone was watching or not. The three girls were just outside the elevator where they'd dragged Sophia, a bloody trail smeared across the floor. A bag was open beside her and Emily was wrapping gauze around Sophia's shoulder.

"We've got to go! Now!" Jonathan yelled, shoving the phone and gun into his pockets. He ran over to them and moved to pick Natalie up. She pushed his hands away.

"No, Dad. Help Sophia," Natalie said.

Jonathan could still hear Lew shouting from his phone but he couldn't stop to explain. An explosion reverberated from outside. The complex hadn't been the target. At least not the primary target.

"What the bloody hell was that?" Emily asked.

"Our luck running out," Jonathan said, picking Sophia up. Her blood-soaked shirt was gone and she was wearing just a black sports bra. He noticed that Emily's field dressing was almost textbook. Not bad for a writer.

"My . . . bag," Sophia said, wincing.

"Got it!" Natalie said. Jonathan was shocked and proud at his daughter's behavior, but he didn't have time to tell her.

"Let's go!" Jonathan said, running out of the complex with Sophia in his arms, Emily and Natalie behind them.

Thick, black smoke rose up over the hill, just about where the landing strip was. Suddenly not having a pilot didn't matter. Apparently the attack's first strike was to destroy the target's egress. The plane was gone. As he ran toward the edge of the courtyard, Jonathan heard the drone's engine again. Up to the right, he saw *two* rocket engines ignite.

"Faster!"

They reached the edge of the courtyard just as missiles slammed simultaneously into one of the outbuildings and the main complex. The blast wave knocked everyone into the jungle like paper dolls in a wind.

Jonathan's head rang and it took him a second to realize someone was yelling at him. Slowly the ringing faded and the world swam back into focus.

"Dad, you're hurting me!" Natalie said in his grasp. He didn't even remember grabbing her.

"Sorry, honey," Jonathan said, releasing his grip. Sophia was in the vegetation a few feet away looking no worse than she had. Even her bandage had held. Emily was on her feet, leaning against a tree, shaking her head. At first he thought she was trying to clear the ringing in her ears, but then he saw she was crying and her head shaking was from despair, not physical pain. She was looking behind him.

Jonathan turned and saw what was affecting her. The smoke was still clearing, but they could see the flattened complex now. He felt like he'd been kicked in the gut. He fumbled the phone out of his pocket.

"Lew! *Lew!*"

The line was dead.

Jonathan looked up at the carnage again. Chances were the levels had pancaked all the way down to the vault. It was a miracle the natural gas holding tanks down there hadn't ignited. Even unignited, they had probably been breached. If Lew had survived, his good fortune would be short-lived. And the attack wasn't over. He tried to call Lew back, but there was no answer.

"Where's Uncle Lew? Was he in there?" Natalie asked.

"I . . . I don't know, baby," Jonathan said, fighting to keep any quavers out of his voice. Then, over all the mayhem, he heard the buzzing again. He pushed up to his feet. If they were lucky, they had a few minutes while the drone reconnoitered the damage. The hangar and one of the outbuildings were still intact.

"Sophia," he said, helping her sit up. "Is there a boat or any other way off the island?"

"There's no boat, but there's a helicopter about a kilometer to the east," she said. She rooted through her bag and then gave herself an injection. "For the pain," she said when she saw Jonathan watching her.

"You wouldn't happen to have a pilot in that bag, would you?" he said.

"I can fly it, if it's still there," she said.

"Is it out in the open?" Jonathan asked, wondering why there hadn't been an attack down there.

"It's stored under some camouflage netting," she said. They still had a chance. But was she in any shape to fly? Then he thought of something that put a pit in his belly.

"Can your sister fly it?" he asked.

"Yes," she said. She started to get up and almost fell back down. Jonathan caught her and helped her up to her feet.

"Do you think that's where your father and Lara are headed?" Jonathan asked.

"There's nowhere else to go, especially with that thing flying around," Sophia said. "If he's alive he's headed there and he'd need Lara to fly him out. I'd say it's a safe bet." Jonathan nodded, noticing Sophia's lack of concern about whether her father was alive or not. He turned his attention to Natalie.

"We've got to go, baby. Emily, are you going to be all right?" Jonathan asked. He was trying not to think about what was devastating her. The only thing that mattered now was getting Natalie off this island before the drone fired its remaining missiles.

Emily took a deep breath and managed a nod. She was far from all right, but she knew the situation they were in. Jonathan wanted to try to call Lew again, but he was afraid of what the act would do to Emily. Maybe the vault's reinforced walls . . . but that was just wishful thinking. And it was distracting. He needed to focus.

"Let's go," Jonathan said. The foursome skirted the edge of the courtyard and then headed up the road that led to the chopper pad, Jonathan with his arm around Sophia in the lead, Natalie and Emily trudging behind them.

High overhead, he could still hear the buzzing, but he ignored it.

Looking would serve no purpose. From what he could tell, the drone had launched three of its *smaller* missiles. His military knowledge was pretty rusty, but they looked like Hellcats. And it still had one left. A direct hit would be deadly, but what concerned him more were the two larger tubes hanging under the bird. Hellcats were twenty-pound firecrackers compared to what looked like five-hundred pound bombs. Just *one* of those would give the entire island a very bad day.

As they walked, he tried not to think about Lew. But it was impossible. Lew was more than a friend. He'd lost a brother.

"WHAT DO YOU mean, you killed her?" Nathan said as he motored his way up the road in his wheelchair with Lara trotting beside him. Lara felt the electronic question as if it were a slap in the face, blinking and rocking her head back. "You idiot."

She was sure it was the disease slipping through. After receiving a look that had approached pride when she'd killed Thomas, Lara had expected more of the same or congratulations for killing her disloyal "sister." He had to hate her as much as she did. Even so, she'd had more than her limit, money or no.

Over the past few days, Lara had done things—incredible things—she would never have thought she was capable of. She felt accomplished, significant, and dangerous. Her father should be treating her as such.

"You've got the item," she said, gesturing toward the cryocase in Nathan's lap. "What do we need her for?"

"This is useless without your sister's research. I might as well have your brain here." Nathan said. Lara got the implication and winced yet again.

"She . . . she had a backpack," Lara said, looking at the rising smoke in the distance that used to be her home. Then she looked back at the cryocase in Nathan's lap. "How did you get that in your lap?"

Nathan shakily raised his arms and showed her he was able to move. The limbs looked unstable and weak, but this was the first time she'd seen him physically move without the serum in years. She could tell that while he could move, he was shamed by the indignity of shaking and not being in control.

"When your sister destroyed her lab, she destroyed my regimen, as well. It's been hours since I had a neuro-blocker injection," Nathan said. "Now go back down there and find your sister's research. Don't come back without it."

"What about the guards at the helipad?" Lara asked. They hadn't finished the cleanup job. There were still four guards alive—assuming they hadn't run off into the jungle when the attack started.

Nathan reached a shaky hand down beside him and struggled to pull a gun up, showing her he was armed.

"You don't even look strong enough to pull the trigger. How are you—"

Nathan grunted and shot a bullet into the ground at Lara's feet. The look on his face after seemed to say he was surprised he'd been able to do it too.

"Now get going. Go through the jungle in case anyone is following us. And no heroics," Nathan said. Lara's eyes brightened for a moment. "If anything happens to you, who's going to fly me off the island?"

8:00 A.M.

LEW PULLED HARD on his leather belt, cinching it tight around his thigh, just above where a six-inch piece of rebar jutted out. The pain was bad, but nowhere near as bad as it was about to get. He took off his duster and tore several long strips out of the lining before removing the canvas belt. Then he took what remained and hung it up in one of the empty displays in Kring's vault. He couldn't admire his work in the oppressive dark, but he imagined it was breathtaking. The duster wasn't very old, but it was a mess. This was the perfect end for it. He just hoped he wouldn't suffer the same fate.

He coughed from the dust in the vault and wiped sweat and grime off his face with a forearm. The attack aboveground had sent concrete crashing down from the ceiling, deadly rebar spears set free as the huge chunks exploded on impact. He dove out of the way of most of it, losing his cell phone in the process, but a short, energetic length of rebar had bounced around the vault until it found a home piercing his thigh.

"No time like the present," Lew said, putting the cloth belt between his teeth. He clamped down hard, gripped the rebar, which was slick with blood, and after mentally counting to three, he yanked it out. He knew you weren't supposed to do that until you were in the ER, but his chances of climbing out were pretty slim and would be even slimmer with a spike through his leg.

Lew howled and grunted from the pain, biting so hard on the belt his jaw hurt. He panted and spewed saliva out around the edges of the material, taking deep, hard breaths through his nose until the waves of pain and nausea finally passed. He wrapped several strips of the lining around the hole in his leg with shaking hands, glad he couldn't actually see the wound. He'd need real medical treatment soon if he was going to keep his leg, but one limb was the least of his worries right now.

He felt around the room, tripping and limping over piles of

debris, until he found the vent. No dice. It was blocked on the other side, the tunnels now just a container for detritus. He threw himself against the wall, grimacing from the pain, and tried to catch his breath.

"Think, Lew."

After a minute or two, he felt around until he found a hunk of rebar about three feet long. Then he felt along the walls until he was back at the elevator. He took a few deep breaths and then shoved the rebar into the seam in the elevator doors and struggled to pry them apart. They slowly parted and he inched them open. Battery-powered emergency lighting from the elevator shaft cut through, seeming as bright as laser beams, his priceless addition to the vault highlighted across the room.

"Nice," he said, giving the duster a final two-finger salute.

A few hunks of concrete lay at the bottom of the elevator shaft, but for the most part it had weathered the attack unscathed. Lew looked up and saw the elevator car hanging above him in the short, two-story tube. He reached in and yanked on the ladder attached to the wall. It seemed solid.

"Now the hard part."

Lew stuck the length of rebar through his belt loops at the small of his back and then stepped onto the ladder with his good leg, gripping the rung above his head. He bent his leg slightly and then launched himself up to the next higher rung, grabbing it with his relatively good hand and pulling himself up. After a moment's rest, he repeated the act—again and again—until he was high enough to drop down onto the elevator car's roof.

He took a minute to catch his breath before opening the trapdoor there. Sitting on the edge of the opening with his legs dangling into the car, he grabbed the opposite edge, and then let himself hang down, dropping the last few inches to the floor on his good leg. Pulling the rebar out of his belt loops, he used it to pry open the elevator doors.

Dust and smoke spilled in from the level four hallway, making him cough. He hopped in anyway and tried to get his bearings.

Rubble and small fires were everywhere. The emergency lighting was working here as well, but the cloudy air made it of little help for more than a few feet. Lew heard something behind him and spun around, grabbing at his empty holsters. He'd lost his weapons in the attack and hadn't even noticed. Unarmed, he raised the rebar over his head as the noise moved toward him. Several mice, rats, and a few rabbits emerged from the din and ran past him, disappearing down the wrecked hallway.

"Yeah, okay," Lew said and followed the mini stampede, figuring they were headed for the closest exit instinctively. At one point there was so much debris he had to dig out a passage before he could squeeze by, but he managed to work his way the full length of the corridor, finally reaching the other elevator that led to ground level.

He summoned his strength and proceeded to pry the doors open. They were more stubborn than the other ones and when he finally got them open he saw why. Rock and debris had fallen down the shaft, crushing the elevator car like an aluminum soda can. With the doors open, it all came spilling out into the hall. Lew dove to the side, howling in pain as he landed on his wounded leg.

When the avalanche stopped, he coughed and waved at the air. He struggled back to his feet and climbed up the small mountain that had spilled out of the shaft and dug a space big enough for him to fit through. Looking up at the four-story tube over his head, he whistled. The echo sounded like a bullet ricochet.

"This will be harder," he said, wiping sweat and dirt off his face before grabbing the ladder that led fifty feet straight up. The ladder wiggled in his hands, some of its moorings likely having come loose in the attack. "Perfect."

With little choice, he stuck the rebar in his belt loops again and started the long, rickety hop-climb. If a second attack came now, he knew it would all be over, but chances were he wouldn't notice for long.

8:10 A.M.

"HOW'S THE PAIN?" Jonathan asked.

As they walked up the road, he'd noticed Sophia wasn't leaning on him as much. He held her arm around his shoulders, slouching so she didn't have to reach up, and his other arm was around her back, his hand on her side, his fingers lightly gripped her bare abdomen.

"Better," she said, "but if I don't get to a medical facility soon, I'm going to be in trouble. Who knows what the bullet dragged into the wound with it." Jonathan nodded. He'd been thinking the exact same thing, but hadn't wanted to make matters worse by saying so.

He looked over at Emily. She'd been quiet ever since her breakdown at the sight of the complex collapse. And she was hanging on to the gun as if it held the cure for cancer. He felt sorry for anyone she came across. Natalie was holding her free hand, as if she could sense that Emily needed human contact at the moment.

"If your father and Lara beat us to the chopper, any ideas about how we're going to convince them to fly us out of here?" Jonathan said. "Assuming he's still on the ground by the time we get there." His Plan A was to just kill Nathan and Lara and then take the helicopter, but they were Sophia's family, and Jonathan wasn't all that sure he could kill someone with his daughter watching anyway. In fact, he knew he couldn't.

"In my bag there's a blue vial. He'll do just about anything to get it. And, of course, there's this," Sophia said, grimacing as she pulled the USB drive out of her pocket and showed it to Jonathan.

"What's that?"

"All the research. The only copy, in fact. Without it, he could have God's brain in that box and it wouldn't help him. Believe me, he's not going anywhere until he gets this," she said, sounding angry and almost vengeful. She put the drive back in her pocket.

"You think he'll really transport us out of here for it?" Jonathan asked.

"We need to find another way," Sophia said. "There's something about my research I didn't tell you before. Something I only recently confirmed."

"What is it?" Jonathan said, worry nibbling at him.

"The injected proteins do more than just unfold the prions back into healthy proteins," she said.

Jonathan recalled what Sophia had told him in her lab, how replicating folded proteins had caused Nathan's disease.

"What else do they do?" Emily asked. He hadn't even noticed that she was listening. He'd almost completely forgotten she was a journalist. Wrapping her mind around a new puzzle was probably exactly what the doctor ordered. Besides, when she drifted back to hear them, Natalie had let go of her hand and was now holding his. He felt his heart slow and his whole body calm.

"The proteins seem to transfer the electrical impressions they were imprinted with in their host. They get mixed with the existing impression base, but there's a definite retention happening while experiencing the protocol," she said. Sophia told him about the anomalous mice that could run her maze perfectly without ever seeing it before just by injecting them with the altered proteins from donors who had run it.

"Impressions," Jonathan said. He stopped in his tracks and turned to face Sophia. "Wait a minute. You're talking about *memories*. Jesus, he's retaining the memories of the donors?!"

"More or less," Sophia said, looking at the ground.

"What do you mean, more or less?" Jonathan said.

"My research was nowhere near complete, but aside from memories, there may have been some transfer of raw intelligence. Basically, the mice didn't just have new knowledge, their ability to apply that knowledge increased as well."

"Oh my God," Emily said. "Einstein." Jonathan had been thinking the exact same thing.

"Jesus," Jonathan said, thinking about what it would mean if Nathan used Einstein's brain for one of his treatments. He was going to make sure that didn't happen. "Let's see what we can barter with the serum and take it from there."

"I think that's wise," Sophia said.

"But if he won't play ball . . ." Jonathan trailed off, looking down at Natalie, but she didn't seem interested in what they were talking about.

"What is it?" Sophia asked.

"You have to understand that my only concern right now is getting Natalie to safety. If your father refuses to help . . . I'll need to convince him," Jonathan said. Sophia looked at the ground again and nodded.

"I know. You probably won't believe this, but Natalie is my main concern right now too," Sophia said. Jonathan looked her in the eye. She looked like she was telling the truth. She also looked like there was something she wasn't saying.

"What is it?" he asked. She stopped walking and took a cleansing breath.

"Nathan isn't my father."

"What? But I—"

"He's been lying to me my whole life," she said as she continued walking toward the helipad. "But worse than that, he somehow convinced my mother to lie to me. Lara and I were barely out of diapers when he showed up, but I still remember my mother telling us he was our father and we were going to go live with him in a big house and never be hungry again. I've always thought of that day as the greatest day in my life. I've lost everything now. Even my history."

Jonathan didn't say anything, just held her a little tighter, pretending he didn't see the tears snaking down her caramel cheeks. He felt a burning rising up inside him. Nathan was anathema to everything he touched. Jonathan had been hoping they were wrong and when they got to the helipad he wouldn't be anywhere in sight. Now he was looking forward to meeting this bastard one last time.

"What kind of resistance are we looking at when we get there?" Jonathan asked, changing the subject when it was obvious she didn't want to talk about it anymore right now. Sophia told him about the four posted guards. The attack might have scared them into the jungle, but he doubted it. The guards they'd seen so far seemed to be ex-military hard cases. It would probably take more than a few bangs in the distance to send them running.

"Why does he have so many guards?" Jonathan asked.

"I've never had much to do with that side of things. When we were kids, there was always Thomas and a few bodyguards, but that was it. But even before he got sick, his style of business tended to attract a considerable amount of animosity and revenge seekers. When I came back from university, he'd replaced the bodyguards with ex-soldiers and their numbers had doubled. Over the past ten years it's just gotten worse. The paranoia of the disease over the past five years once the symptoms showed up has exacerbated things as well. There was rarely a month that went by when we didn't hire more guards. I tried to ignore it all and just do my work, I'm ashamed to say."

They walked on in silence for a while. Jonathan hadn't meant to open a wound for her, he just wanted to know what he'd be facing. But with her past, maybe opening a few wounds wasn't such a bad idea.

"I can't believe she tried to kill me," Sophia said out of the blue. Jonathan held her a little tighter under his arm.

"There is a silver lining, if it's any consolation," Jonathan said.

"What's that?"

"They probably think Lara was successful," he said. Sophia seemed to take little comfort in the fact.

"How you doing, baby?" Jonathan asked Natalie.

"Good," Natalie said, but she sounded tired and looked even more so.

"I can walk on my own for a while if you want to walk with Natalie," Sophia said.

"You sure?" Jonathan asked. She seemed steady enough. "Just shout out if you need help," Jonathan said. Natalie reflexively took his arm.

"We'll be out of her soon," Jonathan said.

"I know," Natalie said with a smile.

"You do, do you?"

"Don't say anything," Natalie said, leaning in conspiratorially to Jonathan. "But I had the dream again last night."

"You did?"

"Yes, but this time I saw the woman's face!" Natalie said.

"Who was it?"

Natalie nodded toward Sophia.

Jonathan smiled and hugged Natalie with one arm. He figured Sophia's saving Natalie in the complex had probably placed her image into Natalie's dream.

What if there's more to it?

8:20 A.M.

LARA COULDN'T BELIEVE that this was where she had lived.

The complex was gone, nothing but uneven rubble remaining. One side of the main level had collapsed into the second level, leaving a kind of ramp that led from where Lara stood to the elevator shaft. The elevator for both the first and second levels was visible now, the first level door looking bizarre as it hung up in the air with no floor leading to it.

Lara kicked through the debris, looking for her sister's body, her head snapping up at the slightest sound like a pigeon eating breadcrumbs in the park. The others were nowhere to be seen, but she took comfort in the sight of Thomas still lying on the ground on the other side of the courtyard, partially covered with debris. She'd had some crazy idea that when she got down here he'd be standing against a tree waiting for her, cleaning his nails with the knife, a look of disappointment on his face. She'd never actually believed that Thomas loved her, not until the final moments of his life when he'd looked her in the eyes as he died. Her father never would have let him live knowing that. And if he had to die, she was glad it was she who had done it. She thought it was romantic.

It was comforting to see everything where she'd left it—except for the complex, of course. There didn't seem to be anything under the rubble, but more rubble. She rationalized that if Sophia had somehow survived, it might get Lara out of trouble with her father. But she knew that was foolish thinking. Her father was never going to be pleased with her, no matter what she did or didn't do. He had always been hard on her, but something had changed after he told her she wasn't really a Kring. Not by blood, anyway.

You're being paranoid. Some bits of concrete tumbled down behind her and she spun around. Nothing there. But a few feet away she saw something sticking out of the debris on the ground. She made her way to it and knelt, pulling the black material out of its hiding place. It was Sophia's backpack.

Lara smiled slightly at her success. She examined the pack, seeing three holes through it. *I knew I hit her.* Though just three holes was disappointing. She touched one of the holes and her fingers came away wet and red. Her smile grew.

She stood, swinging the backpack over her shoulder, and carefully made her way out of the disaster area. A twisted ankle was the last thing she needed now. It would impede her ability to fly the helicopter. Yet another disappointment for her father. Not that he needed a reason.

She heard a scraping sound and stopped, looking around. She

didn't see anything and was going to continue her climb out of the wreckage when she heard it again. At the bottom of the rubble ramp she saw something stick through the seam in the elevator doors. A bar of some sort. She watched as it wiggled around, like it was trying to escape whatever was on the other side of the doors.

"What the . . ." Then slowly the doors parted, the inside too dark to reveal anything from this angle with the morning sun behind the shaft. The doors opened all the way and a moment later a strange man leaped into view, his back half still hanging inside as he gripped the sliding gravel under his fingers, trying to pull himself out of the hungry elevator. Lara just stared, eyes wide and mouth agape.

Who the hell is that?

Resting from his struggle, the man panted for air, his gasps sending dust pluming up from under his mouth. Then he looked up and saw her. For what seemed like minutes, they just looked at each other, waiting for the other to make a move. The man made it finally, which sparked Lara to action.

"Hey . . ." he said, reaching a hand out as if to ask for help. Lara pulled her gun and fired wildly as she ran out of the rubble field. "No!" the man shouted before he fell back into the elevator shaft.

Lara kept running, still pulling the gun's trigger as she ran, hollow clicks the only reaction from the weapon. She finally tossed it aside and ran into the jungle, the bloody backpack bouncing over her shoulder.

LEW'S FINGERS FELT like they were going to snap off, the pain of the broken ones slowly challenging the stabbing in his leg. He'd fallen several feet before he'd managed to grab hold of the ladder, avoiding plunging to his death in the rubble. He kicked his uninjured leg, looking for something to step on, finding nothing but smooth concrete on the wall of the shaft. Almost fully exhausted, he dug deep and growled as he pulled with his less injured hand, his chest slamming down onto sharp hunks of broken stone. He wiggled from side to side until he managed to pull himself completely out of the gaping pit and roll onto his back. His head swam from the pain and he had to will himself to stay conscious.

"Crazy . . . fucking. . . . bitch," he muttered, catching his breath. He wanted to stay there, let the blackness take him and sleep forever, but Lara might be his only chance of getting off this damn island.

Lew got to his feet and limp-hopped his way out of the destruction. He saw Thomas lying on the other side of the courtyard and shook his head. "Love stinks, brother," he said, looking up the road, squinting from the glare of the morning sun. Lara was nowhere to be seen, but about halfway up the rising hill in the jungle he saw vegetation moving. *Of course. Couldn't take the fucking road, oh no.*

Lew headed off into the jungle, stopping on the edge of the vegetation when he heard a buzzing overhead. He looked up and saw the drone that had caused the destruction. He knew that somewhere—probably hundreds of miles away or on a ship off shore—there were soldiers watching him through the cameras that hung beneath the drone's nose. What the hell it was doing here, he had no idea. Nor did he care. Knowing wouldn't help him. The only thing that would help was to not be here if the remote piloting soldier decided to finish what he started. He flipped the craft the bird and limped into the jungle.

If they were going to unload one of the five-hundred-pound bombs he could see hanging from its belly, he was going to make sure he was standing right beside psycho bitch when they did.

8:30 A.M.

JONATHAN CRAWLED UP to the crest of the jungle hill, slipping between the trunks of two trees until he could see the helipad below. He understood now why it was so far from the complex. The helipad was a natural, flat stone outcropping at the very edge of the island, as if Mother Nature had put it there for helicopters to land on. The far edge of the platform dropped off, the sea a hundred feet below. The road they had been on—fifty feet below him—was blasted out of the jungle so it ran neatly onto the helipad. A single small hut sat at the edge of the helipad, and through the big windows Jonathan could see two guards and Nathan in his wheelchair. In the center of the helipad sat a Bell 407 single-rotor helicopter perched beneath camouflage netting attached to four posts on wheels. Another guard was busy rolling the netting back.

It was a risk with the drone still flying around up there somewhere, but it was necessary. Jonathan knew the helicopter needed time to rev up before it could make a run for it, and the netting had to be out of the way for that to happen. But to rev it up they needed a pilot, and Lara was nowhere to be seen.

LEW'S HAND SLIPPED off the tree he'd been aiming at and he fell to his knees, pain shooting white spots into his vision. He turned to the side and dry heaved, spitting stringy bile onto the jungle floor. Using the tree as a crutch, he managed to get himself back up to his feet. He held his hands out in front of him and watched them shake.

Looking up the hill, he tried to find the vegetation movement he'd been following, but the jungle was deathly still. He had no idea how much farther this mountain rose, but he could hear the ocean now, crashing somewhere in the distance. Either that, or it was what little blood he had left pounding in his ears. He suppressed another bout of retching and pushed on.

Where the hell is she?

"ARE YOU SURE?" Sophia asked, reaching into her bag.

"Honestly?" Jonathan said, back down with the girls after reconnoitering the helipad. "Not in the least. But it's the only chance we've got."

She handed him the glass vial filled with the blue serum.

"What else do you have in there?" Jonathan asked. She opened the bag up so he could see. It was a myriad of junk, most of it useless. But he reached in and pulled one item out.

"What do you need a—"

"Dad?" Natalie said.

"Honey, I told you, it's going to be okay," Jonathan said.

"You stay with Emily. No matter what, okay?"

"M'kay," she said, moving over to Emily who put her arm around her.

"Be careful," Emily said.

Sophia leaned over and kissed Jonathan on the cheek.

"For luck," she said. Jonathan looked at Natalie, who was grinning from ear to ear. He winked at her, despite what had happened to Lew when Emily had given *him* a kiss for luck. He handed Sophia his gun and then headed down the road toward the helipad.

"SIR!" ONE OF the guards shouted when he saw Jonathan walking onto the helipad with his hands over his head, the vial sticking out of one and a small black rectangle sticking out of the other. Nathan turned and saw what he was holding as the guards brought their guns to bear on Jonathan.

"Don't shoot. Don't shoot," Nathan ordered.

"I want to make a deal," Jonathan said as the guards walked toward him and Nathan rolled behind them. "That's far enough!" Jonathan raised the vial up as if he were going to smash it on the stone at his feet.

"No!" Nathan shouted, actually using his voice, which was a slurred sound like someone coughing. Even the guards turned to look at him.

All but one fell back into line behind Nathan.

"Sir, don't listen to him. I can just—"

A gunshot rang out and the guard fell to the stone with a hole in his head, the gun in Nathan's hand still smoking.

"What kind of deal?" he asked with his calm electronic voice.

"The serum for passage on the helicopter," Jonathan said.

Nathan raised an eyebrow and seemed to mull over the offer, his eyes never leaving the vial in Jonathan's hand.

"Choose," Nathan said.

"What?"

"Choose. The serum for one seat on the chopper," Nathan said. Jonathan had expected nothing less from this monster.

"How many seats for the serum and Sophia's research," Jonathan said. He held the black rectangle up for Nathan to see, praying he was far enough away for the disposable lighter to look like a USB drive. There was no way in hell he was letting Nathan anywhere near the real thing.

Nathan's eyes widened.

"Deal," Nathan said. "Bring them to me and they can get on the chopper."

Jonathan took a few steps and then threw himself to the ground, throwing the serum up in the air. The guards and Nathan followed the vial up with their eyes and Jonathan made his move.

LEW FELL AGAINST another tree, catching his breath. There was only about twenty feet of jungle left before he reached the edge of the cliff, and still no sign of the crazy woman who had shot at him. Had he missed her? Was she already down the other side?

Rested as much as he dared, he stepped away from the tree and heard a rustle overhead. He looked up just in time to see Lara pounce on him from her hiding place up in the branches over-head. He managed to dodge most of the attack, but even a glancing blow in his condition sent him reeling. He turned over just as she recovered from her attack and leaped on him again, striking him again and again. Her fists slammed into both sides of his head over and over. Then she pulled a knife and plunged it at his chest.

Lew caught the thrust in time, but his strength was gone. It was all he could do to hold the blade in place over his heart. She reached back and slammed her thumb deep into his thigh wound.

His howl masked the sound of gunfire in the distance.

ONE OF THE guards caught the falling serum just as gunfire rained down from the trees overhead. Jonathan realized that Sophia hadn't lied; she couldn't shoot worth a damn. Emily had wanted to do it, but she was a little bloodthirsty at the moment. Still, accuracy wasn't the point and in Sophia's defense, she'd hit one of the guards, though just in the arm. Jonathan continued counting and when Sophia had expended all the bullets in his two guns, he vaulted up off the ground.

He grabbed the wounded guard and spun around behind him, turning him into a shield. Using the guard's submachine gun, he fired at the other two guards. They fell like straw men, dead before they hit the stone. He watched the guard holding the serum slam to the ground, the vial rolling away from his dead fingers toward

Nathan. Then Jonathan's shield fought back, slamming an elbow square into Jonathan's face, stunning him. He fell to the stone, shaking the buzz in his ears away.

The guard took back control of his gun, turning and pointing it at him. Jonathan kicked up and sent the weapon flying. The guard pulled a knife and leaped onto him, but Jonathan caught the knife hand before it hit home. But this was a well-trained mercenary. Jonathan had more training than most, but his skills had atrophied over the years. His conditioning had given way to late night bill-paying sessions and backyard barbecues. He was no match for the attacker, but he fought on.

LEW, OUTMATCHED AGAINST Lara, was no longer fighting but just trying to get away. He still had the size advantage and with a little leverage, he bucked her off him and scrambled up toward the crest in the jungle hill. He had no idea what was on the other side, but it had to be better than this.

Less than a foot from breaking through the wall of vegetation, Lew slipped and fell. He knew she'd be on him and he spun around to see her leap toward him, knife in hand. He mustered all the energy he had and kicked with his good leg, sending the knife flying into the bush. From the cracking sound and the accompanying howl he figured he'd probably also broken her hand. The pain just seemed to piss her off, though, her attack nothing more than frenetic.

Lew slipped around behind her and got her in a headlock, squeezing. If he could hold her long enough, she'd pass out from lack of blood making it to her brain. But it was like riding a bucking spider, legs and arms reaching back, kicking and clawing at him.

SOPHIA WATCHED NATHAN reach a shaking hand for the approaching serum, as she brought her foot down to stop the vial's roll. He looked up and saw her standing a few feet away. She thought she must have been quite the sight with her shirt gone and her bandaged shoulder, though she guessed he was probably more focused on the gun in her hand.

"Sophia—" Nathan started.

"Shut up," Sophia said louder than she'd meant.

"I didn't say anything yet," Nathan's cool electronic voice said.

"I don't want to hear anything from you ever again. Drop the gun," she said when she noticed his shaking hand raising it toward her. "*Now!*"

Never having heard her speak like that to anyone must have had an effect on him, because he instantly complied.

"Please, Sophia. Let's be reasonable. You're not going to murder me in cold blood. We both know that." She ignored him, bent down, and picked up the vial, wincing from the pain in her shoulder.

"I don't have to shoot you to kill you, Nathan," she said. "We both know that. All I have to do is smash this and destroy the research and you're dead."

"Sophia, honey. You're not thinking straight. I didn't tell her to hurt you. That was all Lara's doing! Please, don't—"

"Take it from me," Sophia said calmly. When Nathan looked at the gun in her hand, she tossed it aside. "Go ahead. You're always having someone else do everything for you. Let me see you do something for yourself. Just once. Take it."

"How can I take anything?" Nathan's electronic voice said, his panicked eyes juxtaposed against the calmness of his tone.

"We both know you can get out of that chair, now. You just shot a man. There's no neuro-blocker left in your system by now. I can tell from your shaking. Get up and take it or I swear I'll smash it."

"Wait! All right, all right!" Nathan mewled with his natural voice through his malformed lips. He fumbled for a moment, but then slipped his feet off the chair's footrest and rose from the seat.

Sophia slammed the fist of her free hand into Nathan's face. Blood and teeth exploded out of his mouth as he crashed back into his chair. When he finished coughing and spitting he looked up and saw Sophia had picked up his loaded dropped gun. Then she flicked the stopper off the vial with her thumb and turned it over, letting the blue life-giving fluid drain out onto the stone at her feet.

"*No!*" he screamed. Nathan vaulted himself out of the chair for the final time and landed in the puddle at her feet. "No, no, no, no."

He pawed at the fluid on the ground like he could somehow convince it to not be spilled. Crying and mewling, he bent down and pressed his lips to the serum. Sophia pointed the gun at him and cocked the hammer back. Then he wasn't crying any longer. He was laughing. A maniacal, insane laughter that sounded like a funhouse's soundtrack. He looked up at her, his eyes dead of emotion but his maw continuing to howl. Sophia turned her head and considered him, like a cat considering a mouse it had pinned under its paw, the outcome inevitable.

"Please, please," Nathan managed between gasps. Sophia would never know if he was begging for a reprieve or for an end. And she didn't care.

She pulled the trigger.

JONATHAN AND THE guard both looked up at the sound of a gunshot.

Jonathan kneed the guard in the groin, taking advantage of the moment, kicked the knife out of his hand and slammed his head into the stone. The guard was either out cold or dead, Jonathan didn't care which.

Exhausted, he pulled himself to his feet and went to Sophia's side. He understood what she'd done and didn't blame her at all, but as much as he cared about her, he was more worried about Natalie. If Sophia couldn't fly them out of there, they wouldn't be very far behind Nathan.

"Are you—"

"Get Natalie and Emily," she said, handing him the gun. "Let's get the fuck out of here."

"STOP . . . FIGHTING," Lew managed. "Don't make me . . . kill you."

"I . . . I hate you!" Lara screamed. "I've always hated you. Even when you were fucking me, I just wanted you to die on top of me. Die and smother me!"

"Lady, you need a vacation," Lew said, realizing it wasn't even him she was fighting with. He was just the weapon.

Lara made a noise that might've been a growl and continued her defense. Lew was tiring, but he still had enough strength to do what he knew he should. Still, crazy or not, he just couldn't bring himself to shift the leverage and snap her neck. Chivalry wasn't dead, it just felt like it.

Finally Lew let her go and rolled off before she could come at him again. He unsteadily got up on his feet, standing up the hill from Lara, who was up on her feet, crouching like an animal stalking its prey.

"Don't," Lew said, holding a hand up like he was stopping traffic. "Just hang on a—"

She attacked as if he was speaking a foreign language. This time she didn't try to take him down. She drove him back until they smashed through the jungle crest, gripping each other as they flew into the unknown.

JONATHAN WAS DOING his best to stay focused, but it was hard with everything that had happened, everything he had lost. They weren't out of the woods yet. He lifted Natalie up into the helicopter's rear cabin where Emily was waiting to help buckle her into her seat.

He turned to close the door, but stopped when he saw a rock on the ground. Impulsively, he picked it up and scratched The Monarch's butterfly symbol into the side of the helicopter. Jonathan wasn't sure who he was forgiving: himself for killing, whatever the reason, for the first time in years; Sophia for going along with her "father" for so long and for what she'd just done; Emily for helping Nathan when this all started. He just wasn't sure. One thing he did know was it wasn't for Nathan. He'd never forgive that bastard for what he'd done.

He stepped back and looked at the image, the image he'd carved so many times over the years trying to do the right thing. The image that had started the dominoes falling on this horror. He blinked to clear his blurring vision when he finally realized who it was for. He was forgiving Lew for dying. It was ridiculous, but necessary.

"You're not getting away that easy," a voice said behind Jonathan.

The rock slipped from Jonathan's fingers and fell to the ground. He turned around and his breath hitched in his chest. A half-dead Lew hobbled toward them, his leg painted red.

"Uncle Lew!" Natalie shouted from the cabin.

Emily turned around and poked her head out of the chopper, vaulting to the ground a second later at a full run. She hit him so hard with her open arms he almost fell over. She kissed him, tentatively at first, but then harder as she realized he wasn't a dream.

Everyone walked over to greet him. Emily finally let him go and Lew watched Jonathan approach, a few tears slipping down Jonathan's exhausted, grinning face.

"Jesus, if you're going to be a baby about it," Lew said with a big smile.

"Shut up," Jonathan said, throwing his arms around him— moments before Lew's eyes rolled back in his head and he collapsed.

9:15 A.M.

"YOU'RE SURE YOU can do this?" Jonathan asked for about the fourth time from the copilot's seat. They had to use headsets to communicate over the roar of the chopper's engine, which Natalie thought was the greatest thing since the Internet.

"And if I can't?" Sophia said with a forced smile.

Jonathan looked behind him at Lew, belted unconscious into one of the five seats, next to Emily and Natalie. Emily had bandaged his leg, but they weren't out of the woods. He'd lost a lot of blood and looked about three shades too pale.

They should have been winging toward the mainland, but they still had the drone buzzing around. They were waiting for it to either drop one of its remaining bombs for cover or to simply leave. Jonathan knew the latter was unlikely.

They had no idea where Lara was, but every minute on the ground seemed like a bad idea.

Suddenly the ground rocked from two huge explosions and a fireball shot up in the sky where the hangar used to be. The drone had dropped *both* of its five-hundred-pound bombs.

Somebody wants this island gone.

"Go!" Jonathan shouted.

They lifted off as hell spewed up from the earth. Jonathan was sure the half ton of ordinance had touched off the natural gas pooled at the base of the island. Trapped by the decimated complex, which was acting like a giant cork, the energy was finding other avenues of escape.

Rock and fire exploded into the air all around the helipad like someone had set off a sequence of claymore mines hidden in the dirt. Most of it arced over them to the other side, but gravel pelted the chopper like machine gun fire. Jonathan held his breath in the midst of all the screaming. If any of the larger chunks hit the rotor, they were done.

They skimmed the helipad, headed for the drop-off, then suddenly the helicopter rocked and threatened to slam down into the stone. Sophia had no choice but to try to gain altitude, but the chopper didn't rise, it just rocked back and forth.

"What's wrong?" Emily asked.

"I don't know! It's like . . . there," Sophia said, pointing out the side window as she winced and fought the controls.

Jonathan saw it. The explosions had blown the camouflage netting up in the air and it hooked onto the landing strut. The chopper's down-draft was threatening to send it into the tail rotor.

Jonathan unstrapped himself and headed into the back of the helicopter. "Be careful!" Sophia shouted after him.

Jonathan nodded as the swing of the chopper almost sent him flying. He made his way carefully over to the door.

"I've got it," Jonathan said, pulling it open. The second he did, a hand reached up from below, grabbed him by the shirt, and yanked him out the helicopter's door.

"Dad!" Natalie screamed.

Hanging on to the landing strut, Jonathan was face-to-face with Lara. He looked down and fought to keep calm. *Not now, not after all this!*

Lara hung on with one arm and pounded on him with the other, the helicopter swinging back and forth, threatening to leap from his grasp. Her eyes were empty, the pupils huge saucers, the whites scored with red. Jonathan knew he had no choice, he just prayed Natalie couldn't see him.

He gripped the strut with both hands, waited for the next swing of the chopper, and used the momentum to kick. He slammed his boots into her, knocking Lara off, and watched her plummet toward the stone helipad. Before she hit, another gas explosion blasted a beach ball-sized boulder out of the cliff. The projectile took most of Lara over the cliff and down where her father's body lay. Jonathan unhooked the netting and dropped it down.

He waited for the chopper's movements to calm slightly before he tried to climb up into the cabin, but just as he did, he saw the drone heading straight for them, the single remaining Hellfire missile seeming to stare at him. They had only one option now.

Emily helped pull him back inside and he slammed the door shut before stumbling over to his seat and strapping himself in.

"*Go!*" he shouted into his headset the second it was on, pointing out the window. Sophia looked out the window behind them and saw the drone. She immediately throttled up.

"We'll never outrun her!" Sophia said, despite trying to do just that. Jonathan knew she was right. He wracked his brain, but could come up with only one solution. He leaned over and flipped the switch controlling Natalie's headset so she couldn't hear what he was about to say.

"We need to make her shoot at us," he said.

"What!" both Sophia and Emily said at the same time.

"It's our only chance. We can't outrun her or fly higher, but she only has one missile left. Once that's gone the worst she can do is follow us."

"Follow what? We'll be sprinkled all over the Indian Ocean!" Sophia said, still trying to outrun the jet as it closed in on them.

"Hellfires are air-to-surface missiles. They're designed for stationary targets, not moving ones. If we can get her to fire, we can dodge it," Jonathan said, though he had no idea how easy it would be to dodge a missile, even if the logic in his theory was good.

"You're bloody crazy!" Emily said. He didn't bother to refute her.

He reached out and put his hand on Sophia's.

"Trust me," he said looking into her eyes. For the longest time she looked back, then she looked at Natalie behind them. He knew she was thinking that if he was willing to try this with her back there, then it really was their best chance.

"So how do I make her shoot?" Sophia asked.

"Oh Jesus," Emily said.

"The smoke," Jonathan said, pointing back at the island. "Fly toward it. She'll be afraid of losing us and fire when we duck in. The second we're in, climb. *Fast.*"

Sophia swung the chopper around in a slow arc, trying not to let the drone figure out what they were up to until the last possible moment.

"She's on to us," Sophia said as she throttled up and headed for the smoke. The drone came into line behind them.

Jonathan flipped Natalie's headset back on. "Hang on, baby," he said, looking back at her.

The second they hit the smoke, the drone bucked up and fired her final missile. Jonathan watched it scream across the sky toward them at incredible speed until it was blotted from view by the column of smoke they'd entered.

"Climb!"

The massive G force threw them back in their seats as the chopper lurched up in an almost vertical climb. Jonathan could feel his blood rushing to his torso from his extremities. If he passed out it wasn't a problem, but Sophia was a different story. After an eternity, they leveled out and exited the smoke in time to see the missile miles in the distance, still waiting to hit something.

Cheers echoed in the helicopter. They banked and headed off toward the mainland.

"See? I told you she was from my dream!" Natalie said over the headset. Jonathan laughed.

The drone followed them for about twenty minutes, but eventually broke off and disappeared into the clouds. They might have a welcoming committee waiting for them when they landed, but that was fine by Jonathan.

The more the merrier.

Epilogue

Smithsonian Institute
Washington, D.C.
Two Weeks Later

Dr. Tasha DiZazzo, special acquisitions curator, slugged back the remainder of her energy drink, already feeling the familiar headache approaching. She had finally worked her way through the week's donations so that the rest fit in her messenger bag, even if it felt like the strap was trying to sever her arm from her body. She just wanted to grab her coat and head home to a bubble bath with her name on it.

"Rats!" she said as she pushed into her basement office. More donations had come in while she was upstairs. Mostly envelopes she could squeeze into her bag, but there was one medicine ball–sized crate her assistant had graciously left in the middle of her desk. "Thanks, Krisi."

Against all common sense—and a desperate desire to leave and pretend she didn't see it—Tasha dropped thirty pounds by putting her bag down, cracked open another energy drink, and headed to her desk armed with a crowbar. She knew if she didn't deal with this now, the pile would be twice as big in the morning.

Once she'd squeaked the lid off the crate, she found another case inside, but this one had a keypad on it with a red glowing LED.

"What the heck?"

An envelope was taped to the top. She detached it and read the handwriting on the front:

To whom it may concern:

The preserved brain, eyes, and letter of authentication in this case belong to the world. Please make sure it stays that way.

The note was signed with a symbol that looked, for all intents and purposes, like a butterfly. Tasha opened the envelope and reviewed the letter of authenticity, the tingle up her spine rivaling the energy drink buzz tickling across her scalp.

"Oh. My. God." She fell back in her chair.

The only bubbles she'd see tonight would be squirting out of a champagne bottle.

Tallahassee Memorial Hospital
Tallahassee, Florida

"Up for some company?" Jonathan asked from the doorway of Lew's hospital room, a police officer seated just outside the door behind him.

During their two weeks at the Aga Khan Hospital in Mombasa, Kenya, Lew had been pronounced dead twice, but he'd stubbornly contradicted the doctors and kept on living. Sophia's shoulder wound wasn't nearly as severe, but it had been touch and go for her emotionally as she came to grips with what she had done and lost. They finally got the okay for Lew to travel, and now he was recuperating at Tallahassee Memorial while everyone else started putting their lives back together.

No one had been there to meet them when they landed, and aside from having to call in a few favors to explain why a helicopter had landed on a sports field across the street from the hospital, it seemed like it was going to remain that way. There were still rumblings of The Monarch on the news services, but with the "terrorist attack" in New York, that was to be expected.

As it turned out, that was going to be good for them. The interest in The Monarch meant not only was Emily going to get to finish *The Monarch Reigns* with the infamous missing chapter, but her agent had called with a deal to pen a sequel, *The Monarch's Fall*. At first she'd wanted to refuse, but Jonathan and Lew had talked her into doing it—with a lot of poetic license. When the book came out they would be cleared and The Monarch would finally be well and truly dead.

Sophia seemed to be in the clear, as well. At least legally. Her only connection to everything had been her last name, but since it was never revealed that Nathan was behind the New York killings, she wasn't even being sought for questioning.

"Sure," Lew said, sitting up as best he could with the pain he still felt and the handcuff tethering him to the bed's rail. Jonathan came in and sat at a chair beside the bed, putting a folder of papers on his lap.

"When do you testify?" Jonathan asked.

"Already done," Lew said with a half smile. Unlike everyone

else, Lew had some answering to do when they got back, for walk-ing out of prison three months early. But even that turned out better than they'd expected. He turned state's evidence against Warden Quinn and once he was well enough to travel he'd only have to serve his remaining time. No new charges.

"They did it right here?"

"Easy-peasy," Lew said. He was less than thrilled about having to return to prison, but he knew it was far better than looking over his shoulder for the rest of his life. He'd even been able to keep Miguel Colero out of it by playing dumb. Being on his bad side would have been even worse than having a warrant on his head.

Lew could tell Jonathan felt bad about the situation and that he was going to try to say something about it, so he quickly changed the subject.

"So you're really doing it?" Lew said, nodding toward the papers in Jonathan's lap.

"Yeah," Jonathan said softly. "It's the only way I can be sure she'll be safe."

"I get it. And it's not as if boarding school is like, you know, prison, but do you have to change her name?"

"Change it back, you mean. She was Natalie Webster longer than she's been Natalie Hall. It's a good thing. And if she has to change her name, what could be better than her mom's maiden name?"

"I know, but jeez."

"She'll be safe and that's all that matters. Besides, no matter what her name is, she'll always be my daughter." Lew didn't say anything, but he thought it sounded like Jonathan was trying to convince himself more than anyone.

Silence drew out between them. It wasn't that they didn't have anything to talk about, but everything they wanted to say wasn't supposed to have happened. So they settled for silence.

It was nice for a change.

FCI Yazoo City
Yazoo, Mississippi
Three Months Later

IT WAS JUST after noon in August when Jonathan saw Lew as a free man. Sitting in the rental car, running the AC in a futile attempt to beat the Mississippi summer heat, Jonathan watched his partner come strolling down the path toward the parking lot like a commuter on his way home from work, except for the duffel bag over his shoulder. He was dressed in the same off-white button-down shirt and gray slacks as he had been when he went in. His sleeves were rolled up and his collar button was open, which was about as much as Lew ever did when it got hot.

"Hot as balls," Lew said after putting his bag in the backseat and getting in the car.

"Nice to see you too," Jonathan said, shaking his hand. He reached down and pressed the button to pop the trunk. "There's some sodas in a cooler in the trunk. Grab us a couple and we'll get out of here."

Anybody else would have whined about just getting in the car out of the heat, but Lew nodded and got out. Jonathan smiled and got ready to open his door. They had some serious things to talk about, but they had time for a moment of fun first. When the trunk opened all the way to hide him, Jonathan eased his door open and got out.

"Are you fucking serious?!" Lew called from the back of the car.

Jonathan stepped around the back of the car and saw Lew holding up the duster Jonathan had bought for him, a grin on his face like he was holding a newborn.

"It might be a little hot but I figured what the—"

Lew ignored him and shouldered his way into the heavy coat. He ran his meaty hands along the oilskin lapels and then popped the leather collar.

"Daddy's home."

Back in the car, the rental company's air freshener fighting with the oilskin scent, Jonathan knew it was time to get down to business. He pulled a folder out of the pocket between the seats. Lew saw this and rolled his eyes.

"Aw, crap. The bastard popped up, did he? Okay, let me have it," Lew said.

With everything that had fallen into place and all they had finagled three months ago, there was one piece that had remained out of their control—Canton George. No body was ever found in the remains of his destroyed mansion, but his empire just kept chugging along like the little red choo-choo. They'd hoped it was nothing but they couldn't afford to turn a blind eye to the possibility. Jonathan opened the folder and passed a photo to Lew. It was a picture of a middle-aged white man in a navy uniform.

"Who the hell is this?"

"That is the late Colonel Rudyard Maitland, U.S. Navy. Apparently he was wanted by NCIS when his body popped up in a Capetown slum. They found him with two raped minors and a couple of bullets in the back of his head. They'd been dead for a while too."

"Ick. What was he wanted for?"

"Classified. But get this, he was base commander of the navy's air base on Diego Garcia and the warrant went out the day after the attack on Tartaruga."

"Holy shit," Lew said. "This is the fucker who—"

"He fired it, but it wasn't his idea. When they found him his wallet had been cleaned out, but they missed a necklace with a key on it. A key that fit a post office box. They found a diary inside documenting years of blackmail by your friend and mine . . ." Jonathan trailed off and handed another photograph to Lew, this one of a pristinely dressed, short black man.

"Canton fucking George," Lew said.

"None other. NCIS has had a global warrant out on him for a month, but nothing. I've got some feelers out, but you can bet if the navy can't find him, we're not going to."

"Until he wants us to, you mean," Lew said.

"I don't know. Even for someone with his resources, he's left a pretty huge wake. He might stay underground for a good long while," Jonathan said. He was lying.

"Then why is Natalie in boarding school?"

"I'm just being cautious, and she's not in boarding school for another couple weeks."

"Yeah, yeah, whatever. How's about you kick this pig into gear? If I don't see Emily soon you're not going to like what I do to you."

"All right, all right," Jonathan said, putting the folder away. They drove out of the parking lot and headed to the airport in Jackson.

Emily had actually wanted to come, but her deadline kept her chained to her desk, most days. She had taken an apartment in Tallahassee near Jonathan so they could all give her help with the fiction in her sequel, but she didn't have near enough time to fly out, pick Lew up, and fly back to Tallahassee. But she did have time for a little surprise Jonathan had cooked up.

And maybe a little more.

Jonathan's House
Tallahassee, Florida
8:15 P.M. Local Time

"SURPRISE!"

Sophie, Natalie, and Emily jumped up from behind the couch when Lew and Jonathan walked through the front door. Jonathan flicked on the lights and Lew saw a huge cake on the dining room table. The room had banners, streamers, and balloons saying things like "Congratulations" and "Welcome Home." Lew was starting to get a little misty until he took another look at Emily. She had her hair pulled back in a ponytail, a pencil behind her ear, and was wearing a speckled-pattern sundress. She was about the most beautiful thing he'd ever seen.

Lew took the time to say hi to Sophia and tousle Natalie's hair, but he made a beeline for Emily's outstretched arms. Emily wasn't just getting misty, she was full-blown crying.

"Welcome home, baby," Emily said with a big smile, dabbing at her tears.

Lew kissed her deep and hard. He could feel her knees buckle slightly under his embrace and he held her against him. When the kiss when on too long, Natalie put a stop to it.

"Uncle Lew! Gross!"

It broke the spell and he pulled himself back, parting from

Emily but hanging on to her with one arm when it looked like she was going to lose her balance.

"Don't make me get the hose," Jonathan said.

"Hey, I've been in prison, ya know," Lew answered. Everyone laughed and settled in to a great night of music, food, and conversation.

A FEW HOURS later, with Natalie grudgingly taken up to bed, they lowered the music and the four of them sat on the sofa drinking wine. Lew had his arm around Emily and noticed while they were sitting together, Jonathan and Sophia weren't touching at all. He asked if they'd had a falling out or something.

"I didn't want to say anything during the party," Sophia said.

"About what?" Lew asked sitting forward.

"Sophia's taken a job as a university professor," Jonathan said.

"Hey, that's great!" Lew said. Then he got the point. "Wait. Where?"

"Sri Lanka," Sophia said.

"*Yie*. Tough commute," Lew said.

"No, it's good," Jonathan said. "It's her heritage and a great opportunity. They're even going to let her continue her research. We just decided we didn't want to start anything, you know . . ."

"That you couldn't finish?" Lew said.

"That we couldn't continue, funny man," Sophia said.

"Sorry," Lew said when Emily elbowed him.

"But what about you guys," Jonathan asked Lew.

"Yes, what about us?" Emily asked Lew.

"Any big *plans*?" Sophia asked.

"Um. Uh, that is . . . we just got, you know—"

"Oh God, let him off the hook before he has a stroke," Emily said. Everyone laughed. Except Lew.

"Hi-larious."

As Emily drove her and Lew to her apartment, Lew inhaled the night air and sighed. Free air really did smell better, he thought. Of course, the beer and wine in him didn't hurt.

He looked at Emily again and felt his chest thump. He was acting like a bloody teenager, and he didn't care. Then he noticed the manila envelope in her sun visor with "LEW" written on it in black marker.

"What's that?" he asked.

"No idea. Jonathan handed it to me as we were leaving. He said to give it to you in the morning," Emily said.

"Like hell," Lew said as he grabbed it. He tore it open and found a folder inside marked "September." He opened the folder and couldn't believe his eyes. It was filled with pictures of a villa in Spain, vault schematics, security timetables, and finally a photo of a Renoir. Across the photo Jonathan had written "Stolen in '98."

"I'll be a son of a bitch," Lew said, knowing exactly what it meant.

"What is it?" Emily asked.

"Nothing," Lew said, closing the folder and putting it back in the envelope. "Legal papers and stuff to do with my release." He kissed the back of her hand as they drove into the night.

The Monarch might be dead, thanks to the book Emily was finishing, but Jonathan and Lew still had work to do.

But not tonight.

Acknowledgments

THANKS TO MY editor at HarperCollins, Chelsey Emmelhainz, for her incredible support, advice, and patience. Without you I never would have found the book within the book and I'll forever be grateful.

Thanks to Barb Einarsen, Julia Borgini, Brian Gallucci, and many other unnamed victims for the early reads and feedback. You guys have no idea how much you helped.

Thanks to Robert J. Sawyer and Dan Perez for their support and nurturing of my writing when it was well and truly terrible. You're braver than me, boys.

A special thanks to the National Novel Writing Month (NaNoWriMo) annual event. Much of the early part of this book was written during a NaNoWriMo event and it's doubtful there would be a novel without the community and support I found there. You guys are fantastic and a light in the dark where it's most needed.

Thanks to my daughter for drawing the Kring sisters when even I wasn't sure what they looked like.

Thanks to my parents for buying me a typewriter for Christmas all those years ago when all the other kids were asking for bikes and train sets.

And finally, thanks to the love of my life, Tasha DiZazzo, without whom this book couldn't have made it down the home stretch. Thanks for the multiple reads, for listening and for the "curtain of solitude." Thanks for being the first person to preorder it online and being more excited about that than me. You believed in me and this book when even I didn't. You rescued me, Tash. I'll love you forever.

**Ready for more action-packed suspense?
Keep reading for a sneak peek from
Jack Soren's next thriller**

Dead Lights

Coming Summer 2015 from Witness Impulse

IT WAS THE strangest kidnap and recovery mission Hoyt Randall ever had.

He peered through the binoculars down at the cookie-cutter industrial plaza that looked like it had been designed by an architect with a LEGO obsession. Five businesses were held within the repetitive tan stucco frontages, accented with a burgundy sawtooth pattern, identical bushes in front of the smoked glass doors set into each entrance. The light stands in the empty parking lot provided just enough illumination to discourage amateur thieves, but not enough to dissuade a professional. Nothing moved. All was still.

Hired by Arlo Perez and his wife, Hoyt was here to retrieve their daughter, Linda.

Hoyt fingered some notes into his forearm-mounted computing device before he put the binoculars away, pulled a black balaclava down over his face, and stood up. Dressed all in black and wearing latex gloves, he double-timed it down the hill, coming to rest behind the sign that said "Cry-Stasis Foundation." He checked the area one last time, then he jogged across the parking lot. When he was halfway, he slowed to a walk and stopped looking around.

This is ridiculous, he thought. *You could break-dance across this parking lot in fluorescent yellow and it wouldn't matter.*

Hoyt went around the back of the plaza, counted units, and took out his lockpick kit. After selecting the right tools, he inserted the picks into the lock one at a time, rotated them, and popped the lock in less than thirty seconds. He put the picks away, withdrew his automatic pistol, and entered the building.

Linda Perez had been gone for almost six months, now. She'd gone willingly, but that wasn't unusual in Hoyt's experience. Her parents wanted Linda back. They had plans for her.

Inside, Hoyt let his eyes adjust to the minimal lighting before checking the floor plan on his forearm device. Then he noticed that the security camera up in the corner wasn't even connected, network wiring hanging down from its base. He moved to the next area and saw the same thing again. Cooking inside his mask, he pulled it off and wiped his eyes before stuffing it into his waistband. A few corridor turns later and he was at his target, two large metal doors that gleamed even in the low light.

Hoyt pushed through the doors and felt like he'd walked into a science fiction movie. The room, about the size of a high school basketball court, had a couple dozen shiny chrome tanks around its perimeter. A weird hiss and hum throbbed from the ten-foot-tall cylinders.

"Jee-zus." Hoyt holstered his gun and slowly walked halfway into the room.

He hadn't really known what to expect, but this wasn't even close to what he'd imagined. The Perezes had said Cry-Stasis had their daughter's body. Hoyt had assumed it was some sort of cult that was blackmailing them after their daughter died. It never even occurred to him she was a Popsicle waiting for the future.

And the size of the canister was going to be a problem. He approached one and rapped on it. A solid *thud-thud-thud* sounded. He perused the pressure gauges on the outside of the tank, along with cabling and tubing. The temperature gauge read –320 F.

This was not going to be—

Hoyt's chest tightened as he finally noticed an extra device on almost all the canisters. Unlike the cryonic hardware, these he recognized. They were magnetic, timed charges. And with the Semtex each of them had packed inside, someone was trying to put this place on the moon.

"*No!*" Hoyt yelled as he turned and ran toward the doors. The red digits on the charges were all synchronized and counting down—*finishing* counting down.

8 . . . 7 . . . 6 . . . 5 . . . 4 . . . 3 . . . 2 . . .

He was still ten feet from the doors when the rockets launched. The blast wave slammed him through the doors, metal shards from the destroyed canisters slicing him to ribbons before what was left of his body slapped into the far cinder-block wall with a wet crunch.

Hoyt was dead long before he came to rest. Just as dead as the frozen body parts that peppered him on the wall.

THE WOMAN WHO had watched Hoyt enter the building had not stopped him from going to his death. Death was a necessary part of life. Stopping someone from dying would be the greatest irony for her. She stepped from the shadows once the explosions had stopped, dressed not unlike the late Hoyt, save for the bright red hair that peeked out from the sides of her black hoodie.

She ran to the front of the building, pulling a can from her pack as she did and shaking it. It sounded like a rattlesnake in a tin can. She then wrote on the wall with orange spray paint. When she was done—sirens just starting to sound in the distance—she tossed the can aside, took out her phone, and dialed.

"It's done," she said in Japanese.

She put her phone away as she ran back to the bushes. She wheeled her black Ducati motorcycle out of its hiding place. Straddling it, she lowered her hood and shook her flaming hair back from her Asian features before pulling on her gleaming black helmet. She revved the motorcycle's engine a few times and then sped off into the night. Behind her the flames illuminated what she had written on the front of the building:

DEAD LIGHTS.

About the Author

JACK SOREN was born and raised in Toronto, Canada. Before becoming a thriller novelist, Soren wrote software manuals, waited tables, drove a cab, and spent six months as a really terrible private investigator. He lives in the Toronto area.

Discover great authors, exclusive offers, and more at hc.com.